WILDLY INAPPROPRIATE

A Wild Bluffs Novel

Emma Kate

Flirtation Point Publishing
Emma Kate
www.authoremmakate.com

Cover Design by Emily Wittig
Editing by Kelly Siskind
Copy Editing by Claudette Cruz, the Editing Sweetheart
Proofreading by A Coleman Book Editing Services

This is a work of fiction. Any names, characters, places, or incidents are products of the author's imagination and are used fictitiously. Any resemblance to actual persons, living or dead, places, or events is purely coincidental or fictional.

Ebook ISBN: 979-8-9908678-2-6
Paperback ISBN: 979-8-9908678-3-3
Discreet Cover Paperback ISBN: 979-8-9908678-4-0

Contents

To the readers who saw their life go a completely different direction than they intended, and to the ones who saw one dream come true only to realize another had been lost along the way. To the five- and ten-year plans made with so much hope, and to the realities that are so much better than the plans—even though they are nowhere near where the timeline said they should be.

***

Welcome back to Wild Bluffs.
You will always be enough here.

Chapter One

JT

Seven Months Ago

"Only losers read books in bars," someone says, pulling out the stool next to mine. I glance over my shoulder at the interloper and...Lila Walker. Of course it is. She haunts my dreams, why not my daytime hours as well?

"I didn't realize Lucifer gives his demons a day off," I reply, taking a gulp of my scotch. With her dark black hair, sinful body, and wicked tongue, I'm not that far off with my comparison. She's temptation in a pint-sized container.

"Mother Lilith insists her favorites are allowed to come to Sin City at least once a week to collect new souls to torture."

I almost spit my drink out but catch myself before it's too late. "Um, when did you start learning things about the mother of demons?"

She rolls her eyes. "I've told you I read. Is it really so hard to imagine I might've learned a thing or two?"

When I don't reply, she continues, "Fantasy—well, romantasy—is one of my favorite genres. There's a lot of Hades/Lucifer/demons lore that gets brought in."

"I thought you preferred romance novels?" I ask, realizing too late that I'm dragging out a conversation I don't want to be in.

"I do. Romantasy is essentially the result of fantasy and romance having a baby. I like fantasy, but I'm much more down to jump into the world of fae, kings, and battles if there is a decently significant romance component."

"Oh. Huh. I haven't read much fantasy or fantasy-adjacent books, I suppose."

Lila and I have been at each other's throats since the fall after she turned 18, and after six years of arguing every time we're near each other, it feels weird to be having a normal conversation—even one that started with some light "you're a demon" insults.

We've been on a temporary truce the last few months since we were forced to work together to help her brother—my best friend—get his life back together. I met Jameson Walker when we were both playing in junior golf tournaments across the country. We were some of the top-ranked golfers heading into our final year on the Tour, and in a strange turn of fate, we ended up at Cal State, where we became team-mates, roommates, and friends. Now we both play golf professionally.

This summer, Lila was so worried about her brother hitting rock bottom that she all but forced me to visit Jameson in the little Colorado town he'd been holed up in: Wild Bluffs. I will never admit this to her, but Lila was right—Jameson did need someone there to support him. I don't mean to toot my own horn, but I'm, without a doubt, one hundred percent responsible for giving him the push he needed to get together with his current girlfriend, Bryn.

Lila looks down at the gray, coverless book I'm holding. "What are you reading? Is it one of the books I recommended?"

"Yeah. *A Devilish and Dastardly Duke,*" I say, picking up the book and flipping through the pages.

"Wow. Turns out you can listen to reason. Who knew?" She smirks. "It's such a good story!"

Lila signals for a drink—I guess we are hanging out now. I'm not particularly pleased to be spending time with one of my least favorite people in the world, but I'm not going to be the one to show weakness by leaving.

"Wait. That one is like the third book in that series. Did you start with book three, or have you already read the other two?" she asks.

"I'm not a monster, Lila. Of course I've read the other two. Who reads books out of order?" I leave out the fact that I've also read two other series since she first dared me to read a romance novel. She also annoyingly suggested that if I was embarrassed to be seen reading them, I could remove the dust jacket or buy an e-reader. Coincidentally, my e-reader arrives at my house in California this week—I need the convenience of e-books with as much time as I spend on the road, traveling to tournaments. To be clear, it's not that I'm embarrassed per se, but *romance reader* doesn't exactly align with the image I've carefully cultivated for myself.

"Well, technically, they are stand-alones in the same universe, so you could read them in any order you want," Lila says.

"Do you do that?" I ask.

"God, no. That falls into the chaotic evil bucket for sure."

"It feels more like chaotic neutral to me."

Her nose twitches in disgust. "Blasphemy. Seeing the end of someone's story before reading their book is the worst. But then again, so are you. So maybe you do read them out of order."

I ignore her dig. "But you know they end up together anyway. It's a given for the genre."

"Trust me on this. You want the backstory so you're invested when the author gives you little snapshots into their HEAs in the later books."

"HEAs?" I ask.

"Happily ever afters! Come on, JT. Learn the lingo if you're going to read romance like the big hitters."

"I think you're overselling yourself a bit."

"Romance readers are taking over the book market. Almost half of romance readers finish a novel within a week. We *are* the big hitters in publishing these days."

"You're such a nerd."

"Takes one to know one," she shoots back like a child.

I finish my scotch and signal for another. I don't typically drink more than one on the night before I have to golf, but for some reason, possibly self-flagellation, I'm not ready to call it a night yet either. My group's tee time is late enough tomorrow that I should be okay with just one more drink.

"So, update on Project Don't-Let-My-Brother-Get-Back-Together-with-Alexis: I met Bryn today," Lila says. I know most people would say she looks excited, but I know better. She's smug about meeting her before me.

"I think we need to workshop that project name a bit more," I reply. "Jameo mentioned Bryn might be here. I'm glad she came." I intentionally don't ask her anything more, knowing she's dying to tell me.

"Aren't you going to ask me what I think of her?"

I sigh, pretending not to care. "I suppose. What did you think?"

"Oh, she seems awesome. We just finished having dinner together."

Lila dives into the story about meeting Bryn on the course today while following Jameson's group, and I try to ignore the prick of jealousy that hits me at her words. Jameson was out with his sister and girlfriend while I sat here alone at a bar. Not that I couldn't have my pick of women. I'm a professional golfer and have been successful for several years now. I have women I can call in all the major cities if I'm interested in a night of fun. Unfortunately, fun just isn't doing it for me anymore. Instead of leaving me satisfied, my last few hookups have left me feeling empty. I blame these damn romance books Lila recommended. Fuck. I wonder if she knew this would happen and did it on purpose. I wouldn't put it past her.

Lila orders another drink as well, definitely not limiting herself to two tonight. Though I suppose that's fair. She doesn't have anything to do besides watch golf all weekend and then head back to Denver for her classes on Monday. She's 24. Why shouldn't she get drunk on a Thursday night in Vegas?

Unfortunately, I'm annoyed to find that drunk Lila is a lot more fun than the Lila I'm usually dealing with.

"You're a lot more fun when you're not around Jameson," she says, mirroring my sentiments.

"I'm fun all the time, Pipsqueak. You're the one who went from being my pal when you were fourteen to not being civilized four years later. That wasn't on me."

It *might* be on me, though. That party we went to together during Thanksgiving break her freshman year of college—I know I didn't handle things like I should have. But she didn't either. And when she came out punching when I showed up at her house for Thanksgiving the next day, well, I wasn't just going to lie down and take her insults, clever though they usually were. Now, we can barely be in the same place without getting into loud arguments, no matter how inappropriate the setting. Except for tonight, apparently.

I watch her as she continues to tell me about Jameson and Bryn, distracted by the flecks of light reflecting off her eyes, the dark green that is unlike any I've ever seen. I know people say they're just like her brother's, but—nope. The thought of her brother pulls me back to reality. This is Lila. The girl who turned from cute tag-along to feisty foe to enemy. I know we've been on friendlier terms lately as we try to save the sinking ship that is Jameson Walker, but no way am I going to let her catch me with my guard down.

"So why are you here alone?" I ask. "Couldn't get that nerd boyfriend of yours to fly to Vegas with you on Jameo's dollar?"

Lila slowly swivels on her stool to face me, and I swear someone put her in slow motion. Even her dark eyebrow lifts at an irregular pace. "Rude, JT. We were being civilized."

I take a long pull from my drink, realizing as I swallow that the bartender replaced my empty second glass while I was thinking about Lila. Well, too late now. I guess I'm having three tonight. Luckily, I ate...nothing. I was going to grab dinner before Lila sat down. Shit. I may be a bit tipsy the night before a tournament. Not a good choice on my part. Fucking Lila.

"What? Did this one not live up to your expectations either? Did he run before you asked him to marry you, or after?" I ask.

"Wanting to date someone who isn't a complete asshole isn't that high of an expectation to have for a man, JT. I'm not asking them to marry me today, I just want to know it's on the table."

"It's a lot to ask when they're 24."

She huffs out a non-reply, finishing her drink.

"He's 26."

"It's the same thing. Not a lot of 26-year-old men are interested in shackling themselves to someone permanently."

"Wow. You've got such a high opinion of love," she says, laying the sarcasm on heavily.

"I think, of the two of us, my opinion of love and marriage may be more correct."

"Doubtful. Plus, look at my parents. Look at your parents, for shit's sake."

"Your parents are the anomaly, Lila. You have to know that. My parents, on the other hand, prove my point exactly. I think they like each other okay, but saying it's a love match would be a bit strong."

She snorts into her drink. "You said 'love match.'"

I glare at her. Of course I said *love match*. She's been polluting my brain with tales of romance for months now.

"So what happened with your most recent not-love-match?" I ask.

"He dumped me."

"Ouch."

"Well, technically, he just 'clarified we weren't dating.'" She fiddles with the little black straw in her cup, her eyes fully focused on the row of TVs behind the bar.

"Tough look for you," I taunt.

"You did sort of help me save face in the whole thing," she admits begrudgingly.

I raise an eyebrow, and she sighs before continuing, "It was that first night you texted me about Jameson, and Andrew may have noted that I was talking to another guy."

"And?" I press.

"And when he saw a man's name—your name—on my text messages, he jumped to the conclusion I was talking to some other guy. Oh God, you should've seen his face. He was so relieved he didn't have to break up with me. And since I didn't want to look like a loser who thought we were more than we were, I just went along with it."

"Wait. He was glad you were texting another guy? Not jealous like any normal guy would be?" Like I would certainly be if I were in his place. *Wait. What? No. I didn't mean that. I would be relieved, just like him, that Lila Walker didn't think we were dating.*

"Yep. So, in a way, you actually made something better for once in your life."

"Except for now that asshat thinks we're dating," I say.

"No. He thinks I was talking to some guy named JT two months ago."

"It's still possible he put two and two together."

"He is getting his master's in engineering, so I would hope it's at least possible."

"Do you still like him?" I ask, not knowing why I care.

She lets out a low, self-deprecating laugh. "I don't know. It's humiliating, though. Can you imagine if he *had* realized I thought we were dating?"

Before I have a chance to answer, she continues, "And now I'm clearly inebriated enough to be telling this to *you*, which means it's likely time for me to go to bed."

She's not wrong. I'd normally be all over embarrassing information about Lila. I don't know if it's the alcohol, the slice of tan skin peeking out under the edge of her skirt, or the lack of our usual chaperone tonight, but I don't feel the spark at the thought of taking her down with a barb right now. Instead, I extend my hand, helping her off her stool.

"Come on, Pipsqueak, I'll walk with you to the elevator."

CHAPTER TWO

LILA

JT JOHNSON TOWERS OVER me as I unstick my legs from the stool I've been sitting on for the last few hours. He's officially six feet two, which I know because I've studied professional golfers' height, weight, and age statistics on more than one occasion. It's not as creepy or unrealistic as it sounds—with a brother who's a top ten golfer in the world, I have the opportunity to run into a potential professional golfer boyfriend at any time.

"You good?" he asks as I settle a bit unsteadily to my feet.

I nod, but I'm definitely not sober right now. Certainly not drunk, but if forced to pick one of the two...

"How are you feeling about tomorrow?" I ask, realizing he is likely up way too late for a work night. "It's a bit late for an old man like you to be out gallivanting."

His eyes cut to me as he leads me onto the casino floor, taking a shortcut to the elevator. "I'm not old."

I smile at him before catching the toe of my heeled sandal on the carpet. JT reaches out, steadying me, and I jump slightly as his large hand grips my upper arm, heat shooting from the point of contact throughout my body. Glancing up at his face, I see my reaction mirrored back in his eyes.

He drops my arm, backing away slightly.

"Thanks," I say, trying to hide my embarrassment. Nothing like being the slightly drunk girl who needs her enemy and brother's best friend to watch out for her. Unfortunately, the second I take my eyes off the path, a large man wearing navy running pants and a white tank top knocks into me from the side.

I grunt, grimacing as my shoulder connects with his sweaty arm. JT pulls me to him, wrapping his arm around me. The fact that we both stumble at the move suggests JT is not quite sober either. This time, I'm more prepared for the fire his contact ignites, and I snuggle into his warmth. Sober me is going to be revolted by this, but tipsy Lila likes a good cuddle.

JT shrugs as if he's going to pull away, but as a large group cheers next to us, he moves his hand to my lower back, directing me past the craps tables and into the elevator bay. I brace myself for the cold casino air that will find me again when he moves his hand, but it never comes. Instead, he moves me with him, keeping his hand on me as he pushes the Up button.

"Lila?" a voice asks from behind.

Shit. Please tell me that isn't— I glance over my shoulder. Ugh. Why in the world is Andrew Caldwell here?

JT must feel my discomfort because he shoots me a confused look before turning to face the group of five guys headed our way.

What have I done in my life to deserve this? To be embarrassed in front of the one man certain to taunt me with it for the rest of my life?

"Hey, Andrew," I say, trying to play it much cooler than I feel right now—or ever, if we're being honest.

"Are you out here watching your brother?" Andrew asks.

I don't typically go around telling people who my brother is. Not because I'm ashamed, but because it just seems easier when I don't have to question everyone's motives for being my friend. Unfortunately for me, I thought Andrew and I were dating, so of course he knows my brother is a professional golfer.

Before I can answer, he notices JT—though how he could've missed the man's imposing presence from the beginning is beyond me. "Holy shit. You're JT Johnson!"

JT smiles, and I recognize it as his TV smile, not the real one he surprisingly let loose tonight. "Hey, man. Nice to meet you." He reaches out to shake Andrew's hand, and I feel the loss of his warmth like I just lost a limb.

A group of people pile out of the elevator that finally made its way to the ground, but, before we can get in, a bachelorette party in leather skirts and cowboy boots pushes in front of us, filling the entire car.

"Oh, man. You're JT!" Andrew exclaims.

JT and I both glance at each other. I can only imagine he's thinking the same thing I am: Is this kid losing his freaking marbles? He just did this whole "you're JT Johnson!" bit.

Andrew notices our faces and laughs. "No. I mean, that night, I was all worked up to tell Lila we shouldn't see each other anymore. I'd heard around campus she thought we were dating, and I mean, we definitely weren't. I thought it was going to be the whole embarrassing thing where I had to break the heart of the poor girl who thought we were together, but turns out, the rumor mill had it wrong—she'd been talking to some other guy too."

He gestures to JT with his hand before continuing his one-man act, hell-bent on making this situation as embarrassing as possible. "I can't believe I didn't put it together before now. I guess I just never really thought the JT she was texting with was you. Damn, Lila, really hitting above your weight class, huh?"

I want to die. Please, Lilith, if you can hear me, now would be the ideal time to call me back to Hell. Though, on second thought, it's distinctly possible I'm already in Hell.

JT looks at me before pulling me back to his side. "I'm the lucky one. I can't believe I get to date someone as amazing as Lila."

I'm sorry. What? Is JT...helping me? I gape at him, and his eyes widen as he panics. Luckily, I think I'm the only one who would pick up on the doubt raging in his mind, though I'm also the only one who knows just how similar this situation is to the one that set us on a crash course to enemies.

Fortunately, we're saved by another elevator arriving. Unfortunately, Andrew's group of friends plus another group all shove their way in, so it's a tight fit. As people shuffle around to make space between the groups, JT pulls me to him, my chest millimeters from his. JT asks the lady in front to push his floor, and I remain quiet, sober enough now to recognize it would be a dead giveaway to our ruse if JT and I weren't sharing a room. I catch Andrew openly watching us from the opposite corner. JT must notice him as well, because he gives a small nod in Andrew's direction before wrapping his arms around me and placing a quick kiss on the top of my head.

The sweet move is surprisingly nice for a bottom-feeder like JT Johnson.

As the elevator dings, letting a single rider out, Andrew is still watching us. I know from experience that I'm playing a dangerous game with JT, but all I can hear is Andrew's voice saying JT is out of my league. What a dick. So I do the only logical thing: I lean my forehead into JT's chest, breathing in his clean, masculine smell. He must have sprayed on some cologne before heading down to the bar. Or maybe he took a shower. Yeah, a long, hot shower, all lathered up— I jolt back from my tipsy fantasy as his arms settle around my waist. I lean into him further, wrapping my arms around his neck and taking a deep breath. For the show, of course.

The elevator stops, and the other group exits. The door closes again before Andrew's voice comes from the corner, "It is weird, though. I heard from a couple of different people in our engineering cohort that Lila thought we were dating." JT's body goes stiff as Andrew keeps talking, "That's why I decided I needed to say something. It's just weird that—"

JT grabs my chin, tilts my face up to him, and kisses me. My lips. The ones attached to my face. *What is happening?* At the contact, Andrew's voice fades away, the hot embarrassment morphing into a fiery burn that pulses through my chest and straight to my core. I grab

JT's face, pulling him down to my height and deepening the kiss. He matches my intensity, and I let out a small gasp. Taking advantage of my open lips, he slips his tongue inside, and I'm gone. There is nothing and no one. Only this.

There's a cough, and one of Andrew's buddies says, "Um, this is your floor."

JT and I break apart, and I glance at Andrew's stunned face. I want to care I just won, but honestly, I am shaken by the fire spreading through my body. I distinctly do not like JT Johnson. We aren't friends. We can barely stand to be in the same room.

But fuck. I'm not sure if the buzz is from the tequila or the spark that ignited when our lips met, but I can't seem to catch my breath thinking about doing it again.

JT looks just as shocked as I feel, so I grab his hand and pull him off the elevator. We stop on the dark purple carpet just past the elevator doors, and I turn to face him, uncertainty warring with desire as my slightly addled mind argues over what should come next. As the doors start to close, I pull his head back down to mine, capturing his lips.

Time ceases to exist as JT bends down without breaking our kiss and, looping his hands under my ass, lifts me as if I weigh nothing. Which, to a man who exercises as much as he does, is likely the case. I wrap my legs around his waist, groaning as my center meets a very hard ridge. Shifting my hips slightly, I give over to my need for friction.

"Fuck, Lila," JT breathes, my name like a prayer and a curse on his lips. "I don't like you."

His eyes meet mine, and I briefly wonder if my pupils are as large as his. "I don't like you either, Pretty Boy. Trust me."

Then he's kissing my neck and rocking his hips, and the part of my brain once capable of cognizant thought is pulled back under, lost to the tide of lust.

A door down the hallway opens, and we pull apart, our eyes locked as our chests heave. I know I should leave. I know I shouldn't do what my body is telling me to. But, for the life of me, I can't remember why I shouldn't do it. I can give in to this spark and still hate this man in the morning.

I grab JT's hand and start maneuvering him down the hallway. "What room are you in?" I ask.

He pulls back a bit, clearly questioning the decision we're about to make. Still holding his hand, I look back into his eyes, letting him see the heat in mine. "What room, JT?"

He pauses for a second longer before taking the lead, pulling me this time. "It's just over here."

I let out a little 'whoop,' hustling to keep up with his long strides. We walk for a minute before he finally stops, pulling the key card out of his pocket.

"This means nothing," he says, fidgeting with the gray key card.

"Less than nothing," I agree. "Just like you."

"We can't ever tell anyone."

"Never. I'd die of embarrassment for stooping so low."

"But, it's...it's so good, right?" he asks like he, too, needs someone to explain the energy flowing through his body and why it's so much more powerful than it's ever been before.

"So fucking good."

Chapter Three

Lila

Three Months Ago

"So, what's up with your game these days?" I ask JT as my brother heads to the bathroom yet again. Apparently, I'm unable to stop myself from poking the bear when left alone with him. It's the same impulse I had when he was at our house for Thanksgiving, but this time I don't have the parental oversight to keep things from getting out of control.

Not that it's weird to be sitting in a bar across from the man who rocked my world and never thought about me again—*it's fine*. He promised it meant nothing, and so did I. So I'm sure I'll stop replaying it every chance I get any day now, too.

We are in Phoenix, waiting for my brother's girlfriend, Bryn, to show up after a major blow-up placed her relationship with Jameson firmly on the rocks. Watching my brother pace between the table and the bathroom would be funny if he didn't look so wrecked. Even though he's trying to keep calm, the way his gaze flicks to the door every few seconds says it all: He knows he messed up and is scared of losing her.

JT messes with his hat before taking a long pull of his beer. "If I knew what was wrong with my game, do you really think I'd be missing the cut every other week?" he asks.

"Do you think you're just over the hill? How long until you can start playing in the senior league?" I fake a grimace, pretending to sympathize with his plight.

"I'm not old, Lila."

"Aren't you, though?"

"I'm not even thirty yet."

"Hmm," I say, tapping my chin. "If you're not getting too old, then maybe you're just distracted by something. Maybe a certain bathroom counter—"

"How long until they are here?" Jameo asks, his sudden appearance causing JT to turn his head so quickly that he might be able to blame neck pain for his terrible golf scores moving forward. *Sucker. I knew he'd get worked up about the reminder of what we did in his Vegas hotel.*

I make a show of checking my watch. "Any time now. Like I told you two minutes ago before you stomped off to do god knows what in the bathroom."

I'm trying to distract him, and it thankfully works, because he replies, "What, exactly, do you think I'm getting up to in there, Lila?

Do you have some nefarious bathroom exploits you'd like to share with the class?"

JT snort-coughs so hard, liquid flies from his nose. Tough time to decide to take a drink. "Actually," I start, planning to take full advantage of the ammunition JT just confirmed I have. "Now that you mention it, there was this time in a hotel room, and the countertop was juuuust—"

"Jesus Christ, Lila," Jameo cuts in, passing a wad of napkins to JT, who is about to die from inhaling his beer. "I obviously don't want to know the details of your sex life. In my mind, you are and will forever be an asexual blob."

"Oh, really?" I ask with a smirk before turning my attention to the man who forever changed my opinion of bathroom sex. "What about you, JT? Do you see me as an asexual blob?"

"What? You? I mean... I try not to think about..."

I feel the evil smile pull across my face as he struggles to find the right words. I'm not sure how Jameo would feel knowing his best friend hooked up with his little sister, though if I get a few more drinks in me, we might just find out.

Fortunately for JT, my brother's attention has been drawn to the front of the restaurant, where Bryn and her sisters are walking through the door. JT and I follow Jameson over, saying hello to Bryn's sisters, Kelsey and Izzy, as we all awkwardly gather between the bar and an empty four-top. Jameo and Bryn clearly need to go have it out somewhere private, so after we assure them we can find our own way back to our various hotels, they take off. Uncertain what else to do, I invite Kelsey and Izzy to join us for a drink, and we head back to our table.

As JT breaks away from the group to grab another round, I consider telling him I don't need one. I haven't had enough to eat today, and the two drinks I've had are going straight to my head. On the other hand, I am now awkwardly stuck at a bar with the guy I'm *definitely not* obsessing over and my brother's girlfriend's sisters, one of whom interviewed me a few weeks ago for a job at her company. So maybe another drink won't hurt.

JT returns from the bar and slides into the booth next to me, the Harper sisters having taken the other one for themselves. My thigh sparks where his leg meets mine, and I quickly pull away, making myself as small as possible. We most certainly do not need any sparks catching fire again. The rest of the table falls into the natural rhythm of conversation, talking about work and upcoming travel, but I can't focus on anything but the warmth emanating from the body next to mine.

"When do you finish your grad program, Lila?" Izzy asks as JT excuses himself to use the restroom.

"Oh, um…" I force myself to focus on her, my mind trying to focus on JT's ass as he walks away rather than her question. "May. I graduate in May."

"Oh, cool," she replies. "Well, I hope you'll be moving to Wild Bluffs then."

"Yeah, me too, though obviously no pressure to hire me, Kelsey," I say.

Kelsey sighs. "Way to make it awkward, Iz."

"Only a little," I joke. "Though, why should we deviate from the norm at this point?"

We all share a laugh, the kind where a group acknowledges things are uncomfortable, and somehow that acknowledgment eases the weirdness.

"You know what? I should probably pee before JT gets back and blocks the booth again," I say as I slip out of the leather seat and head toward the little hallway with the Restrooms sign above it.

JT emerges from the men's bathroom, and as he walks toward me, I know I should move to the side so his stupid, big shoulders can fit through, but instead of shrinking against the wall like I normally would, I continue walking, my left side bumping against his firm body as we pass by each other. I wobble at the impact, and JT grabs my shoulders to steady me.

"Been walking long, Pipsqueak?" JT asks as I regain my balance.

I know I should respond with a retort of some kind, but all I can think about is the feel of his strong hands, so close to touching my skin through the thin fabric of my shirt. My gaze travels to his eyes, and they look so dark, they could almost be a dusk sky. But somehow, it's the gleam in them, the one that tells me he's about to argue with me, that causes me to break. I push up on my toes, slamming my mouth against his, my arms wrapping around his neck for stability. His lips meet mine without hesitation, his body responding like it's been waiting for this opportunity. Never breaking the kiss, he moves us to the dark back corner of the hallway, away from the prying eyes of anyone who might be watching.

Our kiss is desperate, like a forbidden fruit we both know we shouldn't indulge in. The bar around us fades away, leaving only the sound of our erratic breathing and thundering hearts. His hands trace fire along my spine, my sides, my ass, igniting a flame within me that threatens to consume us both. My body is no longer under the control of my brain as my hips press into JT. Our mouths continue to collide until, to my horror, my right leg hooks around JT's waist, pulling us even closer together. He bites my lower lip and lifts my skirt, tracing his fingertips up my inner thigh.

"We can't ever tell anyone about this," he says, and I nod in reply.

His knuckle finds my throbbing center, and I bite back a moan. He teases me, gently tracing my pussy through my underwear. He lets out a dark chuckle and pulls his hand away, dropping my skirt back down before grabbing my hand and tugging me toward the bathroom.

As I start to follow him, the door next to us opens, yanking me back to reality. As a bartender steps in from outside, JT drops my hand, and my stomach falls. Regret is written all over his face, and suddenly, I'm 18 again.

Just as he opens his mouth, Izzy walks into the hallway, and we both take a quick step away from the other. Unwilling to endure his rejection again, I turn away without a word, vowing that *this time* I'll forget about JT Johnson.

CHAPTER FOUR

JT

Now

"It's been a rough six months, JT. You've only been in the final hunt one time since you won in Vegas," my agent Jon says through my phone.

"I know. I know. I just can't seem to dial in my short game. It's like any time I get close to the green, my swing is struggling." I let out a short laugh, trying to ease the tension in this conversation.

Jon, however, isn't the type of man who worries about putting others at ease. You don't become a professional sports agent of his caliber without enjoying the stress and pressure that come with uncomfortable conversations. So he forges ahead with his point. "Have you considered seeing someone? I know you've been opposed to seeing a sports psychologist in the past, but I think it could be helpful. You know how helpful it has been for Jameson."

He's not wrong, but I also think he might be giving the good doctor a bit too much credit and not enough to Jameson's girlfriend, who has settled him like no therapist ever could.

"No. There is nothing wrong with me that a few thousand practice putts won't fix. I don't need a therapist." Plus, my dad would likely disown me if he ever found out I was lying around on a couch somewhere, bitching about my problems, rather than out on the course, working to fix them. I've heard his rants about it before.

"Look, I'm not sure your standings would agree nothing is wrong with you. You're clearly struggling with the mental aspect of your game. You can't just stay holed up in California, wearing yourself down on the putting green, expecting to fix something that isn't physical."

"My game is getting better. Phoenix was in February. I placed second. You're acting like my game is dead. You know how golf is. It's rare to be number one every week."

What I don't mention is Phoenix and Vegas are part of my current problem. Because those two tournaments? The only ones this year where I was in the top twenty? They happen to be the two tournaments where I hooked up with Lila fucking Walker. I shake my head, telling myself yet again that two times does not make a pattern. Let's not confuse coincidence with causation. Lila Walker is a walking, talking demon, not a good-luck charm.

Jon, choosing to ignore my very valid point, continues like I never said anything. "If you're not going to talk to a sports psychologist, maybe you should consider doing what Jameo did. Step away from your daily life for a while. Shit, maybe you should go to Wild Bluffs. It might be something in the water there."

I laugh, a real one this time. I had a good time with Jameson when I stayed out there last year, and I enjoyed my last visit, but I'm a big-city, California guy. Tiny, landlocked Wild Bluffs is not the solution.

"Sure, Jon. I'll think about it," I tell him. We chat about the business side of things for a few more minutes before wrapping up the call. I hate letting anyone down, and Jon is included in that. So I will think about it. In the meantime, I'll turn my game around so I don't actually have to go to Wild Bluffs.

Unfortunately, now I'm also thinking about Lila Walker, which is always a frustrating experience—in more ways than one.

Lila is everything I shouldn't want. If you happen to overlook the fact that she is my best friend's *little sister*, which, if I learned anything from the last time I dated a friend's relative, is enough in itself to stay the hell away from her, she also happens to be a huge pain in my ass. She does exactly what she wants, and somehow knows exactly which of my buttons to push to set off a fiery wave of anger any time I'm around her. She's just finishing up grad school, and she has a professional golfer for an older brother who buys her whatever she wants. It's like she has no idea how the real world works. Which maybe she doesn't. She dates guys who—*damn it.*

All of a sudden, I'm pulled into the past, reliving it like I'm a ghost in a goddamn Christmas movie. I see the way Lila's shoulders slump when that fuckboy approached us by the elevator in Vegas. I feel my arm wrap around her, my body offering to be her fake boyfriend without my mind ever agreeing to help. I smell her coconutty shampoo as I pull her against me.

Stop, I tell myself, pressing the heels of my hands into my eyes before the next scene plays, but I know it's useless. I knew this would happen once I started thinking about Lila. Damn demon magic.

Now she's sitting on the countertop in front of me, her legs spread wide. It's just the right height for us, and I take full advantage of it. The memory of watching her in front of me and in the mirror makes my shorts grow a bit tighter, and I mentally slap myself. Just as the memory shifts to my hotel bed, my front door slams, and a metaphorical cold bucket of water is thrown on me in the shape of my mother.

"JT!" she calls, walking into my living room.

I walk over to meet her, giving her a brief hug and a light peck on the cheek, the one without the scar. "Hi, Mom," I say, wondering what brought her to my house this time.

She looks me over, her eyes catching on every detail of my face before working their way down my white golf shirt and navy blue golf shorts. "You aren't using that face cream I bought you, I see," she says, her eyes narrowing in on the faint lines next to my right eye.

"I do use it," I say. And I do. I, like basically any other 30-year-old man, don't care about the wrinkles, but Patricia Johnson cares. So I use the face cream...when I remember. Which is...most of the time.

"Honey, you know we have some very important investor events coming up in the next few months, and I need you to look your best, okay? You are a reflection of your father and me, and we must look good right now. We need to keep bringing new money into the firm."

"I know, Mom," I say. It's second nature at this point to hold in my "I know because you've told me all ten times we've spoken this week." I learned the hard way that saying anything more will cause her to give me the silent treatment for a week while somehow loudly yelling at me with her eyes.

"I just want to make sure you're at your best, JT."

"I know, Mom," I say again. Because I do know. She does want me to be my best, and she's sacrificed a lot to ensure I was able to be one of the best golfers in the whole damn world—including her perfect face and almost her life.

And now I'm letting her down. She and my dad both. My dad has called me almost three times a day with suggestions on how to turn my game around. Unfortunately, neither my dad nor my real coach have any useful ideas on how to turn my game around. My coach recommended I take it easy, while my dad suggested I double up on my daily lifting sessions. Needless to say, I've been hitting the gym a lot lately.

My mom stops her perusal of my house, her fingers tracing the gray and black cover of my e-reader. "You...read?" I'm confused by the disgust lacing her tone, as she was the one who monitored my grades and education like a hawk the entire time I was making my way through junior tournaments.

"Yes?" I reply, though I'm not sure why it comes out as a question. I've read over thirty books since I switched to the e-reader last year. I love that I can read on my phone when I'm sitting in locker rooms or am in the back of a rideshare and then switch to the exact place I finished on the larger e-reader when I get to my house or my hotel.

"Interesting. What do you read?"

"Romance novels."

She pauses, her eyes searching my face before she lets out a tinkling laugh. "Oh, dear. I almost believed you. Hilarious. Romance novels."

"I do," I say, but she's already moved on to examining a vase she bought me three years ago and either doesn't hear me or chooses not to listen.

After an uncomfortable silence, I speak up, asking, "So what brings you by? Not that I'm not glad to see you." I would prefer if my mom stopped showing up at my house unannounced and letting herself in, but there is no way I could ever suggest such a thing after everything my parents gave up for me.

"I need to talk to you about the Ferguson Golf Tournament."

"The what?"

"The Ferguson Golf Tournament," she says again, but with a little more volume this time, like my confusion is due to a lack of hearing, not a lack of understanding.

"I don't know what that is."

She draws in a deep breath, making it clear that my not knowing this is unacceptable. "It's only the biggest announced purse in professional golf tournaments history, JT. The Ferguson brothers announced it almost an hour ago, and everyone is talking about how startling the award amount is. It is going to be in Las Vegas this year, and according to Carol Hearst—you know, of that Hearst family—they are going to have a dinner the night before that is going to be a who's who of investors."

I smile. I can help with this. Even though I'm sure I'll only be able to bring one guest as a player, one quick text to Bryn, and I'm sure I can get my parents into the dinner as well. "I'm on it, Mom. I can get you and Dad tickets for sure."

Pulling out my phone, I start to fire off the text that will make my mother happy when the sound of another deep breath stops me. "It's not about getting *tickets*, Justin Theodore."

I cringe, as much at my mom's tone as at her use of my full name—which I hate.

"Okay, sure," I say, trying to keep the peace.

"*You* need to win."

"Why? I mean, I'm definitely going to try, but we both know I've been off my game lately. Why is this specific tournament so important to you?"

"You know your father and I have been working tirelessly to bring in new investors to grow Johnson Investments, well, we—" she cuts herself off abruptly. "Anyway, you winning such a prominent new tournament that will have the focus of the business world all over is the exact publicity we need. And after all the negative press you brought our way with your being friends with Jameson Walker—"

"Mom, I never had bad press—"

"You were besmirched by association, and you know it. I do not have the energy to have this discussion with you again, JT. Your father and I gave up a lot for you to get where you are." She reaches up and traces the thin white scar under her right eye as if remembering her car crash and the cause of it before continuing. "I don't think it's unfair of us to ask you to help us grow the business we put off because of you in return. Unless you're ready to invest another few hundred grand of your own money to bolster our portfolio?"

"Of course. If winning the tournament will help you and Dad, of course I'll try. And, as soon as I win my next tournament, I'll make sure I send you more money to invest for me."

My mom walks over to me then, her golden hair so much like my own shining in the light from the windows. "Well, your best is all you can do, I suppose. Your father and I did our best with you, and that got you here. So I'm sure your best with this one small request will be enough to help with what we need."

I stop my shoulders from drooping at her reminder of how much I owe to my parents for sacrificing their happiness and time to make my dreams of being a professional golfer come true. I have never wanted the fame of golf—though it doesn't bother me most days—but if it's important to my mom, I'll do whatever I can to try to make sure I win the Ferguson Tournament.

"Of course."

"Excellent. And just one other thing, I need you to get to Wild Bluffs. I've heard Conrad Ferguson is out there regularly—God only knows why—and it can't hurt to have some face-to-face time with the man before the event. Having one of the brothers introducing us around at the event would be everything."

"Mom, I—"

"It'll be great, JT. Plus, your father and I have decided to get our kitchen remodeled and a sauna added on, so we're planning to stay here while you're gone. The contractor promised it wouldn't take more than six weeks."

"Mom, you can't just—"

She talks over me again as she swings her oversized sunglasses on her face, "We'll be here next week."

Well, fuck. I guess I'm going to Wild Bluffs.

CHAPTER FIVE

LILA

"No. Mark Grant is a terrible choice," my roommate, Elise, says as she sorts through clothes in her closet. It's two days until we graduate from the engineering master's degree program at Denver College, and Elise—like the killjoy she is—is systematically rejecting every single one of my potential "date" options for the party hosted by one of our classmates tomorrow night.

"Elise! I need to go with someone. Everyone knows the only reason you take a date to a party like this is so they take you home that night. I *need* someone to take me home tonight."

"You know you sound like the horniest girl on the block right now, don't you?" she asks as she examines a red tank top that I've seen her wear exactly one time in the last four years. Unsurprisingly, she adds it to her "maybe" pile. Elise has a distinct inability to make decisions.

"I may be aware of that, yes," I reply. "And, if we are being honest, my libido may be part of my need for a date for the party tomorrow.

However, *as you know*, the real motivation is the fact that my five-year plan has fallen completely off-track this year between the Andrew snafu and the other thing with the worst man alive."

"What casual names for a miserable ten months with not one but two guys completely fucking with your head."

"Eww. JT, that ass, did not fuck with my head. Plus, he and I are back to our usual hatred since Phoenix. No sexual tension whatsoever. Just good old-fashioned disdain. He remains a giant, hairy ball sack."

She peers around the jean skirt she is examining so I can see the skeptical look plastered on her face. "What?" I ask. "We teamed up and saved Bryn and Jameson's relationship. That's it. Jameson still owes me for that, by the way."

"Didn't you end up with an amazing job opportunity out of that whole ordeal?"

"Yes. But he had nothing to do with it. Don't take this future boon away from me, El."

"Normal people don't say boon, Lila. You've got to stop throwing historical-romance words into your everyday conversations."

I wave my hand, dismissing her opinion on the subject. "Back to my problem. I don't want to just date around. I don't want to move to a new town and have to start from scratch finding a boyfriend. The plan is to get married and live happily ever after. I can't do that if I'm single. As you know, you have the highest chance of finding your spouse in college. If not, the next years—"

"Yeah, yeah, yeah. You've given me your old-fashioned dating sermon before, Lila," Elise cuts in. "And while it seems logical in theory, I think you're missing the important part." Elise stands to grab a stack of dresses out of her closet before sitting back down between her piles. "You can't force yourself to fall in love, and you certainly can't force someone to fall in love with you."

"I understand that. But that's why I've got my list of potential dates prioritized based on three factors: if they're planning to stay in Colorado after graduation, their previous interest in long-term relationships, and our general relationship as of now."

"And Mark is at the top of your list?"

"Yup! He's staying in Denver after graduation, he's talked about dating some girl during undergrad for three years, and we got along well when we were in a group last semester." I lift a finger as I say each of the three points in Mark's favor.

"You've literally never mentioned him before today. Are you even attracted to him?"

"Just because I've never considered him before doesn't mean I might not start to find him attractive if I get to know him better," I reason.

"But could it ever be bang-you-on-the-counter-of-his-hotel-room-in-Vegas levels of attraction?" Elise asks.

At the mention of my night together with JT in Vegas, my brain pulls up the montage of memories from that fateful night. Of JT's hands gripping my hips to find the perfect angle as I sit on his bathroom counter. Of the two of us twisted up in the sheets of his bed. Of his thick cock hard and heavy as I suck it into my mouth. Of us repeatedly declaring our unending dislike for one another, even as every cell in my body screamed at me to find a way to be closer to him.

It was the best night of my life with the one person who makes me want to pull my hair out every time we're in the same room. Though, when JT pulled my hair, it was...very different. *Very* different.

"You're thinking about it again, aren't you?" Elise asks, pulling me out of my head.

"Ugh. Yes. How can I not? And that's not fair. No, Mark doesn't currently give off counter-fucking vibes, but he also doesn't give off complete-asshole vibes, which is likely a better foundation for a loving relationship."

"I just don't think you should give up on JT. For as much romance as you read, it really feels like you're letting yourself fall into a miscommunication trope. You guys made out in Phoenix!"

"You realize how delusional you sound right now, don't you?" I ask. "What about me waiting for him to show up to an early breakfast the next morning so we could talk about it like adults sounds like miscommunication?"

"You left him a note, Lila. A handwritten note. And you put it on his pillow as you slipped out of his room after he fell asleep."

"He was in the middle of a tournament! Of course I left so he could sleep. And, yeah. My phone was dead by that point. I left him a note asking him to meet me for breakfast the next morning at six, or to at least shoot me a text so I knew he wasn't going to make it. He did neither."

"Which suggests he didn't get the note. That guy is a notorious people-pleaser. He's not going to ghost his best friend's little sister after hooking up with her."

"He does if they agree to go back to hating each other afterward. Plus, he's never been that guy with me. It's like he enjoys pissing me off."

"Oh, kinda like you enjoy pissing him off? Or do you not recall your evil plan to, and I quote, 'make that asshole hard all through Thanksgiving dinner' by wearing your fuck-me boots?"

"Fine. I do like pissing him off. It's fun. And he deserves it. He's the worst. And it was the only way I could get him to stop treating me like a 14-year-old."

"Well, based on what you told me about what happened in Vegas and then again in the hallway in Phoenix, I can confidently say that the man does not think of you as a little kid."

"And!" I say, continuing my rant about our time in Vegas from earlier, not really caring if Elise is keeping up at this point—she's heard it all before. "Sunday morning when we had breakfast with Bryn and Jameson—which he *did* show up for—I asked him what happened yesterday morning and he said, 'You've been around long enough to know what happened, Lila. I'm not proud of it, but it—'"

"'—is how it is.'" Elise finishes the last part of the quote with me. Okay, I may have talked about this one too many times.

"Ugh." I flop back onto Elise's bed with a dramatic sigh, thinking through my options. She's right. Mark isn't the best choice. I have been in four classes with him throughout my master's program and have felt nothing but baseline friendliness toward him. Exactly zero sparks or hints of attraction felt. I guess I could just wait until I get to Wild Bluffs to find a guy to date.

I sit up quickly, causing Elise to drop the pair of leggings she is folding. "Okay, change of plans. No dates for tomorrow night."

"No. What will I ever do? All I wanted was a date," Elise deadpans.

"Sarcasm noted," I say. "But now I'm on board too. It doesn't make sense for me to have a date for tomorrow. We're graduating this weekend anyway."

"Wow, it's like I've been saying that for the last week or something."

"Have you?" I tease. "Okay, then. New plan. We'll get dressed up, we'll get a little bit tipsy, and we'll celebrate with whatever guy sparks our fancy. Or we will celebrate sans guys and treat ourselves to a late-night ice cream run. It'll probably be more fun anyway."

"Because you've been ruined by counter sex?"

Because I've been ruined by JT Johnson sex. "Because these fools act like boys, and we deserve real men," I say instead.

"And you're going to find a man in Wild Bluffs?"

"Certainly."

"As a small-town girl, I feel I must warn you again that dating is much more complicated in a town the size of Wild Bluffs than you think it is."

Elise is from a small town on the western side of Colorado and has been filling me in on the political maneuvering that is required to live in a town where everyone knows everything about everyone. She somehow thinks I'm going to both be swarmed by single men and all the married women trying to set me up with said single men, and, at the same time, be totally alone after offending every person in town somehow. I can only hope she's exaggerating.

"It will be fine. I can casually test out the dating pool without offending everyone I meet."

She sits down next to me on the bed, her larger frame dipping the mattress down and pulling me into her side. I accept my fate and lay my head down on her shoulder. "I wish I could believe you, but you just don't understand. Unfortunately, you can't understand until you get out there. At least you'll have the Harper sisters to help you navigate it, I guess."

"Or you could just ask your big, fancy job if you could work remotely and come live with me..." I plead for what is likely the hundredth time.

"If only I could. Unfortunately, I will be stuck living downtown, working in a building that holds more people than my entire town growing up."

"You can come visit me anytime you want. Especially for the first six weeks, when I'll be living in Jameo's rental on the golf course."

"I cannot believe how lucky you are," Elise says, leaning her head on mine.

I swipe one of her curly blonde hairs out of my face before replying, "What do you mean?"

"You are the only person I know who finds an awesome house to rent and then, when it won't be ready for the first six weeks you're there, your brother 'just happens' to be out of town traveling that whole time. And, *and*"—she's really on a roll now—"instead of you having to ask him if you can stay there, he asks *you* to stay there and even offers to pay you if you watch his girlfriend's dog for them."

I pat her leg in a consoling gesture. "It must be hard being best friends with someone as awesome as me."

"You mispronounced *annoying*."

"Can't be that. I exude awesomeness. It leaks from my pores."

"Gross. You should really get that checked out."

"Nothing can be done about it. They tried to tone it down, but the awesomeness just keeps shining through."

I swear I can feel Elise's eye roll from where her cheek still rests on top of my head. But instead of engaging again, she lets it go, tugging me back into a hug before getting to her feet and staring at her piles of clothes.

"Why is my maybe pile four times larger than the other two?" she asks.

"Because you're terrible at making decisions," I offer.

Her shoulders slump before she lowers herself back to the ground and starts sorting her maybe pile again.

"I hate packing."

"You and me both. Though at least yours is all either going straight into your apartment or into the trash. I have to figure out what I need for the next six weeks so I can store the rest until my place is ready."

"It's nice your new landlord is willing to let you store your stuff in the garage while the work is done, though," Elise says.

"True. I got pretty lucky with Tim. He seems like a decent guy to rent from. I mean, it sucks that I have to continue to rely on Jameson's handouts, but it's not like anyone could have predicted the pipes bursting and flooding the entire first floor. And housing options are slim in Wild Bluffs."

"And you get to stay in a swanky house on a golf course with a dog...and get paid for it..."

"You make a good point. Things really are looking up for me."

Chapter Six

LILA

"I CAN'T BELIEVE IT'S over," I say to Elise as we stand on the front lawn, staring at the little tan house that holds so many memories. Our parents were here yesterday, helping us pack things up after our graduation ceremony in the morning.

"I'm going to miss it," Elise says, nodding toward the house.

"I'm going to miss you," I reply.

"I may just miss you too. Luckily, we're only going to be three hours away, so we can see each other all the time."

"We better," I threaten before looping my arms around her middle and pulling my tall friend into a tight hug.

After a long embrace where we both pretend not to notice the other one is tearing up, Elise lets go of me and climbs into her truck.

"See you later!" she calls through her open window.

"Bye!" I yell as I wave.

I climb into my navy blue SUV, and after a mental pep talk about how capable I am of pulling a trailer, I shift into gear and slowly creep out onto my street.

Luckily, traffic is fairly light, and I manage to navigate the city portion of my drive without incident. Once I'm on the highway, it's practically a straight shot to Wild Bluffs, so I loosen my grip on the wheel and turn on my audiobook.

I'm just reaching the third-act breakup when I pull into Wild Bluffs. With the help of my map app, I navigate to the single-story, square house with a cute wraparound porch I'll be renting for the foreseeable future. There is a concrete driveway from the street to the attached garage, so I pull forward, intent on backing the trailer into the spot before I let Bryn's sisters know I'm here. There is nothing more embarrassing than trying to back up a car into a spot with people watching.

After a few unsuccessful attempts at getting the trailer going the direction I need it to be, I finally give up and pull straight along the curb. What's a few more feet to the house? I make my way to the porch, only to stop halfway there. Four people are sitting on chairs on the deck, drinking what appear to be beers.

"We didn't want to interrupt your work," Izzy Harper says, standing from her chair and heading down to me. I feel my cheeks turn pink with embarrassment as I realize they watched my horrible trailer parking.

Bryn's other sister, Kelsey, who also is about to be my boss—yes, it does seem a bit awkward, but I'm told these types of complex relationships happen all the time in small towns—stands from her chair as well. "We brought help," Kelsey says, gesturing to the man and woman making their way down to us. I wave, realizing the two middle-aged people must be their parents. I haven't had a chance yet to meet Jen and Ken, but with names like those, I at least remember them from the stories I've heard.

"Hi," I say. "Thanks so much for coming."

"Of course. You're practically family now," Jen says.

"Mom," Kelsey says in a warning tone.

"What? I know they are 'just dating.' But it just seems like they are going to get—"

"No." Kelsey cuts her mom off as Ken chuckles from next to her.

"You know how kids are these days, Jen. They like to take their time. Let's not put any carts before any horses." He turns his full attention to me then. "Plus, we would be happy to help move in Kelsey's employees, even if they aren't related to Jameson."

I nod my head in thanks before Kelsey asks, "So where should we start?"

It takes the four of us just shy of an hour to move all my boxes into the garage. It shouldn't have even taken that long, but Izzy insisted we stop halfway through to walk through the house and make a list of all the furniture I'm going to need to buy. While I knew I was moving into an unfurnished place, it hadn't hit me just how much I was going to have to find to fill the place. Thankfully, Jen knows of a few families in town who have some of the bigger things in storage, so I won't have to worry about somehow getting a table and chairs or a bed frame delivered out here. And, apparently, you can now get mattresses delivered directly to your house in a normal box, so that won't be quite as big of a challenge as I worried it might be.

After we finish unloading, Ken invites me out for a bite to eat, and I almost jump for joy at the offer. Now that I'm here, heading out to Jameson's house and eating dinner alone seems kinda...sad. Kelsey hops in my car with me and, on the way to the restaurant, we return the rental trailer to what is apparently a field behind someone's house.

"How is this associated with a national moving-vehicle chain?" I ask.

"No idea," she replies. "But it's super handy for the few times that you need to move something out here from Denver but don't want to have to drive the trailer all the way back to the city to return it. It's why I suggested this company to you when you asked about moving out here. It's the only one with a return spot in town."

After unhooking the moving trailer, I navigate to Main Street, pleased by how much I remember from when I was here for my job interview. I park across the street from the two-story brick building that houses the bar and restaurant, and we head up the steep steps to the dining area on the second floor. Kelsey glances around, and I follow her to a long booth against the front windows where the rest of our group is waiting for us.

I slide in next to Kelsey, noting walls covered in neon beer signs and TVs turned to the sports channel before noticing the curious faces of people watching me. I accidentally meet eyes with a middle-aged woman across the room, and, to my horror, she takes it as an invitation to come over and say hello.

"Well, hello. You must be Lila. I'm Trish. My husband and I own the hardware store just a few buildings down from where you will be working. I just wanted to come over and introduce myself to a fellow Denver College alum."

Um...what? Is this lady stalking me? I wouldn't have guessed it with her slacks and polo, but maybe the quintessential-mom vibe is her sneaky way of staying under the radar.

Kelsey coughs pointedly, and I realize I've been staring at her. I quickly rearrange my face into what I hope is a friendly smile. "Hello. It's so nice to meet you, Trish," I say.

"Well, anyway, I should let you all get back to dinner, but I had to introduce myself, since we are practically working next door."

"Oh, sure. Um, thanks."

As Trish makes her way back to her table, I take in the table, each and every face trying to cover up a laugh.

"Is she stalking me?" I whisper, and the Harper family loses their battles against the amusement they've been trying to suppress.

"You've been the hot gossip for a couple of weeks now," Izzy says when the laughter dies down, leaning forward so she can see me around Kelsey. "Not to worry, though. They're just excited because you're a new, young, single person moving to town. You'll be old news in like a week." She pauses to consider. "Well, you moving here will be old news in a week. You never know what kind of gossip may or may not follow after."

"How do they even know about me?" I ask.

"Kelsey is the biggest gossip in town."

The sister in question levels Izzy with a glare that could take out a small hippo, but clearly this isn't the first time Izzy has been the subject of Kelsey's ire. Instead of cowering like I would, Izzy's face transforms into a shit-eating grin, and the entire table devolves into laughter.

"Small-town gossip is like a big game of telephone," Ken explains after we order our drinks.

"The coffee men are the worst gossips in town, Lila," Jen cuts in. "So you're really getting the lowdown from an expert."

Ken shoots a good-natured glare at his wife. "The information spread starts out fine and with the best of intentions. People are excited and truly want to know what is happening in the lives of others. But then the speculation and judgment start. And that's what gives small towns a bad rap. People start wondering *why* you would move here or *if* you are single and want to date their nephew. And because the information is passed from person to person just like in the game of telephone, people hear the speculation and think it's the truth, and then that's what gets passed around town. Before you know it, you're a vagabond from South Africa who is living in Tim's house and buying Kelsey's business."

Kelsey takes a long drink from the glass of white wine the waiter delivered during Ken's monologue. "That was surprisingly accurate."

With the complexities of small-town gossip solved for the night, the Harpers fall into a relaxed conversation about their lives, what's going on at work, a couple of relatives I've never met, and so on. Finally, when we're mostly done with our food, Jen turns the conversation back to me.

"So, are you dating anyone, Lila?"

"Mommm," Izzy and Kelsey both groan.

"What? It's a valid question."

"It's an inappropriate question," Kelsey says. "Especially considering she's my employee."

"She's not *my* employee," Jen replies with a shrug. "And I'm curious."

"She does this on planes too," Izzy offers with an eye roll. "She really can't help but pry into the lives of others."

"I like to get to know people," Jen says as she snags one of the two remaining french fries from her eldest daughter's plate.

"That's okay," I say. "Nope. Not dating anyone." I catch a look that passes between Izzy and Kelsey, but I don't speak Harper sister well enough to know what it's about. Probably just typical daughter exasperation about their mom.

"Really?" asks Jen. "That surprises me. You seem like such an outgoing, lovely girl—"

"Mom," Kelsey groans again. "Maybe Lila doesn't want to be dating someone. How many times have I told you that not everyone wants to be in a relationship?"

Well, this is awkward. I don't necessarily want to contradict Kelsey, because that is definitely a true statement, but it's also not me.

"Well..." I say. "I do agree with Kelsey. I have some friends who say they won't even consider dating someone seriously until they are in their thirties. I am, it turns out, just not one of them. I've maybe read one too many romance novels, but I'm a sucker for love. It just didn't end up working out for me at school." I shrug as if my soul isn't crushed by the knowledge that I may not ever find someone who likes me enough to be with me.

You're worthy of love, I remind myself. *There is someone out there who loves you for you.* I read somewhere that positive affirmations are supposed to help with anxiety and mental wellness, and I have embraced these two over the last six months. Okay, fine. I heard it in a Snoop Dogg song for kids, but it doesn't change the fact that sometimes when I say them enough, I can revert to the naïve version of myself who believed I wasn't actively repelling men with my personality.

We wrap up dinner, and Ken insists on paying even though his daughters and I all offer and even suggest we split the bill. So, with a full stomach and a to-go carton to use as my lunch tomorrow, we head back downstairs. Kelsey and I finalize our plans to meet up at Izzy's office in the morning to get me settled at my new workspace. I may not be exactly where I want to be with my love life, but I am so excited about my job. I will never admit it, but I do owe my brother a big thank you for connecting me with the Harper sisters.

With that thought, I climb into my car and then carefully navigate to my home for the next six weeks. Wild Bluffs Country Club isn't too far out of town, but it's dark out, and with no streetlights, it's easy to miss the turn onto the country roads. Luckily, I've been out to visit Jameson a few times, so I manage to find the first turn without much trouble.

I'm surprised when the headlights of the car that has been following me since town also turn onto the dirt road, but I tell myself to stop being paranoid. There are a lot of people who live out here, even if their houses aren't visible from the road after all. As I turn into the golf course road itself, the dark vehicle behind me turns as well, always staying just far enough behind me that I can't see the driver's face inside. *Okay, now this is getting creepy.* I consider calling Elise just to be safe, but then I remember she's likely out to dinner with her parents tonight. *It's all right, Lila. You can do this. Be brave.*

I pull into the driveway in front of Jameson's house, forcing myself to stay calm and think as the pickup pulls into the spot in front of Jameo's garage.

Oh, no. Oh, no, no, no. I frantically search my car for anything I can use to protect myself, somehow deciding on the small flashlight I keep in my center console. Unsure if I should wait in the car or try to make a mad dash for the house, I grip my keys with the pointy ends sticking out between my fingers like I saw in a movie one time and push open my door.

CHAPTER SEVEN

JT

"Thanks for the directions, Mary. I'm in front of the house now. Do you know who this other car might be?" I ask the helpful concierge, Mary, from Wild Bluffs Country Club. It's nine thirty at night, and this poor woman had to guide my dumb ass to a place I've been multiple times before. Which, for the record, is why I wasn't using my phone for directions. Unfortunately, when I realized I was lost—I'm blaming it on the lack of moonlight tonight—my phone didn't have enough service to pull up directions. Turns out that one little bar may not work for the internet, but it will still make phone calls.

"I'm not certain, Mr. Johnson. The Harper sisters have dropped by a few times to help out with the dog, but I really can't say. It most certainly shouldn't be any staff. We are one of the safest places in the world. There has never been any criminal activity out here since we opened almost twenty years ago. That said, I would be happy to call the bartender on duty and see if he can have someone come out to make sure you're safe." My attention is drawn to the car as a small figure darts from it to the house.

"Oh, no. No need to burden anyone, Mary. You've already done enough. I'm sure it's one of Bryn's sisters."

I thank Mary again before hanging up and grabbing my small suitcase and duffle bag out of the backseat. I make my way to the front door, stopping to grab the key under the gray rock to the left of the front door, just where Jameson told me it would be.

I unlock the door and push my way into the house. A woman's scream greets me the second I walk inside, a figure rushing at me before tripping on a lone dog toy in the middle of the entryway. I, like the hero I am, drop my bags and throw my arms out, moving at supersonic speed to catch her shoulders just before she slams into the ground.

"Holy shit," I say, my heart pounding from the adrenaline. I pull the woman up to stand, and I'm so distracted by her tan legs sticking out of her athletic shorts that I don't realize whose shoulders my hands are on.

"What the fuck are you doing here, JT?"

I force my eyes to find her face, and all my worst fears are brought to life—it's Lila Walker. "What am I doing here?" I ask. "What are you doing here, Pipsqueak?" Her eyes narrow at the nickname, and I get a zing of enjoyment from the easy hit. She hates it when I make fun of her height, so I do it whenever possible.

"I asked you first," she says, moving a step away from me. My eyes are drawn back to her legs, and I mentally slap myself and refocus on her face. She seems uninterested in talking, and every cell in my body begs me to break the silence, to smooth this over, but I resist that urge. Not with Lila. Never with Lila. So, instead, I spread my legs and fold my arms across my chest. I complete the I-can-stay-here-all-day look with a slight smirk, the one I know annoys her to no end.

She glares back at me a moment longer before breaking. "Ugh! You are such a child. I'm here watching Bryn's dog while she and Jameson travel the next six weeks." She mirrors my stance as my mind runs with this new information. Lila is staying at Jameson's house for the next six weeks? Why wouldn't Jameson have told me? You tell someone if they're going to have a roommate while staying at your house. That's just common courtesy. And Jameson knows Lila and I can't stand each other. He wouldn't let us stay here together. We might burn his house down.

"Well?" Lila asks after a long pause.

"Well, what?"

"Why are you here?" She asks the question really slowly, like I'm not able to keep up with her intellectually. Though, at this exact moment, maybe I'm not. I feel like I'm struggling to catch up.

I'm not sure what I'm going to do about this whole situation, but I know I can't let Lila see how frazzled I am. "I'm staying here too," I say, shrugging and turning to pick up my bags from where I dropped them by the door in my hustle to save Lila. Though, if I had known it was Lila at the time, I would've let her fight it out with gravity herself. *Okay, I would've still tried to help, but I would've had a snarky comment ready to go once she was safely upright.*

"Tonight?" Lila asks, and I turn back to face her.

"Yeah, tonight. And for the next few weeks."

"No."

"Didn't Jameo tell you?"

"Of course he didn't. You aren't staying here. You're just trying to annoy me."

I raise my right eyebrow. "Why else would I be here?"

She doesn't answer, clearly unable to come up with a logical reason why I would be in a house, alone with her, in the middle of nowhere. Honestly, I'm having a hard time remembering why I'm here too. However, one thing is certain: if Lila is staying here, there is no chance I will be. I'll find a place to stay in town or, hell, in another state. Wild Bluffs doesn't have magic golf properties. I'll just find Conrad Ferguson or one of his brothers somewhere else. New York, maybe. The biggest city in the country is more my style anyway.

"But not to worry," I say. "I'm here now, so I can take care of the dog." I look around, realizing I haven't seen or heard a dog since getting here. "Where is Jack, anyway?" I met Bryn's dog last time I came to visit, and while he didn't give off wagging-tail, be-my-best-friend-forever vibes, he seemed like the type of dog to come say hello when someone walks through the door.

"Why do you remember his name?" Lila asks, as if my question wasn't important enough to answer.

"I made a joke about how Bryn's taste in men was remarkably similar to that of her taste in alcohol...named after whiskeys."

Lila snorts a laugh but then quickly catches herself.

"Also, he's important to Bryn, who is important to Jameo, who is my best friend, so of course I would remember his name." I cross my arms again, wondering if we're going to stand in the dead space between the front door and the kitchen all night. "But you didn't answer my question. Where is he?"

"The Harpers'."

"The parents or Kelsey's? What are the parents' names again? I know they rhyme…"

Lila stares at me, her mouth in a straight line, like she is trying to figure out my angle. Unfortunately for her, I don't have one. I just like to make sure I know the people who are important to *my* people. Plus, I'm sure I'll see Bryn's sisters around town, and after spending some time with them when we were all in Phoenix with Bryn and Jameo, I feel like I should make sure to say hi and ask about the things they mentioned last time I saw them.

"Jen and Ken. And yeah, Jack is with them."

"Okay, well, I can figure out where their house is in the morning. I'm sure there are no less than twenty people in town who would be willing to tell me where the Harpers live. So no need for you to stay here."

Lila glances at the door like she might just make a mad dash out of it right now. "I, um…" She coughs before starting again. "I actually don't have…"

My hand unconsciously moves forward at the sound of her anxiety. *Do not comfort her!* I warn myself as I pull my hand back to my side in a fist. *Remember what happened last time you tried to help her? She cursed you with her demon magic, convincing you that you were in ecstasy, ruining you for all mortal women, and then flying away on her broomstick. Demons do not apply to the normal rules of polite society.*

Okay, I've got to stop reading paranormal romances. Those are clearly too much for me right now.

So I do what I've done with Lila for the past eight years. I don't pull my punches—metaphorically, of course. "What? Nowhere else to go? Aren't you supposed to be living here now? Or are you just mooching off your brother until you can find a local to sweep you off your feet and into his house?" Honestly, I'm not even sure where that last part came from, but I'm on a roll now, so I might as well go with it. "I really thought you were smarter than that."

Her hands are on her hips, her little chin tipped up defiantly. "Oh, JT. I'm so much more intelligent than you that you can't even comprehend the difference. And no, I have a house in town, but I sure as shit won't be leaving here just because you showed up and decided to act like you own the place. I was here first. And I'll be staying."

OH. She wants to throw down now? Mmmkay. Well, two can play that game. "Well, I'm not leaving either," I say, making my way into the living room and flopping down on the couch, manspreading in a way my mother has criticized me for numerous times in the past. "I think I like it here."

She stalks out to stand in front of me, her hips swaying as if she really is made from smoke and wisps of brimstone. "What's wrong, JT? Are you out here trying to find a local girl for yourself like Jameo did? Maybe another one of the Harper sisters so you can move out here, buy the house next door, and live a perfect little life with your bestie?"

"And if I am?" I ask, knowing it will piss her off more.

She stares at me, and I can see the moment she calls my bluff. "Then let me help. I'll even put a good word for you...with Kelsey." And damn if I don't feel a shiver go down my spine. Kelsey is beautiful, smart, and really fucking scary if I'm being honest. She has never once been anything but fun and kind to me, but I have no doubt that if I tried to date her, she would eat me alive. Apparently, Lila feels the same way about my chances with Kelsey.

"Anyway, JT. You're a professional golfer. Go get a room in the hotel. Rent another one of the houses. Do anything but be in my space. See you never."

She offers a little wave of her fingers over her shoulder that she smoothly transitions into just the middle finger. Riiight. I guess she's staying in that room. This house is set up for a foursome of golfers to stay in for a week or so, with each room having its own bathroom. They are located on the four corners of the house, with the kitchen, dining area, and living space in the center. I peek into the two rooms on the other side of the house from Lila, but one is clearly Jameson's, and the other appears to have a bunch of Bryn's stuff stored in it. I grab my bags and throw them into the closet of the final room. The one that shares a wall with Lila, though luckily the bathrooms act as a barrier between the two rooms themselves.

Not wanting Lila to overhear the phone call I'm about to make, I slip out the back door onto the patio and drop into one of the Adirondack chairs surrounding a stone firepit.

"Jameson," I say when he answers my call right before it goes to voicemail.

"What's up, JT? I'm kinda busy over here." As he is with Bryn and it's even later where they are, I can only imagine what kind of busy he is, but I don't care. He knowingly sent me into my own personal hell without even the slightest heads-up.

"Um, did you know Lila is staying at your house?" I ask, trying to stay upbeat about the whole thing. Jameson is a moody guy sometimes, and I've always been the golden retriever to his black cat. You can't have two black cats in a friendship.

"Yeah. She's watching Bryn's dog while her place in town gets repaired."

I wait for more, but apparently, that's all he's going to say about it.

"You weren't going to tell me that your sister, the girl I fight with more than anyone in the world, was going to be my roommate for two months?"

He laughs and says something low to Bryn, who also laughs.

"I was going to tell you, but Bryn thought you would both find reasons to be somewhere else if you knew the other was going to be there. And we thought this would be a good time for you guys to figure your shit out. What—" He pauses as Bryn says something behind him. "Sorry, Bryn feels it's important to clarify—for a reason she won't explain to me—that she says you all need to 'get it out of your systems.'"

"Okay, well, that sounds miserable. I'm not going to stay here so I can fight with your sister for six weeks straight. That feels like my living Hell."

"Aren't you going to be gone for tournaments anyway?"

"No." I tug at the back of my neck. "I'm sitting the next month out. I tweaked something and don't want it to get worse." I hate lying to my best friend, but he doesn't need to be worried about me. Psychological issues with your game can be contagious, and I don't need to bring him down when he just made it back to the top. I'm still not pleased that my agent Jon talked me into sitting out these next couple of tournaments.

"Oh, shoot, man. Well, let me know if there is anything I can help with, okay?"

"Okay," I say.

"And, JT?"

"Yeah?"

"Please just stay there with Lila. I know you guys don't get along anymore, but at one point you spent almost as much time with her as you did with me."

"She was a kid then," I say quickly.

"I know, but she's moving to a new place, starting a new job, and while she would kill me for saying it, I know she's anxious about it all. Please just stay there and try to be there for her?"

Well, shit. How am I supposed to leave now? Especially without telling him about us hooking up the last two times we were together in the same place, let alone the same room. No, Jameson can never find out about that. He might be cool with it at the time, but the first sign of things going south, and I'd lose the only real friend I've ever had.

CHAPTER EIGHT

LILA

"You need to leave," I say as JT walks into the living room. I'm sitting on the couch, trying to force my heart rate to slow, but the thought of him staying here keeps ratcheting it back up. The last thing I need while I'm starting a new job—one I had never even heard of before I met Kelsey—and trying to integrate myself into a new community is JT Johnson messing with my head.

He casually strolls to the armchair. "No, I don't think I will," he says as he sits down.

I want to punch him in the face, but that would be admitting he's getting to me, which I can't allow to happen.

"You need to leave," I repeat, narrowing my eyes as JT lounges in the armchair like he owns the place. The audacity.

He leans back, resting his ankle casually on his knee, and smirks. "Sorry, but Jameo invited me. You know, the guy who actually pays for the place."

I glare at him, crossing my arms over my chest. "Well, Jameson isn't here right now, so technically, as his blood, this is my territory."

He tilts his head, pretending to consider my words. "Territory? What are we, wolves?"

"Considering how you've all but peed on that chair, yeah, I'd say so," I shoot back. "Now, unless you want me to call Jameson and let him know you're harassing his little sister, I suggest you find somewhere else to be. Like maybe your house. Or Siberia. I truly don't care as long as it's not the one place I am."

JT chuckles, low and infuriatingly confident. "Harassing? I'm just sitting here, Lila. You're the one getting all worked up."

"I'm not worked up," I lie, feeling the heat rise in my cheeks.

He raises an eyebrow. "Oh really? You've been glaring at me like you want to rip my head off since I walked in."

"Because you're infuriating," I bite out.

He shrugs. "Some might call it charming."

"They would be idiots."

He grins, that infuriating, cocky grin that makes me want to simultaneously scream and—no, I'm not going there.

"No, you're definitely not," he says. "You've always been…special."

I narrow my eyes. "Special? That's rich, coming from the guy who thinks he's God's gift to golf."

He laughs, a genuine sound that throws me off for a second. "Not even I can convince myself of that these days."

For a moment, there's a strange silence between us, filled with the tension of unspoken words and too many shared memories. I shake my head, determined not to let it affect me.

"Seriously, JT, just go. I've got work to do, and I don't need you lurking around, distracting me."

He leans forward slightly, his expression softening just enough to make my heart do an unwelcome flip. "Lila, I'm not here to distract you. I'm just trying to figure things out too."

I scoff, leaning back into the couch. "Figure things out? Like what? How to be more insufferable?"

He sighs, running a hand through his hair. "No, how to be less of a screw-up."

That throws me for a loop, and for a second, I don't know how to respond. But I won't give him the satisfaction of seeing me soften.

"Well, good luck with that," I say, standing up and brushing past him toward the kitchen. "Maybe consider flying to your golf tournament early instead of bothering me here."

He watches me go, and I can feel his eyes on my back, the weight of whatever tension lies between us growing heavier. But I refuse to look back, even as my heart races with the mixture of anger and something else I can't quite name.

***

"Don't do this to me!" I plead into the phone.

On the other end of the line, Jameson and Bryn both laugh. I sneaked out of the house this morning after getting ready for work in complete silence, choosing not to make myself breakfast or coffee out of fear it would call JT to the kitchen like a smoke signal. But now I'm hangry, uncaffeinated, and on speakerphone with two happily in love people. It feels like the world is ganging up on me.

"Lila, the guy needs somewhere to be," Jameo replies.

Bryn continues as if they are part of a hive mind now, "He's been playing like shit recently, and he has to sit out due to an injury. You don't want him sitting at home stewing with his horrid mother, do you?"

"Bryn!" my brother chides his girlfriend lightly. "You've never even met his mom."

"Yeah, well, she sounds like a real piece of work from what you've told me. And JT is the sweetest guy ever."

"Hey!" Jameo says, before the sounds of a scuffle and good-natured laughing come through the phone.

Ugh. People in love should have to keep their cuteness locked down until at least ten in the morning. I hear Bryn say "You know I would never want to be with the sweetest guy ever," and I consider hanging up on the two of them, but instead, I yell, "Back to me, please!" directly into the phone, startling the woman walking on the other side of Main Street from me.

Great. Now I'm going to be the crazy new girl who yells into her phone—not the image of professionalism and poise I'm hoping to maintain.

"I'm one minute away from my first day of work, and you have not taken care of the pest problem at your house yet."

"Just be nice to him, Lila. He's going through a rough time. And you two were once buddies, remember?"

I hate when my brother decides to be all logical about things. But if I keep complaining now, I'm going to look like a petulant child who is throwing a temper tantrum.

"Fine. He can stay," I say.

"And you'll try to be nice to him?" my brother prompts.

"And I will do my best not to kill him or destroy his already fragile ego."

"I suppose that's all I can ask. Okay, Sis, well, I'll let you go. Have an awesome first day of work."

"Say hi to everyone for me!" Bryn yells as I hang up on them.

I am so excited about my job, but at the same time, I don't love that I'm working for my brother's girlfriend's sister and, on top of that, working in the same office as her other sister and other sister's best friend. It just feels like a lot of nepotism at play, and since the marriage portion of my life plan isn't going well, I feel like I need the professional half to really step it up. I'm worried people are going to think I got the job because of Jameson—something I've been trying to avoid my whole life. I guess I'm also the tiniest bit worried that I actually did only get the job because of Jameson. I hadn't even known what a project manager for a cybersecurity firm was until I met Kelsey a few months ago, let alone what one actually does. I feel woefully unprepared for my job, though I've been doing my best to project confidence and competence.

I walk into the office to find Izzy and Becca already there, dressed in business casual and in deep conversation with one another, looking to all the world like the successful consulting business owners they are.

Seeing the two of them like this makes it a lot clearer why Flat Roads Consulting is being pursued by multiple venture capitalist firms.

"Morning," I say, slipping my backpack off my shoulders and moving toward the empty desk. "This one mine?"

Both women jump up from their seats, rushing toward me to say hello. Their desks sit next to each other with their backs to an exposed brick wall and about five or six feet of space between them. My desk isn't far away but is set with the back to the wall opposite of the front windows rather than perpendicular to them like theirs.

"Morning!" they both say as Izzy leans in to give me a quick hug. "You remember my friend Becca, right?" she says by way of introduction.

"Of course. Hi, Becca."

"So excited to have you as a new officemate, Lila."

"I picked up some coffee and scones from the coffee shop for us," Izzy says, moving back to her desk before handing me a to-go coffee cup like the absolute queen she is.

"Oh, this is just what I needed," I moan as the first splash of coffee hits my bloodstream. Taking in the lack of branding on the side of the stark white cup, I say, "I guess when you are the only coffee shop in town, you don't have to have your logo on your cup."

"Wild Brews gave it up a few years ago now. Much cheaper this way," Becca responds. "Plus, everyone just refers to it as 'the coffee shop,' so why bother?" She shrugs before continuing, "How is your morning going? How's the house?"

"Great!" I force a smile onto my face.

"Really?" asks Izzy. "Because word on the street is that JT Johnson is also staying out at Jameson's place. And if I remember Phoenix correctly, there's a lot of...tension...between the two of you."

"Ugh." I let out a groan and sink into my new office chair, taking a sip of coffee to steel myself. "How can you possibly already know that? I just got off the phone with Bryn."

Izzy laughs. "Oh, you poor, naïve newbie. This is Wild Bluffs. I don't need Bryn for this information, though, if we're being honest—which I always like to be—she told us you might both end up staying out there like a week ago. No, we ran into Mary at the coffee shop this morning."

Becca must notice the confused look on my face, because she says, "Mary is the manager and concierge out at WBCC. I guess JT got lost on his way last night and had to call for directions."

I giggle and file that away to torture JT with later.

"Sooo?" Izzy asks.

I drop my head into my hands. "It's so much worse than you could possibly imagine."

"Oooo. This sounds juicy. Tell us everything," Becca says, settling back into her chair behind her desk. Izzy does the same, and I notice the three desks are situated so the occupants can easily see and chat with each other, the computer screens positioned to offer a view between them.

"Oh, it's my first day of work. I don't think I should be exposing all my deepest, darkest secrets."

"Now I know it's juicy," Becca says.

"You don't work for us," Izzy adds. "Not that that would stop us from prying into your personal life, but we would feel worse about it."

"We aren't prying, Iz," says Becca. "If she doesn't want to tell us, she definitely doesn't have to."

I know I shouldn't tell them about JT and me. We are way too connected, and they literally just demonstrated how fast gossip moves in this town. But, at the same time, Elise is also just starting her new job, so I'm not sure when we are going to be able to debrief this whole JT thing. I feel like if I don't tell someone, I'm going to explode. And, based on the way Jameson and Bryn have been acting toward each other lately, Izzy and I are essentially sisters-in-law in everything except name.

Still. "I don't know..."

"Fine," says Izzy. "I won't pressure you. But just know, if you do want to talk about anything, like, say, the fact that you and JT disappeared for a while at the same time in the bar in Phoenix but then acted like you hated each other when you came back, Becca and I actually can keep a secret. We can gossip with the best of them, but if we are ever told something is a secret, our lips are sealed."

I take a deep sip of my coffee and then look at my watch. I arrived fifteen minutes early today, so I should have enough time to at least give them the highlights. But where to start?

"Well...if you're sure you can keep it a secret?"

"Of course," says Becca. Izzy pantomimes locking her lips and throwing away the key.

"Well, to really understand, you have to start a lot farther back. JT and Jameson knew each other when they were playing in Juniors and then both ended up joining the same college team. They became inseparable, and Jameson would invite JT home every holiday and any time we were having a party or some family event. He's been to every Thanksgiving of ours for the last ten years."

"Does he not have parents around?" asks Becca.

Izzy shushes her. "That's a question for a different day, Beccs!"

"They are both still around," I say, answering her question anyway. "They are just...different from my parents or the Harpers. They..." I trail off, unsure how to describe the complicated relationship between JT and his parents. "...have different priorities, I guess."

"Okay, now we *have* to dig into that later," Izzy says. "But for now, keep going. We are like ten years away from the juicy details."

"Well, long story short, JT and I became friends too. He was around at every holiday, and he would let me tag along with him and Jameson even if I was four years younger than them and a very mediocre golfer. And sure, I had a little girl crush on him, but who wouldn't? I mean, you've seen the man. They've literally published articles about how good-looking he is."

Becca nods her agreement, but Izzy shrugs. "I see his appeal, but the blonde surfer boy look has never really done it for me."

I gape at her with wide eyes and notice Becca doing the same.

"I...I don't know how to respond to that. Though there is a not-small subset of the romance community who would agree with you. They hate blonde main characters for unknown reasons," I say.

Breaking apart one of the scones from the bakery, I continue my tale, purposely downplaying the horrible party where everything went wrong when I was 18, and focusing on the enemies-to-elevator-kissing-to-banging-in-Vegas story.

"And we went back to fighting about everything. I think it was our most insufferable Thanksgiving yet," I conclude with a sigh.

"Bryn may have mentioned something about that," Izzy says, and I'm not sure if she's joking or not.

"It wasn't my best moment." I wave my hand as if my intentional goading of JT to fight with me about our hookup could be dismissed as nothing. Maybe it was nothing. He definitely never took the bait.

"And then we were at that bar together in Phoenix. And, well, you were there, Iz. We all had a few beers waiting, and I had had a few before that, and we just happened to pass each other in that little hallway back by the bathrooms. And I swear, our shoulders bumped, and it was like a switch inside me was flipped. All of a sudden he was pulling me into the dark back corner, or shit, maybe I was pulling him, but either way, we were making out with some serious hand action. And then one of the bartenders pushed into the back door and...we weren't anymore."

"And then?" Becca asks.

At that moment, Kelsey walks through the door, carrying her laptop and the world's smallest cup of coffee.

"And then nothing," I say. "The next time we talked was last night when he showed up unannounced and declared we're going to be roommates for the next six weeks."

But maybe, just maybe, I have a plan for how to get rid of him sooner.

CHAPTER NINE

JT

"Hey, Dad," I answer my phone on speaker before setting it on the grass next to my ball so I can continue to line up my putt. To be clear, I would never answer my phone—let alone put it on speakerphone—at a normal golf course. I'm a strict rule follower and always leave my cell phone in the locker room. But unsurprisingly, Wild Bluffs Country Club doesn't have the same rules as most courses. While I'm guessing it technically has a no-phones policy, no one abides by it. However, I admit my knowledge is limited because you rarely ever see another human while playing out here—unless you both happen to be a long way into the rough, that is. So it doesn't really matter either way.

"JT, your mother informs me you are sitting the next few tournaments out due to an injury. Are you sure that's the right move for your career?"

It's a classic question from my dad, so I should've been expecting it. Calling him "involved" in my career is like calling the universe "big."

It's technically true, but at the same time, it doesn't come close to encapsulating the magnitude. He gave up his lifelong dream of playing professional golf himself when I was 7, choosing to coach me instead. Since then, he has dedicated every minute of his life to making sure I'm the best golfer I can be, even though he hasn't been my coach since I left for college ten years ago.

"I talked with all my people, Dad. We all agree this is best." I pause, considering if I should tell him the truth, but I decide against it, so I add, "Based on my injury." Do I wish I had the type of relationship with my dad where I could admit that my "injury" is ten percent a physical ache in my lower back and ninety percent the mental cluster-fuck that my mind is? Sure. But I don't. My dad, like the media, tends to handle physical ailments much better than mental ones.

"And are you sure your team has your best interest in mind? I cannot imagine how taking a month off from tournaments can be beneficial. Plus, as your financial advisor, I feel the need to remind you that it's important to keep bringing in additional earnings. A few of those investments you suggested have been underperforming."

"I'll still be out on the course, Dad. It's not like I'm going to be sipping margaritas on the beach for a month. I'm—"

"I've got to go, JT. Some of us still have work to do." He chuckles at his joke before continuing, "But I told your mother I would call and make sure you were able to make contact with one of the Ferguson brothers. I also had Penelope put together my thoughts on your putting, including a few videos of your last three tournaments with a voiceover from me."

"Okay, um, thanks." I'm sure his assistant enjoyed every minute of that task. Who doesn't join a finance firm to splice together golf videos for their boss?

"Oh, you'll also be getting a few notifications about a couple of transfers I made in your accounts last week."

"I'll look them over and sign whatever you need to move the money."

"No need. I had Penelope go ahead and start making the changes, since I'm on your accounts."

"Oh, well, that's...convenient." A classic Ronald Johnson move. Make it sound like he's doing you a favor when he's just forcing you to do whatever he wants.

"You're welcome, Son. Well, I've kept my next meeting waiting long enough. Make sure you don't take your foot off the pedal. You only get one shot at this thing, and you don't want to miss it because you weren't willing to push through a little pain."

And with that lovely goodbye, he hangs up.

I pick up the extra golf balls I'd been practicing with and swing my bag over my shoulders. The worst part about this course is that they don't allow golf carts. I like walking, but I don't like walking *all day* if I'm not in a tournament—and then I have my caddie along to carry my bag.

Knowing I'm going to hate the conversation I'm about to have with my assistant, Sam, I call him anyway.

"Hey, JT. I just got the best email from your lovely father. How is it that the money you invest through him always returns far less than the money you invest yourself or in the S&P? You really need to start asking more questions, JT. You know your stuff when it comes to investing, and your parents are actively losing your money. Oh, and speaking of losing money, your mom called to let me know you're paying for their home renovation."

"Sam," I say, trying my hardest to stop his rant.

"Your parents suck."

"They are good parents. I would most certainly not be where I am today without them. It takes a lot of parental support to become a professional golfer, you know?"

"Yes, which they remind you of any time they want something from you."

"That's not true."

"Remember when your mom pulled that card so she could use the jet you already had booked to go to New York for one of her friends' art show openings?"

"I was happy to lend it to her," I say, setting down my bag by the large cooler stocked with waters and grabbing one out.

"She met you at the tarmac with her other friends in tow as you were getting ready to leave. You ended up having to fly economy to get to Florida when you needed to."

"Economy is fine. The flight from California to Florida isn't so bad."

"We are not discussing whether or not economy is fine, which it isn't, by the way, some of us just don't have another option."

"Do I not pay you enough, Sam? You know I'll give you a raise."

"JT, do not distract me with shiny things. This is about your parents taking advantage of you. They can book their own flights and pay for their own renovations. They were the parents. They *chose* to drive you all over the country to go to all your golf stuff."

I hear a rustle in the long grass and now am only giving about a fourth of my attention to Sam. If I'm attacked by a rattlesnake out here, I'm packing up my bags and living out of a hotel for the next six weeks. I cannot stand snakes. No living thing should be able to move their body the way they do. I swear I had a minor heart attack last time I was on a course and one slithered in front of me.

"My dad also gave up his future as a professional golfer to let me have the dream instead. He reminds me about it frequently. 'I could've been a better golfer than you, but I wanted my son to have the dream, not me.'"

"What?" Sam asks, his voice full of anger.

"Um, what?" I say, not sure what we are talking about because...well...there is a snake that is about to pop out of the grass and wrap its far too bendable body around my leg before biting me and leaving me for dead in the middle of nowhere.

"Did you just say your dad frequently suggests he would be a better golfer than you?" he asks again slowly, in a tone that is far too controlled for Sam.

Shit. Did I just say that? It's something I've kept to myself, particularly with Sam, who already judges my parents far too harshly. Not everyone can be as amazing as his parents. I still tear up a little thinking about how supported Sam felt when he told his parents he was interested in men. When Sam first told me the story, I wanted to track down his dad and give him the world's biggest hug. Sam's parents are essentially the definition of unconditional love. He is amazing at his job, smart, quick-witted, and takes shit from no one. I don't know how anyone could be anything but supportive of him. But Sam's parents have also not had to give up their lives for him to be who he is. On the other hand, I've caused my dad to sacrifice his dreams, and my mom to sacrifice her face.

"JT?" Sam asks.

"Oh, um. I mean, he's mentioned it once or twice. And he was about to get on the Tour when I started showing promise."

The grass moves again, and fuck it—I can't stand here and have a real conversation and keep an eye out for the snake. I climb on top of the cooler, sitting cross-legged, ensuring no part of my body is exposed to any possible snakes passing by.

"You make it sound like you forced your parents to give up their lives for you. You know that's not true, right?"

"Nope. That is one hundred percent true," I say.

"Leaving your dad and the outrageous claim that he was suddenly going to make it as a professional golfer at the ripe age of like forty aside, your dad *chose* to give up on his golf career to coach you."

I can practically hear the quotation marks around the term "golf career."

"To *help me* become a professional golfer. *Which I am*," I respond.

"And what guilt exactly do you feel toward your mom? The lady who seems to think that what's yours is hers, including your checking account."

I pick at the top of the cooler as I picture Sam's ice-blue glare right now.

"JT?"

"It's my fault she has the scar across her face."

"What scar?" he asks, as if the thin white stripe that traces her cheekbone isn't the first thing anyone sees when they look at her face.

"The one on her cheek, just under her eye," I say, my voice a bit softer.

"Okay, I may remember that. Though, to be clear, it's not noticeable. And even if it were, how could that possibly be your fault?"

"She was working two jobs to pay for everything after my dad quit his job to coach me."

"And?"

"And one day, after working the night shift, she got home and had to drive me to meet my dad at the course where he had been trying to get in a couple of rounds himself that morning. I could tell she was exhausted, but I made her drive me anyway."

I cough, trying to hide the emotion that finds its way into my voice any time I think about that morning. "On her way home, she fell asleep behind the wheel. The car hit a tree, and the windshield broke. One of the pieces of glass cut her face. Because we were so short on cash at the time, she didn't go to a plastic surgeon. Now, it's too late to make it go away."

"Oh, JT," Sam says, sympathy in his voice. "That's not—"

"Sam," I cut in. "I appreciate that you care about me, I do. But my parents love me. I like being able to pay them back for all their sacrifices by lending them my jet time or by investing in the business they started."

"They've lost half a million dollars of your money, JT."

"*What?*" I ask.

"Your accounts with your dad lost 500,000 dollars this year while the stock market has soared. And it's not just that I'm concerned about *how* they managed to lose so much money, it's also going to make a substantial impact on your cash flow for the year...especially since you aren't bringing in a lot of money right now."

Here's the thing about being a professional athlete: we make a lot of money, but we spend a lot of money too. I have a substantial number of people on my payroll and spend a lot on traveling across the world to play. I'm working really hard to not be one of those athletes who end up broke because of their spending habits, which is why I have a lot of my net worth tied up in investments. Unfortunately, it means cash flow can occasionally become an issue when I go for a while without bringing home money from a tournament.

"Will the winnings from Phoenix cover what we need?" I ask.

"Yes. Of course it will. But we were talking about investing it in that—"

"Okay, well, as long as I have the cash flow to pay you all, then I'll be fine. I don't need to invest in another start-up right now."

Being an angel investor is one of my favorite things to do with my money. The one time I brought it up to my dad, he told me I should leave the investing to the professionals. Unfortunately, my parents' investment firm doesn't invest in start-ups, so I've been keeping some "fun money" on the side to try out a few investments that speak to me. Sam and I are both interested in new business opportunities, so he spends a ton of his time finding one or two perfect investment opportunities each year for me. It's not a fail-proof system, so while we've had a couple of really good returns, we've also invested in two companies that went under completely.

And while I appreciate it as an investment vehicle, it isn't truly about the money for me. It's about seeing passionate people finally have the resources they need to make their dreams come true, kinda like when I was able to invest enough money with my parents that they could start their own firm.

I've never felt something as amazing as the first time I met with the CEO of a company I had just invested in. Her excitement was palpable, and it felt like that moment a roller coaster starts racing down the hill you just climbed—pure euphoria.

"Are you sure? We'd found that baby bottle company with the screw-on bags. It seemed really good."

"I know. And it is a really good one. Keep monitoring it. I'll win another one soon, and we can make sure everyone has the money they need."

But for the first time ever, I start to question if I will ever make enough money for my parents to have what they need—what they deserve for the sacrifices they've made for me.

CHAPTER TEN

LILA

"Wait. You didn't see him at all?" Izzy asks. It's only been two days, but I can already tell Izzy is going to be a highly entertaining officemate.

We are seated in the small coffee shop on Main Street, the smell of baking bread making me wish I'd ordered a cinnamon roll in addition to my iced latte. Becca was on a call with one of her clients, so Izzy and I decided to take a quick break. I'm already realizing I'm going to need to bring in my headphones if I'm going to have any chance of getting any work done. Not that I've had to focus on anything too intense. I spent yesterday morning with Kelsey going through my tech setup, an onboarding packet with company policies, and a detailed list of our current and past clients and the type of work we did for each.

As the first project and account manager for Kelsey's cybersecurity firm, it's my job to make sure our clients are happy and our projects are completed on time. From what I can tell so far, I'm mostly just a go-between for our clients and the developers, installers, and security personnel on our team of twenty. I feel like I'm drinking from a firehose of information, but I'm doing my best to make sure no one can tell I have no idea what any of the acronyms they are using mean. The last thing I want is for Kelsey to think she made a mistake in hiring me or that I can't handle the work.

I pick at my cup lid, thinking about Izzy's question. "It's weird, right? I mean, it was our first real night living in the same house, and it's like he purposefully timed it so he was never in the common space at the same time as me. Jack kept getting up and walking over to JT's door too. His doggy sense could tell something was happening. At like seven, I finally felt like I had to do something, so I just curled up with Jack in the living room, reading my book."

"Ooo. What book are you reading?"

"It's a pirate romance. It's so good. I'm trying out doing fancy annotating on it, and I feel like I'm really getting into it a lot more because of the underlining and notes."

"Oh. I could never do that. I like to fly through the books I'm reading. I barely remember the characters' names once I'm done. Having to stop and write something does not sound fun to me. But I love it for you." She takes a drink of her hot vanilla latte before continuing. "But that's beside the point. What are you going to do about JT avoiding you? Do you want to do something about it? Maybe it's just less awkward if you both stay holed up in your own space. I mean, you were kinda pissed that he was there in the first place. Maybe he was just trying to stay out of your space."

"That definitely could be the case, but it seems unlikely. I mean, the man lives to torment me. You'd think he'd be the one staking out the living room so that he could annoy me all night." I don't mention that *I* had been lingering in the living areas, doing everything I could possibly think of to annoy him. I played Taylor Swift as loud as my phone speaker would play, though I swear I heard him singing along at one point. I purposely made the smelliest dinner I could think of by heating up a frozen steak of salmon in the microwave, but all that did was get Jack all spun up. I left my dirty dishes sitting out, but after two hours of him not coming out, I couldn't take it any longer and had to wash them. I guess he's more immune to terrible-roommate behavior than I am.

She raises her eyebrows, but instead of voicing her skepticism, says, "I need to get to know JT more, I guess. Why don't we all plan on dinner on Friday night or something? You guys could come into town, or I could come out there. I'm sure Becca and Kelsey would join."

"That sounds—"

"Oh, shoot! I forgot Friday is my parents' annual BBQ. You guys definitely have to come to that."

"I'd love to come. But no way am I inviting JT to come with me. That's a sure way to ruin the night not just for me but for everyone around us."

"Come on, Lila. He can't be that bad. Plus, he can't possibly want to stay out at the course all alone."

"I, in fact, think that's why everyone goes out there: to be alone." I pause. "Except me. For the record, I would love nothing more than for you to set me up with some hidden gem of a local."

"Noted. I'll put some thought into someone for you. But, in terms of people wanting to be alone, they may think they want to be alone, but if I've learned nothing in my thirty years, it's that the people who say they want to be alone are often the ones who most need someone to be there for them. Look at Jameson. Coming out here did nothing for him until he met Bryn. There aren't a lot of people in small towns, but they are some of the most engaged communities. People aren't left on their own, not really."

Why is JT in Wild Bluffs, really? I'm pulled from my wonderings by the sound of the door opening and the man in question walking in.

Izzy notices him at the same time as I do, and I hate that I note his signature golden curls are hidden under a black baseball hat, likely to try to keep from causing a scene in town. Though Wild Bluffs is mostly used to professional golfers wandering around at this point.

Or maybe not. The barista's eyes are lit up in glee as JT makes his way to the counter, and I fight the odd urge to yell "mine" like a toddler with their favorite toy. Luckily for my insane moment of jealousy, a middle-aged woman steps up to JT, cockblocking the poor high schooler at the cash register.

"Yesss," Izzy says with a laugh. "JT is about to meet the leader of the Wild Bluffs welcome crew."

"Is that an official title?" I ask.

"It depends on how you define *official*. She definitely thinks she's the queen of Wild Bluffs." Izzy sighs. "We should go save him before he is unknowingly married to Janice's 45-year-old daughter. She just moved back to town after her divorce, and her mom is ruthless in finding her a new man."

We don't move, though, instead watching their conversation. As usual, JT is being warm and friendly with everyone but me.

"He might be interested."

"He would be lucky to have Sarah, but word on the street is that she's got her eyes set on an older guy in town. Janice just isn't a fan because he happens to be her neighbor, and they fight constantly about a tree that is between their two property lines."

"Why do you know all this?"

"Small towns, Lila. You'll see soon enough."

I sit back, content to let this play out, but Izzy clearly disagrees, because the next thing I know, she's popping up and walking over to the counter where Janice is still talking to JT. I internally evil laugh at the fact that he hasn't even been able to order his coffee yet.

"Hi, JT!" Izzy's voice is a little too loud and a little too bright for it to seem normal, but the look JT shoots her is like she's saving him from an especially painful round of bamboo torture.

"Izzy!" he exclaims. "So good to see you."

It's clear he means it when his face breaks into a full grin and he steps forward to hug Izzy. Since they are both so tall, the two of them standing there look like one of those couples that would be featured in magazines. It's...gross, really. Yeah, definitely. I'm *glad* JT has never once smiled at me like that or been glad to see me. Ew.

"We're so glad you could make it into town! Our table is just over there." Izzy points in my direction, and it's only Janice's gaze moving to me that keeps me from flipping JT off in greeting. I offer a casual nod instead. JT must be able to read my annoyance, though, because the left side of his mouth lifts into a smirk.

JT turns back to the woman and says, "Well, Janice, it was so nice to meet you. I will definitely be back in touch if my schedule opens up, but I really have to join my friends now."

"Not a problem. So nice to meet you," she replies.

JT orders a black coffee and makes his way over to our table.

"Jameson's coffee maker not doing it for you?" I ask as I scoot my chair in so he can slip around to the empty seat by the window.

"Just thought I'd come into town and see what's going on. I've barely seen another human since I arrived. It's starting to creep me out."

"I'm a human. I was in *our* living room all evening yesterday."

"I don't know, I'd say you only count as half a human, size-wise at least."

"I'm *not* that short!" I hiss. "I'm the average size for a woman in the United States."

"That's just what they tell you so you don't get worked into a rage and start biting people's ankles."

I hear a snort from Izzy and look over to find her staring at JT and me, her mouth hidden behind her entwined hands and her eyes alight with glee. I realize how close JT and I have gotten since we were both leaning in as we whispered insults, and I pull back.

"Just because I happen to spend all my time around giants doesn't mean I'm small. You are the abnormal ones," I say, aiming my glare at both Izzy and JT.

"Rude," Izzy says. "First I can't be a theme park princess because of my height, and now this. What did I ever do to you?"

I can tell she's joking, but I do feel a bit bad about bringing her into it. But to be fair to me, I did warn her that there is often collateral damage when JT and I are together.

"Sorry," I say.

She waves her hand, indicating my apology isn't needed.

Instead, she turns her attention to JT. "Did you agree to go out with Janice's daughter?"

"How could you possibly know that's what she was asking me?"

"It's what she asks every single man she meets these days."

"Dang, and here I was feeling special by the offer."

"You should. Sarah is awesome. That said, she is like fifteen years older than you, so I'm not sure where your age gap line is."

JT looks at me quickly before looking away and fidgeting with his hat. My eyes narrow at the move—everyone knows it's what he does when he's nervous. "I mean, I'm not opposed to a bit of an age gap."

"Well, she's also in love with her mom's neighbor, so that could also throw a wrench into things," Izzy says.

"I do try to avoid dating women who are in love with other men," he says with a chuckle.

"Smart," Izzy replies.

"Well," I say, making sure to slurp the last bit of my coffee up through the straw. "I'd better head back to work." I stand up and slide my phone into my jeans pocket.

"I'll meet you back there," Izzy says, smiling up at me innocently.

I don't like the looks of that smile, but it isn't like I can sit back down now or force Izzy to come back with me. Instead, I offer a quick, "Okay, see ya," to Izzy and a middle finger to JT before heading out the door.

As the door is closing behind me, I hear Izzy say, "So my parents have this thing on Friday night..." *Ugh.*

Chapter Eleven

JT

"Ten minutes!" I yell, knowing it'll piss Lila off.

It's Friday night, and I'm waiting for Lila to change so we can head into town together for the Harpers' annual BBQ. Izzy sent Lila and me a group text yesterday afternoon, telling me to ride in with Lila so I'd know where the house was. Apparently, sending the address would've been too difficult. I asked Lila if she'd rather go in alone, but she'd just shrugged and said, "It's fine" before curling back up on the couch to read.

She leaves her book out in the living room every night when she goes to bed. It's one I haven't read yet, and I've been tempted every day to crack its pink cover open and read it. I finally broke this afternoon when I was taking a break from golf to escape the heat. I'd just finished the series I was reading, and the dreaded moment when I had to pick what to read next just felt like too much for a Friday afternoon. So I'd started hers. It's a pirate romance, and I'm hooked. I may have decided to skip my planned session at the driving range this afternoon to read instead. I have to admit I also really enjoy seeing Lila's notes and colorful underlines throughout the book. It feels strangely intimate to be reading the same romance book as someone else.

Noticing a fancy marker under the couch, likely one Lila has been using as she reads, I pick it up before flipping to the place where I stopped this afternoon. A minute later, I turn the page to realize I've now passed Lila's farthest spot. Glancing at her door to make sure she's not about to catch me, I pull the top of the marker off with my teeth and start reading. She's been underlining the female main character's quotes in pink and the male's in blue, but that's not really what I'm here for. I'm more interested in having a conversation with the book. So, with one final glance at her door, I write in the left-hand margin. *Why don't these pirates say "Argh, matey?" more?* I chuckle to myself imagining the eye roll that is going to break Lila's face when she reads it. I keep going, leaving a few more comments throughout. Most of them are serious thoughts, questions, or predictions, but I sprinkle a couple of one-liners for my own amusement—and, maybe, if I'm being honest, a little bit for Lila's amusement as well.

"Oh, so *now* you're hanging out in the living room?"

Lila's voice startles me, and I slam the book shut, hastily hiding it by my thigh. Jack lifts his head up from his bed, eyes narrowed at me. Fortunately, Lila makes her way to her shoes lined up nicely by the door, putting her back to me. I quickly stick the book back in its rightful place and jump up to join her.

"What do you mean?" I ask.

"You've hidden in your room every night this week."

I tug my baseball hat on my head and open the door for us both. "I'm not hiding. I've just been tired. I've been playing a lot of golf."

"Aren't you supposed to be injured?" Lila asks as we both climb into my rented navy blue pickup. I'm pretty sure it's the same one I get every time I'm here. Lila is so small, she has to use the oh-shit handle to pull herself up and in, and the move gives me a view of her toned hamstrings peeking out from under the black shorts she changed into.

"What?" Lila asks, catching me watching her. "This is what Kelsey recommended I wear. I asked if this was more a jeans party or a sundress party, and she said, and I quote, 'Jeans or shorts. Definitely not a sundress.'"

"Sure," I say. "I'm sure Kelsey knows what she's talking about." I look down at my collared golf shirt and salmon-colored shorts. "Do you think I'm okay?"

"Well, you look like you just stepped off a golf course. And, as you're a professional golfer, that feels appropriate for any occasion."

We drive in uncomfortable silence until we reach the paved road that leads into town. Lila turns to look at me, scanning me from my flip-flop-clad toes to the top of my head. "You aren't really hurt, are you?"

"I tweaked my back," I say, the lie tasting a little worse in my mouth when I tell it to Lila. But Lord knows Lila would use my inability to perform to make my life a living hell. I mean, shit, even my mind immediately goes to impotence jokes. No—Lila, like the rest of the world, is best left at arm's length. I can still be one of the best golfers in the world with a tweaked back. It's a rite of passage for golfers over a certain age. But a guy with the mental yips? That's not someone worth the sacrifice my parents have made.

"Suuuure," she says. "If that's what you want to go with. It's definitely not—" She slams her mouth closed and smacks a hand across her lips like she has to physically restrain herself from saying whatever was about to burst out of her mouth. "Never mind."

"Are we pulling punches now, Pipsqueak? I'm not that injured."

"No. No, it's just that I...I need to ask you a...favor." The last word comes out like it's the most disgusting thing Lila has ever said.

"You don't say?" I reply, not knowing where this is going but loving every second of it. "And what, exactly, is important enough to make you be nice to me?"

"I'm not being nice to you, I'm just not *not* being nice to you."

"I'm not sure there is a difference besides one being grammatically correct."

She takes a deep breath, squaring her shoulders like she's about to do battle. She clearly doesn't want to ask me whatever she's about to.

"Can we pretend not to hate each other tonight?"

I'm caught off guard by the term *hate*. I've never *hated* Lila. Sure, she annoys the hell out of me, and I definitely don't want to spend more time around her than I have to, but it doesn't sit right that she thinks I hate her. "I don't hate you," I say.

"Come on, JT. Of course you do. We fight all the time."

"I really don't, Lila. I..."—I'm not sure how to explain the complex web of our relationship—"I know I said I don't like you, but I've never hated you."

She pauses like she's considering the difference between the two, but then she shakes her head like it doesn't matter. "Okay, well, either way. I promise to be on my best behavior tonight, but can you please help me? I can't have these people thinking I'm some kind of shrew, and I'm pretty sure Jameson has actually used that word to describe me when you're around."

"Okay," I say.

She still doesn't seem content. She's fidgeting with her necklace, her eyes staring blankly ahead. "Is there something else?" I ask. "We're almost to town."

"Can-you-not-mention-to-anyone-that-we-hooked-up?" she says it all in one go like any break between words would make her incapable of getting the whole question out. Which is fair because, fuck. I thought we would both take that right to the grave with us and never, ever speak of it again. I'm pretty sure we actually agreed on that while I had her pushed against the wall in Phoenix. Bryn's sister had almost caught us about a minute later, and at that realization, I swore to myself that I would never touch Lila again. Jameson is my only friend, and there is no way he would continue to be my friend if things between Lila and I ever went south—the only direction that things have ever gone between us.

"Um. Sure." I fidget with the brim of my hat. "I actually thought we weren't ever speaking of that again."

"Right," she says, her tone sounding surprisingly dejected. "Oh, you need to turn right up here."

I make the turn, but my mind won't stop picking at the sound of her voice. The vulnerability in it. I'd only heard it one time before—when we got breakfast with her brother and Bryn in Vegas. She had asked me about a mic catching me cursing during my first couple of holes on Saturday morning, and apparently, she didn't like my answer. Her tone confused me then, and it's confusing me now. I'm about to pull into the empty lot in front of what appears to be the hospital when she points to the left.

"It's just up this way a bit."

She directs me to a red brick house set off the street with a big lawn and a couple of nice trees out front. There are already about fifteen cars lining their driveway, so I pull in behind the last one.

"Why don't you want people to know we hooked up?" I ask, worried that maybe she, like my dad, is embarrassed by me now that I'm not playing well.

"Honestly?" she asks, and I nod.

"Izzy mentioned there are a couple of single guys who are going to be here tonight, and I don't want them to think we are dating."

"Don't want me to besmirch your good name? I get it," I say.

"Yeah...something like that," she says, climbing out of the pickup and making her way to the front of the house.

Jameson asked me to look after his sister, so I will certainly help Lila make a good impression with her new neighbors. However, I also know Jameson wouldn't want Lila trying to hook up with some rando. So, like the above-average friend I am, I make my way inside, fully intent on stopping any guy from getting too close to Lila tonight.

Chapter Twelve

Lila

"No way! That doesn't count!" I yell, pointing to the 3-year-old neighbor of Ken and Jen who just dropped JT's bean bag directly into the hole on the board across from us. Kelsey and Izzy spent the last hour filling me in on all I need to know to survive a BBQ where each of the seventy-five guests is related, feuding, or both. I can't keep it all straight, but luckily Kelsey has stayed by my side the whole night. She's not a bubbly person, but I really have enjoyed working for her. She's smart and driven and seems to really care about her company and her employees—even if I'm the only one she sees in person most days.

Now, Kelsey and I are playing corn hole against JT and one of the three single guys in town who's here. After mentioning I wanted to start dating the other day to Izzy, she's made sure to point out any single man we've seen. She even confirmed a couple of times if I was sure I wasn't interested in women, since that would increase my pool of potential dates. Unfortunately for my odds, we are sticking to the single men. Izzy orchestrated this game for me to get to know Carter Mitchell, the brother of the owner of the competing security firm in town. I was shocked to learn there were two security firms in Wild Bluffs, but as it turns out, remote work has really allowed some locals to move back home and still have the careers they want. Similar to Kelsey's firm, Mitchell Security works with clients worldwide.

Carter apparently didn't get the memo we are supposed to be using this time to meet, and he all but ran to stand next to Kelsey before I had the chance to send JT her way. I hissed at JT to go ask Carter to change, but JT just shrugged, giving me a "what can I do about it?" face. Now JT and I are stuck competing against each other the whole game. The problem is that I'm very competitive and so is JT, so being on our best behavior is proving to be a challenge.

Kelsey and Carter look like they are having an okay time. They've mostly just stood there in silence, occasionally commenting on the game or the weather or other inane things. Kelsey is currently asking him a question about a new earpiece their guys in the field are using when providing personal security. We stick more to the technology side of the security field rather than boots-on-the-ground, but Kelsey mentioned this morning that she was considering expanding to offer more services. I'm not cut out to be a bodyguard, but Kelsey with her military background could probably kick some crazy fan's or stalker's ass if needed. Carter seems to only be responding in grunts or head shakes, but it's still more than I've seen from him the rest of the game.

"Hey, kid!" I yell at the little ankle-biter who just helped JT score three points. "Come back here!" The kid in question stops running away from us and looks back at me. "Come put this one in that hole too!"

"No way!" JT makes a quick grab for the red bag in my hand, but I hide it behind my back as the kid in question chooses to ignore me and restart his mad dash around the yard. "I didn't ask him to do it," JT continues. "He just decided he didn't like where it was sitting on the grass. And you can't blame him. It looked sad down there."

"That's on you. You're the one who is remarkably bad at this for being a professional golfer. Your job is literally to get things in holes."

JT wiggles his eyebrows at me.

"Eww," I say, giving his arm a shove.

"No one has paid me for that...yet," he teases.

"Have you considered that you're just earning what you're worth?" I toss my bag to the other side of the yard, doing a little dance when it lands on the board. It's Kelsey's and Carter's turn to throw now, so as they start to pick up the bags, I take a long swig of my beer before turning to look at JT's stunned face.

"I can't believe you just said that," he says.

"It's hard to hear the truth sometimes." I nod. "I understand."

"Was that your experience?" he asks, his tone lowering in pitch and volume.

"I'm sure—based on the rules we set less than two hours ago—that I have no idea what you could be talking about."

"I'm sure—based on the way you moaned my name—that you know exactly what I'm talking about."

A bag smacks down on the corn hole board between us, and we both jump apart. I hadn't realized how close we'd drifted as we'd talked, but, thankfully, Kelsey and Carter are both focused on their throws, clearly unaware of the inappropriate conversation happening at this end of the game. I take a long look at Carter, trying to imagine my night if it had gone to plan, with me on the other side of the board, talking to Carter. He's a good-looking guy with dark hair and dark eyes. He's a bit shorter than the men I'm usually attracted to, probably not quite six feet based on the difference between him and Kelsey.

"We can't talk about it, JT."

His gaze is on me, a flinty glean to his normally sunny blue eyes. "Right. I remember the lecture. I'm not an idiot. I'm aware that you are trying to hide who you really are so you'll have a chance of convincing one of these townies to date you."

There's a hint of anger in his tone. I'm a bit taken aback by his shift in attitude, and I briefly wonder what caused him to have such an unkind response, but then I remind myself that I really don't care. He's being a judgmental prick...to both me and the men from Wild Bluffs.

"Are you sure about that?" I ask him. "You sure seem pretty dumb to me. But, whatever, let's just get this game over with. I didn't want to hang out with you tonight, anyway, and if you're going to be a jerk, then honestly, I want nothing to do with you."

He doesn't say anything, but his shoulders are tense as he finishes off the rest of his drink in one long gulp. Getting along was the other thing I'd asked of him, and he's already proven he can't keep from talking about us hooking up. And, for the record, that was one of the most humiliating asks I've ever had to make. But I *needed* to be clear that I can't have people in Wild Bluffs thinking I'm either not serious and just hooking up with random guys or that I *am serious* with JT. Both would ruin my chances of getting set up with men who are interested in long-term relationships.

Kelsey, luckily, sinks her final bag through the hole, winning the game for us. I put on a smile I don't quite feel like wearing and go insert myself into her conversation with Carter. JT congratulates Kelsey on his way back into the Harpers' house but doesn't stop to talk, claiming he needs another drink.

"So, Carter, how did you get into the security field?" I ask.

His eyes shift to Kelsey before he looks my way. "I wanted to come back to Wild Bluffs, and my brother was looking for someone to help him out with managing the team. It just made sense."

"Oh, that's great. Is it hard working with your brother? I love mine a lot, but I can't imagine working for him."

Again his eyes shift to Kelsey, even though she's staring out at the kids playing, not at all paying attention to our conversation. "It's mostly okay. He can be a bit intense, but the pay is good, and I don't have to go on assignment too often."

I chat with Carter, learning he was in Kelsey's class in high school and went to a prestigious university back East. He's clearly smart and kind, but there is no spark between us. Plus, if I'm reading things right, he's already interested in someone else. I wonder if all the Harper sisters secretly have men in town in love with them. Maybe I should warn my brother.

Izzy and Becca make their way over to our little group a couple minutes later, inserting themselves into our conversation with ease. Izzy widens her eyes, slightly nodding her head toward Carter as if to say "What do you think?" I shrug, pulling my lips to the side, trying to indicate the slight indifference I feel toward the man. He's handsome and pleasant, but there is no way I want to go to battle against a high school crush that is still alive and well today.

We chat for a while, the Harpers and Becca continuing to give me the rundown on all things Wild Bluffs, from the people, to the history of various events and feuds, to the importance of showing up for the high school sporting events once they get started in August. It's a lot to take in, but it feels more like watching a "last time on..." clip montage at the beginning of a soap opera episode than truly understanding what's happening.

"Well," Carter says, looking at his phone as the sun starts to slip below the horizon line about an hour later. It's the first thing he's said since the other women joined the conversation. "Unfortunately for me, it's time I head home. One of the guys on our monitoring team called in sick, so I'm filling the six-to-noon shift tomorrow. It's amazing how guys always seem to get sick and need coverage for the early-Saturday-morning shifts."

"And here I thought all you big bodyguards would be able to hold your liquor," Izzy jokes. Kelsey gives Carter a knowing smile and says, "Maybe if you guys would stop trying to make your field staff work on the monitoring side of things too, you wouldn't have that problem."

He doesn't quite smile, though a hint of one peeks through. "Maybe."

The temperature drops quickly after that, and not too long after Carter's departure, we all head inside, looking for sweatshirts and jackets. I spot JT chatting with Kelsey and Izzy's dad and a couple of other middle-aged men, a genuine smile on his face. I guess maybe it's just me he's grumpy with tonight. He must feel my eyes on him because his gaze meets mine, hardening when he sees me standing there watching him. Holding up a finger to indicate I should wait, he says something to Ken and the group before heading in my direction.

"I'd like to get going. I need to spend some time on the course tomorrow before it gets too hot."

"'Kay," I say, as it's clear I don't have much of an option. He is my ride, and making someone else take me would require them to make a thirty-minute round-trip detour.

We both go in search of Jen and quickly say our goodbyes before climbing into JT's pickup.

It's a quiet drive home. I'm not sure if it's that we are both tired or if our squabble from earlier is still lingering, but it's awkward now. We pull into the driveway after saying nothing for fifteen minutes, and we both climb out of the car.

I suddenly understand JT's desire to be anywhere but in the same space together. So, instead of letting him be the one to leave me, I speed walk into the house, making a quick detour to the living room to grab my book, and head straight into my room without saying a single word.

After getting ready for bed, I climb under the covers, grabbing my book and an extra pillow to prop my back up while I read. I flip the pages until I reach my bookmark and am shocked to find that someone else has written in the margins. My first thought is "Whoa, what possessed journal magic is this?" followed quickly by, "I can't believe I bought a book someone has already written in." I start to read the comment on the first page of the chapter and am hit with the truth—JT read my book! *Duh, Lila. That's clearly the obvious answer to writing in your book.* I'm about to go yell at him when I realize the comment is actually pretty clever. I flip to the next page and see the notes in the margins are all interesting in some way: funny or insightful or just a glimpse into JT's psyche.

It makes me feel like I'm 14 years old again, and JT's convincing Jameo to let me tag along with them while they go to the driving range or just cruise around town after Thanksgiving dinner. *Don't be silly. If anything, this is your book. You're letting* him *tag along for the ride!*

But that doesn't stop me from grabbing my fancy markers and annotating the book like before, underlining and adding little hearts or exclamation points next to the parts I like. Except this time, I also reply to his comments.

As I read, I feel like it's someone else entirely who is talking to me through the pages. It's not the guy who lost his cool during the cookout tonight, and it's definitely not the man who sits at a different table at Thanksgiving dinner because we can't stop fighting with each other. Unfortunately, it might be the JT who worshipped my body in Vegas. The one who not only brought me pleasure like I'd never experienced before but also made me feel like he cared about me with his words and his actions. Though, as I found out the hard way, that JT is short-lived. The real JT is the one who returned when we came up for breath, the one who didn't feel anything about us being together, who acted like we were still enemies. The one who stood me up. The one who kissed me in the hallway of a bar like I was water in the desert and then pushed me to the side like he found out I was contaminated with a deadly virus.

I'm not sure what it means that I want to keep responding to his messages in my book. I've spent this entire week getting more and more frustrated with the man who insists on staying where he isn't wanted all while acting like an uncivilized brute, unable to even exchange pleasantries with me before squirreling himself away in his room.

I'm not sure what it means when I reach the next chapter and find it missing his thoughts, so I add mine in instead.

And I definitely don't think about what it means the next morning, when, without saying a word, I leave the book in the living room and slip out of the house before I can accidentally run into JT.

CHAPTER THIRTEEN

JT

"WHAT CAN I GET you to drink?" the barista at Wild Brews asks as I find myself in the small, teal-colored shop for the fourth time in a week. The country club has coffee. It's just not busy yet on the course, and it turns out I need people around to stay sane. I have no idea how Jameo handled the isolation. If I didn't know I was a big-city guy before now, this is definitely proving it to me.

It doesn't help that Lila and I have successfully avoided each other for an entire week now.

I order my usual black coffee and grab a seat in the far corner just as Kelsey Harper walks through the door. Noticing me, she waves at the girl at the counter before heading in my direction. I stand up and give her a quick hug, inviting her to join me. Amazingly, at just that moment, the barista brings over a small coffee mug and sets it in front of her.

"Thanks, Laura," she says, giving a name to the young woman who serves me most days. I mentally catalog it so I can remember it for next time. The other thing I've noticed in small towns—no one wears nametags. It makes it much harder for a guy like me, who likes to call people by name.

"Did you call ahead or something?" I ask, nodding toward what appears to be a kiddie cup of black coffee that she certainly didn't order when she arrived.

"One of the perks of being a local: They know your order. And they know that I won't drink a whole cup of coffee, so they just give me one of the kids cups."

"They obviously aren't worried about you skipping out without paying either."

"I have a time or two on accident, but they just write it down and I pay the next time."

"Small towns are so weird," I say.

Kelsey nods. "That they are. I always thought I would be one of the people who moved away and never came back, but after moving regularly with the military, I realized I needed Wild Bluffs."

"Really?" I ask. "It seems so lonely."

"Lonely? That's not...ahh." Her face changes from one of confusion to a small, knowing smile. "Let's be clear, staying for a couple of weeks at the country club is not the same as living and working in Wild Bluffs. When you're part of the community, it can be, well, honestly, smothering at times. Everyone knows everything about your business, and everyone has an opinion about what you should or should not be doing. Now, staying out at the course, I can imagine that's lonely." She plays with one of the wisps of hair that has escaped from her blonde ponytail and now hangs next to her temple. "How's Lila handling it?"

"Fine, I'd imagine," I say. "You'd likely know more than I would."

"I doubt that. I don't really ask her about her personal life—not because I don't care, but because I've never had an employee I see in person every day, let alone one I'm likely going to be related to. I'm still trying to figure out the balance, and I'm not sure I'm handling the line between personal and professional well."

Kelsey doesn't seem like the type to share personal information very often, let alone hint at a weakness, so I decide to share my own truth. "We don't really interact much."

"Oh really? Why's that?"

"We've never really gotten along."

"Huh."

"What's that mean?" I ask, leaning forward to rest my elbows on the table between us.

"Nothing."

"Oh, come on. It meant something. I promise not to cry if you tell me," I joke.

She rolls her eyes but decides to answer me. "That's just not how I would've described it. But what do I know? I've been around the two of you together a grand total of two times. If you say you don't get along, who am I to say otherwise? You both just seem to be friendly, outgoing people, and you are her brother's best friend...and you're living together for the summer...so I assumed you guys would at least get along somewhat well."

"Yeah, well, Jameson thought it would be fun to not tell either of us that we'd be staying at his house."

"That sounds like an awkward surprise. Does he know the two of you don't get along?" Kelsey asks.

"Honestly, it feels like you're the only person who has ever been around the two of us together for more than a minute without picking up on the fact that we drive each other crazy."

"Oh. Huh," she says again, her nose crinkling as she looks at the ceiling.

"You said it again."

She rolls her eyes but doesn't make me ask again this time before answering. "That time, you said you drive each other crazy. The first time, you said you didn't get along. They're not quite the same, I guess."

Are they not the same? I've never really considered it before. Lila and I push each other's buttons, that's for sure, but I was pretty shocked in the car when she thought I hated her. If anything, being around Lila is like a session in an ice bath—all of my synapses fire at once, the feeling so overwhelming, I just want to jump out, but once it's over, I feel energized and like I'm back to the real me. No one likes an ice bath, but you understand the role it plays. You don't hate the ice bath for being an ice bath, but that doesn't mean you want to spend all your time in one.

"Huh."

"Now you're saying it," Kelsey jokes. "Well"—she gathers up her little cup—"I've got to get back for a meeting with my East Coast team, but if you ever need a friend…well, my dad and I could probably come out and golf."

It was almost a friendly offer. I appreciate that she threw her dad into the mix too.

"Thanks, Kelsey." I get up as well, following her to the place by the door where you can bus your own dirty dishes. "Hey, do you know if any of the Ferguson brothers are in town?" I ask as I hold the door open for her on our way out of the coffee shop.

"No. I think Bryn mentioned that Conrad would be out at the club sometime this summer, though. You would probably have better luck asking out there."

As we turn out of the corner store and onto Main Street, I spot Lila talking to the woman who tried to set me up with her daughter the last time I saw her. Lila is wearing a pair of black pants today, the ones that are wide from her thighs to her feet. She has a striped, short-sleeved shirt tucked into it, giving her a nautical feel. I've made sure to stay out of her way since the Harpers' party last week, so I can't help but absorb the details about her even as I continue walking. She has a smile on her face, and her hands are moving animatedly as she talks. The women are far enough away they don't seem to notice Kelsey and me. Lila's smile somehow grows with whatever Janice says. I make for my vehicle, doing my best to avoid both women. Just as I'm climbing into my vehicle, I hear Lila say, "That sounds amazing. I'd love to meet Matthew."

I slam the door shut, and both Lila and Janice look my direction at the noise. Noticing it's me, Lila's happiness melts into a look of distaste, and for some reason, a small piece of my heart feels like it's about to cry.

***

"Who's Matthew?" I ask when Lila walks into Jameson's house that evening.

Lila screams, tossing her keys into the air.

"Jesus Christ, JT. What are you doing just sitting there?"

I could tell her that I've been sitting here reading our book, leaving her messages about the logistics of the most recent sex scene and what I would've done differently, but we don't address the book. The Lila and JT who write those notes back and forth aren't us. They can't ever be us. They are the little pieces of our personalities who were friends once upon a time, and I'm not ready to send them back into hiding by addressing the personal comments we continue to leave for each other.

I'm also not going to tell her that I've barely been able to focus on the book because the stupid name *Matthew* keeps popping up in my brain.

"Just hanging out," I say instead.

She snorts. "Right. You've been hiding in your room for the last two weeks, but now you happen to be 'hanging out' in the living room at the time I get home every night?" She kicks off her shoes before stopping at the edge of the living room, her arms crossed.

"So are you really not going to tell me who Matthew is?" I ask as I move toward her. Shit. Just like in Phoenix, I'm unable to resist the pull she has on me. The one I've been trying to avoid for the last two weeks. The one that only pops up when we are in private.

"Why would you possibly care?" she asks.

It's a valid question. One I've asked myself multiple times since I drove away from her and stupid Janice. So I give her the only answer that makes any sense to me.

"Your brother asked me to keep an eye on you while he was gone. I just want to make sure you're not doing anything stupid."

"Wow. Thank you so much. I am just a naïve little country mouse who just wouldn't know a good seed from a bad one."

"Your Southern accent is terrible."

"Did Jameson really ask you to keep an eye on me?"

"Something like that."

"I'm going to kill him," she says, pulling out her phone.

I capture her wrist, staring into her bright green eyes. "Are you going to answer my question?" I ask.

She licks her lips before pulling a defiant mask over her face. "It's none of your business. I don't need anyone to keep an eye on me. I'm 24. I have a master's degree. I'm involved in cybersecurity for some of the top corporations around the world. I can decide whether I want to go out with Janice's nephew, okay?"

I move closer, our lips just a few inches apart.

"Janice's nephew, huh? Sounds like a real winner."

"You don't know anything about him."

"I know his name is Matthew. What kind of name is that?"

"What kind of name is *Justin Theodore*, JT?" she asks, pushing me away.

It's hard to argue that point because I dislike the name so much that I officially go by JT. So, as any good debater would, I decide to skip right over her question and continue with my point. "I know Janice is out there just trying to set people up all willy-nilly. She tried to set me up with her daughter, for fuck's sake."

"Well, it doesn't speak well for her track record that she would try to set anyone up with you, let alone her own flesh and blood, but she doesn't know you that well. I'm sure she knows her nephew much better."

"I'm a catch, Lila," I say.

"Really?" she asks. "Then why don't you ever have a girlfriend?"

"Oh, trust me, I could if I wanted to. I could have a girlfriend tomorrow if I wanted one. I don't know if you know this, but I've always had a knack for getting women into bed quickly."

She rolls her eyes, seeming not to care that I just equated her with the other women I've slept with. Though, *fuck*. She's definitely not in the same category as any of them. My time with her meant so much more than that.

"Fucking isn't the same as dating," I say, terrified at the thought of Lila meaning something to me. *You cannot risk losing your best friend, JT. Get it together.*

"Oh, I'm quite aware." She glares at me one last time, and it takes all my self-control not to capture her lips with mine. To make her forget the name Matthew ever existed.

CHAPTER FOURTEEN

LILA

"I CAN'T SEE ANYTHING," Elise says from the speaker on my phone.

"Ugh." I groan. "It's a lot harder to have you help me pick out clothes when you're hundreds of miles away."

"I don't remember getting this motion sick when we did it in person. Maybe you should just set your phone down until you pick something out and then I can approve or not."

"Fine," I say, walking over to prop my phone against the lamp on my nightstand. At least this way Elise can still see me as I inspect my closet. How is it that I own all these clothes and nothing in here seems to be remotely close to what I want to wear? Who was I when I bought these? To be fair, I only have two suitcases' worth, but it still seems like a lot of options that I hate.

"So we are thinking no on the summer dress?" I ask, pulling out the cute light blue dress with puffy sleeves and a floral pattern on it. It was my go-to dressy outfit in college, so it feels like a good fit for a blind date with Janice's nephew Matthew.

"You said you haven't seen anyone wearing a dress since you came into town."

"True."

"And that dress is what the youths are wearing these days."

"Are we even considered youths at this point?"

"Doesn't matter. I assure you that style has not reached rural Colorado."

"Don't be mean, Elise."

"I'm not being mean! Small towns just tend to be a few years behind on fashion trends, and even then, most people's fashion just freezes the minute they move back to town. I'm not hating on it. It's very practical. My mom wore the same clothes my entire life. Actually, now that I think about it, I'm not sure if it's practical or sad." She considers it while I stare into my closet as if more options might magically appear.

When nothing new materializes, I move on. "Okay, so no dresses. That helps narrow things down," I say. "Next question: Jeans or dress pants?"

"It's not a business interview, Lila."

"Hey, I've got some cute wide-leg pants I could wear."

"Nope."

"So...jeans?"

"Yes. I feel ninety percent sure jeans are the correct option," Elise confirms.

I hear JT's door to his room open, followed quickly by the sound of him leaving through the front door. I've continued to avoid him since his little outburst yesterday. Fuck him for knowing exactly what to say to make me question everything about myself by making it clear no one could ever love *me*. I'm embarrassed by how distracted I was at work today. I was creating a monitoring schedule for a new client's online accounts, and it took twice as long as it should have because his words continued to play in my head. It likely didn't help that I was trying to do it all myself without reaching out to Kelsey for guidance—she hired me for this job, so I should be able to do it.

I also refused to open our—*no, my*—book when I got home today because I didn't want to see that version of JT. No, JT Johnson is a complete asshole, and I will not let myself believe anything else.

I grab a pair of my dark jeans and a silky, emerald-green blouse with a deep V-neckline. The shirt is just elegant enough to make it look like I dressed up, but the jeans and casual black slide sandals I plan to wear should make it look like I'm not trying too hard. I slip off my white blouse from work today and change quickly before stepping into Elise's line of sight again.

"What do you think?"

"Perfect! That color looks amazing with the slight tan you're getting and your dark hair."

"Like I'm trying but not too hard?" I ask.

She gives me one more full-body sweep. "The exact right amount of trying."

"Perfect," I say, bringing the phone with me into the bathroom so I can do my hair and makeup. Janice immediately followed up our conversation yesterday by sending me and another number a group text introducing me to Matthew and him to me. It's clear he's been set up by his aunt a time or two before, because when he responded, it was to the whole group and politely asked me out for the next night. Once I agreed, he switched to a private text chain with me, apologizing for including his aunt but assuring me it was the only way to get her to leave us both alone. I trust him on this one. So here I am, one night later, getting ready to go out for pizza with a complete stranger who is "my age." I considered asking Becca and Izzy for the rundown, but they weren't in the office today, and I'm not sure if we're the kind of friends who randomly just text each other yet, so I'm flying blind on my date with Matthew at the pizza place in town, Wild Crusts.

"It's amazing how quickly I got set up with someone in Wild Bluffs," I say. "I really thought it would take much longer for me to find a date."

"Really? I'm surprised it took so long for some local matchmaker to get her claws in you. You *want* to be set up. You're like every mama's dream."

"That's an exaggeration. I just have life plans, and getting married and having kids is an important part of mine."

"You know you give people the ick when you say that, right?"

"I can recognize I don't *need a man* to be happy and successful and still want to be in a loving relationship."

"Yeah, but..."

"But what? It's not like I've dated complete losers or lowered my standards just to be with someone, have I? No. I just know dating is a numbers game, so if I'm not out there meeting people, how will I ever find my person?"

"Fine. Fine." Elise holds her hands in front of her in the universal sign for "I give up."

"As long as you aren't lowering your standards, I say have as much fun as you want with all the locals."

"Thank you. That's the kind of support I'm looking for."

"Well, I mean, don't have too much fun with too many of the locals. That shit will get around, and you will not like the impact it has on your reputation."

"Oh, come on. I'm not planning on sleeping my way through Wild Bluffs."

"I'm not saying not to do it, I'm just saying make sure they know how to keep it on the DL before you do."

I nod but don't reply. Sleeping my way through town sounds like the worst. Though, after that moment with JT last night, I have been looking forward to some male companionship this evening. Why must JT be so good-looking? It's like being in his presence does something to my senses that causes half of my brain cells to turn to mush. Luckily, I caught myself in time last night. God forbid we add Wild Bluffs to another one of our random hookup locations. Jameson would never forgive me if he found my ass print on one of his bathroom counters. Oh God, Jameson knowing we were hooking up would be completely embarrassing, especially since he still sees me as a child. I mean, he's paying me to dog sit right now.

"Sooo... How is it going, living with JT?" Elise asks after a long pause, clearly guessing where my thoughts have drifted. "Still just avoiding each other like children?"

"Why is giving each other the space we both so clearly want childish?"

"You guys had sex on a counter in Vegas. Not talking to each other when living in the same house is immature. Did you all even clear the air about the hookups?"

"It was mentioned."

"And..."

"We decided not to talk about it and to pretend like it didn't happen."

"Wow, really proving me wrong," Elise says. I know she's staring at me with a smug smile on her stupid face, but I choose to ignore her and focus on my mascara instead.

"You need to talk to him, Lila. I know you care about him in some dark recess of your heart. I'm not telling you to sleep with him. Just be his friend."

Ugh. The same thing Jameson told me to do. Why does everyone want us to be friends?

"I'll think about it, but hey, I've got to run if I'm going to make it into town and not be late for my date. Keep your phone on you in case I need a fake emergency call."

"I'm always happy to be your grandmother's nurse letting you know she isn't doing well."

"Love you. Come visit me soon!"

"Love you too," she says, and we both hang up.

CHAPTER FIFTEEN

JT

"JT Johnson, what are you doing here, man?"

I look up and smile at Conrad Ferguson. Mary, the club manager, let me know he would be arriving tonight. She also mentioned he had dinner reservations for him and one of his brothers at the club's restaurant, so I've been waiting at the bar for the last thirty minutes to ensure I don't miss them. I may also be avoiding listening to Lila talk to someone about her date tonight. I can't believe she's going out with a guy named *Matthew*.

"Conrad. Good to see you again. I'm staying at Jameo's place for a few weeks while I'm recovering from a tweaked back."

"Oh, no. Sorry to hear that. When do your doctors think you'll be able to be back playing in tournaments?"

"Unless anything major happens, I'm planning to be at the tournament in two weeks."

"Ah, that's not too terrible, then. Though I know any time away from your job can feel like too much."

A snort of laughter draws my attention to the man who just walked up behind Conrad.

"Do you know my brother Tyler?" Conrad asks by way of introduction.

Tyler looks a lot like his brother. Both have dark brown hair that's slightly longer on the top and neatly trimmed on the sides. They're both roughly my height, so somewhere between six feet two and six feet four, though Tyler is a bit taller than his brother. He's also a bit bulkier. While it looks like Conrad likes to spend his time out running, Tyler has the build of someone who spends time in the gym, lifting weights.

I shake Tyler's hand. "Good to meet you." I gesture toward the bar where I've been posted up. "Want to join me for a drink?"

Conrad shakes his head, and I feel my stomach drop. I didn't expect much more from him than idle small talk, but I also didn't think he'd turn down the invitation for a drink.

"We golfed all day, and I've barely had anything more than a candy bar to eat. If I don't get some real food in me, I'm going to pass out."

"Okay," I say. "Well, it was good to see you."

"You want to join us?" Tyler asks.

"I don't want to intrude..."

"Not intruding at all. Please, we'd love to have you join us for dinner," Conrad says, heading toward a table in the corner where two walls of windows meet. "I like this table best. Everyone gets a good view."

"Great, then, I'd love to join you." I grab my drink and cross the room to sink into the seat next to Conrad's.

He's right. The view is spectacular. The sun is setting, and it looks like a flaming ball of fire resting on the horizon, swathed in layers of orange and yellow. There is a foursome of middle-aged men out on the grassy area in front of the restaurant playing bocce ball, each with a drink in their hands.

"So how are you liking Wild Bluffs Country Club, JT?" Conrad asks.

"The course is amazing." Remembering that I'm supposed to be out with a tweaked back, I backtrack a bit, saying, "Not that I've been able to play too much golf."

"What have you been doing to keep yourself occupied, then?" Tyler asks.

"Jameson said his sister was moving out here this summer. Do you see her very often?" Conrad asks before I can answer his brother's question.

"We're both staying at Jameo's place right now. But she's working, so I don't spend too much time with her. We mostly just do our own thing."

"I don't think I knew Jameson had a sister. Is she older or younger?" Tyler asks. Even though I know it's a polite, normal thing to ask, I can't help the irritation that pricks at the back of my neck. *Why does he care about Lila?*

"She just graduated from college."

Conrad tilts his head. "I thought she was finishing up a graduate program. Engineering or something like that."

Good God. Is this man secretly stalking Lila? Why would he possibly know that?

"Uhm, yeah. Something like that," I say, though I know very well it was a master's in engineering from Denver College.

The waitress arrives, greeting us with a warm smile as she takes our orders. With a quick nod, she departs, leaving us to our conversation. Conrad picks up right where we left off, leaning in slightly. "Bryn was telling me about Lila's graduation ceremony. I was bummed Bryn's sister had a chance to snag her as an employee before we did."

You're an idiot, JT. Of course one of the wealthiest men in America is not stalking Lila Walker. He works with Bryn. It makes sense she would mention Lila's graduation and her moving out here to work for her sister.

"Yeah. She's a bit fiery, but I'm sure Kelsey wouldn't have hired her unless she knows her stuff."

"Fiery, you say?" Tyler asks with a smirk.

"Tyler." Conrad has on a big-brother face if I've ever seen one.

"What? It's so hard to meet a girl who doesn't work for us and isn't just after me for my money. Plus, I like a girl with a bit of fire in her veins."

"You're starting to sound as bad as Xander."

Alexander Ferguson rounds out the Ferguson brothers trio. The youngest of the family, he's rumored to be quite the playboy. I've never met him before, but his face does have a tendency to land on the front of gossip magazines at least a couple of times a year.

"I am not. I was just considering if I should ask her out on a date."

My beer goes down the wrong pipe, and my eyes water as I cough.

"You okay?" asks Tyler.

I nod and croak out, "Yup."

"Sorry. I didn't mean to make the Lila thing awkward," Tyler says. "Does she have a boyfriend or something?"

I know she doesn't, and despite his interest in Lila, Tyler seems like a decent guy. As I go to tell him she's available, something else comes out instead. "Yeah."

What the actual fuck was that?

"Ah, well. All the good ones do these days. Is it serious?"

"I think they started dating last year when Jameo and I played in Vegas. So probably pretty serious." *Why are these words coming out of my mouth?* I'm not even supposed to be talking to these men about Lila. I'm supposed to be making friends with them so they can help my parents connect with potential clients. Instead, I'm sitting here lying to them about Lila's love life.

"Ahh, well. You win some, you lose some," Tyler says.

Our food arrives then, and we get wrapped up in eating and making small talk about golf, California, and Jameson's recent rise to greatness.

As our plates transition from full to empty, I navigate the conversation to their work. "I'm looking forward to the Ferguson Tournament this year. I'm especially excited for the event the night before."

"Oh really?"

I hate having to navigate this delicate balance of asking about the event without it coming across like I'm asking them for a favor or am trying to help my parents poach their clients. This is the realm where my parents thrive, but I've never quite been able to figure it out.

"Yeah. I mean, I'm not at the level of the Ferguson Brothers Investment Firm, but I dabble with some angel investing. Sam and I have been doing a lot of research into how we might want to expand some of our angel investments to better support the leaders we are investing in. It's been eye-opening for us just within our small portfolio, I can't imagine what I can learn talking to some of the guests."

"You're an angel investor?" Tyler says at the exact same time his brother asks, "Who's Sam?"

"Sam is technically my PA, but he does so much more than just manage my life."

"Like help you with your casual angel investing hobby?" Tyler teases.

I grab one of the few fries left on my plate and pop it into my mouth. "Exactly."

"Don't your parents own an investment firm?" Conrad asks.

"They do," I answer, not sure where this is going.

"I thought that's what Bryn said. I guess I assumed they managed your wealth for you." *Why were Bryn and Conrad talking about* my *finances?*

"Oh, well, they do manage the majority of it. When they started out, it was just my money they were investing, but they've expanded into a full wealth-management firm since then. The angel investing is just a very small portion of my portfolio. Only one or two investments a year."

"That's great that you have your parents to help you out. Managing investments for your family can be tricky, though. We stick to private equity investing and don't do much wealth management, but I know it can be challenging for my colleagues who manage their parents' or friends' money. It's a lot of pressure, particularly when the investments don't perform as well as they expect. You know, now that I think of it, the reason I know about your parents is because Bryn mentioned it when I suggested she ask Jameo about investing in one of the start-ups she's working with. She quickly let me know she wouldn't be mixing business with pleasure."

"It adds a different dynamic to the relationship for sure." Although it doesn't seem my parents feel particularly guilty about losing my money.

"That it does. But just so you know, there won't be many investors at the Vegas event. I know that rumor went around when we first announced the event, but my brothers and I are starting to focus on sports investments—like the Ferguson Tournament. To help balance the investment, we are also going to start giving a large portion of our philanthropic dollars to sports programs for underserved kids. We'll primarily be inviting people who run those programs and a few of the families they serve. We hope that by connecting the programs across the country, there will be more collaboration and less duplication of services."

"That's amazing," I say. And it is. It's just not the people my parents are hoping to meet that night. Although it might be a smart long-term play for them if they can create connections with the parents of golfers on track to play professionally someday.

"Well, thanks. We're excited about this new avenue for the firm," Tyler says in what can only be described as his interview voice.

Crap. I somehow managed to turn this casual dinner into a work event. Wanting to dispel that immediately, I shift into fun-guy mode. "But enough about work, tell me about what Xander is up to these days. He seems like the type of guy I should be spending more time with. Is it true he went skydiving naked? That seems...cold?"

The brothers laugh and regale me with stories of their wild younger brother. When we finally decide to call it a night, we're all a bit drunk, but I feel like I've possibly made enough of an impression to help my parents with introductions at the event in Vegas—even if it's not with the exact clients they are hoping for.

I walk with the brothers out of the restaurant, saying goodbye outside the front doors as they head to their house that's in the opposite direction of mine. I make my way to Jameson's place using the path that follows the first fairway, only stumbling once as I navigate the dirt walkway in the dark. I stop outside the house, my impaired brain trying to understand why the lights are off. Shit, I guess Lila isn't home yet. Unwilling to go inside to sit and stew about what Lila is up to and where *Matthew* is or is not touching her, I turn the firepit on and drop into one of the chairs facing it.

Realizing it's not too late to call my mom in California, I pull out my phone to let her know I made progress on her request. I'm excited to finally be able to give her some good news after letting her and my dad down so much lately.

"JT," my mom says as her greeting.

"Hello, Mother."

"Are you calling to let me know you've finally been able to meet with the Ferguson brothers? Or that you finally decided to give up on this ridiculous 'injury' and start golfing again? You know your dad does not agree with your decision."

I do know, he's called me at least twice a day about it since I've been here.

"I'm not—" I cut myself off, recognizing how fruitless it would be to explain why I need a break. My mom needed a break twenty years ago, and she worked through it. Worked so hard to earn the money we needed for me to play golf that she fell asleep at the wheel and drove into a tree. "I actually just finished up dinner with both Conrad and Tyler Ferguson."

"Oh, darling, that's fabulous."

"It is!" I say excitedly. "I think we really hit it off. I'm sure they'd be willing to introduce us to a few people at the event. However, just so you know, they did mention it will primarily be young athletes and their parents in attendance."

"Oh, JT," my mother says, her tone making it clear just how displeased she is.

"I know it's not the demographic you were hoping for, but I think it could be a smart long-term play. The parents of junior players will appreciate your insight, and you can start building connections that may pay off in a huge way in five or ten years."

"Five or ten years will not work, JT. We need the investments now." And with that cryptic statement, my mom hangs up on me.

Why do they need money so badly?

Chapter Sixteen

Lila

Matthew leans forward, his arms crossed with his elbows on the table. We're sitting out on the back patio at Wild Crusts. We finished our meal a while ago and, somehow, we've had enough to talk about that we're just getting to what we do for a living. "My job isn't too exciting. I work on the family farm."

"Oh, that's cool."

He smiles and, dang, the man has a nice smile, one that feels like a hug from your best friend after a long day. Not necessarily the feeling we are hoping for with a date, but it's better than the alternatives. Plus, I'm not ready to call it a night, and this is just our first time meeting. Maybe the sparks and butterflies will surface once I get to know him a bit better.

He's got on light jeans and a white button-up with boots. It's a good look in general, and Matthew wears it well. He clearly spends time out in the sun, with his tan skin and sun-kissed short brown hair. I guess that makes sense if he works on his family's farm.

"You must be new around here if you think working on the farm is cool. It's what most of my classmates are back doing at this point."

"Oh. You don't like it?"

"No, I do. Don't get me wrong, it's a great job, and I'm lucky that I enjoy working with my dad and brother. Not every family deals well with passing the baton on to the next generation, but my dad is great and has a really clear process for how and when ownership and leadership will get passed to me and my brother, Chris."

"That's...wow. I guess I've never put much thought into succession planning for family businesses. It seems like it's a field of interconnected landmines just waiting to explode."

"It sure can be. But enough about me. Tell me more about working with Kelsey. How did you end up working for your brother's girlfriend's sister? That feels like it might have just as many landmines to navigate as my work does."

"It's been great. And, yeah, I met Kelsey last year through Bryn, but it was just normal families meeting stuff. Then, when Kelsey heard I was graduating with my master's in computer engineering, she suggested I apply for a position she was about to open at KH Security. The job sounded too good to be true, even if my degree isn't exactly in cybersecurity. Plus, my brother was living out here, and I thought it would be fun to be closer to him again. So I applied and the rest, I guess, is history."

"That's amazing. Kelsey Harper has always slightly terrified me." He glances over his shoulder as he says it, as though he's afraid she might pop up behind him. "I mean, she seems really cool, but also like she could kill me with her pinky, ya know?"

"Oh, I know."

"So tell me about what you do at KH Security."

I give Matt a rundown of my job as a project and account manager at a cybersecurity firm. My days are a whirlwind of timelines, coordination, and constant communication. I'm the go-between for clients and our technical teams, ensuring that everyone is on the same page. I juggle multiple projects at once, setting deadlines, tracking progress, and troubleshooting any issues that arise along the way. There is definitely a point in there where I get overly detailed about the work Kelsey and I are doing as she considers expanding into personal security. I tell him about the proposal I've been putting together for Kelsey to submit to a potential client, but I leave out how confused I am about the specifics I'm supposed to be including, not wanting to admit that I'm failing at the first major task Kelsey has assigned me.

Realizing I've been talking about the proposal for way too long, I switch the conversation back to him.

Matt tells me more about going to college out of state, trying everything to escape the small-town life, but then graduating and knowing there is nowhere else he'd rather be than in Wild Bluffs.

He's a super nice guy, and I'm having a great time hanging out with him, but it feels really...platonic. There's no tingling when he looks at me or a flutter in my stomach when his hand gets closer to mine on the table. Nothing like the buzz I feel when I'm around JT—and that will be the last time tonight I make any comparisons between the two, I promise myself.

Matt glances at the shadows in the corner of the patio before setting down his beer and looking at me with the most serious expression he's worn all night. "Look, Lila, I should've told you this before, but I'm not looking to date anyone."

"Oh," I say, because what else do you say to a statement like that?

"Aunt Janice keeps setting me up on dates, and I've found that if I agree a couple of times a year, she actually tones it down a little. And I am excited to meet you. I'm just—"

"Oh, it's okay!" I say, a little too loudly. I don't understand what I did to make this go south so quickly, but I most certainly will not be causing a scene about it.

"No. It's really not okay." He pulls his hand through his hair, causing the strands on top to stand on end. "Look, the truth is that I'm in love with another woman, and…well, let's just say she doesn't love me back. I keep going on dates mostly to get my aunt and family off my back, but also because I'm hoping that I'll suddenly stop feeling this way, but…all they end up doing is making me want her so much more."

Damn. I now want to know everything about this woman and how she managed to ensnare this kind, handsome man so thoroughly. Is it rude to ask him for some tips?

"That…sucks?" I ask it as a question, though I'm unsure if it's actually a bad thing. I would give anything to be loved like Matt loves this mystery woman.

"It's my fault. And now, everyone keeps telling me to move on, but I just can't. And you seem like an awesome person, and I really hope we can be friends, but I just don't want to lead you on."

"That's totally okay. I'm actually very jealous of her, if that's not too weird to say." He just laughs, so I keep going. "I've had this life plan, which, as lame as all my friends tell me it is, has always included being married and in love by this age. Not some trad wife situation, though, more power to them, but just in a healthy relationship where we love and support each other. I hate I'm so very single. I'm not willing to settle for some jerk who isn't worth my time, but I don't feel like it's too hard to ask to find someone who loves me like you love your mystery woman."

His smile is so sad that I want to hug him. Instead, I pat his arm a couple of times.

"You don't want someone like me, Lila. Trust me. I'm the jerk who isn't worth your time." We're both lost in our thoughts for a moment, listening to the babbling of the river as it runs past the side of the patio.

"But, hey," Matt says, breaking the silence. "Want to come to the high school football scrimmage with me next Friday? A couple of the coaches are single. I may not be boyfriend material, but I make one hell of a good wingman."

"That sounds surprisingly fun," I say, pulling out my wallet to leave some cash for the bill.

"I've got it. It's the least I can do."

"Well, thanks," I say as we both stand to leave.

As we pass the bar inside, I realize I know the three women whose backs are to me.

"Mind if I go say hello real quick?" I ask Matthew, and we say a quick goodbye, promising to touch base about the football scrimmage before Friday.

"What are you three doing here?" I ask as Becca, Izzy, and Kelsey turn around.

Izzy scans me from head to toe, but apparently, my outfit passes inspection, because when she meets my eyes, she's wearing a pleased smile. "We're here to spy on your dinner, obviously."

I laugh but slowly let it fade away when I realize neither of them is laughing with me.

"Why does it feel like you're not joking?"

"We learned with Bryn and Jameson that it's best if we're just here for the start of it. Otherwise, our phones start blowing up, and then by the time we arrive, there aren't any good seats left, and we've already missed the action," Izzy says.

"Et tu, Kelsey?" I joke.

"Thing One and Thing Two invited me along. To be clear, I'm here for the pizza. I couldn't care less about you and Matthew going on a date."

Then it hits me. "I didn't tell any of you about this date. How did you know we would be at Wild Crusts?"

All three of them send me looks that say "Really?" but then Becca takes pity on me and answers, "Janice, Izzy. I thought we warned you about the speed at which small-town gossip moves."

"I guess I'm still trying to wrap my mind around everyone knowing my business."

"How was the date?" Becca asks as I slide onto the bar stool next to her, suddenly feeling exhausted.

"Well, he's great. Doesn't wear women's underwear or show people his collection of baby teeth, but I don't think it's going to work out."

"Ew," Becca replies as Izzy just says, "No."

Kelsey shakes her head slowly before she says, "I clearly should've done a psych test on you before I hired you."

Izzy still has a look of disgust on her face when she says to me, "I'm actually worried about why you would say that. Obviously we wouldn't let you go out with someone who collects baby teeth."

I laugh but then climb back off my stool, unable to muster the energy to have this conversation. "I'll tell you guys about it later. I'm beat."

And for some reason, I really want to curl up with my book and let myself be embraced by the fictional version of JT.

Chapter Seventeen

JT

I'm still out by the firepit when I hear the door close, indicating Lila is home from her date. It's late enough that I know the date went well, though not so late that I'd given in to obsessing about the fact that she went home with *Matthew*. I know she's upset with me from our exchange last night. If her silence wasn't enough to indicate it, her reading habits definitely do. Her bookmark has moved a few chapters, but she hasn't left any annotations, let alone any comments meant for me. Hell, I would take a squiggly line under a quote she likes at this point.

I didn't think avoiding each other would somehow leave a gaping hole in my chest, but not having her thoughts there next to mine as I read about finding love and making it work is...well, it's lonely.

I'm surprised when the door to the patio opens and Lila walks out with two beers from the fridge.

"Hey, Pipsqueak," I say in a teasing tone. "What brings you out to the ol' firepit tonight?" God. When did I become an 80-year-old man?

"I wanted to watch the storm roll in." She points her beer bottle toward the clouds forming in the southeast.

I've been sitting out here stewing in my failure for a while now, not even noticing the temperature drop or the big thunderheads start rolling in. My dad called me fifteen minutes after I hung up with my mother, and he spent a solid thirty minutes dissecting my last three putts in Phoenix and comparing them with my putting since then. Then he proceeded to ask me for more money, saying he found a fail-proof investment he wants me to get in on. When I told him I don't have much spare cash, he lectured me on being fiscally responsible and not letting down the family. He ended the call with "If I hadn't given up my career for you, your mother and I would have our own money to invest, so maybe think about that next time your 'back is bothering you.'"

I called my coach, suggesting I was ready to go back for the upcoming tournament, but he convinced me to stick to our original plan. I agreed half-heartedly because I truly do believe it's what's best for my game, but at the same time, I hate feeling like I'm disappointing my parents.

The lightning flashes behind one of the big cloud formations, lighting it up from behind, and it's one of the most mesmerizing things I've ever seen. I look over at Lila, her face lit by the firepit, and I want to tell her about my parents. I want to unburden myself, but I know I can't. It's not just that we fight all the time—I just don't want to be a burden to someone else. And Lila deserves so much more than having to carry the weight of my burdens. So I crush that feeling, the one telling me to open up to her, to have a conversation with her about real things.

"Does your connection with Hell also allow you to call forth storms?"

"I'm pretty sure that's not a demon thing," she replies, sliding the second beer over like she brought it for me.

"Sky demons?" I ask, knowing I'm way out of my depth here.

"Maybe? I'm pretty sure there are a couple different fantasy series where the bad guys control lightning. But now that I think about it, lightning-wielding is regularly associated with the heroes or heroines. There's a very popular dragon series out right now where the heroine can wield lightning. Maybe it has something to do with Zeus's lightning powers? So it's like a 'godly' trait? But...Zeus was kinda an asshole, so maybe that's not it."

I don't know anything about Greek gods (or are they Roman?), so I decide to skip over the last part of her analysis. "Should I read it?"

"I'm not sure if you're ready to take the leap into romantasy, my guy."

"Oh, am I your guy now?" Fuck. My chest tightens at the thought. I know it's just a phrase people are saying these days, but it kinda makes me *want* to be her guy. "And why the hell not? If I can handle alien romance, I can certainly handle romantasy."

"You read *alien romance*?" She basically shouts the last part. Thank goodness none of our neighbors live close by. "Tell me everything. How? Why? Did you like it? I have never been brave enough to read one, but—gah!—you have?"

"It was an accident," I admit, hoping to let the topic die there. Unfortunately, Lila has other plans.

"Oh, no. You're not getting let off the hook that easily." Her eyes are wide with delight, and she's shifted in her chair. Her legs are tucked up under her, and she's leaning toward me, her elbow on the arm of the chair, her chin resting on her hand. It's making her flowy green shirt gape a bit, giving me an unimpeded view of her cleavage.

Damn. I shake my head, trying to clear the thoughts of her breasts in my hands, her nipples hardening as I run my thumbs over them.

"JT!" she says, snapping me out of my fantasy. "Tell me more about how you accidentally read an alien romance! How did the algorithm even serve that up to you?"

"Well"—I sigh, leaning back in my chair and staring into the fire—"I was at a tournament in New York a couple of months ago and had just finished the book I was reading. Unfortunately, it was only like seven o'clock, so it was too early to actually go to sleep, and this was the final book in the final series of an author I'd been reading. So I was facing the dreaded book chasm and had no idea what I was going to read next. Well, my Kindle popped up an advertisement, and I was like, hey, Amazon knows what I like better than I do at this point, I trust it. So I just bought it and started reading. No questions asked."

Lila giggles next to me, clearly anticipating what is coming next, but tries to hide her smile behind her beer bottle.

"I started getting suspicious about twenty pages in, but at that point, I was in, so I decided to see where it went. And now, fuck, I'm not sure I can ever unsee it. There were multiple penises. Peni?"

Lila full-on snorts this time, she's laughing so hard, but she manages to choke out, "I'm pretty sure it's *penises.*"

I narrow my eyes at her, but that just makes her laugh harder.

"Anyway, multiple blue and green penises that changed color depending on how, uhm, aroused the alien was."

There is a good chance Lila is going to either suffocate or fall out of her chair, she's laughing so hard. Tears are streaming down her face, creating little trails from her makeup.

"Did you...finish...it?" she asks between gasps for air.

I want to be annoyed that she's finding this so funny, but I can't muster any indignation when she's clearly enjoying it. "I did. And the love story was excellent, thank you very much."

She's leaning back, feet on the ground, taking deep breaths, trying to get herself under control. I watch her chest rise and fall in a steady rhythm, my eyes locked on the curves of her body.

"That's amazing," she says once she can breathe again. "What's it called? I want to read it now. You've inspired me."

"I'm not sure. I'll have to get my Kin—"

I'm cut off by a loud crash of thunder and a sudden cold splash on my shoulder. I look up, surprised to see the storm has gotten so close so quickly.

"Rain!" Lila yells, her voice a mix of glee and warning.

Lila grabs the bottles sitting out on the lip of the firepit while I find the dial to turn the darn thing off. It takes me a minute to get it fully turned off, and by the time I make it inside, the sky has opened up, and I'm drenched.

"Oh, shit!" Lila exclaims. "That's a storm."

Jack, who is honestly such an easy dog that I forget about him most of the time, is out of Bryn and Jameson's room, howling along with the wind raging outside the window.

"Shhh," Lila says, going over to comfort him.

I shiver, the cold, air-conditioned house chilling the rain on my skin in a thoroughly unpleasant way. "I think I'm going to go grab a quick shower to warm up," I say.

"I don't think you're supposed to shower when there is lightning."

"Is that true? I thought that was just an old wives' tale."

She shrugs. "No idea. Are you willing to risk it?" As if Zeus is on her side, a huge bolt of lightning streaks across the entire expanse of the sky.

"Great point. I can figure out another way to warm up."

She cocks an eyebrow at me.

"I didn't mean that!" I say, feeling my eyes go round in my head. "I'm just going to go change into some dry clothes. And get under my covers. Alone. Yup. Just me."

She laughs, turning back to Jack, who has started up his conversation with the wind again.

***

I'm pulled from my sleep by a loud crash and my phone ringing. It's pitch-black in my room, and it sounds like the house is being pounded by baseballs.

"Hello!" I shout into my phone, trying to be heard over the noise.

"Mr. Johnson? It's Mary with Wild Bluffs Country Club. Are you and Ms. Walker both okay?" Shit. *Are we okay?* What's happening?

"Uhm. I'm not sure. I was sleeping. What's happening?" Christ, is this a tornado? Am I about to be picked up like Dorothy?

"It's a bad hailstorm. It just went through the outskirts of Wild Bluffs, and I guess it broke a ton of windows there. Don't go outside, and try to stay away from any southern-facing windows. I've got to go, JT. We've got a few more guests I need to get a hold of. Can you make sure Lila is okay?"

"I'm on it," I say, pulling on a pair of shorts before throwing open my door.

I have no idea how I've stayed asleep so long in this. It feels like I'm standing in front of a vacuum cleaner, the roar of the wind making it impossible to hear my own thoughts. Jack is pacing in front of Lila's door, whining loudly. From the way the wind is blowing into the room, it appears at least one window in the living room is broken. A flash of lightning burns across the sky, and I catch a glimpse of snow on the ground outside the window. Wait. No, not snow. Hail. Inches of white hail cover the course outside. I feel my way along the wall, hoping to find Lila's door. I breathe a sigh of relief when I do and ease it open, desperately trying to find the light switch inside. My fingers make contact, and I flip the switch but...nothing happens. Right. Power is likely out. Shit. Where is Lila? Maybe I can call her? I look at my phone and realize how big of an idiot I am. I turn on the flashlight and point it at her bed. Her room is a mess, little pinpricks of glass lighting up the floor and her bed. Fuck, fuck, fuck. Where is she?

"Lila!" I call out.

I hear a noise that could be her response from inside her bathroom. Clearly, Lila makes better decisions than I do when woken by a breaking window. I rush toward the bathroom door, stopping when I realize small pieces of glass have made it over here too.

"I'll be right back!" I call out, uncertain if she can hear me over the roar of the wind and the constant pounding of the hail against the windows and walls. This is...terrifying.

Jack follows me back to my room, where I throw on a pair of tennis shoes, leaving them untied, the tongues wide open. I all but run out of my room before realizing I can't have Jack walking on the broken glass that is covering the floors. My windows face north, so my room should be relatively safe, but I decide not to risk it. Following Lila's lead, I shut him into the bathroom. He immediately starts howling, but I can't deal with that right now.

I rush back into Lila's room, the glass crunching under my now-covered feet. I hope Lila made it into the bathroom before she had to cross a field of razor-sharp shards.

I throw open the bathroom door. "Lila!"

"Here!" She's huddled in the bathtub, wearing nothing but a skimpy tank top and little sleep shorts.

"Come on!" I yell. "My room is okay!" I move to help her stand, grabbing her hand as she steps over the lip of the tub. I start to open the door to the bathroom when I realize she's not wearing any shoes. "I'm going to have to carry you!" I yell.

"No way!" She shakes her head vehemently. "I can walk."

I turn back toward her, getting my face right next to hers. "Like hell you will! There is glass covering the floor out there. You have bare fucking feet. No." With that, I bend down and scoop her up into my arms. As I shove out the bathroom door, the wind picks up, and another window breaks, throwing pieces in our direction. Instinctively, I turn my back toward the window, pulling Lila tighter to my body to protect her from any shrapnel. I feel one piece cut the back of my bicep, but I keep moving, navigating through the living area and into my room. I slam the door shut and set her down, grabbing her arms as I check her over from top to bottom, making sure there isn't anything broken or bleeding. When I lift up her foot to check her sole, she gently shoves my hands away, grabbing my face and holding it inches from her own.

"I'm okay."

"Fuck. I was so scared when I saw your bed covered in glass."

"I'm okay." She runs her hands down my arms, and I wince when she comes in contact with a piece of glass that apparently lodged itself in there earlier.

"Shit, JT." Her eyes are wide. "Is that...glass?"

I swallow hard, trying not to think about it. "I think so."

"Come on." She grabs my hand and pulls me into the bathroom. Jack stops howling and presses up close to my legs, clearly just as frightened as I am. Taking my phone from my fingers, Lila sets it on the edge of the sink, filling the basin with light and illuminating the small room.

"That's a fancy trick," I say.

"I'm very smart, JT." She is inspecting the back of my arm, using a piece of toilet paper to catch the small stream of blood running down toward my elbow.

"I never doubted it, but if I had, the fact that you knew to hide in your bathroom would've proven it to me."

"It's like tornado safety 101."

"I don't think this is a tornado."

"Tell that to my sleep-addled brain."

I laugh. "It was a tough wake-up call."

"Do you have any tweezers?"

She takes the pair I offer her from my bathroom bag I've just left sitting on the counter and picks the phone back up from the sink. "Can you hold this right here while I pull this out?" she asks.

I grab the phone, angling it just the way she asked.

"One, two—" She pulls before she gets to three, but it's not as painful as I was expecting. She holds the toilet paper on the cut and shines the phone back into the sink before inspecting the rest of me for cuts. Her free hand runs so gently over my back that I'm not thinking about hail, broken glass, or injuries anymore. It's peaceful, and as the adrenaline leaves my system, all I want to do is go back to bed with Lila cuddled in my arms.

"I think you're good," she says.

We open the door to my room, and the storm seems to be calmer than it was before. Lila looks at me, and then at the bed, and then at the door to my room. Like hell I'm letting her out of my sight tonight.

"Come on," I say. "You can sleep with me tonight."

She looks at me for another second before climbing into bed. Her adrenaline must be wearing off too. I can feel her body shaking, the vibrations making their way to me through the mattress.

"You're okay," I say softly, and, without thinking, I pull her against my chest, wrapping my arms around her.

Lila tenses for a second before relaxing into my touch. We stay like that, our heartbeats slowing down in tandem until we're both asleep.

CHAPTER EIGHTEEN

LILA

I BURROW INTO THE warmth, trying to fully cocoon myself in its embrace. A small piece of my mind tells me to wake up, but I quickly silence it. I've rarely felt this content, and I plan to keep consciousness at bay for as long as possible. With a deep sigh, I press my body into the source of the heat next to me. I hold on to this sense of calm, this feeling that everything is exactly where it should be. Then, the realization hits me that the solid bulk under my cheek is not, in fact, my pillow. Startled, I blink my eyes awake.

The sun is shining through the windows, and I slowly take in the unfamiliar room and the far too familiar body I'm currently draped over. Damn, that man looks good asleep, his long eyelashes resting on his cheeks, his lips slightly parted. I track the lines of his body, down his bare chest to the arm that's wrapped around me, the bandage from last night peeking—shit!

Last night comes rushing back to me. Waking up to the sound of something battering against the side of the house, having no idea what could possibly cause that all-encompassing sound.

And then JT was there, carrying me to safety. Protecting me as another window gave in to the constant beating of the hail.

When he invited me to sleep with him, I'd almost balked, but where else was I going to go? And then he'd pulled me against him, and it had felt right. Safe. So I'd fallen asleep in his arms.

And if I'd known how amazing it would be sleeping next to the man, I don't know if I would've had the willpower to leave all those nights ago in Vegas. In spite of everything, I think those few hours might've been the best sleep of my life. It's so nice, in fact, that I'm having a hard time convincing myself to get up, even though I know there is so much that has to be done today to even begin to clean up from the storm.

JT's phone starts vibrating from its spot on his nightstand, and he jerks upright, a worried "Lila?!" escaping from his lips as he glances around frantically. I slip off his side at the movement, still not functioning enough to process the fact that I'm the first thing he was thinking about this morning. His hand fumbles around next to him before coming up with his cell phone. He answers the call with a husky "Hello."

I sit up in bed next to him, not at all sure what the proper protocol is, but I'm nosey enough to want to stick around to see what this phone call is all about. His eyes slip over to me, silently scanning me as if checking for invisible injuries.

"Thanks for the information, Mary, and for the call last night. We're both okay, but yeah, we have at least two broken windows, one in a bedroom and one in the living room. I haven't explored enough to know what other damage we have."

Ahh. The course is calling him to make sure we are all right. I wonder why they didn't call me. I search the bed for my phone before realizing I hadn't grabbed it in my dash to safety last night. *Dang it.* I should've thought about grabbing my phone before I rushed to the bathroom. What if something had caved in, and I was stuck in there? What if someone needed to get a hold of me? I should've known better—JT clearly did.

JT's listening intently, and I catch pieces of information about the havoc the storm wreaked both in Wild Bluffs and at the course.

"Okay, thanks for the information. We really appreciate it. And don't worry about us. We can sweep up the glass here."

His fingers pick at the comforter while he stares out the window, nodding in apparent agreement with whatever Mary is saying.

"Sure. We will head into town to see how we can help, then. Thanks, Mary."

He hangs up the phone and looks at me, clearly prepared to handle the fact that I'm in his bed now. I, however, am not, so I decide to take control of the conversation.

"What'd she say?"

"Apparently, the power is still out at the course and in town, but someone brought a generator to the coffee shop. They're making a bunch of eggs and coffee for breakfast for anyone in town who needs it. I guess the storm destroyed an unbelievable number of the southern-facing windows in town, including those at the hospital and nursing home. The hardware store and a couple of the families who own construction companies are putting together teams of volunteers to help patch all the broken windows in community buildings or seniors' homes if we want to join."

"Oh, that would be good. I'd love to help," I say, jumping out of bed. "Should we try to get ours patched up first?"

"Mary said that, for liability reasons, they'd prefer we leave everything as it is, and they will have a team in here as soon as they can to get things boarded up and cleaned."

Okay. I can work with that. I am nothing if not flexible.

"Okey-dokey, smokey," I say, before mentally face-palming at using such a juvenile expression. "Let me just go get changed, and we can head into town."

I turn to exit, but JT calls, "Wait!"

I guess we are going to talk about us sleeping together after all.

"You can't go out there without shoes on."

I look down at my bare feet like I've never seen them before. How does my lack of shoes have anything to do with us sleeping in the same bed, curled around each other?

"There's glass everywhere out there," he explains.

"Oh, right. Of course." Duh, Lila, you buffoon. *We aren't talking about it.* "I'll just..." I look around, searching for an answer. "Can I borrow your shoes?"

"Yeah, of course." He points to a pair of tennis shoes by the foot of the bed, and I slide my feet in. I feel like a kid dressing up in my mom's heels. My feet are so much smaller than JT's that I have to flex my toes with all my might to keep the shoes from falling off as I walk. My exit turns into a shuffle, and my face burns as JT lets out a light chuckle. Jack sniffs at my feet, making it even harder to get where I'm going. Well, not the stride of pride one would want after spending a night with a guy, but I think I'm hiding my embarrassment pretty well.

I open JT's door, and my worries about looking like a fool vanish at the sight of the living room. Jack tries to slip past me, but I shove him back into JT's room, shutting the door behind me. There is glass *everywhere*. One of the doors to the patio has a large, jagged hole right in the middle of it. The carpet is covered in shimmering shards of glass, and I can even spot some on the couch itself. Outside, everything is covered in a layer of melting hail. The few flowers that poke through the layer of white are decimated, all broken stems and missing petals. A lone evergreen tree stands across the fairway from me, half of its branches missing.

JT slips out his door behind me, and I feel him pull up at the sight.

"Fuck," he whispers.

His words are the final knock, and my walls come crumbling down. I can't take it anymore, the terror of last night, the devastation of this morning, and so I start to cry, my shoulders shaking with built-up emotions. JT steps up behind me, turning me into his chest and wrapping his arms around me. I know I should stop; I shouldn't let him see this side of me, the one that isn't perfect or tough. Plus, I'm getting snot and tears all over his shirt. Unfortunately, I can't help it. The stress of graduating, starting a new job, moving to a small town, trying to date, living with a guy I slept with and now just fight with all the time, and then being woken up in the middle of a fucking act of God is just too much for one girl to process.

"You're safe," JT mumbles into my hair, lightly stroking my back. "You're safe."

We stand like that for I don't know how long before I finally pull myself away from him, wiping my eyes with my fists.

"Sorry. I don't know what came over me. I'll pull myself together."

"No need to apologize, Lila. It was terrifying. I thought I was going to lose it when I walked into your room and saw your bed empty."

Well, that's...something I will need to process at another time.

He continues, "But you might want to prepare yourself. Your room is going to be just as bad, if not worse."

I nod, forcing myself to take a deep breath before shuffling my way to my door. When I open it, I realize he's right. The floor sparkles like a kid has been playing with silver glitter, and my bed is somehow worse.

"Shit," I say.

JT heads to my closet. "What do you need for today? If you have any boots, those might be a good idea if we're going to be helping clean up glass."

I shake my head. "My boots are in storage. I have some running shoes in there that will have to do." I move over to the closet, which fortunately had been closed last night, and grab what I want off the floor.

I head to the bathroom to change when I notice JT sticking things into my suitcase. "What are you doing?"

"Well, you're obviously not staying here tonight, and it may be a while before they can get the window fixed. You can stay with me until they do."

I want to say I can stay in Jameson's room—assuming none of those windows are broken—but I can't seem to offer it as a suggestion. There's always tomorrow.

Instead, I follow JT's lead and pack up my toothbrush and assorted bathroom paraphernalia and move them into his room as well. After a quick change into jeans, a T-shirt, and shoes that actually fit, I exit the bathroom to find JT in matching attire.

"No boots for you either?" I ask.

"Not something I thought I would need for this trip."

"Let's check out the rest of the house before we head into town," I suggest.

The room Jameson has been using for storage looks a lot like mine, though the window that broke was slightly smaller. Jameson's room faces the same direction as JT's, so it's fine. Neither of us mentions the fact that I could sleep there.

Instead, we head outside, and I groan at what I see. My poor car is totaled. The front windshield was facing directly south, and it's now completely shattered. The body looks like a golf ball, it's so covered in dents.

JT's pickup, luckily, is better off, and by that I mean it's covered in divots from the hail, but no glass appears to be broken.

"I guess I'll drive, then?" he says.

"You don't want to ride in mine? Everyone loves the wind in their face."

"I'm just not a huge fan of glass in my ass."

"Weird. I thought for sure that'd be one of your kinks."

"Jesus, Lila. That...nope. Not even going to think about it."

"Let me just take a few pictures so I can submit an insurance claim, and then we can go."

We both snap a variety of pictures of our vehicles, capturing the destruction from all different angles. I take longer than JT, and while he waits, he walks around the house, commenting on the damaged siding, the broken fake logs in the firepit, and the bent gutters.

"Ready?" he asks when he gets back around to the vehicles.

"Yup. Let's go board up some old people's windows," I say, looking forward to having something to do to put things back together.

CHAPTER NINETEEN

JT

THE SMELL OF COFFEE and breakfast sandwiches mingles with the low hum of chatter in the coffee shop. The place is packed, with people crowding together, bundled up against the morning chill. It feels like half the town has shown up, all bleary-eyed and yawning, but ready to get to work. I take in the scene—the familiar faces, others I've only seen in passing—and it hits me that everyone here is up this early just to lend a hand. There's a loyalty in Wild Bluffs I'm not used to seeing in the city.

Lila hands me my coffee, her fingers brushing against mine, and gives me a quick grin. "Ready for a day of cleaning and construction, Pretty Boy?"

I smirk, taking a sip. "If you can handle it, Pipsqueak, I'm sure I can. Though I'd like to get some food into me first."

We find a spot near the door, and I dig into my egg sandwich. The Harpers show up a few minutes later, Ken giving me a nod before he heads to talk to a group of men. Kelsey and Izzy both make their way to us, their mom pulling both Lila and me into hugs.

The organizer calls out assignments, sending us off in groups to places around town that got hit hardest by last night's storm. Lila and I get paired with the Harpers and a few other families and head to Sunshine Hills, the local nursing home.

When we pull up, there's already a small crowd gathered outside, families pulling toolboxes out of their cars, everyone ready to pitch in. I recognize a few of the faces from around town—a lady who is at the coffee shop with Janice most days and one of the waiters from the country club. Mr. and Mrs. Abbott, the couple who run the local hardware store, are unloading supplies from the back of their truck.

Lila ties her hair back, the same focused look in her eyes that I've seen a hundred times when she's set on something. I'm half tempted to make a comment that I know will rile her up, but the whole scene has me feeling too...comfortable.

Ken walks over, offering me a red-handled hammer. "Think you're up for a bit of work today, JT?"

I chuckle, grabbing the hammer. "I think I can handle it, Mr. Harper. Just don't expect me to go easy on you."

He laughs, his eyes crinkling with genuine amusement. "That's what I like to hear."

The first task is boarding up broken windows, and Lila, predictably, is quick to remind me that I'd better be careful not to hurt my back trying to reach the high windows. I pretend not to notice the challenge in her smirk and grab a piece of plywood, hauling it up with Ken's help. Lila snaps a picture of us as we press the board into place. I stick my tongue out at her, and she mouths *focus* back at me, rolling her eyes.

As I work alongside Ken and the Harpers, the conversation flows easily, and we swap stories about the tornado that hit the next town over a few years back, last year's fishing trip disaster, and—of course—the sports teams this year and how they are going to fare. At one point I realized they were discussing the high school team's volleyball record from twenty years ago and quickly let my mind wander again, my eyes following Lila as she hands out water bottles to the group.

"You know," Kelsey says, squinting at me as Ken and I line up the next board, "I was pretty surprised to see you here to help, JT. I thought you mentioned you're a big-city guy through and through. Pitching in to clean up the town is definitely a small-town thing to do."

I shake my head, but there's something in me that wants to agree. "Maybe. It's not like this in the city—everyone just minds their own business there."

Ken nods. "Well, that's the thing about small towns. We may know far too much about each other, but when things go sideways, we come together."

The work goes on, and I find myself surprisingly content in the rhythm of lifting, hammering, and chatting with the people around me. After a while, I take a quick break and snap a photo of the group hard at work, sending it off to Sam. A few seconds later, he responds: *Nice work, man. How much are you thinking of donating?*

I stare at his message, and it takes me a moment to realize he's right. Sure, the nursing home's insurance will cover the repairs, but something about today, about the people around me, makes me want to do more. I type back a response, telling him to set up an anonymous donation, something that feels substantial enough to make a difference.

As the day wears on, the shenanigans inevitably start. At one point, Ken and another guy, Dale, start arguing over the best way to nail the plywood, and I can't help but laugh as they bicker like a married couple about it. Lila and Jen catch on and start placing bets on who'll give in first. Unfortunately for Ken, Dale never backs down, and I've never seen someone more committed to winning a bet involving a hammer.

When we finally finish boarding up the last window, Lila and I meet up near the entrance, both of us covered in dust and probably looking as exhausted as we feel. She grins, brushing plywood dust off her shirt. "Not bad, Johnson. Didn't think you'd last this long."

"Oh, please. I did all the heavy lifting," I tease, nudging her shoulder with mine.

"Maybe so, but I'm the one who kept everyone hydrated," she says, flashing that smug smile of hers. "Dehydration is the *enemy*, JT."

The rest of the crew starts gathering their things, and Ken walks over, clapping a hand on my shoulder again. "Good work today, JT. You know, you might just make it in this town."

"Thanks, Mr. Harper," I say, feeling a strange warmth in my chest. "Means a lot coming from you."

He chuckles, giving me a nod. "Anytime, son. And hey, you ever get tired of golf, there might even be room in one of these construction crews for you. It's going to be a long time before everything is repaired from this storm."

I laugh, shaking my head. "I'll keep that in mind."

As we head out, the group of us tired but satisfied, I glance back at Sunshine Hills, at the work we've done today. It's hard to explain, but something about it feels right, like I'm finally where I'm supposed to be.

CHAPTER TWENTY

JT

"I'M WORKING WITH THE pilots to get your flight finalized," Sam says Monday morning as I'm on my way back from dropping Lila off at work. Her car is inoperable, and as all the rental cars in the area—what few there are—are being used by other people whose cars were damaged beyond repair by the hail, I told Lila I was happy to be her driver.

"What do you mean?"

"Are you not...are you not planning to go back to California?"

"No. Why would I?" I ask as I pull into the driveway of Jameson's house.

"Well, because you can't golf at Wild Bluffs right now," Sam's confused reply comes through.

Huh. I hadn't even considered the fact I can't practice until the grass on the golf course recovers from the damage done by the hail. Lila and I had walked down to the restaurant yesterday after finishing up with the town cleanup crew, and I'd been shocked by how much damage an ice pellet the size of a baseball could do to a fairway, let alone the more fragile area on and around the greens. But the fact that I'm supposed to be returning to golf in less than two weeks hasn't crossed my mind once since the storm started.

"I'm sure I'll be able to practice soon," I reply. "No need for me to head back to California. Plus, I'm Lila's ride right now, and I wouldn't want to strand her without a vehicle."

"If she drops you off at the airport, I'm sure I can get your rental switched over to her name." Of course he can, because Sam is the most competent person I've ever met. Unfortunately, I'm actively not looking for ways to solve this problem right now. Similar to Lila and I sleeping in the same bed the last two nights. Did I realize as soon as we walked into Jameo's glass-free room that Lila could stay there instead of with me? I sure did. Do I also suspect that Lila has realized it as well? I can't imagine it hasn't crossed her mind. And yet, we both pretend like it's her only option and that she'll be moving back into her room just as soon as they can get the glass out of her bed.

They had the window covered the first afternoon, but the cleaning crew has been extra busy trying to get the common areas to be glass-free, which apparently takes a professional-grade vacuum making multiple passes over an area and then it being mopped if possible. After seeing how long it took to get our living area to be usable, not to mention listening to the sound of the vacuum for that long, we assured the cleaning crew that Lila's room could wait.

I'm trying to smother the part of me that hopes it never gets cleaned, but every time I wake up with her ass snuggled into me as

I spoon her and a huge fucking smile on my face, it gets harder and harder to deny. It turns out the spark between us can ignite more than just annoyance and bickering.

"That's okay," I say in response to Sam's suggestion to switch the car over to Lila's name. "I've really dialed in my game out here, and I don't want to get out of this headspace before my first tournament back," I lie to Sam.

"Oookay. You sure there isn't something else going on that I should know about?"

I roll my eyes even though he can't see me. Sam doesn't need to know about the personal goings-on in my life, but unfortunately for me, our relationship often strays into the realm of TMI. He's really more like the brother I never had than my assistant.

"I'm not sure what's happening, but I just feel like I can't leave right now."

"Are you finally rethinking your stance on relationships?"

I scoff. "Please, Sam. Let's not get carried away here. You know I need to be focused on my game now more than ever. My cashflow needs an infusion, and on top of that, my parents have an investment they need additional funds for. Besides, I've stuck around cities before when I had someone I was enjoying spending time with. That's all this is."

"And is it someone from town, or…?" He trails off, but we both know exactly how he wanted to finish that question. Or is it Lila, the little sister of your best friend?

"Do you really think I'm stupid enough to risk losing Jameson as a friend?"

"I don't think you want me to answer that question. Also, Jameson is not Luke. He's not going to just dump you as a friend if you and his sister try dating and it doesn't work."

Maybe, maybe not, though. And I'm not going to risk losing my best friend. I also didn't think our friend on the golf team would stop hanging out with me when I broke up with his cousin after dating for five months during my freshman year of college, but I was wrong about that.

"Why have I not fired you yet?" I ask, avoiding his comment.

"You need me far too much. You actually have no idea how to do anything without me."

"I'd still know how to golf."

"Yes, but I'd love to be a fly on the wall as you're trying to get yourself to the golf course."

"I could do it."

"I sincerely have my doubts."

We exchange a few more quips, finalize my schedule for my first tournament back after my "injury" in a few weeks, and hang up.

I let myself into the house, surprised when Jack runs over, tail wagging, excited to see me. He's not an unfriendly dog, but he's the dog version of shy for sure. Just as I'm sitting down to read a few more chapters of our pirate romance—I'm getting so close to the good part—my phone rings again. I glance at the screen and see my mom's name. *Elated* is maybe too strong of a word to use to describe my feelings, but my mom never reaches out to me after I've disappointed her. She either makes my dad call me and guilt-trip me into calling her, or she just waits me out until I finally miss her enough and feel guilty enough to call or visit her, usually with an expensive gift in tow. Maybe we're turning over a new leaf.

"Hey, Mom," I say, my excitement coming on a little too strong for my mom's more restrained attitude.

"I didn't think you had it in you, JT." Her voice is as polished as ever, but there is a hint of warmth seeping through.

Well, that was not what I was expecting. "Didn't have what in me?" I ask.

"Using a natural disaster to help you make inroads with the Fergusons? Brilliant. I don't think I could've thought of anything better."

"I'm not following. How do you know about the hailstorm?"

"Oh, please, JT. You don't have to play innocent with me. You helping board up windows at the nursing home in Wild Bluffs is trending on social media. Not to mention donating additional funds 'anonymously' to help repair the important buildings in town? Your father and I are both so proud."

I feel...dirty, and, frankly, pissed at Sam. I wasn't out helping clean up around town because I wanted any sort of praise or recognition. It was the right thing to do. So was donating money so the real repairs could begin immediately rather than having to wait for insurance to come through. I told Sam those donations were supposed to be anonymous. I meant it.

My mom has told me she's proud of me several times in my life: when I won my first junior championship, when I won my first major tournament, and when I signed my first big endorsement deal. Each of those times, it filled me with joy and pride knowing I finally was someone my parents could be proud of. That their sacrifices were worth it.

But this, this doesn't feel that way. I'm proud of myself for helping because it's something that a good person would do. So I'm proud of myself for being a good person, but I'm not proud of it becoming a publicity play to try to win favor with the Ferguson brothers. I hope Conrad and his brothers don't think I was the one behind leaking it to the press, though I suppose my "people" were. Shit. I hope they think less of me for that. Not that I want them to think less of me, but I want them to be the types of men who see through that bullshit and lose a little bit of respect for someone who would use a town's disaster to their own advantage.

"I didn't realize Sam was publishing that," I say.

"Well, that boy must have more brains in his head than I gave him credit for."

That *boy* was about to have a considerable amount of wrath headed in his direction. Okay. I don't actually do wrath well, but I am going to let him know I'm extremely disappointed. Well, disappointed. Though he was just doing his job. I'm sure he had my best interests at heart. So I guess I'll need to call Sam and talk this through with him.

My mother continues her monologue about how smart it was to be seen taking an interest in the town for another five minutes, before changing tactics and grilling me about when I'll be back to playing. Apparently, she and my dad are really excited about this new investment, and my inability to line up the cash they need is causing them a lot of problems. I apologize again, promising to focus on nothing but golf for the next two weeks so I can have the funds after my first tournament back.

Once I hang up with my mom, I consider calling Sam back but decide I'm better off just shooting him a quick text asking him to run any stories he's releasing to the press by me first. I can't have Sam getting upset with me and taking another job elsewhere.

Me

> Next time, please run any stories you're sending to the press by me first.

Sam

> I didn't leak this one. I posted the photo of you helping out on your socials but didn't mention the donations anywhere.

Me

> How did it get out, then?

Sam

> My guess? Penelope. She called from your dad's office asking about the photo. I didn't tell her anything about the donations.

Sam

> But also, anyone who knows you would know that you were going to donate to that nursing home.

Sam

So I assume she made the leap. The articles do just strongly suggest that the donations were made by you. They don't conclusively say it was you.

Me

My mom thought it was you.

Sam

Penelope likely didn't fill your mom in.

Sam shared his theory that my dad was banging his assistant exactly one time with me, and that was enough for both of us. I can't imagine my dad would do something like that. Not because of his relationship with my mom, but because it could seriously hurt his career if it got out. Well, it could hurt his career, or it would bring him even more firmly into the old boys' club that he runs with.

Entirely disgusted with society as a whole by this point, I shift my attention to someone with ethics—pirates. I pick the book Lila and I are sharing, and warmth spreads through me as I realize she's started her annotations again. I know I should be focused on winning that money for my parents, but right now, all I want to do is let myself fall into a story with Lila.

Chapter Twenty-One

JT

"Hey, Pipsqueak," I say as Lila walks into the house a few days later. She and Kelsey have been out golfing the par three with Izzy and Becca this afternoon. Unfortunately for my game, the main course is still too banged up to play on.

I would normally have picked her up from work, but she caught a ride out with her officemates. The extra space in my schedule is making me feel a bit off my game, and for some reason, my mind kept slipping to Lila the whole afternoon, wondering how her day was. I know she's excited about the proposal she's working on for Kelsey, though, based on the way her shoulders tighten any time she talks about it, I think she might be struggling with it more than she is letting on.

Lila slips her shoes off with an exhausted sigh before joining me in the kitchen.

"Hey, Pretty Boy. Whatcha working on there?" she asks, pointing to the pile of chicken I've been cutting up for fajitas for the last ten minutes.

"Chicken," I say with pride.

"Are you sure? It looks like a pile of mush."

"Oh, I'm sure. It's for fajitas. They always slice it like that."

I look at said pile quizzically, and—damn it—she has a point. Why is it so mushy?

Her lips are pinched together, clearly trying and failing to hold back a laugh. "You know most people cook the meat and then cut it into strips, don't you?"

"Only people who are terrible cooks," I reply. Except I didn't know that. Makes sense why it was so fricken hard to cut. I'm not much of a cook-my-own-food kind of guy.

"Or anyone who wants their meat to be edible."

"Trust me, no one has ever complained about having my meat in their mouth. Especially the women." I give her a quick wink for good measure.

She stares at me for a second, her eyes alight with surprise, before she lets out a strangled sound. "Oh God. That was the douchiest thing anyone has ever said to me." She's laughing now, so hard she's bent double. I start to move back to my cutting, but she holds up her hand to stop me.

I wait patiently for her to get it together, but Lila doesn't seem to be able to stop her laughter. As I turn away, she chokes out, "Do the men tend to complain?" She's laughing again. "About your meat in their mouths?"

"Let's just say I've never had any complaints and leave it at that."
That shuts her up, and I can feel the curiosity in her gaze burning a
hole through my back.

"No way! I'm not leaving it at that! Tell me, tell me, tell me."

The woman is bouncing up and down on her toes in glee.

"I was joking, Pipsqueak. Unfortunately for the male population,
I'm a women-only kind of guy. Though my PA Sam often tells me I
should reconsider my options."

"Boo. I was hoping for a scandalous story."

"Sorry to disappoint."

Lila starts heading to our bathroom, yelling behind her, "I'm going
to take a quick shower."

I hear the door lock and try not to think about her very naked form
behind it, forcing myself to focus on how to cook this chicken instead.
Unfortunately, my mind keeps wandering to the naked woman currently in our room.

Lila and I have been sleeping together for almost a week now. We
never do more than basic cuddling, no matter how annoyed my dick
is at me each morning as I force myself to roll to my back, abandoning
the warmth of her ass. But it's nothing more than...well, I don't know
what. Similar to the book, we've both—without ever talking about
it—agreed to act like it's not happening. Even if it's the best part of
my day.

I grab my plate and walk to the table, forcing bites of mushy chicken
and peppers into my mouth. As I'm searching for how to tell if chicken
is going to give you E. coli, my phone vibrates, and I look down to see
a new message from my mom.

I've lined up my friend Bethany's daughter to be your date for the Ferguson event.

Shit. I've met Bethany's daughter Morgan before. The dinner our moms forced us to attend together was utterly miserable. Morgan spent the whole time talking about purses and shoes or something like that. I was bored out of my mind and mortified by the way she treated the serving staff at the restaurant. When the condensation dripped off our waitress's water pitcher and onto the lap of Morgan's dress, Morgan went as far as asking to speak to the poor girl's manager. I added an extra twenty dollars to her tip. It was the least I could do. I told my mom about it, hoping it would cause her to drop the whole thing. Apparently not.

I already have a date. Sorry!

My phone rings, and without looking, I know it's my mom. I hate lying to her, but I also cannot go with Morgan.

"Hey, Mom."

"Who is your date, and why have I not heard about her?"

Cutting right to the chase, I guess. Smart, really. It doesn't give me any time to come up with a plan.

"I just asked her recently. We're going as friends, of course." The latter part is more for me than my mom. My mother feels a wife could be "very beneficial for my overall image and future career success." Then she likes to use her relationship with my dad as supporting evidence, which is unconvincing at best.

"And her name is...?"

"And her name is…" Just then, I hear the door to the bathroom open, the easy answer coming to mind. "…Lila. Lila Walker."

"Jameson's sister? Isn't she a child? Good God, JT."

"She's twenty-four, Mom."

"That's practically an infant."

"I'm not even five full years older than her. And we are going as friends." I mean, probably. As soon as I convince her.

"I think you should consider backing out and going with Morgan."

The thought of it makes me shiver a bit in disgust. Nope. I would grovel at Lila's feet before agreeing to go with Morgan. Plus, I'm offended on behalf of fake Lila. She deserves to be treated so much better than a placeholder until someone better comes along.

"Sorry. Lila really wants to go. I can't back out on her now." I can tell I'm not making any headway, so I play the one card I know will work with my mother. "Plus, Jameson is considering coming"—also a lie—"and I wouldn't want him to be upset if I showed up with a different date."

"I suppose you don't want to upset Jameson. It's wonderful he's playing well again. I've always had a soft spot for that boy. Is he still happy with his wealth-management team?"

I roll my eyes, glad my mom can't see me. She's back on the Jameson Walker train these days, but there was a rough couple of years recently when she regularly tried to get me to stop spending time with him. Now he's playing well, and she's back to trying to use our friendship to her advantage.

"He's not interested in switching, Mom."

"Well, if something changes, let me know. About Jameson or your date. I'm sure Morgan can be available if you need her."

Yeah, right. Pigs will be flying around the golf course before I take Morgan with me. I'm sure I can find some way to convince Lila to go. Maybe she can be bribed with a trip to a bookstore while we're there.

I say goodbye to my mom and stare down at my food. Completely inedible. I take it and dump it in the trash, then grab a protein bar from the cupboard instead. Yum. Dinner of champions.

"What are you wearing?" I ask when Lila emerges thirty minutes later. She's wearing jeans and a navy blue T-shirt with the letters WBHS stamped above a picture of a charging horse.

"Did you get your fajitas made?" she asks instead of answering me, suspiciously eyeing the plate in front of me.

"Yep. They were fucking delicious too."

She looks around. "You didn't save any for me?"

"No. Did you think I was going to?"

Her cheeks flush a bit pink, and, to be fair, she's had quite a bit of leftovers the last few days, so we've taken to sharing meals. But we've both been very clear that it was just because there were leftovers. Definitely not because we enjoyed the verbal sparring while she cooked dinner.

"Okaay," she says, pulling her phone out of her pocket before typing on it. Whomever she's texting responds right away, and she types something back before turning her face back up to me.

"No worries. Matthew confirmed there will be food at the game tonight."

Suddenly, her shirt makes sense. WBHS is Wild Bluffs High School. Their mascot isn't the Stallions, though I think one of the Harpers mentioned it was something horse-related.

"You're going out with that guy again?" I ask, my voice harsher than intended.

Lila looks at me for a second, her head tilted to the right, her eyes searching my face as if trying to decide something. She just shrugs. "Just because you find the idea of dating me repulsive doesn't mean everyone else does."

"I don't find the idea of dating you repulsive," I say, all thoughts of asking her to join me at the Ferguson event slipping from my mind. She scoffs, so I continue, "I find the idea of dating *at all* inconvenient. I have to focus on my game right now."

"Well, then. There you go. Since it's an inconvenient time for you to date, I clearly shouldn't ever go out again." She lightly smacks herself in the face. "Oh, wait! I just remembered. I don't care what you think."

"Maybe you should. I'm doing pretty darn well for myself."

"Are you, though?" she asks, her lips downturned as she shoots me a pitying smile that immediately makes me want to rage.

And in a way I only ever do around Lila, I let that rage break free. "Fine, then. But good luck pulling the pieces of shrapnel out of your back after he fucks you on your glass-covered bed."

"Wow. That escalated quickly. Luckily for me, he has his own house. Maybe I will bring him back here, though. I bet I could figure out some creative ways to avoid the bed. The bathroom counter is safe..."

Like fucking Hell she will. I almost bark at her that the counter is our fucking place, but I catch myself, my hand tightening into a fist instead.

I force a smirk onto my face. "Don't set the poor guy up for failure by giving him such *stiff* competition." I raise my eyebrows at the word "stiff" so she knows exactly what I'm talking about.

"Oh, I'm sure he can handle it. The bar is very low." She stares right at me, her expression flat, her body language not giving me anything. And, even though I know I'm being gaslighted—gaslit?—my confidence wavers. She had a damn good time on that counter in Vegas. I made sure of it. Shit, I made sure of it twice. But maybe she didn't? Could she fake ecstasy like that? No. I shake my head, causing her to huff out a sigh of displeasure. Lila would never fake something like that. She would bust my balls until I gave her exactly what she wanted.

I'm too busy mentally backtracking through our entire night together to respond, and the next thing I know, Lila is pulling the door open to the house, the sight of a white pickup just visible through the opening.

"Don't wait up!" she calls.

I would never dream of waiting up for Lila to find out how her stupid second date went. I'm sure the guy is some weird local who can't find anyone new to date so is pulling out all the stops to woo Lila. Though, if a high school football game is the best he can do, the poor guy doesn't stand a chance. What a terrible second date. Maybe he and Lila deserve each other.

I look around the empty house, suddenly feeling more alone than ever, even though I've lived by myself for half a decade at this point.

A look at the empty bed in our room—fuck, *our room*—and a wave of nausea rolls through my body. Hoping the feeling is just a bit of light food poisoning from the terrible chicken I made, I force myself to drink a big glass of water. Maybe getting something else into my stomach will cause me to feel normal again. "Dilution is the solution to pollution" and all that.

CHAPTER TWENTY-TWO

LILA

Small-town football games…live up to the hype. And this is just a summer scrimmage.

Honestly, some of the best times of my life. The slight chill in the air. The crappy hot dogs and hamburgers. Wearing my boyfriend's jersey as I cheer from the stands. The football pants *drooling smiley*

Gross. They're like 16.

Elise

I haven't been to one since I was in high school, but I see now that commenting on the 16-year-olds is not appropriate. I take it back.

Me

Yes. Please stick with ogling football players at the college level and above.

Me

Shit. Do you think we're too old to check out the college football players now?

Elise

Why do you ruin everything for me?

Me

It's why you love me.

Elise

Speaking of ruining everything for you. How go things with your sleepover buddy?

Me

Still annoying as fuck.

Elise

And by that you mean you're still annoyed you haven't fucked?

Me

I plead the fifth.

Elise

How is new boyfriend going to feel about you living with your one-night stand?

Me

The one-night stand I can't stand?

Elise

The one-night stand you definitely want to sleep with again.

Me

Those two things are not mutually exclusive. Plus, I told you Matthew and I are just here as friends.

Me

But, to be clear, I will not ever be telling anyone about JT and me.

Matt—who told me only his aunt calls him Matthew—stands next to me on the Wild Bluffs side of the grandstands. We're both wearing Wild Bluffs Mavericks shirts, though mine is mostly hidden behind the light jacket I pulled on at the end of the third quarter. Tonight has been a lot of fun. Matt has introduced me to a lot of locals, always letting me know if their kid is playing and what number he is. I appreciate the gesture, as I wouldn't want to upset any parents by saying something less than positive about their kid's performance, but I'm being on my best behavior tonight regardless.

The football stadium is way more impressive than I would've imagined for a high school team. Set at the foot of the bluffs that surround the town, towering cliffs of sand-colored stone are the perfect backdrop for one endzone. There's a large WB made from white stones on the grassy hill between the bluff and the field, and a fire truck sits next to it, the firemen setting off fireworks each time the Mavericks score. It feels like I've been transported into one of the romance movies I love so much, with the sun setting in shades of red, yellow, and orange behind us. If only I were here with a real date like I let JT believe.

Stupid JT Johnson.

The crowd cheers loudly as the Mavericks march their way down the field, the score tied seven-seven with fifty-four seconds to go. I haven't spent a ton of time watching football—my brother is a professional golfer, after all—but I follow sports in general enough to understand what's happening in a high school football game. Even if I didn't, the energy in the air is enough to turn anyone into a fan. There aren't as many cheerleaders down on the track that circles the field as I would've expected, and when I ask Matt about it, he shrugs, saying cheerleading isn't particularly popular in Wild Bluffs, and even fewer cheerleaders come to the scrimmages.

I follow up by asking if Kelsey or Bryn were cheerleaders, and he laughs so hard, I swear soda comes out his nose. When he gets himself back under control, he says, "Christ. Can you imagine Kelsey or Bryn as cheerleaders? Actually, don't. Kelsey might murder you just for picturing her in such a bubbly role."

With twenty seconds left, Wild Bluff's quarterback makes an impressive throw to his tight end in the back corner of the endzone. I clap along with Matt, the two calmest fans in the entire stands. I swear one mom is considering doing a flip on the field.

"Well, that's good luck," Matt says.

"Why's that?"

"Now the coaches will be in a good mood when I introduce you to them."

Matt promised to introduce me to his two single friends in town, Austin and Bobby. They both help coach the high school football team, Austin helping with the receivers, Bobby with the defense.

We make our way off the bleachers and start the downhill walk to where Matt parked his vehicle. Earlier this week, I'd offered to have JT drop me at the game, but as it turned out, I was glad it looked like Matt was picking me up for a date.

We pull the tailgate of his pickup down, and I sit on it as we wait for his friends to leave the locker room. Soon, high school boys start trickling out in ones and twos, most of them being hugged by the high school girls who've been waiting around the large parking area.

"Ah, here they come."

Two men walk out the door, heading in our direction. Both are in navy blue polos and black dress pants, their hair hidden beneath matching Mavericks ball caps. Luckily, one is fairly short—though still taller than me—whereas the other is definitely above six feet tall, so I may have a chance of telling them apart, regardless of their matching outfits. They are attractive, though neither is as good-looking as JT with his broad shoulders and deep blue eyes. Not that it matters how they compare to JT.

"Austin, Bobby, hell of a game tonight." They all do the bro hug, back slap thing in a way that makes it clear they've done it about a thousand times before.

When they're done hugging, Matt introduces me. "Meet my most recent date, Lila Walker."

"Gosh, you sure know how to make a girl feel special," I joke as I shake both men's hands. "For the record, I was totally going to turn him down, he just beat me to the punch."

"Oh, really?" the short one, Austin, asks.

"Nah. Janice scares me way too much for me to bail after one date. I was sure I was going to have to go on at least three."

"And as far as the town of Wild Bluffs is concerned, we've now gone on two," Matt points out.

"Doesn't the entire town know you're still pining after some lost love?" I ask.

Both of his friends nod, but Matt shakes his head. "Everyone knows I let a girl go that I shouldn't have. Not everyone knows how hung up I still am on her."

He turns to load up in his pickup so we can go to the house Bobby and Austin share for a couple of drinks, but before I climb in the backseat with Austin, I turn to Bobby, who is making his way to the passenger door, and ask, "Everyone knows, right?"

He just nods solemnly. Bummer for my guy Matt.

I can't help but imagine what JT's response to my question would've been—something about only blind people not being able to see it—but I shut down that line of thought, shoving JT from my mind.

A few minutes later, we pull up in front of a house just across the street from where I'll be living in a few weeks. "Woah. We're going to be neighbors," I say, holding my hand out for a high five.

Bobby smiles as he gives me one. "I just moved in a few months ago."

Though in my mind I hear JT finish the sentence with, *so it seems like the street is really on an upswing.*

I smile but internally add "next-door neighbor" to both guys' Cons lists. Living across the street from your boyfriend? Definite upsides. Living across the street from your ex? Just go ahead and sign me up for the next train leaving town.

We head into the house and all grab beers before the three men drop down on the couch to watch sports highlights.

"So what do you do for fun?" Austin asks.

"Work has been taking up a lot of my time lately, but I'm a big reader."

"Oh, really? What do you like to read?"

"I'm a big romance fan. Well, romance, romantasy, that type of thing."

Bobby snorts a laugh. "Wait, you're kidding, right?"

"Nope," I say, mentally adding another large mark to the Cons column for Bobby.

"I thought only my grandma reads that. Isn't it unrealistic smut geared at women who have nothing better to do with their time than sit around?"

"It's the most popular genre of books, and at all ages, not just older women."

"Huh. Who knew?" Austin cuts in, clearly trying to stop Bobby before he says anything else.

Bobby shoots me a remorseful smile. "Sorry, that was rude. I didn't mean to offend you. I'm sure there are some great romance books out there."

I know there are a lot of people who don't understand romance, and open-door romance in general, but I can't help but think of how JT has never once made me feel frivolous for enjoying them. Hell, he's read a spicy *alien* romance.

"I also like to golf," I say a few beats later to dispel the awkward lull that's fallen over the group.

"Oh, cool. I guess that makes sense, with your brother being who he is," says Austin.

"Have you gotten to play much since you moved here?" Bobby asks.

"Yeah. I've played a couple times with Kelsey, Izzy, and Becca."

"That sounds like fun," Bobby responds.

I take a swig from my beer and feel a smirk pull at my mouth as I ask, "Did any of you ever date a Harper sister?"

Matt snorts. "No."

"What? Not even in high school? Why not?"

"They're pretty intimidating, if you haven't noticed," Bobby says.

"More so than other women?" I ask.

"We all grew up with them being good at everything. They were athletes, they were smart, and they'll argue with you about the color of the damn sky. They dated in high school but not a ton. I think all the guys were a bit scared. I know I was. And now, I think that aura just hasn't gone away, even though we all know how amazing they actually are."

"Unfortunately, your brother had to go and steal one from us. I think Austin was just about to work up enough nerve to ask Bryn to coffee too," Matt jokes.

"Really?" I ask.

"No. Not really. He never would've had the balls to handle Bryn."

I laugh. "That's crazy. Bryn is awesome."

"Oh, trust me, we all know how awesome she is. Kelsey and Izzy too. We're all friends with them. Dating them...it's just the next level," Austin says with a sigh.

That doesn't bode well for me. I may be even more to handle than Bryn is. I think of the way JT has never once made me feel like I was too much for him but quickly push JT from my mind for what feels like the hundredth time tonight. No need to focus on that spark just waiting to burst into flames.

The conversation flows smoothly from there, and it feels like I'm one of the guys. While I'm super excited that I can stroll across the street in six weeks and have a buddy or two to hang out with, I can also say without hesitation that I've cut two more potentials from my dating-possibilities list. As much as I want to find a partner and settle down, I'm also starting to realize how much I need there to be a little fire, that slightly dangerous spark, in a relationship. Unfortunately, JT Johnson seems to have thrown sand over all the men in my life, dimming the sparks of every interaction I have except for the ones with him. *And he doesn't date.*

CHAPTER TWENTY-THREE

JT

I WALK TO THE bar at the back of the restaurant, a bit more relaxed from the walk over here. The crisp summer night air will do that to a guy. I've been sitting at home for the last four hours, a bundle of pissed-off energy. It's just a bad mood in general, definitely not something to do with Lila, the woman who is sleeping in *my bed, my arms,* being out on a second date right now.

"JT!"

I hear my name called from a table in the corner and plaster on what I hope is a friendly-looking smile before turning to see who is calling to me. The locals and the staff here mostly leave me alone, but occasionally a member and their friends will be in for the weekend and will ask for an autograph or selfie. I'm typically happy to oblige, but the great outdoors didn't impact my mood that much.

Spotting motion at one of the tables, I find Izzy Harper waving at me from her seat next to Kelsey. Both women are still in their golf attire, Izzy in a bright pink golf skirt with a black collared tank top and Kelsey in a full black golf dress. It looks like the sisters decided to hit up the restaurant after their round of golf rather than head home like Lila. Though I suppose Lila had her *date* to get ready for. I feel the irritation start to flare back up inside of me at the thought of Lila out on a date but push it back down as far as I can.

"Hey, Izzy, Kelsey," I say as I reach their table.

"Hey. Want to join us?" Kelsey nods at the empty seat next to her.

"Oh, no. I don't want to intrude."

"It's not an intrusion, but also, if you'd rather be alone, I completely understand," Kelsey replies.

I don't want to be alone with my confusing thoughts right now. If I sit by myself, I know all I'm going to do is stew over the fact that Lila is out on a second date tonight with someone who may or may not be better in bed than I am. Though I'm pretty sure she has no way of knowing that. There definitely wasn't enough time on their first date for her to sleep with him. Plus, Lila doesn't strike me as the type that hooks up on a first date with someone she might be serious about. An image of Lila and I in the hallway of the bar sneaks into my mind at the thought, and I feel my hand tighten on the back of the chair I'm standing behind. Shit. I'm not sure if I'm more upset that the memory has reminded me 1. How good Lila feels pressed up against me; 2. That she did, in fact, have enough time for a quick hookup with Matthew; or, 3. That, by my own reasoning, she never saw me as someone to be serious about.

Number three convinces me to sit down with the Harper sisters.

I need something to banish the thought of me not being someone she could be serious about—and the fact that it makes my chest feel like there is a gaping hole in it—from my mind. I *do not* care that Lila would never be serious about me. *I* am the one who needs to be focused on his golf game right now, not a serious relationship.

"You okay there, bud?" Izzy asks, her dark eyes full of concern and sympathy.

"Yeah. Just have a lot on my mind."

"Want to talk about it?" Kelsey asks. I still don't feel like I know Kelsey all that well, but she's really growing on me. She's not as outgoing and loud as Bryn or as openly kind as Izzy, but she says what she means and, while she seems to realize she impacts the emotions of people around her, she doesn't seem to carry the same feeling of responsibility for others' emotions like I do. It's refreshing to see someone who is so loved by their family and friends even though she isn't always a ray of sunshine. Real black cat energy, that one.

"I'm not even sure where to start," I reply honestly. "Plus, it'll just bring you guys down with me."

Both women shrug in an identical move that is either genetic or has been nurtured in them since a young age.

"We might not be best friends, but I assure you, we can handle listening to you work through whatever you're dealing with." Kelsey pauses. "Unless it's murder. I'm not interested in going down as an accessory," she jokes.

"Don't listen to negative Nancy over there, JT. I'm sure Kels actually has some really solid tips up her sleeve to help you get away with murder."

"Luckily, murder is not yet one of my issues."

We sit in silence for a minute, and I want to fill it, but I'm not sure how to make the transition.

"How about this?" Kelsey says. "We will talk about work, Bryn and Jameson, and the hot town gossip while we get two drinks in you. Then, we'll go out to the putting green—the course was in decent shape today when we played, and they put up glow-in-the-dark flags at night—and you can tell us what's going on while we all get a little practice in. That way, you don't have to look at us while you talk about whatever is going on with you. It's always harder to unburden yourself when you have to confront the ugly truths staring back at you in someone else's eyes."

It does seem like it would be easier to talk through what I'm feeling if I have a golf club in my hand, my head focused on my ball rather than their reaction to my words. Though it is getting pretty late, and the Harpers have been here for a long time now.

"Are you sure? I don't want to make my problems your problems."

"If it wasn't clear you're an only child before, that statement alone just really did it. Of course you should make your problems our problems. It's what family does to help lighten the load for everyone. And while you aren't technically family, we'll take you in anyway," Izzy says, and the open look on her face makes it seem like she truly means it.

"Okay," I say, still not convinced they won't see the dark side of me and realize they have somewhere else to be. But I suppose it's worth a try. The Harpers do seem like a family who have each other's backs. "But drinks are on me."

"Obviously," Kelsey replies, signaling for the waitress. "I sure as shit don't make pro golfer money."

We sip on whiskeys. *All of us.* I feel Ken Harper deserves a medal for somehow instilling solid fucking taste in alcohol in his daughters. When I ordered my drink, the women both just requested the same. With Kelsey's scowly nature, it was almost like I was sitting here with Jameo, but instead of talking golf the entire time, I'm regaled with stories about one of the teens in town who ran face first through a glass door, Jen and Ken's trip to France last summer, and a possible international security project that Kelsey is working on submitting a proposal for. One I've heard quite a bit about from Lila.

Finally, Izzy tips back her glass to get the final drops of her drink, the last of us to finish.

"Putting, then?" she asks, setting the engraved glass down on her coaster.

"Are you sure?" I ask one final time. "I totally understand if you two need to get back to town. It is getting pretty late."

"Nah. I only had one drink, but I should still burn off a bit more alcohol before we head out. You're not getting rid of us that easily," Izzy replies.

I sign the bill for the table, paying for the drinks and the appetizers, and we make our way down the stairs of the restaurant to the putting green. We find our golf bags in the storage area by the clubhouse and grab our putters and a few balls. Izzy is the first on the putting green, so when I join her, she's already tapped a golf ball toward the hole, missing by a few inches to the right. I'm about to tell her it's her grip that's causing her to push the ball, not her read of the green, but I decide to remain silent. No one really wants unsolicited advice, even from a golf professional. She looks up at me when I drop my four balls to the grass a few feet away and leans her weight on her putter, giving me her full attention.

"I thought you said you weren't going to look at me while I talk," I say, uncomfortable with her focus.

"To be clear, Kelsey was the one who said that, *and* she said you didn't have to look at us, not the other way around. But, fine." She takes a half-hearted attempt at her next ball. "Happy?"

"I suppose I'll take it if it's the best I can get."

"Smart man."

Unsure where to start, I just keep focusing on my putting. When I've hit all four of my balls into or very close to the hole, I walk the five steps to pick them up before starting the routine again.

Izzy lets out an impatient sigh, drawing my attention to the silent conversation she seems to be having with her sister. Kelsey shakes her head before returning to her balls. Apparently, the strategy is to let me decide on a conversation. I think through all the things I'm worried about right now, and even though I can't rationalize it, I ask what's most pressing right now.

"So tell me about this *Matthew* guy Lila's out with tonight."

I swear I can hear Kelsey's eye roll, but I keep my focus on my putting. It does help.

Izzy replies, "He's a local guy who moved back after college and now helps run the family farm. He's a good guy. And going to the high school games is a good way for Lila to get involved in the community."

"Not your type, though?"

"What do you mean?"

"Why aren't one of you two dating him if he's such a catch?" I know I should be less of a dick about *Matthew*, but I can't seem to be able to.

"What do you—" Izzy starts again but is cut off by her sister.

"Lila isn't dating Matt, JT."

"What?" I stand up and look at the sisters, the putter dangling from my hand.

"She told me they were." Right?

"Did she? Because she told us he was going to introduce her to a couple of his single friends."

"It seemed like a date to me."

"Well, *Matthew*"—Kelsey mocks the snobby way I've been saying his name—"is notoriously still hung up on another woman. A fact he told Lila about at the end of their dinner together the other night, so I really doubt either of them would've said this was a date." Shit. I wrack my brain, but I don't actually remember Lila saying she was going on a date, though she definitely went along with it once I reminded her she couldn't invite someone over to sleep in our bed.

"Huh." It's all I can think of to say. My mind is spinning as it tries to realign everything I've been feeling the last few hours to incorporate this new information. I'm not sure what it means, so I drop my focus back to my golf balls.

"Why does it matter if she's out on a date with him?" Izzy asks gently.

I don't know. And, damn it, that's the problem they are supposed to be out here helping me work through. So I give her the easy answer.

"I may have told my mom I was taking her as a date to this golf event I have coming up in a couple of weeks."

"Why?" Kelsey asks at the same time her sister says, "And?"

"I needed to ask her about it, is all."

Both sisters chuckle.

"I'm not going to talk to you about it if you're going to laugh at me," I say, sounding like a petulant child, even to my own ears.

"Unrelated question," Kelsey says. "Where has Lila been sleeping this week?"

"What?" This time it's Izzy and me asking the question at the same time. I can tell Izzy is gaping at her sister, but I remain focused on putting the white ball into the small round hole.

"You heard me. She mentioned her window broke in the storm, but she's been surprisingly quiet about where she slept. And she hasn't mentioned anything about her room since that next day when I was talking to her, even though every other person in Wild Bluffs who had a window broken has given me unsolicited, daily updates about the state of getting back in their rooms." Damn. Kelsey missed her calling as a lawyer. She's really laying this all out methodically. "The staff in the restaurant told us at dinner that most of the rooms still weren't ready, since they'd been focused on the public areas. Now, all of this would be circumstantial at best, but then you thought Lila was out on a date with another guy and you are clearly more upset about it than a typical roommate would be."

Well, shit. "That's not—"

"Damn, Kels. You nailed that," Izzy says, the pride in her voice evident.

"Didn't you give me a speech an hour ago about helping me carry my burden? This feels like adding to it," I say, giving them my full attention so they can see the disappointment on my face.

Izzy snorts. "I think this is exactly the family treatment you were promised. You know how you have to clean a wound out before you let it heal so the little rocks and shit don't become ingrained in your skin? Well, imagine this as the antiseptic portion of your journey."

"Okaaay," I say, kind of grossed out by the visual, and not at all interested in having my emotional wounds cleansed.

Kelsey crosses her arms, still holding her putter in one hand. "Let's try this a different way. I'm going to ask you a question, and you answer with the truth—the first thing that pops into your mind, okay?" Kelsey asks.

"Yesss," Izzy breathes, fist-pumping a little. "I love this strategy. Plus, bonus points for stealing it from a TV show. Bryn would be so pleased."

Kelsey and I both glare at Izzy, who seems a bit taken aback by our lack of enthusiasm.

"Have you and Lila been sleeping together since her window broke?" Kelsey asks, not waiting for me to agree to her game.

"Yes." I guess we're just diving right into it. But to be fair, Kelsey already figured that out. If I wasn't already slightly scared of her and her "ninja skills" as her sisters call them, I sure would be now.

"Are you *sleeping* sleeping together?"

"No."

"Are you more than friends?"

"I'm not even sure I'd call us friends."

"Do you want to be?"

"Yes." Shit. I'm surprised by the answer. Maybe this strategy works.

"What's your favorite color?"

"What?"

"You were overthinking it. I'll start again. What's your favorite color?"

"Green." Like Lila's eyes. Shit.

"Do you like pizza or ice cream more?"

"Pizza."

"Boo," says Izzy, but Kelsey shushes her.

"Do you want to date Lila?"

"No."

"Why not?"

"I have to focus on my golf game and winning the next tournament, and Lila deserves to have the husband and kids that she's always dreamed of. Plus, she's Jameson's sister."

"Shit," Izzy says, and it snaps me out of the trance Kelsey somehow put me under with her questions.

"We're going to come back to the sister thing, but why does focusing on your golf game keep you from being in a relationship? You know lots of golfers who have serious girlfriends and wives, right?" Kelsey asks.

They do have serious girlfriends and wives, but they also don't have a mom with a scar on her face and a dad who calls five times a day reminding them of the sacrifice they made.

"I owe my parents so much more than the average golfer," I say.

"Why?" Izzy asks.

"Because my dad gave up his own dream of being a professional golfer to coach me, and my mom had to work two jobs to support the cost of my dad and I traveling everywhere and all my golf equipment. She was working so hard, she fell asleep and drove into a tree when I was younger."

"Shit."

"That's scary."

"Yeah. She has a big scar on her face from it. She was trying to make it as an actress at the time, and it completely ended that career for her. And now I try to pay them back by offering them everything they've ever wanted, on my dime, but since my game has gone downhill lately, my cash flow has been...tight."

"You know you're not responsible for the decisions your parents made when you were a kid, right?" Izzy asks.

"They made them for me. They gave up the lives they wanted, for me."

"I'm not sure I agree, but either way, it doesn't mean you have to give up the life you want for them," Kelsey says.

"You hooked up with Lila in Vegas and in Phoenix and played well in those tournaments, didn't you? You can be in a serious relationship if you want one, JT, with Lila or with someone else. Or you can be in a casual relationship and try it out. Lots of relationships start out casual and go from there. Hell, I even had a friend where she and the guy agreed to a six-week trial period."

Fuck. Even though I'm annoyed Lila told Izzy about us, her conclusion isn't wrong. In fact, it'd been staring me in the face this whole time. Being with Lila makes me play better. We are living in the same house. We can casually date while we are in the same place and it's convenient. I can make the money my parents need to live the lives they want, even if I can never truly pay them back for giving up so much when I was younger.

After a long pause, Kelsey asks, "Why does it matter she's Jameson's sister?"

Izzy continues like she's got a lot to say on the subject. "You're one of his best friends. You'd think he'd be happy for two of his favorite people to date. I've never understood why brothers wouldn't want their sisters to date their friends. Well, maybe it'd be awkward if they date more than one of their friends— Has Lila dated another of Jameson's friends?"

"No."

"Then are you actually a bad dude and Jameo just pretends to be your friend for some weird reason?" Izzy continues.

"No."

"Then...I don't understand."

"Jameson is my *best* friend. He's one of the only guys I actually consider to be my friend. Yeah, I'm friendly with a bunch of people and am happy to grab a beer or a bite to eat with almost anyone, but I have a very high bar for the people I consider my friends. Jameo is basically my brother. His family is my family. My parents have given up everything for me, but they are rightfully bitter about it. So they don't love spending a lot of time with me doing normal family things like Thanksgiving or big Christmas parties. I spend most of my holidays with the Walkers. They're some of my best memories."

"And...you see Lila as your sister?"

"God, no. No." I shake my head for emphasis. "No. She is about as far from my sister as someone can be. The problem is that if I were to date Lila, and we were to break up—which odds say we would—I would lose not only my girlfriend but my best friend and family too. It's too big of a risk."

"That seems like a bit of a stretch," Kelsey says.

"When I was in college, I dated my friend Luke's cousin. After reading Lila's romance novels, I understand that I was a pretty mediocre boyfriend, but I tried to give her as much time as I could, despite having a crazy schedule between class and golf. She eventually grew tired of me not being able to go to parties with her on Friday night or walk her to her classes, and she broke up with me. It was fine, I wasn't heartbroken or anything, but Luke basically broke up with me too. We stopped hanging out, texting. He cut me out when things ended with his *cousin*. Do you really think it would be less with someone's sister?"

"It sounds like Luke was kinda a dick, but also, he was a friend in college. Those friend groups change like the fricken wind," Izzy says.

"I don't think you're giving Jameson or the Walkers enough credit," Kelsey adds. "I think they would be excited you were dating Lila, and I think if you broke up—as long as it wasn't for like cheating on her or something—they wouldn't kick you out of their lives. From the conversations I've had with Jameo, it seems like you're just as important to him as he is to you. Plus, it's not like you and Lila can fight any more than you currently do. Or at least that's how it sounds from what I've been told."

"That's the other thing. Lila and I don't get along. We fight all the time."

"Do you, though?" Kelsey chuckles. "They say there's a fine line between love and hate for a reason, JT. It's the same spark—the same energy—that drives them both. It just depends on which way you decide to let it burn. And it is a *decision* you make. So I'll give you the same advice I would give either of my sisters: If you want something, make it happen. Your wildest dreams aren't going to just fall into your lap. Just don't overthink it."

She's right. I know she's right. I can focus on winning for my parents and be with Lila. There is a spark between Lila and me that I can't deny. Jameson is a good guy. He and his parents might be surprised if I date Lila, but they wouldn't cut me out completely. Lila and I already make every family meal awkward, it's not like we could make it much worse.

I've gotten where I am right now by chasing my goals with everything I have. Lila drives me crazy in all the worst ways, but somehow, I can't stop looking forward to every infuriating second with her. What would happen if I leaned into the energy between us instead of fighting it? What if I let myself fall for the girl who drives me insane, who challenges me, who makes me want to be someone better every time I look at her?

The thought leaves me rattled, my pulse thrumming with a mix of anticipation and something close to fear. For the first time, the idea of being with Lila isn't just a distant fantasy I force myself to ignore—it feels real, close, like a door swinging open right in front of me.

Don't overthink it. It doesn't have to be a promise of forever. We'll just set a premeditated end date for when we aren't living together and things would get messy anyway.

Chapter Twenty-Four

Lila

I'M IN A WEIRD headspace when Matt drops me off that night at the door to Jameo's house. I had a great time at the game and am excited to have some new friends in town, but even Matt commented on the drive home about finding other single guys for me to meet. So I guess it was pretty apparent I'm not a good match for either of his friends. Even though I had a lot of fun, I'm feeling a bit dejected as I walk into the house and take off my sneakers.

I can hear the shower running, and the hot-blooded 24-year-old in me casually suggests *but what if you just...joined him?* I consider it for a moment, and my brain tries to entice me by replaying some of our greatest hits from Vegas and Phoenix. Surprisingly, even an argument from last Thanksgiving makes the highlight reel. I'd been on a warpath, and he'd risen to the challenge like an alpha fae in some fantasy novel. I chuckle, knowing he would pretend to hate that comparison but would secretly be preening.

As I open the door to our room, my logical brain finally overpowers my horny one, and I pause. My mind is rapidly firing off all the reasons why joining JT in the shower is a bad idea: JT humiliating me in college, JT totally ghosting me when I asked him to get breakfast in Vegas, JT telling me he is too busy—

Suddenly, the shower turns off, and it's like I'm stuck in a trance as I hear JT grabbing a towel. I try to silently back out of the doorway when I realize he's going to be headed my way soon, but I'm too late. JT steps from the bathroom naked, using his towel to dry his hair, and I freeze, a deer caught in the headlights.

"Uhhhgg sorry" falls out of my mouth, all of my neurons currently occupied with trying to mentally catalog every single inch of this man's wet body. I'm pretty sure I'm drooling as I watch a drop of water slowly make its way past the curve of his shoulder, down between his pecs, and into the divots in his abs. My eyes are just making it to the best part when JT springs to life, using the towel in his hand to cover his junk.

"Shit, Lila. I didn't know you were home." He backs into the bathroom and steps behind the door before wrapping the towel around his waist.

"Yup. Just got here," I say as he opens the door back up to meet my eyes.

He takes me in, a smug smile pulling at the corners of his lips as he leans his muscular shoulder against the doorframe.

"How was your *date*?" His emphasis on the word *date* is wrong, and I cross my arms over my chest as I narrow my eyes at him.

"I had a great time tonight."

"You know, word on the street is that *Matthew* is still pining over some lost love."

Well, crap. How is JT getting access to any of the words on the street?

"Well, he sure doesn't fuck like he's thinking about someone else." Maybe a bit of an aggressive response, but they do say the best defense is a good offense...or something like that.

JT's eyes darken as he tucks his hands under his biceps, and I decide to see just how far I can push him. "I'm not sure if I got all the glass out of my back, though. Oh well, I'm going to be walking funny for weeks anyway, I can't imagine the glass will make it any—"

I'm cut off by him stalking toward me, muttering "make it happen" before slamming his lips down on mine. And, holy crap, when that little spark of ours hits the oxygen in my bloodstream, it ignites, lighting an inferno inside me. I can't breathe. I know all the reasons this can't work, that it won't work. But at this moment, I don't care.

I reach up and tangle my fingers in the damp curls at the nape of his neck, pulling him closer. He mirrors my intensity, one hand trailing down to cup my left ass cheek. He gives it a light squeeze, and I can feel the smile on his lips. He tries to pull back, but I tug the ends of his hair again, pressing myself against his bare chest. I can feel the warmth from his shower radiating from him, and a part of me wants nothing more than to curl up against his wide expanse of muscular chest and bask in his heat. But I can't let him go. I can't allow him to end this before I get to feel the ecstasy of our combined fire one more time.

His tongue dances with mine, a reflection of every argument we've ever had. I press my hips against his, standing on my tiptoes to better align the bulge under his towel with the part of me so desperately seeking friction. JT lifts me from the floor, and I wrap my legs around his waist, knocking off his towel in the process. I let out a small groan at the sight of his stiff cock rubbing up against the cleft of my jeans. Realizing I have far too many clothes on, I drop my legs back down, maintaining contact with his lips while I quickly undo the button on my jeans. I'm afraid if I let even an inch of space come between us, JT will change his mind. It's happened before.

I force myself to forget the past, and I lean into him for balance as I use my feet to finish pulling off my jeans. He lets out a low "fuuuck," the warmth of his breath skimming my lips. JT traces his hand down my side, the light tickle of his fingers in direct contradiction to the desperate violence of our kiss. When his hand reaches my ass, he slaps it, just hard enough to sting. I groan, the pressure in my core mounting at an unsustainable rate. He doesn't stop there, though. His hand slides between us, his fingers circling my clit a few times before one sinks inside me.

I shudder, letting out a soft cry as he bends his finger forward, stroking the spot on my inner wall in a way that makes my body tighten and go limp at the same time.

His erection is hard, a constant, begging presence against me. I untangle my hand from his hair, moving my body aside so I can access his bulge, wanting to pleasure him like he is me.

He stops my hand, pulling his lips away while continuing to stroke me with his finger. I'm disoriented by the contradiction between the lack of contact and the orgasm that continues to build at his touch.

"Me first," he says, his voice deep and gruff.

"I know, I'm try—"

"No. I get to get you off first."

"But—"

He adds a second finger, making me convulse forward into his chest.

"Good girl. Take my fingers, and after you've come at least once, then, if you're really good, I'll give you my cock. Now, take your shirt off."

Woah. The dominance in his voice...damn. I'm seconds away from coming on his fingers, but I grab the bottom of my shirt, pulling it and the sports bra I had on off in one go. He leans back, taking in the sight of me before leaning his head down, his back bending to reach my nipple and suck it in his mouth. There's nothing I can do to stop the wave of desire that flows through my body. My walls flutter. JT looks up at me, his face a savage grin, before he lightly bites my nipple at the same moment he plunges a third finger into me.

I break. My orgasm hits, wave after wave of pleasure pounding into me. When my insides finally still, I find JT there, holding me up and lightly kissing my face, my neck, my lips.

"That was...holy fuck," JT whispers, his lips against my temple. "You're perfect."

And yeah, that does something to me in a way I never, ever wanted it to. I'm not sure if it's the words themselves or the aftereffects of the powerful orgasm, but a small piece of my heart breaks off, turning coat to declare its alliance to JT.

Instead of acknowledging those feelings, though, I do the predictable, irrational thing. I tempt the Devil in him with words I know will keep this flame alive between us. "I've had better."

"You've…" He looks into my face, and the flash of devastation at my words quickly turns into a predatory grin as he realizes I'm teasing.

In one swift movement, he lifts me, smashing his mouth against mine as he carries me to our bed and throws me down on it. I giggle as I bounce, but my laughter quickly dies as I take in the half-undone man standing in front of me. His sandy blonde hair's usual curls are disheveled from my fingers running through them, and his wide, tanned chest is rising and falling from exertion. His pupils have taken over his irises, the black shoving out the vibrant blue. I can tell he's assessing me the same way, so I give him a deviant smile before reaching between my legs, using my wetness as a lubricant as I circle that tight bud of nerves. JT raises his eyebrows, and, calling my bluff, takes himself in his fist, matching my pace stroke for stroke.

The chords along the side of his neck tighten as he closes his eyes and tips his head back, and as good as the view is, I want him with me, in me, not standing there with this distance between us. I drop my hand to the mattress, the sound loud enough to draw his attention. When he realizes I've stopped, his hand stills, his thumb slowly moving over his tip.

"Prove me wrong," I taunt. "Prove you're the best I've had." Great, I'm outright poking the bear now. Blood, please start flowing to my brain again.

JT's eyes burn with desire as he grabs a condom out of his bag, sliding it on before he stalks the final two steps toward me. Climbing onto the bed, he places a knee on either side of me before scooping up my legs and lowering his head to my ultrasensitive flesh. He nuzzles his nose against the inside of my thighs, taking a deep breath before lowering his mouth to me and feasting on my sensitive clit. My back arches off the bed at the contact, my body warring between trying to run away and to get closer to him. He presses down on my lower abs, adding pressure to the storm already building inside me. He continues to torment me with his gifted tongue as I run my hands through his pretty hair.

It doesn't take long until I'm on the edge again, my legs clenching around his head in a way that makes me somewhat concerned for his well-being. I tug on his hair sharply and, giving in to my demand, he ends with one long lick up my slit before sitting back, his mouth covered in me.

"I want you," I say between gasping breaths, and I swear I see shock flash behind his eyes before they shift into a cocky glint.

He doesn't take the need in my voice as seriously as I feel he should, so I reach forward and grab his hips with both hands, pulling him to me. He falls toward my chest, catching himself on his arms before lowering his lips down to mine. The kiss is slow and tender and everything I want but nothing I need. As he kisses me, I slide my tongue into the warmth of his mouth and grip his cock, lining it up at my entrance. I press my hips into the air, and I let out a deep moan of pleasure as he gives in to my demand.

My body relaxes for him, welcoming the length of him as if it's welcoming home a long-lost friend. Two thrusts and he's fully buried inside of me. I lift my hips, unable to stop myself from encouraging him to move.

"Fuck me," I whisper, and I'm not sure if it's a curse or a plea, but JT answers it regardless, moving with a steady rhythm.

Time halts in the movements of our bodies, and we live on the edge of the cliff, dancing together, for minutes or hours or—I'm pretty sure not days—until a loud noise from somewhere on the course makes its way to us. We both pause, coming back into our bodies, and JT's gaze quickly turns feral.

He grabs my waist and flips me onto my stomach, pulling my hips up and back to meet his. Without pausing, he slams back home into me, the change of position bringing me right back to the precipice. JT's movements become uncoordinated, his hips pumping with abandon, and as I look over my shoulder and see him start to tense, he reaches around, his hand sliding between my legs to find my clit with his two fingers. He circles it once, twice, and as I break and cry out for the second time, he follows me over the edge. JT crashes down onto the bed next to me. He moves closer to me, his fingers slowly tracing small circles on the inside of my hip bone.

My chest still heaving from the second orgasm, I look up at the ceiling, trying to figure out where to go from here. I take a deep breath and try to figure out what I want from this. Where I want it to go. Unfortunately, it's not just up to me, so I turn onto my side, looking at the five o'clock shadow on JT's jaw, and ask, "What does this mean? What does it look like when we wake up tomorrow?"

"I can't promise you forever, Lila, but I can promise you now. We both want this. Shit, we both need this. There has been this building need between us ever since that damn first kiss of ours. Can we just forget about our past and our future and see what happens? Please? A preset end date so neither of us gets hurt. We're together while we're both living here and then we go our separate ways, no feelings hurt, when we move out." He reaches out and runs his finger lightly down the length of my arm. "I can't keep holding the attraction at bay now that I know what it feels like to sleep with you in my arms in this room—our room. I want to wake up with your ass pressed against my morning wood."

I let out a giggle, but he continues, "I want to kiss you when you get home from work. I want to fucking talk to you about the book we're both reading instead of leaving you notes. No, not instead of, because I still want to do that. But I want to stop pretending the version of us who are friends, who get along, aren't the same people as the ones who bicker constantly. I want to be both."

He paints a really nice picture. Sure, it's not a picture of forever, but it's one too hard to turn down. The logical part of me knows that this isn't going to end well. I'm not the type of person who can just walk away after dating someone for a month. It's going to be like sticking my hand in a flame when JT leaves. But it's already too late for me. I'm already burning.

"I want that too." I press my lips against his. "A few weeks of taking everything we both want, and then we're done."

"And then we're done," he agrees.

CHAPTER TWENTY-FIVE

JT

"Outside of about twenty minutes of putting, I don't know if I've ever golfed with a woman except you," I say.

After a full day yesterday spent in bed and in each other's arms, Lila suggested we come out and play golf to get out of the house for a bit. I wasn't a huge fan of the suggestion, mostly because leaving the cocoon of our little house felt unsafe—like everything that had happened the last day and a half could be exposed as a dream in the harsh light of day. It also might be because I can't stand it when I'm not touching Lila. I don't think I went more than five minutes yesterday without touching at least some part of her body. Even as we lounged in the living room, talking about our pirate book, reading out loud some of our favorite lines, she was either in my lap or snuggled against my side. Unless we were testing out some of the spicier passages, that is.

This utter infatuation is a completely new feeling for me, and when I realized I may be entering into clinger status, I agreed to play eighteen with her. I also desperately need to spend time working on my game before my tournament back this weekend.

Lila is standing on the tee box of WBCC's second hole. Her dark hair is pulled into a high ponytail that my fist is begging to have wrapped around it, and she has on a black golf skirt that hugs the muscular curves of her ass as she takes a practice swing. I watch with fascination as she brings her club back around, executing an all-but-perfect-looking swing.

Every fiber of my being wants me to find something wrong with her form so I can step up behind her and "show her the right way to do it," but leave it to Lila Walker to have such a technically perfect swing that I can't find something to correct.

Actually, now that I think of it, her swing doesn't have to be bad for me to help her with it. She might call me out on my true motives, but I'm beginning to realize just how much *fun* verbally sparring with her really is.

"That can't possibly be true," she says, turning around to face me as she stands with her weight on the driver in her right hand.

"Well, I assure you I've never been golfing with my mom." I hold up a finger for some reason and choose to overlook the slightly pitying crease that pulls at the corner of her eyes. "I've also never taken a date golfing." I hold up a second finger. "So yeah...it literally might've been since the last time you tagged along that I actually played golf with anyone of the female persuasion."

"Ew. Don't say 'female persuasion.'"

I laugh and pull her into me, resting my chin on her head as I wrap my arms around her waist.

"And, what about in college, didn't you have to golf with the girls' team then?"

I scoff. "No. We were two fully separate teams." She tilts her head up, butting my chin to let me know what she thought of my slightly scornful tone. "Not that they weren't great, it's just not how it worked."

"And you, a professional golfer, have never once taken someone out on a date to the golf course?" she asks, suspicion lacing her tone. "Was your twenty minutes of putting at Putt-Putt? It feels like a natural way for you to go about picking up women."

I lean down and kiss the top of her head. "Don't take this the wrong way, Pipsqueak, but I don't usually have to put that level of work into picking up women. And I've never wanted to spend much time with them outside of the bedroom."

"You're such a pig," she laughs, shoving me away.

I let her think she's escaped before grabbing her arm and pulling her back into a tight hug. "I want to deny it, but I probably am. But in the nicest way. I've never led anyone on or gotten into a situation where the woman I was with thought we were going to turn into anything more than a fun night or two."

"How Jameo got painted as the womanizer while you walk around with a reputation for being the golden boy of golf is beyond me."

At the mention of her brother, I flinch slightly. I know I'm trying to give Jameson the benefit of the doubt, but I'm terrified how this is going to impact my friendship.

"Speaking of Jameo," I say, and Lila buries her face in my chest, groaning.

"Do we have to speak of him?"

"I mean, I'd rather not, but also, yes. It feels like the responsible thing to do."

"Okay. Well...since you brought it up...why don't you share your thoughts first?" she suggests.

I twist my baseball cap backward, and Lila chuckles at my outward sign of nerves. She twirls one of the curls at the base of my neck around her fingers.

"You don't look terrible with your hat like that," she says, pressing up on her toes to skim her lips across mine.

Thank goodness we don't have to worry about anyone needing to play this hole right now. Most of the club members prefer to start their rounds early—unlike me and Lila, who are just getting started.

"Was that a compliment?" I tease, tightening my arms around her to lock my mouth against hers. We make out for a few minutes, my body hardening under her featherlight touch as she explores my chest and arms. When my length presses against her hip, I pull back.

"Okay, probably inappropriate to fuck you on the tee box."

"Wildly inappropriate, JT." Lila smirks. "Everyone knows the back nine is the only proper place to fuck someone on a golf course."

"Is that why the pace of play is always slower on the second half?" I tease.

"Well, that and the fact that regular people have had multiple beers, not enough water, and hours out in the sun by the time they get there."

"And then some poor schmucks choose to lose even more fluids?" I ask. "Risky."

"I don't think they'd classify themselves as poor schmucks."

"I know I won't if that's what is in store for me this afternoon." I wink at her, and she rolls her eyes.

"Anyway," Lila says, heading back to her teed-up ball. "Tell me what you're thinking about how we handle my brother."

She executes a beautiful backswing, her toned legs shifting and muscles flexing as she hits the ball, and the drive is straight down the fairway. It doesn't have the same length as the women on the ladies' tour, but I'd be lying if I said it didn't turn me on how good she is. How good she looks in golf clothes doesn't hurt either.

I think about the question of how to handle her brother. My primary thought is that we just don't tell him, but I'm worried that will offend Lila...and it's maybe a bit naïve.

"Well, we both agree we are ending this when he comes back and we aren't roommates anymore, right?"

"Right," she says, swinging her golf bag on her shoulders as we start walking down the fairway to her ball. It's a bit awkward to walk next to someone when you're both wearing golf bags that stick out to either side of you, but we stagger a bit to make it work.

"So, I don't love the idea of telling him something that might be weird for us all when it won't even be an issue by the time he's back."

"Makes sense." Lila shifts her hand, placing it on the heads of her clubs to keep them from rattling as we walk.

I continue, voicing my concerns with not telling him. "That said, I'm worried about the gossip in Wild Bluffs getting back to him. He'd be mad we didn't tell him. I mean, shit, even the staff just casually mentioning we went golfing together while he was away would be a shocking revelation for him."

Lila chuckles lightly. "True, and I'm beginning to learn there is no such thing as a secret in Wild Bluffs. And, while Jameo might not be as connected to the local gossip, Bryn sure is."

"Exactly. So"—I blow out a deep breath—"I'm not sure what to do."

We reach Lila's ball, and I help her figure out the yardage to the green so she can choose the appropriate club. She hits one of her hybrids, and the ball lands about twenty yards off the front of the green.

She slides the club back into her bag, and we make our way toward my ball. If I were golfing in a tournament or with one of my buddies, I wouldn't be walking with her to each of her shots, but it feels kinda intimate spending this time with her.

"I'm leaning toward not telling him and trying to keep it a secret, but I also know I'm one hundred percent not going to be able to keep it a secret...and the only people I know in this town are Bryn's sisters."

"They seem like people who can keep secrets...don't they?" I ask, unable to contain the hint of worry in my voice.

"Kelsey most certainly can. Izzy, I have my doubts. I think we have to assume whatever she knows, Becca also knows, for sure. But I do trust her. She could likely be persuaded not to outright tell Bryn or Jameson anything. We would certainly have to keep it from the town at large. No PDA both in town and on the course..." She trails off, looking around. "Well, I mean, at least in the public spaces on the course. I'd think the back nine is still safe." She winks at me, and I have the urge to tackle her and show her just how unwilling I am to wait another seven holes to publicly display my affection.

"Okay. That seems like a fairly solid plan," I say instead. "No PDA in town or in the public areas of the golf course, which includes any holes people can see from the clubhouse or restaurant. We do everything we can to keep this from getting to Jameo, ever, in his entire life. The Harper sisters are safe to talk to if and only if they swear a vow of secrecy." I'm not sure why I'm spending so much time defining these rules, but it does make it all seem safer. "Our house is obviously fair game, though we should probably make sure we are careful in the living room where people could see us. So no sex against the living room windows."

"As those are mostly still covered with plywood, I think we will be safe. I don't think people can see in, and I'm definitely not going to risk getting a splinter in my ass."

Over eight hundred houses in and around Wild Bluffs had hail damage from the storm, with over a thousand windows needing fully replaced, so we are still working with a lot of plywood-covered doors and windows out here. The golf course offered us rooms with northern-facing windows in the hotel portion of the club, but we both declined, assuring them we're fine in the house.

"I forgot about the plywood. That is handy." I waggle my eyebrows at her. "Lots of living room sexcapades, then."

"You know when you say things like that, it makes me want to punch you in the face, right?"

"Punch me in the face or sit on my face?"

"Punch. Definitely punch. Though I'll never say no to the other option."

"Now, then," I say, and I drop my bag. I stalk toward her like she's my prey, but she squeaks out a yell and runs away from me. I snag the back of her bag, pulling her small frame to a halt. "You said you'll never say no. Ride my face, Pipsqueak."

"JT Johnson, that is *back nine* behavior. Get it together, man," she chides, but I can see the fire that is lighting up her eyes.

Fuck, this is going to be the best month of my life.

CHAPTER TWENTY-SIX

LILA

"Ugh. Elise, we are at DEFCON 1 here! Why are you not answering your phone?" I'm practically shouting at my best friend's voicemail as I walk into the office Monday morning. I sent her a string of text messages every night for the past two nights but haven't been away from JT for long enough to call her until now. Inability to gossip about him with my best friend aside, I could really get used to him shuttling me back and forth to work. This morning, we spent the time in the car talking about his upcoming tournament and his travel schedule over the next three weeks. I knew he was going to be back to playing, but it hadn't sunk in just how much that meant he would be gone in the next few weeks. To say I am bummed would be like saying gummy candy is decent: understatement of the year.

"Oooo, DEFCON 1. Say more," Becca says from her computer monitor. Kelsey hops up from my chair where she's lounging. Even though the third desk in the office is now officially mine, it seems old habits die hard from when the Harper sisters used to use it as their own personal hot desk.

"Nope," Kelsey says. "At least, not until I leave. I have to hold a boundary somewhere, and, based on the conversation we had with JT Friday night, I feel like I have a good idea what this is about."

"What did you talk to JT about Friday night?" I ask, and quickly follow it with, "And why can you talk to him about this stuff but not me?"

"Because I don't employ him." Her brow furrows. "Though maybe it is crossing a line anyway."

"It's not, Kels. You know everyone in this town is involved in their employees' business. I feel like you could live a bit more in the gray," Izzy jumps in.

Kelsey scrunches up her nose like she got a whiff of a particularly sweaty man's body odor, clearly not a fan of crossing any lines with her employees. "Nope. Couldn't be me," she says before pushing through the doors and heading out onto the street.

"We never should've let her hire you," Izzy says.

I put my hand over my heart and fake a gasp. "Excuse me?"

"Not like that. We just should've known she'd get all weird about the boundaries of it all. You could've come to work for us. Becca and I have absolutely no boundaries." Izzy leans over to high-five her friend, but Becca just stares at her hand.

"I am not high-fiving you for that. We have boundaries, or we would if we weren't a two-person company where both employees are also the co-owners. We still don't do things like sleep with clients, steal money, poach clients—"

"Fine, fine," Izzy says. "Though I'm upset you didn't high-five me. It's pretty mean to just leave me hanging like that."

"You'll survive."

"Well, if I don't, I'm going to come back to haunt you for sure. And any time you're with a guy, I'm going to hover over you and offer my critique while also reminding you of all the non-sexy things I can think of, like...hairy moles...or old banana peels."

"There is something seriously wrong with you, you know that, right?" Becca asks, shaking her head but laughing all the same.

"Yeah. I have terrible taste in best friends and business partners, but it's a cross I must bear."

I laugh at my officemates as I pull up the proposal Kelsey asked me to work on. It's a huge potential contract, and I was so excited when she asked me to take point on it. Unfortunately, I'm realizing nothing I did in college prepared me for this. I've spent way more hours than I care to admit Googling different diagrams and information Kelsey included in the proposal outline. I know if I ask Kelsey, she'd walk me through it, but I don't want her to regret her decision or think I'm incompetent. I'm sure I can figure it out myself; I just need to work harder.

I'm trying to figure out how to correctly interpret a mobile security plan so it's understandable in the client mockup when my phone vibrates loudly on my desk. As I read it, my heart speeds up.

JT

Is it ridiculous that I miss you already? Can you sneak away for coffee? And then again for lunch? Do you all do elevensies?

Elevensies. Ha. What a nerd.

> Unfortunately, Kelsey won't let me take off three of the first four hours of the day. Real hard-ass like that. Maybe you should consider doing your job today ;)

I smile at the thought of our golf game yesterday. JT had been on fire, and I could tell it was a relief for him to be playing well again. He was actually enjoying being out on the course. And enjoying some other things on the course. *Damn back nine.*

"Oh my gosh, are you blushing from a text message over there?" Izzy asks. "I know I was the one who got us distracted from the impending nuclear war designation when you came in this morning, but now we must know. What's going on?"

"You first," I say, tilting back in my chair and tapping my pen on the desk. "What did Kelsey mean when she said you guys were talking to JT Friday night?"

"Strong power play. Kelsey would be proud," Becca says. "And, as I wasn't there Friday night—and apparently my *best friend* didn't feel the need to fill me in—I'd also like Izzy to go first."

The woman in question looks between us, her long brown hair falling over her shoulder as she considers it. "Fine. Seems fair. But you better hold up your end of the deal."

I shrug and nod my head in agreement.

"Well, as you know, Kelsey and I stayed after golfing Friday afternoon to get dinner and drinks. We had just wrapped up a very long dinner when who should arrive but our dear friend, JT."

"Why do you sound like you're Pharrell narrating *The Grinch*?" Becca cuts in.

"Do you want to hear the story or not, Rebecca?"

"Damn, she Rebecca'd you," I tease.

Izzy gives us both her best teacher glare before continuing her story. "Anyway, it was clear he was worked up about something and looking to drown a few of those feelings, so Kelsey and I took pity on the poor man and let him buy a few rounds for the whole table."

I chuckle. I'm sure JT was just glad to have the company and would've happily bought a few roundtrip tickets to Bora Bora for the whole table if they'd asked.

"Anyway, Kelsey mind-ninjaed the man once she got his defenses down out on the putting green—"

Becca snorts. "That sounds dirty."

She receives another teacher glare before Izzy continues, "And he more or less admitted he was jealous of Lila's date with Matt. Oh! And he and Lila have been bunking together since the hailstorm." She shoots me a wicked smirk as my jaw drops. No wonder he was okay with me telling Kelsey and Izzy about this—he'd already spilled the tea. Izzy continues, "Actually, Kelsey had already figured out the sleeping together thing."

"What?" I ask. "How? Why? What?!" That lady is too damn good at her job.

"She had a whole line of evidence, but it doesn't really matter, since JT confirmed it."

"You can't tell Bryn and Jameo, Izzy. And you have to tell Kelsey not to either. You too, Becca. This has to stay between us."

They both agree, and Izzy adds, "And you definitely don't have to worry about Kelsey. Secrets are her thing."

"But why is it a secret?" Becca asks.

I let out a groan and slide down into my computer chair until my body is almost at a forty-five-degree angle with the floor. "This is why we are at a DEFCON 1," I say. "JT doesn't do relationships. Like, he is so committed to golf that he might as well be married to it. Not to get all armchair psychologist over here, but the man has some real issues that almost certainly stem from the way his parents treat him like he's a walking reminder of all their failed dreams. If the stories Jameson tells are to be believed, that is. JT doesn't talk about them to me, even though I know he talks to his dad multiple times a day."

Jameson told me a couple stories about JT's dad to try to get me to be nicer to JT. Apparently, JT's dad was critiquing his son's game so hard during college that *Jameson* almost started crying just hearing it. It wasn't that I didn't feel bad for him, even before all this, I just would never want to be treated differently because someone felt bad for me, so I wasn't going to do that to him either.

"Shit," Becca says.

Izzy nods her agreement. "I mean, he didn't get into the parent part of it, but yeah, he essentially said he needs to focus on winning another tournament, and since he knows you dream of a husband and kids, you guys aren't a good fit." She offers me a sympathetic grimace.

"Which is totally true. Except"—I hide behind my hands—"turns out we may fit a little too well, if you know what I mean?"

I look up to see the wicked smiles on the faces of both of my new friends.

"Um, we're going to need *significantly* more details," Becca says. "That man is beautiful, and I need to live vicariously through you. Ugh! Why is everyone in my life hooking up with men out of fucking romance novels?"

Izzy double coughs as if to say, "Um, what about me?" but Becca pays her no attention.

"Please don't compare my brother to a romance novel hero ever again. It will ruin the entire genre for me, and then what will I read? Nonfiction? Get out of here."

Both women ignore my comment, and at their prodding, I tell the highlights: walking in on JT fresh from the shower (Becca almost swooned, and I would not have blamed her if she did); us diving head-first into bed together; our decision to be roommates with benefits until we both go back to our previously scheduled lives; acting like a real couple all day Saturday as we cooked, watched TV, read, and slept together; golfing yesterday and doing date-y things. By the time I'm done telling them about it, I'm more confused than when I started.

"It feels like we're in a relationship," I say. "At the very least, he's quickly becoming a good friend. It's not just crazy hot sex all the time. There is unfortunately also a connection on an emotional level. Though I'm worried I'm not going to be able to be his friend after all this. Even knowing how much fun he is."

"Why not?" Becca asks.

"There is this electricity—this magnetism—between us that has been there the entire time I've known him. When I was younger, it was more of a gentle pull, and it led to him being someone that I always wanted to talk to and be around, but then once I was older, it intensified. We became powerful magnets, and depending on how we are aligned, we are either forcibly repelled or attracted—we cannot simply exist in the same space without having a significant impact on the alignment of the other. We only have two options: fight or fuck."

Izzy snickers at that. "Based on that one time I was in the same room as the two of you, that is actually spot-on."

"So you're just going to date him for three weeks and then go back to fighting with him constantly?" Becca asks. "Because—and I say this with love—that feels like a terrible plan."

I drop my head into my hands, my elbows propped on the table the only thing holding me up. "I know it is. I can see the nuclear explosion coming, but I have no idea how to stop it."

"Shit," Izzy says. "It really is DEFCON 1."

CHAPTER TWENTY-SEVEN

JT

"Morning, Pipsqueak," I whisper, kissing Lila gently on her cheek. She's asleep, one hand on my chest, her head in the crook of my shoulder. I grab her hand and stroke my thumb down the inside of her palm, watching her eyes flutter as the tickling sensation starts to pull her back to consciousness. I hate waking people up, but Lila needs my vehicle, so she has to drop me off for my flight to my practice round in Detroit this afternoon with my caddie. Instead of flying out yesterday like I normally would've, I insisted Sam schedule my flight early this morning so I could get in one more night with Lila. I know we set the three-week time limit on this thing between us for a good reason, and I'm not about to suggest we lengthen it, but I also am damn sure going to take advantage of every second.

I need to ask Lila about coming with me to the Ferguson Tournament event. I know it's technically at the very end of our three weeks together, but I really hope she says yes. Things between us have been so amazing this week that I haven't wanted to risk messing it up by inviting her on this very public date with me. And, really, it isn't so much a date as her saving me from going with someone who makes me want to shove golf tees through my eardrums.

The problem is that the more time Lila and I spend together, the more it feels like it will be a real date—like I'm asking my girlfriend to come to this important thing with me where she will meet my parents and spend the night on my arm as I introduce her to everyone I know.

I don't hate it. And that's the real reason why I haven't asked her. I'm worried *I'll* start to think it's real.

But I also can't leave her for the next five days with it hanging over my head and any conversation I might have with her. So I kiss her again, lightly brushing my lips over hers. As she starts to wake up, she moves her knee from where it has been resting on my thigh and brushes it against my very awake morning wood.

She smirks, her eyes still closed. "Morning."

"Morning," I say again.

"Not talking to you," she whispers, barely opening her one visible eye against the stream of light coming through the window.

I chuckle and my dick jumps, excited she's choosing him over me this morning. Unfortunately, I know I need to ask her about Vegas before we do anything else. "Ah, well, he'd like to say good morning to you as well, but I need to ask you about something first."

"Oh." She tries to sit up, her eyebrows pulled together in concern, but I tug her tightly into my arms.

"It's not like that." I kiss the top of her head, the black strands catching the sun and entrancing me as I work through what to say next.

"I was wondering if you'd be willing to come to the Ferguson Tournament reception event with me in a couple of weeks."

"A reception? As like, your date?" she asks, pulling her lower lip into her mouth and chewing on the corner.

"Yeah. The Ferguson brothers are hosting this huge golf tournament, and there is an event associated with it that is a big deal to my parents. I may have, before all...this...told my mom you were going to be my date."

She chuckles. "Before all this? Were you trying to punish yourself with my company?"

"My mom suggested I take this other woman I've gone out with before"—Lila tenses in my arms, and I don't hate knowing she's jealous, even if she has absolutely no reason to be—"who is *awful*, and I could hear you moving around, so somehow your name just came out."

"When is it?"

"It's that weekend before Bryn and Jameo come back."

"So our last weekend doing...whatever this is."

"Yeah," I say, a sad tone to my voice. "And, I haven't confirmed this, but I'm guessing Jameo and Bryn will actually be in Vegas, since it's a major new tournament with a huge purse for Jameo, coupled with it being Bryn's company."

I can feel her nodding, taking it all in. "Vegas, huh?"

"Is that a good or a bad thing?" I ask, and I genuinely want to know. We haven't talked about our past together at all. There's too much to unpack there for a three-week roommates-with-benefits situation, so I've avoided it like the plague. Plus, I'm not sure how *I* feel about the couple of times we hooked up last year. It was amazing, and it was torture. I'm haunted by the memories, but at the same time, I wouldn't give them up for anything in the entire world. And, somehow, that party before Thanksgiving, the one that all of our animosity stems from, seems like an even more insurmountable conversation.

"I mean, who doesn't love Vegas," she jokes before growing serious. "I don't know, JT. It's pretty complicated, and I try not to think about what happened in Vegas, particularly what happened the next morning, most of the time."

"The next morning?" I ask, confused, but my question is lost to the sound of my phone ringing. My dad's name flashes across the screen. I know I shouldn't answer it, but I can't help but reach out and grab my phone, the need to answer any time my dad calls ingrained into my very being at this point.

I answer the call and slip out of bed, heading out to the kitchen to start my coffee. I've got to keep moving if I'm going to make it to the airport by the time I told the pilots I'd be there. There is a lot of flexibility in private air travel, but I hate making people wait for me. Jack wanders out of Jameo's room as I listen to my father talk, and I make sure to feed him a little extra, just because.

Unsurprisingly, my dad called to make sure I know how important the tournament is this weekend. I've already talked to my entire team about this, from my agent to my PR team to Sam, but no, apparently my dad needs to remind me, the professional golfer, how important it is that I play well. I remind myself that he has positive intentions, but somehow I can't help but imagine how different this conversation would be if it were Jameson talking to his dad or one of the Harper sisters talking to Ken. Neither of those men would've spent the entire time lecturing their kids on how important it is to perform well and win more money. They would've been supportive, maybe even tried to distract their offspring from the stress with jokes or funny anecdotes about their siblings.

My dad ends the lecture with a cryptic comment about "needing that money." I consider asking about the big investment opportunity they're working on that's so timely, but instead I'm distracted by Lila slipping out of our room, fully clothed and ready for her day at work.

"Dang it," I sigh as I hang up, pulling her into a hug and leaning in to smell her freshly washed hair. "I was hoping to catch you before you got out of the shower."

She chuckles, but it sounds off to me somehow. "Well, you snooze, you lose. We've got to get you to the airport for your big return to the game of golf. I heard viewership has been down since they lost the twenty-five percent of viewers who are female and tune in solely to watch your ass as you play."

"Eh. Jameson's a big enough ass to keep the fans interested."

She laughs out loud, and this time it doesn't seem as forced as before.

"You two are certainly the two most popular asses on Tour," she jokes, taking a sip of coffee. "Speaking of ass," Lila begins, her mouth hidden behind her coffee and her eyes focused on the top of the refrigerator. "Uhm, just so we're on the same page and everything, will you be getting any this weekend? Ass, that is."

I start. I hadn't considered what us being apart this weekend would mean for the casual part of our arrangement. "Oh." I run my fingers through my hair, wishing I had my hat on to help me think. "I don't think I will be, no."

I see the smile she tries to hide, and it lightens the dread that pooled in my stomach at her question.

I cough. "Are you?"

She looks conflicted, and I hate she didn't automatically say no. Not that I blame her. For me, it's just a weekend without sex. For her, it's possibly saying no to someone she might want to date long-term. I want her to tell me she's not going to hook up with some other guy at the same time as me, but I know I can't ask that of her. It would be too much like defining this as a relationship. Roommates-with-benefits definitely aren't exclusive, even if the thought of Lila with someone else makes my blood boil to the point that I'm seeing red.

After what feels like an eternity, though is likely only a second or two, Lila smiles. "No. I'm not going to be getting any ass. But, and I'm sorry if this makes things weird, I'm not going to say no to someone if they ask me out and I'm interested. I don't think I'll actively pursue any dates, and I won't sleep with anyone while we are still doing what we're doing, but I just can't...you're...we both know I'm looking for something long-term."

My chest is being squeezed by a giant hand, but I do my best to breathe through it. I knew this. There was not one thing Lila just said that I didn't already know. But hearing her say it and knowing it are apparently two very different things.

"I understand."

"I *am* sorry, JT. I promise I won't actively pursue anything."

"You've got to do what you've got to do, Lila, and—shit—I've got to get in the shower."

I do have to get in the shower, but I also need to get away from the hurt that her words are causing me. I'm not allowed to feel hurt about her wanting to date someone, so I hurry into the bathroom, washing our conversation off with scalding water before quickly dressing and heading out to the living room, where Lila sits waiting for me.

We drive to the airport in relative silence, the awkwardness of our conversation heavy around us. I want to tell her I'm going to keep my options open, too, but I know I'm just hurt and trying to lash out. I also know it's not the truth.

I don't know how I'm going to get over the connection I have with Lila once we aren't in our situationship, and I most certainly can't imagine wanting to be with someone else when I know Lila is a viable option. Even if she's in a different zip code.

We pull up at the little private airport outside of Wild Bluffs, and Lila and I climb out of the pickup. I grab my bag and turn toward the tarmac, but Lila catches my hand. "I'm sorry about this morning, JT. I want to talk about it more when you get back, but let's just agree that, for this weekend at least, we are exclusive roommates-with-benefits, yeah?"

For the first time since she brought up sleeping with other people, the tension in me releases. "That sounds...fuck, that sounds great."

I try not to show her how much it means to me, but I'm doing a piss-poor job of it. Fortunately, that seems to be the right move. Lila throws her arms around my neck, and I bend my head down, praising her for her decision with my mouth. Her kisses stoke the fire in my veins, begging me to carry her onto the plane and have my way with her.

Damn. It's going to be a long, uncomfortable plane ride.

When she finally pulls back, we are both breathing heavily, and Lila is going to have to fix the back of her hair before she heads into town. I'm about to turn away when she darts forward, wrapping her arms around me and snuggling the side of her face into my chest. "You're going to do amazing, JT. You've got this. And if not, I promise I'll still be here for you when you get back."

I kiss her forehead and head to my plane, my heart already flying at her words of support.

CHAPTER TWENTY-EIGHT

JT

"I TOLD YOU WILD Bluffs was the solution to all your golfing woes," Jameo says as he walks into the locker room late Saturday afternoon. It looks like we'll both be in the running for the top spot this tournament, which isn't a surprise for him this summer, but with the way my golf game has been, it's noteworthy on my part. Unfortunately for Jameson, I think we found the same solution to our problems, it just doesn't happen to be golfing at Wild Bluffs.

I'm beginning to suspect the women in our lives are the real difference-makers in our games. It might be a coincidence I did so well at the tournaments after I hooked up with Lila last year, but when you add this one into the mix? I'm having a hard time denying the data.

"It's been a pretty great summer," I say. "Thanks again for letting me crash at your place."

"You know you're welcome any time. I'd prefer I get to hang out with you next time you come to town, though," he says, and I feel a block of guilt settle into my stomach. I'm sleeping around with his little sister. We're intentionally keeping it from him. Maybe I should just tell him now? But no. First of all, telling him the night before the final round would be a shitty thing to do, plus, I'm just not willing to risk our friendship over a three-week fling. My heart rebels against my mind at the term *fling*. Lila and I may be temporary, but it's not a fling, not something I'm going to throw away easily once it's done. No, I know these six weeks living with Lila will have changed who I am at a visceral level, and I may never get her out of my system, even if I never touch her again.

"Of course. How has your time away with Bryn been?"

"Fucking fantastic," he says, pulling his head through his shirt. "The vacation time, seeing Bryn in action at her job, and having her with me at the tournaments have all been amazing, but it's also made us both feel a bit untethered. We actually have some big news. I talked to a couple of local contractors as well as WBCC, and we're going to buy a lot and start building a house of our own at Wild Bluffs."

"What?" I ask, taken aback. They've been together for less than a year. They aren't married. "What's the rush?"

"There isn't a rush, but at the same time, I know Bryn is end game for me, so why wouldn't I start taking steps to make it permanent? Plus, I can't keep renting that house. It was never supposed to be a long-term rental—Conrad was just doing me a favor. And, especially now that Lila is in Wild Bluffs for the foreseeable future, it feels like a good next step. Bryn insists on calling it my house, if that makes your commitment-phobe heart feel better."

"That's-that's great, man," I manage to reply.

I can't imagine throwing myself into something like that. Jameo has been hurt by a long-term girlfriend before, and yet here he is, willing to risk it all again for the woman he loves. Even as I say it, I see Lila's face like it was last night on our video call, her eyes bright as she told me about her day and the work she's doing on her top-secret security proposal. I could see it with Lila—diving headfirst into the deep end of being with her. Unfortunately, I know it wouldn't last. I would need to focus on my game, on earning my parents the life they gave up for me, and she would get tired of not being my top priority. After a week, a month, or a year of being put second, she'd give up on me and leave. And I can't have anything but golf be my priority. It's the only way to pay my parents back for the dreams they gave up to support mine.

"Speaking of Lila." Jameson starts talking to me again, and I force myself to focus on the present. "I haven't been contacted by the police, so I take it you two have kept from murdering each other or burning the house down. How is she? I haven't had much time to talk to her lately between her work schedule and mine."

"Thoroughly satisfied" feels like the wrong answer, but I also smirk with pride at the accuracy of the statement. I wasn't sure what the protocol would be for our time apart, but Lila texted me minutes into my flight, and we've only stopped messaging each other since while I'm actively golfing.

Thursday afternoon, after a good day on the course had me in ninth, I opened my phone to find messages from Sam, Lila, and my dad. I, of course, opened Lila's first. She'd texted me almost twenty times, all string of consciousness thoughts about my attire, excitement at my good shots, and amusing tidbits and gossip about the guys in my foursome. Her comments made me laugh, and I've never felt more supported by someone. My dad's message, on the other hand, had been short and sweet: About time. Call me to discuss your chipping form.

I ignored my father and texted Lila back instead, the first time I didn't call him directly after a round. I ended up texting Lila all night, including falling asleep messaging her. While it wasn't the same as having her in my arms, it was so much better than being alone or lying next to some random stranger like I used to.

Lila and I texted each other all day Friday, and I laughed out loud in the locker room as I read her thoughts from the round. She was highly offended on my behalf that the announcers didn't mention the decline in female viewers during my absence. To be fair to the announcers, though, I'm pretty sure that's a stat that only exists in Lila's head.

The best surprise came Friday night when my phone rang, notifying me of a video call from Lila. She'd been out with the Harpers and Becca—the Mavericks football team was away last week at a summer camp, so none of her "new friends" were there, thank God—and she was a bit tipsy as she lay on our bed, her phone held in front of her face so I could see her beautiful grin.

We'd talked for almost two and a half hours before she'd fallen asleep, and I'd put my phone down on the pillow next to me, tilting the screen so I could sleep with her from hundreds of miles away.

I'd been on fire on the course today, too, and I knew it was thanks to Lila. And fuck me if that doesn't suck, because I know it's going to end, and then what am I going to be left with? A gaping hole in my chest and a golf game that can't function without her, that's what.

I realize Jameo is waiting for me to answer him about the state of his sister, so I force myself to focus on him rather than spiraling about what's to come.

"Honestly, Lila seems to be doing really well. She loves her job, and she's making friends with Bryn's sisters and some of the other people in town." A few too many of the men in town, but I don't mention that to her brother.

"My mom said you've been driving Lila to and from work every day since her car got totaled." He looks at me, and I can't read the look on his face. His arms are crossed, but it feels less like he's mad and more like he just doesn't know what else to do with his arms.

"It's not every day. Izzy and Kelsey give her rides back home sometimes."

"Well, still. I appreciate you helping her out while I'm not there. Bryn's car is at long-term airport parking. If you can get to Denver, I'm sure we can figure out how to get it back for Lila to use. Or I'll just buy her a new car and get it delivered there," he says, considering.

I know Jameo means it, and suddenly it feels like I might lose my time with Lila even sooner than I anticipated. "Oh, no. It's not a problem. I've developed an addiction to the coffee at Wild Brews anyway. Plus, I'm gone most of the next few weeks for tournaments, so no need to figure out a car until then. Even then, I can switch my rental contract over to her name if she still needs something."

Now I know it's suspicion on his face. "Okay, who are you and what did you do with the guy who can't stand to be in the same room as my sister?"

"It was never that bad," I say defensively.

"My mom had to add an extra table at Thanksgiving because you two made the rest of us miserable with your bickering."

"That's not true, there were just more people there for a couple of years."

"There were fewer people than normal two of the three years she did it."

Fuck. I didn't realize how bad we'd gotten.

"Shit. I'm sorry. I didn't know it was that bad. I'll call your mom. I'll apologize. Crap. You should've said something. I never meant to inconvenience anyone. I don't have to come—"

"JT," Jameo says, grabbing me firmly on the shoulder. "It's not a big deal. Of course you're coming this year. If anything, we'll kick Lila out." He laughs at his own joke, and even though I know he's kidding, I kind of want to punch him in the face on Lila's behalf. And I suppose it doesn't matter. I won't be at Thanksgiving with the Walkers this year—the first time since Jameo and I became friends freshman year of college. There's no way I'll be able to face Lila in front of her entire family, to hear about the life I'm no longer a part of, and not completely lose it.

"Right. Sorry." I reach up and shift my baseball cap so it sits backward before reversing the movement so it's forward again.

"Are you all right, JT?" Jameo asks. He's a much better friend than I deserve and is, of course, picking up on my nerves.

"Yeah. I just feel bad about imposing on your family. I feel like such a dick for making your mom do extra work."

"No one has ever felt that way about you. My family loves you, and we all really appreciate you helping Lila get settled into her new life."

"We're friends now," I say. "I'm happy to help."

Realizing there's something I need to tell Jameo about, I continue, "Plus, she's doing me a huge favor by being my plus one to the Ferguson Tournament event, so driving her around for a couple of weeks is the least I can do."

I'm slightly terrified of how he'll react, but he doesn't seem affected at all. "Nice. We'll be there too. Maybe the four of us can get breakfast together or something."

"Sure," I say, surprised with how cool he's being about this.

"But she cannot bunk with me." Ahh. That explains it. He's not even considering she might be going as my date.

Jameo continues, "I'm not losing my alone time with Bryn, even if she'll be busy most of the time with her work colleagues getting things ready."

"Is she involved with the event?" I ask, feeling both hopeful and kind of like a leech at the same time. Maybe she can introduce my parents to some people who might want to invest with them.

"Not really. She just offered to help set up, since she'll be there with me anyway."

"Oh, cool. That'll be fun." Well, there goes that idea.

I offer a grin that comes out lopsided, and Jameo smiles back before heading out to find the love of his life. I sit there feeling inexplicably jealous of my best friend as I pull out my phone and respond to Lila, telling her about the bullet I just dodged with her brother.

CHAPTER TWENTY-NINE

LILA

I am SO sorry I've been MIA this summer. My job is kicking my ass, and I'm so stressed out that any spare moment I have I'm just stress cleaning everything in sight.

Oh no. I'm so sorry it's so stressful. Quit?

Ha. Do you know what a move this early on in my career would do to my employability? I might as well just move back in with my parents now.

Trust me. I get it. Does your boss know?

Elise

One of the updates I haven't been able to talk to you about yet: My boss quit like two weeks ago and now I'm working under this new guy who is THE WORST.

Elise

Though in the spirit of full transparency, I must confess he also might be the most gorgeous man I've ever seen. He looks like one of the models of your romance books.

Me

Damn, girl. Get it. Or don't get it and still quit.

Elise

I know. But he and all his bro friends act like I can't do the job, so I have to prove to them that I can. It's for womenkind, really.

Elise

But I don't want to think about my shit show. Tell me everything about you and JT.

Elise

And I would like to go on the record stating I told you so. I saw this coming from a mile away.

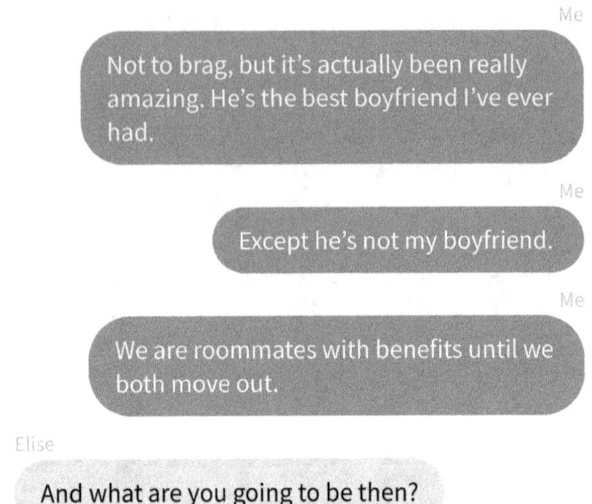

ANNOYED WITH HOW LONG this is taking to text, I call Elise instead, settling in on my and JT's bed. He came in fourth today, which is amazing, especially since he's been struggling so much the last year. He'd come into the day as number two, but a couple of putts didn't go his way and a few guys ended up having a lower score than him by the time it was all said and done. I'm still planning on congratulating him in the sexiest way when he gets home in a few hours, so I stopped by the garage where I'm currently storing clothes and picked through my boxes until I found the only silky pajamas I own. Now I'm showered, shaved, and home alone with nothing to do but lament to my best friend about falling for a guy I'm most certainly not supposed to be interested in.

And if I learned one thing this week, it's that I'm falling hard and fast for the man. He consumes my waking thoughts and chases me into my dreams each night, whispering words of forever I know I will never hear in real life.

Elise answers her phone, and I feel the tension easing from my shoulders as her voice echoes from my speakerphone. Maybe if I debrief my feelings with Elise, I'll be in a headspace to take full advantage of JT once he's home.

"So, what are you going to do once you move out?" Elise leads with her unanswered question from our text conversation.

"Cry," I say. I mean it as a joke, but when my voice breaks, I realize it's likely the most truthful thing I could've said.

"Oh, friend. I'm so sorry."

"That's the thing, I can't even accept your sympathy. He's been so up front about what this is. I've known since the beginning there would never be anything long-term between us." I clasp my hands between my knees, my shoulders bunching around my ears.

"But you're going to keep up this friends-with-benefits thing until then?" she asks.

I laugh. "We're not even calling it friends-with-benefits. There is such little expectation of long-term feelings that we've been referring to it as roommates-with-benefits."

Elise snorts. "Well, at least the benefits are good, no matter what other title is attached to them." She pauses. "They are good, right? It wasn't like a one-time thing in Vegas?"

"Vegas has been seriously upstaged. I swear it gets better every time we mess around."

"So clearly not something you're giving up before the time arrives?"

"Definitely not. I truly think I may be addicted at this point."

"Ugh. I'm so jealous."

"Elise!" I yell at her. "You cannot be jealous of me about this."

"Are you or are you not having life-altering sex with a professional athlete who also happens to look like Zeus's little, less crazy brother?"

"I cannot confirm the Zeus thing, but I get your point. I'm living every girl my age's dream."

"Exactly, and then maybe you two can be friends, or at least friendly, later."

"I don't know. I'm not saying we are going to fight like we used to, but I'm not sure I'll be able to be around him without being pissed at him for being so stupidly against a relationship with me, but—there I go again. I keep blaming him, but in reality, this is on me. JT has been open about what he wants the whole time."

"Maybe he'll change his mind. You two have always had something more than friendship or even annoyance between you. I can't imagine he'd walk away that easily."

"I don't know, he did the first time we kissed. And then again after we hooked up."

"Have you actually confirmed that with him?"

"No," I reply.

"So you still haven't asked him about Vegas?"

"No. What am I supposed to say, 'Hey, remember how after we hooked up in Vegas you completely ghosted me for breakfast the next day and then were a complete ass when I asked you about it? Can you explain that to me? Because I really don't understand how that guy is the same as the guy I'm falling in love with right now.'" Tears push at the corners of my eyes and the back of my throat, begging to be released. I'm so pathetic.

But that is what this conversation with my best friend is for—to get this out of my system before JT gets home. Once he's here, I'll be in the roommates-with-benefits mindset, not this one that wants something more from him.

"Wait, did you just say 'love'?" Elise's voice crackles with disbelief.

I open my mouth to explain, but a sudden, deep thud echoes from outside my bedroom door. My heart seizes as I turn toward the sound, feeling the blood drain from my face.

"What was that?" Elise whisper-yells through the phone.

I press a finger to my lips instinctively, though she can't see it. "Shh," I murmur, listening intently. The silence on the other side of the door is somehow louder, prickling at my nerves.

"Lila? What's going on?" Elise's voice is barely audible now.

"I... I think someone's in my house," I whisper back, gripping the phone tighter. "Stay on the line. Call 9-1-1 if I don't respond to you at any point."

Grabbing one of my high heels from the floor, I creep toward the door, my pulse hammering in my ears. I press down on the handle, pushing as I swing the door open, only to find the house empty, with no sign of what made that noise.

CHAPTER THIRTY

JT

I HURRY OUT OF the house, limping from the pain shooting through my toe. One brave kitchen stool attempted to stop me as I fled from the house, but I'm not one to be deterred when freaking out.

How did me surprising Lila end up as a big surprise for me? Maybe surprises aren't my thing. Yeah, I should stick to letting people know where I'll be and when.

I basically run down the hill to the golf club's restaurant, all the while thinking about what I heard. She's falling in love with me? I can't...I don't know what to do with that. She was never supposed to feel that way about me. I can't lose focus right now on my game. My dad lectured me for almost an hour after my round today about how I let him and my mom down with my performance. They need first-place money for the investment, and I couldn't close. Lila might be my good-luck charm, but she's also a major distraction. All I could think about today was coming home to her, and my round suffered.

I can't let myself get caught up in my feelings for her.

The shittiest thing is that I might just be starting to fall in love with her too. But I was okay with breaking my own heart if it meant I was able to help my parents without hurting Lila. What am I supposed to do now that there's no way to avoid breaking her heart?

I try to force myself to think of anything else, but it keeps spiraling back to the conversation I overheard, a second, far less important portion of the conversation popping into my mind. What the heck was she talking about when she said I completely ghosted her for breakfast and then was a complete ass about it? I would certainly remember it if Lila ever asked me to breakfast.

I head straight for the bar as I walk into the restaurant, secretly hoping one of the Harpers will be there to coach me through this mess that is my life. I feel like Kelsey and Ken would be a solid advice combo right now, but I would take any of them at this point. I wouldn't even turn my nose up at an overly friendly bartender I could work this through,with. Unfortunately, as I plop down at the end of the bar, I realize the man two seats down from me is none other than Lila's date-turned-friend, Matthew Something-or-Another. Perfect. Had to be the one guy whose face I want to smash for no good reason.

"Hey, you're Lila's boyfriend, right? JT Johnson?"

"She's not my girlfriend," I say gruffly.

He chuckles like there's something fucking funny about us not dating. "Right. Okay."

He takes a swallow of the dark amber liquid he's drinking before turning his attention back to me. "Want a drink?" he asks.

"No," I say, and he just smirks at my lie. To be fair, I'm sitting at a bar, alone, at night, so it's not hard to puzzle out that I want a drink.

"Fine," I sigh. "Whiskey on the rocks, please," I tell the bartender, and Matthew signals with his finger to indicate that she should put it on his tab.

"I can get my own drink."

"Did you know this golf course is on land that used to be my grandfather's ranch?" he asks. "My family ran cattle right here for over a hundred years before my grandpa sold off this part to build the golf course. He negotiated memberships for all his children, grandchildren, and great-grandchildren, living or future, as part of the deal too. Since it's the closest bar to my house, I tend to end up drinking here when I'm looking to drown my sorrows or to forget."

I say nothing, nodding my head graciously to the bartender as she drops off my drink.

"Why am I drowning my sorrows? Thanks for asking, JT. It would've been a real dick move not to, of course, but you, the guy they tout as the nicest professional golfer in the world, would never be so jealous of a guy who's friends with your *not girlfriend* that you'd act like that, right?"

A laugh escapes me even though I desperately don't want it to.

"Fine. Sorry. I'm having a shit night."

"Want to talk about it?"

I look at him skeptically because um, yes. I most certainly want to talk about it. But I also just met this guy who went out on a date with Lila like four minutes ago. I'm not sure I can trust him or his advice.

Unfortunately, my mouth has other plans, and without deciding to open up to him, I hear myself saying, "She loves me."

He just stares at me blankly. "Why is that a problem? Most people want their girlfriends to love them."

"She's not my girlfriend!" I practically yell, and am glad it's just the two of us here. Even the bartender headed to the back, leaving us truly alone.

"Right. You did say that, to be fair to you."

"Exactly. So she can't love me."

"Do you love her?"

"I don't know." I drag my hands through my hair. "Maybe?"

"Okay, and are you married?"

"What?" The drink I just took a sip of goes down the wrong pipe, and I start coughing.

Matthew waits until I can breathe again before repeating the question.

"No, I'm not married. Do you think—"

He holds up his hand. "Then why can't she be your girlfriend? Then you can see if you love her or not."

"It's complicated."

"In my experience, saying it's complicated is usually just someone's way of not having to put their heart on the line."

I take in the man again, sitting in a country club bar instead of in town, all alone with a day-old beard and dark shadows under his eyes.

"Why are you drinking away your sorrows, Matt?" I ask, truly wanting to know the answer.

He takes another long pull of his drink, finishing off the glass. "Because I missed my chance with the girl I love. And now, I have to live every day knowing she's out there in the arms of another guy and happy. But also knowing she's not as happy as she could be because there's not a guy in this fucking world who could make her as happy as I could. And that's on me. Because I was too afraid to tell her how I felt, and she got tired of waiting around for me to be the guy she deserved. And so finally she left."

"Shit, man. That sucks. But that. That right there is why I can't do this. She will eventually leave. I have to focus on my golf. I have responsibilities and people who rely on me, and she's going to be at home waiting for me to come back from some tournament or another, and she's going to leave."

His eyes flare in annoyance at that. "If you really think so little of her, then you're right. You shouldn't pursue her."

"What? I think Lila is fucking amazing."

"And yet you also think she's so flighty, so weak that she's just going to give up because you have a job where you have to travel a lot?"

"It's not about that. It's about my priorities. I've made people sacrifice for me, give up their dreams *for me,* their whole life. And I'm not worth it. She'll realize I'm not worth it and will leave."

"No. You don't get it. The girl I love, she didn't leave me because I wasn't good enough. I always had the potential to be the guy she wanted. Shit, I *was* the guy she wanted, I just wasn't able to believe I could be that guy forever. So I always left the door open, giving her out after out so she wouldn't be stuck with me. But all she ever wanted was for me to be willing to take a risk on us. For me to say, yes, she is it. It might be hard sometimes, but she's worth it—*we are worth it.*"

Matthew shakes his head. "She left me because I wasn't willing to fight for her—for *us*. I didn't show up when it mattered, and I didn't make her feel like she was my everything. It wasn't about being 'worth' anything—it was about proving to her that I was willing to risk both of our hearts. But I didn't, and that's why I lost her."

"I...shit. I have to go," I say, throwing a handful of bills down on the bar next to my glass, his words hitting me hard because, deep down, I know they're true. I am so scared of Lila leaving me because she has to sacrifice too much to be with me that I am shoving her out the door myself.

"Good luck," he says, offering me a toast with his glass as I practically sprint out of the doors and back up the path to our house.

***

The door slams shut behind me as I come to a gasping stop inside our room. Lila sits up in bed, startled by my sudden appearance. Her face breaks into a full smile, and I realize maybe I'm not a sacrifice for her. Maybe I'm part of her dreams.

She hops out of bed, and I'm knocked speechless by the sight of her in a black little pajama dress. She walks over to me, and I pull her into a hug.

"Nice work this weekend," she says, and that's it. Nothing about how I could've gotten first. Nothing about how this impacts her. Just a kind comment.

"I missed you," I say.

"I missed you too." She tilts her mouth up, pursing her lips as she silently asks for a kiss.

I oblige, covering her mouth with my own, my heart increasing its pace as she melts against me. My hands move over the silky fabric she has on, skimming the curves of her body.

I paint a line of kisses along her jaw and up to the hollow behind her ear. I reach the sensitive spot, and she digs her fingers into my hair. Her nails scratch against my scalp, and I swear it's like someone is pouring champagne directly into my bloodstream—my head is spinning with a bubbly rush.

"I want you," I whisper, sliding my hands down her back to rest lightly on the swell of her ass, my thumbs gently passing back and forth over the top of the muscles there.

"Take me, then," she says, and I realize I wasn't clear enough. She doesn't understand I'm trying to tell her I don't just want to give in to this undeniable physical chemistry between us, but I want all of her: her heart, her mind, her soul.

Before I work up the courage to speak, her teeth graze my ear and everything in me squeezes with need.

As much as I love the way she looks and feels in that little black dress, it's got to go. I hook my finger under the hem, and Lila raises her arms above her, allowing me to slowly peel it off, exposing her bare flesh. She shivers as the cool air hits her sensitive skin, and I shift her hair over her shoulder, my lips making the journey from her collarbone, down the curve of her breast, and to the peak of her nipple. At the contact, she lets out a breathy moan. The sound pulls all thought from my body except for my need to join with hers and wring that noise from her again and again.

I'm desperate for her, all but coming apart from simply kissing her skin. I realize how ridiculous I was for thinking I could walk away from this after just three weeks. I need her like the grass needs water, like the waves need the moon. I move my attention back to her lips, my hands roaming over her smooth form. Lila deepens our kiss, her tongue stroking mine, our bodies connected. I let out a desperate groan as I feel Lila's heart beating a furious rhythm, just as ready for this as I am. I pick her up, moving her back onto the bed and stepping between her thighs. My fingertips trace the bottom edge of her silky black underwear, a demon incarnate. I skate my fingertips higher as she wraps her legs around my waist.

"I want you so bad it hurts," I whisper.

"Then have me," she commands, lifting her hips and pulling her underwear off.

"Hey," I say, kissing my way down her bare stomach. "That was my job."

She chuckles, and I make my way back to her mouth, pausing to nibble on each rosy bud as I go past. She arches her back, and I pin her with my hips, the feel of her against my arousal making me moan as I automatically grind myself into her.

She fists my hair, pulling my mouth roughly against hers. I need to shed every article of clothing that I have on right now.

Drawing back, I look at Lila spread out before me on our bed. Her dark hair is splayed out behind her head, her green eyes are glassy with lust, her chest is heaving, and I've never seen anything as beautiful in my entire life.

I strip quickly, discarding my clothes into the corner. As I undress, I can feel Lila's eyes on me, moving over my chest and abs. She grins mischievously as she takes in my hard cock raised in a salute to this amazing woman who has us both bewitched. The smile undoes me, and I climb over her, settling my knees on either side of her body before quickly rolling on the condom I grabbed. I lower down slowly, catching her bottom lip between my teeth before plunging my cock into her.

Lila gasps slightly as I slowly drive every inch of me between her legs. She clutches the back of my neck, thrusting her hips up to meet mine, causing me to bottom out on a groan. I hover above her as she's spread out on the bed, making sure I keep most of my weight off her so I don't crush her small body.

I move at a steady pace, sliding into her again and again. As a powerful orgasm starts to build at the base of my spine, I reach between her legs, giving Lila the friction I know she so desperately needs. Her breath quickens, her eyes fluttering closed with each heartbeat.

"Look at me, Lila," I beg, needing to connect with her, to know she is here with me in this moment.

Her brilliant eyes snap to mine, the hunger in them reaching out to steal the very essence of my soul. I drive into her again, her mouth meeting mine as her legs tighten around my hips.

Lila cries out, her walls squeezing around me, her pleasure written across her face. Unable to do anything but follow her to my ruin, I come with her, burying my face into her neck as my orgasm rampages through me.

I'm exhausted and so damn happy. I pull her into my arms and kiss the top of her head. As I'm about to fall asleep, I remember her friend's comment from earlier.

"Hey, Pip?" I ask.

"Yeah?" she replies groggily from her place in the crook of my shoulder, and I realize now is not the time. But I will find out how I hurt her, and I will make it right. I'll also figure out a way to tell her I want this to be more than just a roommates-with-benefits situation for a couple of weeks. I want to do this for real.

"Thanks," I say instead, leaning down and kissing her forehead, hoping somehow the simple gesture conveys I'm not just thanking her for the sex, but for supporting me, for caring about me...for loving me.

Chapter Thirty-One

JT

"What the actual fuck?"

It is far too early for my mind to process anything, but I sit up anyway, every synapse in my brain firing to warn me that something is wrong, very, very wrong.

A shape moves by the door, and I realize what the threat is: Jameson Walker is in our bedroom.

"Shit, Jameo," I start, but am cut off as Lila sits up and yells, "Argh!" her bare chest on display as the sheets slide off her lithe frame. I quickly reach out, attempting to pull the sheet up over her.

"NO!" Jameo yells, turning around quickly. "No. My eyes. My brain. I'm going to have to carve part of my hippocampus out with a spoon to get rid of that image."

I run a hand through my hair, still tangled from my late-night activities with my best friend's little sister. Good God, could this get any worse? Jameson has clearly been shocked back to his human anatomy and physiology classes if he's pulling out words like "hippocampus."

"What the hell, Jameo?!" Lila snarls from the bed next to me. "Get the fuck out of our room!"

"YOUR room?" he bellows.

"Jameo," I say, in a consoling tone. I'm considering getting out of bed, but I think him seeing both of us naked at the same time might be too much for my friend. I hate that this is on me. I should've told him about Lila and me last time we were together, and I have an overwhelming urge to jump out of bed and beg him to forgive me.

I knew I was crossing a line. Shit, everyone knows sleeping with your friend's sister is crossing the line. But I came to a decision last night, and I'm going to see it through, even if Jameson's unexpected arrival just made it far more complicated. So there will be no begging for forgiveness as if there is something wrong with Lila and I being together.

"Are you fucking kidding me, JT? You could have any girl in the world and you're fucking around with my little sister?"

"I...that's not...I don't want just any girl." I don't know how to explain to him that it's not what he thinks. This isn't just a casual hookup for me. Even when it was timebound, in my mind, it was never casual.

The door opens, and Bryn steps in. "What's going on in here?" she asks cheerfully. I take in her shit-eating grin and realize in an instant that Bryn knew, or at least suspected, that this might be happening. Fricken Izzy. No way was Kelsey the one to blab the secret.

But it doesn't matter who it was because all that matters is that it wasn't me. It should've been me and Lila telling Jameo and the world about us, rather than trying to hide it like we're ashamed. Though it's not like we've been dating in secret for months or years or something. We're on, what, week two? If we weren't living together, this probably wouldn't even count as a thing.

My heart constricts at the thought, and it tries to argue with my brain: We are something. I just thought we had more time to define it, to figure out what this could be. Jameson isn't supposed to be home yet. He's not supposed to be back for another week. I've actively fought against any positive feelings I've had for Lila for the past six years because she is off-limits. I decided long ago that as much as I physically might desire a fling with Lila—which was all that it could ever be—it would never be worth the possibility of losing my best friend.

Now? Now the possibility seems worth it.

"These two are sleeping together!" Jameo shouts in response to Bryn's question.

"Yeah, I know," Bryn says, patting him on the shoulder. "You *have not* been quiet about it. Clearly handling it super well." She shoots him a double thumbs up, and I want to laugh, but the look of death on Jameo's face convinces me otherwise.

"Get out, Jameo," Lila says in a menacing growl.

"Really, Lila?" Jameo turns his attention to his sister, who just glares back. "Really, JT?"

"It's not what you think," I say, and I swear all three other people in the room huff in disbelief. Jack may have even let out a little dog huff of disbelief in the living room.

"Oh, really? What is it, then? Have you given up your 'I don't date. I have to focus on my career' mantra? Are you two dating?"

"No," Lila says, and I see Bryn's face fall a bit in disappointment.

"That's not what—" I start to say.

"Don't tell him anything, JT. We are grown-ass adults," Lila says. "We can do what we like with whomever we like." Jameson starts to say something else, but Lila cuts him off. "No. Just get out, Jameo! I'm naked under here, but if you don't leave, I'm going to start getting dressed whether you're in the room or not."

"Come on," Bryn says, grabbing her boyfriend's hand and pulling him forcefully from the room. "I'll get you some coffee, and then we can cover why barging into people's rooms at six in the morning is a terrible idea."

Jameson basically growls in response, but Bryn just laughs.

"I just wanted to surprise my friend."

"Well, you did surprise him. And, as a bonus, it looks like he surprised you too. A twofer, you might say."

Lila stands up, heading to the closet where she's been keeping her clothes with mine. She's upset, but I don't know if it's with me or her brother, or, shit, maybe Bryn? But I do what I always do: I try to make it better. "I'm sorry, Lila."

"For what?" she asks, her tone biting. Soo...me, then?

My sleep-deprived brain is now functioning solely on adrenaline dregs, so I'm having a harder time than normal figuring out how to make this right. I take a deep breath and climb out of bed, joining her by the closet and getting dressed as I decide how to respond.

I've got on a pair of athletic shorts and a T-shirt when I finally say, "I'm sorry your brother is mad at us. I know how important your relationship is with him."

"Yeah, JT. It is important, but so is my relationship with you." I can't help but smile when I hear her call it a relationship. I know I haven't told her how I feel, but it hurt when she denied there being something to her brother.

"You two better not be doing it in there!" Jameson yells from the kitchen.

Lila rolls her eyes before yelling back, "We. Are. Coming!"

"That's what he's afraid of!" Bryn yells back. And I'm pretty sure I hear Jameo choke on his coffee.

"What do you want to tell him?" I ask, my voice a whisper.

"I've been told honesty is always the best policy."

"Do you think I should tell him how I made you come twice in five minutes that one night?" I ask with a smug smile. That had been a damn good Monday night.

"Only if you want him to know how you sit down to pee at night because you're too tired to stand up."

"What? How? I shut the door!"

"Sounds different."

"Why are you listening to me pee, you weirdo?"

I laugh, and that is clearly not the right move, because Jameson barges back into the room, glaring at us like we personally poured itch powder into his underwear. "Do you think this is funny? Get your asses to the living room."

"Yes, Dad," Lila says in a fake apologetic voice, and I do my best to stifle the chuckle that wants to pass through my lips. Lila shoots me a conspiratorial grin, and it feels good, like Lila and I are on the same team.

Jameson points us to the chairs in the living room, making it very clear with his gesture that we are not to be on the couch together. Unfortunately for Jameson, his dick behavior just makes Lila want to push back, so she grabs my hand, sliding her body right in front of her brother to reach the small couch. She nods for me to sit down first, and when the gleam in her eye tells me that she's going to sit on my lap, I tip my head toward the seat next to me. I want Jameo to stay out of our business as much as any other guy, but I don't think we need to poke the fucking bear.

Jameson looks at our entwined hands, and we wait in silence as he decides if he's going to make a big deal out of it or not. Luckily, Bryn must notice the awkwardness from where she's at in the kitchen, and she hustles out three cups of coffee. "Jameo," she says, the couple silently communicating something. Bryn clearly wins, not that any of us are surprised, and Jameson sits down heavily in the chair across from us.

"How did this fucking happen?"

"Well," Lila starts, and I know from her tone this is not going to go well. "When a man loves a woman...well, I suppose they don't actually have to love each other. When a man and a woman are attracted to one another—"

"I know how *fucking* works, Lila."

"Can confirm," Bryn adds helpfully from the place she's taken up at the stove, clearly thinking eggs will somehow improve this situation.

Jameson closes his eyes and exhales before starting again, "How long has this been going on? Oh my God. Is this why you act the way you do together? Is it like some weird kind of foreplay?"

"Vegas!" I all but shout, because I cannot have Jameo or his parents thinking I was hooking up with 18-year-old Lila after spending Thanksgiving dinner with a fucking boner.

"What?"

"We accidentally hooked up in Vegas last year, and then basically nothing happened until we moved in together a few weeks ago," I say in a rush.

"To be clear, the disdain was real," Lila adds, somewhat unnecessarily in my opinion.

Jameson looks between the two of us, his elbows on his knees, a deep scowl on his face still.

"What does 'basically nothing happened' mean?"

It's like I can't catch a fricken break.

Lila curls up to my side, and without thinking, I tuck my arm around her. We've spent so many hours in this exact position, reading together or watching TV, that it's second nature at this point to cuddle her to me.

Jameson, however, looks like he just saw a dog solve a quadratic equation before reciting Shakespeare. "I'm sorry. Are you two cuddling? On my fucking couch? Right in front of me."

I go to pull my arm away, but Lila keeps hold of it.

"Yep," she replies.

"I fucking hate this already."

"Well, no need to get used to it," Lila says. "We're just roomies-with-benefits until the Ferguson Tournament."

"Jameson told me you're coming to that!" Bryn chimes in as she brings out four plates of eggs and passes them around before plopping down on Jameson's lap. The hypocrisy seems a bit strong, but other than shooting them a pointed look, it doesn't really feel like the time to call Jameo on it. "The four of us should go out to dinner a couple of the nights we are all there."

"Bryn," Jameson says, his patience obviously wearing thin with his girlfriend's desire to talk about anything other than Lila and me.

She rolls her eyes in a very Harper way. "What? I don't see what the big deal is. JT is a great guy and one of your best friends in the entire world. Lila is your sister and also one of your best friends. It's obvious to anyone with eyes there has been something between them for a while." We both start at that, but she just shrugs. "At least as long as I've known them. So, I'm not really sure what you're expecting from me. I assumed they were hooking up."

"Fine. But no more fucking in my house."

"No," Lila says at the exact same time I say, "Fine."

Lila turns to me with an exasperated look. "Neither of us have anywhere else to go, JT. We're both going to be sleeping in that bed, and there is no way we aren't going to fool around. My idiot brother can just get over it."

"I could go...somewhere else, if Jameo really doesn't want me here. I could get a hotel room in town or something. Maybe someone in town would let me bunk with them."

Jameson looks between us as if it's finally becoming clear to him this isn't just some one-night thing. "No," Jameo says, though I can tell he's none too pleased about the idea. "It's fine. But if I hear anything, I swear I will ruin you both."

CHAPTER THIRTY-TWO

LILA

"Hey, Pip, before you go, can I talk to you for a minute?" JT asks as I brush my teeth in the bathroom. To be fair, I'm sure we do need to talk. I mean, his best friend who is also my brother just caught us naked in bed together. Thank goodness all we were doing was sleeping. I'm a little confused by JT's reaction to it all. I was sure he was going to chalk it up to a one-night stand, head back to California, and just call it quits, but then he went and said he was staying even if it wasn't here at the house with us. I'm not really sure how to handle it, and Elise is not texting me back. That girl really needs to get her work-life balance figured out.

Jameson insisted he is the one who will be driving me to work today, and I didn't put up a fight, even though spending the drive with my angry brother feels like a real downgrade from my carpool time with JT. But it'll be good to have it out with my brother in the safe confines of a vehicle. Neither of us can walk away, and no eye contact is required.

I spit in the sink and rinse out my brush before giving JT my full attention. He's standing in the doorway, his fingers grabbing the top of the frame as he casually leans into my space. The sun is lighting up his golden surfer curls from behind, and he looks like an angel straight out of Malibu. He's just Ken. Though he's a ten here. "What's up, Pretty Boy?" I ask, reverting to my nickname for him from before we got together. I know "Pipsqueak" has become a term of endearment, but this feels like it's just enough to put up a minor wall in case he's here to end things with me.

He seems to understand, and his body tenses as a sad smile tugs at the right side of his face. Instead of answering, he drops his arms, taking the two steps to reach me, and wraps his arms around me. He kisses my head, whispering, "It's going to be okay." I'm not sure what exactly he's referring to, but I want to believe him, so I melt into his hug.

After a moment, he lets go of my waist, grabbing hold of my hand instead. Looking me in the eyes, he says, "I wanted to talk to you about this last night, but I got a bit distracted." His eyes gleam in boyish delight at the memory of last night before turning serious again. "I've been thinking, and I, um..."—his eyes briefly dart away from mine—"was wondering if maybe you'd want to have this be more than just a roommates-with-benefits situation."

I tense. I'm not sure if I believe him. This feels like him trying to make it seem better in the eyes of my brother.

"Is this because of Jameo?" I ask.

"No." He shakes his head before saying it again, more firmly this time. "No, Lila. It really isn't. I fully planned on asking you this last night. I think I want to try this—a real relationship—with you. One with no end date."

My heart is about to jump its excited ass out of my chest, and I can't keep the smile from my face, even as I seek further reassurance. "Really?"

"Yeah. I don't want this to end. I don't want to be drinking alone in a bar years from now, thinking about what I could've done to keep you."

"What?" I ask, trying to make sense of that last part.

"Not important right now."

I cross my arms, and he lets out a breath of a laugh. "I'll tell you the story another time, but for now, before you leave for work, I need you to know that I don't want this to end in a week or two weeks, and I especially don't want it to end now just because your brother isn't happy about it."

"I'll talk to him."

"I know. And I'll talk to him too. But this isn't about Jameson. This is about us. Can you please tell me you're willing to give this a try with me? Or do I have to beg?"

Uncertainty is evident in every line of his body. How does this man not understand just how far I've fallen for him in an unreasonably short amount of time?

"Of course," I say before rising on my toes to kiss the corner of his mouth. "Of course I want to try this with you."

I give him another long kiss before I head out of the bathroom, giving my hips an extra little swish just for him. The deep chuckle he releases lets me know he saw it.

"Ready?" I ask my brother as I slide my feet into the tan leather mules I left by the door last night. Instead of JT's golf shoes sitting next to them, there is a pair of men's loafers. I guess things have already started to change, whether we like it or not.

"Yep. Bryn is going to come in too. She's going to hang out with her sisters."

"Oh. Okay. Great." I force a positive tone, but the last thing I need is an audience for the argument Jameo and I are about to get into. I like Bryn and all, but she's not my sibling, so I'm going to feel the need to be on my best behavior, which is not what I was hoping for from the car talk. I was looking forward to yelling some things at the jackass who thinks he has any say over whom I do or do not sleep with.

I grab my bag and go to climb into the back of Bryn's black car.

"Oh, no. I'll sit in the back," Bryn says, sliding past me through the door I just opened.

"It's...it's your car," I say.

Jameo climbs into the driver's seat and raises an eyebrow at me, as if to say "Are you getting in?"

I climb into the front, and Jameson pulls out of the driveway, heading toward town.

"Okay, well, I'm going to listen to music back here. Very loud music. So loud, in fact, my watch will likely yell at me and tell me it's too loud, but I'm going to keep it that loud. The whole time. Plus,

I'm tired, so I will have my eyes closed," Bryn says from the back, and I laugh, glad Bryn is such an easy person.

"What are you even doing home?" I ask Jameson. He isn't supposed to be around for another two weeks, and I had big plans for those two weeks.

"The meetings Bryn was supposed to be at this week changed, and I figured with all the drama with the hailstorm and everything, we should come home. Plus, Bryn's going to stay here while I'm gone for the tournament this week so she can get shit done at work. She's worried about falling behind, since she'll be helping the team get ready for the tournament and event next week."

"It does sound like a really cool event. I'm glad I get to go."

"You're...right. I forgot JT mentioned you were going with him. At the time, I thought you were just a convenient date."

"I was just a convenient date at the time."

"Are you sure you're more than that now?" Jameo asks, and I guess the kid gloves are coming off.

"He said he wanted to date me this morning, so...yeah."

"This morning, huh?"

"Yep," I say, popping the final 'p' sound.

"Tough timing on his part."

"He claims you getting home had nothing to do with it."

"Sure."

"Jameo!" I'm annoyed now. JT is *his* best friend. "What the hell? You're the one who's best friends with the guy. Do *you* think it's just because you got home?"

"Honestly, Lila, I don't know what to think. I haven't seen JT with anyone who he even remotely pretended to be more than friends or fuckbuddies with since college." He pounds his hand on the steering wheel. "This is why guys shouldn't date their friends' sisters! I know way too much about how he treats women for me to want you to be with him."

"What does that mean? How does he treat them?!"

"Like they're temporary! He has a girl in every city. They all know he's just interested in them for the weekend, and as soon as he leaves, they don't mean anything to him again."

"Don't act like you weren't exactly the same way until you met Bryn."

"I wasn't."

"Oh really?" I ask, a biting tone in my voice at his lie.

"Okay, fine. I was for a little bit there. But it wasn't who I *am*. I was going through some shit. You know that. But I had long-term girlfriends before. Hell, even my shortest relationship is longer than JT's longest."

"Well, you changed when you met Bryn. Who's to say JT won't change for me?"

I watch as he tries to figure out how to answer the question, and I'm impressed by how much thought he is giving it.

"You're most certainly worth changing for, Lila. But JT has serious mental blocks in that department. His parents' relationship is the weirdest thing to ever witness. It's"—he runs his left hand through his hair—"fucked up."

"Yeah, well, it's also fucked up that you're sitting here basically saying your best friend isn't good enough for me to date."

"I don't think anyone is good enough to date you."

"Okay, Dad."

"If JT were trying this with anyone else, I would one hundred percent be cheering him on and offering any and all support I could to help him figure it out. But you're the one person in this world I side with over JT. And from your side of the equation, dating JT is risky. I don't want you to get hurt."

"Do you really think JT would hurt me?"

"Physically? No. Certainly not. Emotionally? I mean, yeah. I think there is a good chance. He has before, right?"

I raise a questioning eyebrow at him. "What do you mean?"

"I"—he sighs deeply—"I never told you about this, but that first Thanksgiving you were home from college, I heard you talking on the phone about what happened at the party we were all at the night before. It's why I tried not to give you or JT too much shit about the way you act toward each other."

"Oh."

"Yeah. And I know how bad it hurt you. I mean, I may have missed it this time, but it was impossible to miss the crush you had on him as a kid. And I heard how crushed you were when you were talking about him leaving you and never coming back after he kissed you. I mean, I get it from his point of view—you were 18—but I also heard the devastation in your voice. I wanted to break his face and tell him he made the right decision. How do you know he won't do the same thing this time?"

"I don't. I don't know that. But I also know the crush I had on him when I was 18 is nothing like how I feel about him now. He's a good guy. And, to be fair to him, I was 18. He kissed me to save me from some guy who wouldn't stop hitting on me, and then, when I wanted there to be more, he left. I'm not saying it was the right thing to do, but there *wasn't* a right way for him to break my heart at the time. It was going to be crushed no matter what he did. Plus, I was so embarrassed that not only did he feel like he had to defend me with fricken Wes but then he had to explain to me that it wasn't real. The weakness, the imperfection he saw in me, is something I try to avoid at all costs. Him seeing it? It's fueled my rage and need to point out every flaw in him since that day."

"I get it, Lila, I do. But it's not just that. I'm worried he doesn't know how to be in a relationship. It's hard work for anyone, but it's really fucking hard when you're a professional athlete. We travel *all the time*. We leave tomorrow for yet another tournament."

"You think I don't know that?" I say, an unintended venom lacing my voice. "I've watched you go through it. I *helped* you go through it."

"I don't know what to think, Lila. I thought you guys were likely to murder each other when you found out you were living together. I don't understand how it goes from that to...whatever you are."

"Dating. We're dating."

We pull onto Main Street, and Jameson sighs, clearly as frustrated with our conversation as I am.

I decide to extend the olive branch. "Look, I'm really sorry you walked in on us together this morning. That was not intentional. But we've only been together for a couple of weeks, and we didn't know that it was going to turn into something—and before you say anything, no one knows if it's going to be something when you're just a day or two in."

"I did." His eyes flit back to Bryn, and I know that jerk has her music off and is listening to us because her eyes light up like a kid who just heard the ice cream truck's song.

"Gross."

"Just be careful, okay?"

"And don't come crying to you when he hurts me. I got it," I say.

He parks and turns to look at me, a deep furrow between his brows. "No. And if he hurts you, I will be there for you—whenever or wherever you need me. And you can cry as much as you want."

I lean across the console and hug my big brother. "You're the best. And you have good taste in friends. Don't forget that."

I climb out but lean my head back in before heading into the office. "And you'd better go apologize to him for being a child this morning."

Chapter Thirty-Three

Lila

"Vegas, baby!" I yell, grabbing my suitcase from the tarmac as JT does the same with his bag and clubs.

"Vegas!" Bryn echoes as she and Jameson both load their suitcases into the car Sam arranged to pick us up.

The four of us flew to Vegas together, and I spent the majority of the flight trying to distract myself from how handsome JT looked by reading my current small-town romance. Ten out of ten do not recommend reading spicy scenes while on a flight with your sexy boyfriend and...your brother.

"I vote we ditch the girls and make them fly commercial on the way home if they do that again," Jameson gripes to JT.

"Vegas!" I repeat just to piss off my brother. I'm very excited about going back to the place where this all started for JT and me, but the yelling is mostly to get a rise out of Jameo.

"JT, did you remember to bring your girlfriend's booster seat?" my brother asks. "I'm not sure she's tall enough to ride in the car without one."

I stick my tongue out at him. "We'll be lucky if there's enough room in the SUV for all of us with how big your ego is."

"I knew I should've flown commercial." Bryn sighs. "At least then I had a chance of someone trying to airdrop me a dick pic."

"B!" Jameson pretends to tackle Bryn from behind, scooping her up and throwing her over his shoulder like he's a firefighter.

I look over at JT. "Don't get any funny ideas, Pretty Boy."

"About the dick pic or about carrying you like a caveman on steroids?"

"The caveman one, obviously," I joke as I slide into the black SUV and buckle in next to JT in middle row. "I wouldn't want you to throw your old-man back out after only two tournaments. I'd happily receive the other."

Jameson pretends to vomit from his seat in the back with Bryn, and I smile. This is going to be much better than I expected.

It's the height of the golf season, so JT and Jameson had another tournament last week. Unfortunately, Bryn and I both had to stay home rather than travel with them—it's great that Bryn's job lets her travel to his tournaments as much as she does, but I'm not sure what that will look like for JT and me. Kelsey and the company overall are super flexible, but she also hired me specifically to have someone in town with her, so I don't want it to look like I'm trying to get special treatment. Plus, I don't want to put the cart before the horse—we've only been dating for like ten days at this point.

Both JT and Jameson did very well last weekend, coming in fifth and second. While they were out of town, Bryn insisted on a girls' night, and we ended up at Kelsey's place to eat pizza and drink beer. Bryn forced us to regale her with every single piece of gossip she'd missed while she was gone and had taken a surprising amount of credit for JT and I getting together, claiming she knew there was something between us. She supposedly was also the one who suggested Jameo not tell us that the other would be staying there. The woman cackled when she said it. *Cackled.*

Luckily, the time away for golf also gave JT and Jameson the space to reconcile. According to JT, they made up on the flight they shared to the tournament with a simple "hurt her and I hurt you" speech from my brother. I know it was a shock when Jameo found us in bed together, but my brother is genuinely a good guy, and I know how highly he thinks of JT, despite whatever might've come out of his mouth that first morning.

Even though JT has only had two golf events since we started hooking up, we are falling into a routine I wouldn't trade for the world. We text all day and then video call each other at night to catch up. I feel like I've been able to learn so much about him during those calls—about his parents, what it was like for him growing up, his dreams. We've also moved our reading virtual, recommending e-books back and forth with our included notes.

We even spent a night last weekend role-playing a couple of the spicy scenes out of the book he's reading. Luckily, hockey romances are so popular right now, and they contain a lot of phone sex scenes, since hockey players travel almost as much as pro golfers do. I'm glad

Bryn decided to stay in town at her sister's house that night, because I most certainly wasn't quiet.

When the men made it back into town, Bryn and I picked them up from the airport with takeout already in the car. We came back to Jameson's house and sat around the firepit, drinking whiskeys and eating slices of jalapeno and bacon pizza. It was one of my best nights ever, just relaxing and enjoying the company of some of my favorite people on the planet. JT and I went to bed together that night, silently touching each other in all the ways we'd dreamed up while we were apart. It was amazing, but nothing we did felt quite as good as the feeling of falling asleep in his arms again after missing him viscerally for four nights.

Now, we're headed out to Vegas with enough time for the golfers to make it to their practice rounds this afternoon before the tournament kicks off tomorrow. I know this is their job, and I do want them to do well, but I'm kinda hoping both men play so poorly they don't make the cut so we can fully enjoy the Ferguson event Saturday night. If not, they'll have to leave early to make sure they're ready to go on Sunday morning for the final round. JT and I have a date night planned tomorrow night—a homage to our first night together. JT is so excited about his elaborate plans that I didn't want to burst his bubble by telling him our night in Vegas has pretty mixed memories for me. I know I need to ask him about what happened the morning after we hooked up, but I just can't bring myself to. It feels like, even if it has changed now, it's going to hurt for him to tell me how little I meant to him that next day.

Chapter Thirty-Four

JT

"Here we are!" I say, pulling Lila to a stop directly in front of the two bar stools we sat on last October. I'm excited about our date tonight. I don't think I've ever planned an actual date, and I spent way too much time trying to make this one perfect. Sam was a big help. He took his role seriously in coordinating it all, but I don't think he appreciated how many times I texted him confirming various portions of the night.

"It's drinks and dinner—not a choreographed flash mob with a carriage arriving at the end." His words, not mine.

I'm just trying to embrace my main-character-in-a-romance-novel energy. They always go all-out for the first date.

I knew I wanted to recreate our last time in Vegas, but it turns out that night holds a disproportionate amount of space in my head for the time that we spent together. So, at Sam's recommendation, I added in dinner at the steakhouse that's next door to our bar. Yes, our bar.

"Are you going to call me a demon just to get us kicked off the right way?" Lila asks as she slides her small frame into the seat she occupied last time.

"Hmm," I say as I lean in and kiss her on the cheek. "Well, that little black dress is most certainly sinful."

"All the better to tempt you with, my dear."

I slide into my seat and take in the three-inch heels she had slipped her feet into before we left our room. "And those heels were likely invented by the Devil himself."

"All the better to torture you with, my dear."

I laugh. "Are you the big bad wolf now?" I ask, but she just shakes her head, giggling at her own joke.

"But, no, you're most certainly not a demon." I lean in and press a light kiss to her mouth, my hand running up the smooth expanse of her leg. I stop before I reach an inappropriate height for a bar, even if it is a Vegas bar. "You look like a goddamn angel and taste like you were sent down from Heaven just for me."

"But, if I'm a goddamned angel, doesn't that still make me a demon?" she asks, as if she's unraveling the logic of a fallen angel.

"Well, you're mine, whatever you are."

Calling Lila mine is quickly becoming one of my favorite hobbies. Not only does it calm the pacing beast inside of me who wants nothing more than to be with her constantly, but it also makes her face light up like I just gave her the best present imaginable. I love the way the gold flakes in her green eyes sparkle and her lips pull into a wide grin, even when she's trying to fight it.

"Tell me about your round today," she prompts, turning her body toward me and grabbing my hand. I appreciate that she cares enough to ask me for my thoughts rather than diving into what she thinks I should do differently.

I tell her about how nice it feels to finally be playing well again, though I don't tell her my suspicion that it's due to her being in my life. I wouldn't want to put that kind of pressure on her. I know I'm responsible for my own game, even if the fates seem to be telling me otherwise. Though, to be fair, she just pulls me out of my head. When I stand at the tee box, ready to hit my first shot, I'm focused on my game, but I'm not overly focused on it because the thoughts of Lila are cocooning my mind, keeping the worry and anxiety from spreading too far.

I had a great opening round this morning, and I'm looking forward to the next few days, especially since I get to hang out with Lila each night.

"I'm really excited to get to watch you play tomorrow," Lila says.

"I'm not in your brother's group, so if you want to watch him instead, it's no big deal." I'd been looking forward to having Lila come watch me play, so I was a little disappointed when she had to stay at the hotel and work the last two days, but I also understand how important her job is to her. And, since her brother is playing too, I realized she may not choose to follow my group.

"What if I want to watch you?" she asks.

"I would love it. I just don't want you to feel obligated to."

Lila rubs her thumb over mine, taking a sip of her drink before she says, "I love supporting my brother, but I'm an adult. I can look at my options and make the decision that's best for me and my emotions. You are not responsible for the emotions of others."

"I know, but I feel like us dating has put you in an awkward place, and I'd never want you to feel like you have to choose between us."

"And I don't. The truth is golf is not the *most exciting* thing I've ever watched. So it'll be nice to care about more than one golfer there."

"You never cared how I did before?" I ask, and regret the words as soon as they leave my mouth. Of course she didn't.

She raises a black eyebrow. "Are we talking about our past now, JT?"

"Um, yes? I forgot to add it to the agenda for the evening but—" I stop, a text message from Sam coming through to remind me to head to our dinner reservations. "Oh, shoot. We need to head to dinner. Our reservations are in two minutes."

"Dang. I need to get myself a PA. I would never be late for anything again."

I signal for the bartender to bring me our check and chuckle at Lila. "You don't really have a tardiness issue right now. You're always early to work."

"I don't like being late. Plus, that's when I was trying to escape the tension in the house. Now that I've got a reason to stick around..." She trails off.

"What?" I ask, before signing the check and grabbing her hand to walk across the casino to the restaurant.

"I just realized I don't know where you're going to be after this weekend. I mean, I logically knew you were only in Wild Bluffs until after this weekend, but I guess it never really clicked that you likely wouldn't be with me in Wild Bluffs. It sounds stupid when I say it like that."

We arrive at the hostess stand just as Lila finishes her thought, and I follow the two women, both dressed in head-to-toe black—though in very different levels of sexiness—to the table in the back of the restaurant. Lila slides into her seat gracefully and immediately opens her menu to begin scanning it. I think she's trying to hide her face from my sight, but the thing is, I've also put zero thought into where I'm going after this. Back to my house in California, I guess. I'd always planned on going home after this weekend, but now that house no longer feels like home to me. The corner room in Jameo's house feels like home.

"I don't have plans for after this weekend. I...I just assumed I would be flying home with you, Jameo, and Bryn. But"—I search the ceiling as if the answers might be written up there—"I didn't put any thought into it. Sam might've worked with Cathy to figure it out so you all are using Jameo's plane instead of mine." My heart is beating too quickly, and my palms are sweaty as I hold on to my menu like it has the solution I need written in it.

"It's okay, JT," Lila says.

"Yeah. Of course. It's not a problem. I just don't know if we'll be living in the same place or across the country from each other, but it's okay. I'm sure it'll be okay."

I feel Lila place her hand on my leg and realize it's been bouncing up and down too.

"JT, look at me," she says, her voice a soothing tone I've never heard before. I force my eyes to hers, but the guilt continues to gnaw at my stomach. How are we supposed to do this when I'm gone all the time for work, and even when I'm home I'm in a different state? I wasn't sure I could do this before, what could possibly make me think I could do a long-distance relationship as my first one?

She chuckles a little. "Did you not realize when you asked me to date you that your house is in California?" I know she's trying to lighten the mood, but I'm spiraling here, and while I know how ridiculous it sounds, no, I did not put those pieces of information I knew together in such a way.

"No," I say. "Somehow, I managed to remain ignorant of that fact."

She grabs my hand, trying to stop it from the up-down, up-down, up-down motion it's been making on the side of my water glass.

The waitress approaches, but Lila quickly sends her away, asking for more time.

"JT, look at me," she says, and I force my eyes to hers.

"You may not have realized this, but I did. I understand you live in California. I understand I live in Colorado. While it's not ideal, we'll figure it out. Maybe once I get this proposal submitted, I can talk to Kelsey about working remotely a couple of Mondays and Tuesdays so I can come and stay in California with you when you are between tournaments. I was thinking, if it works for you, that when you have longer breaks or are taking a week off, you might come out and stay in Wild Bluffs. I'll have my own house here soon, so you could stay with me. Or in a hotel. Or with Jameo—whatever you prefer."

She's...thought about it. She's been working on finding solutions to our problem before I even realized there was a problem. Fuck, I do not deserve her, and this just serves as a reminder that I have no clue what

I'm doing as a boyfriend. I should've been planning and working on this too. I should've had the answers. Hell, I'm a professional athlete with a private plane at my disposal. This isn't brain surgery. I just had to put one ounce of thought into it. I'm surprised she's not gathering her things and walking out on me right now.

"JT," she says in a way that makes me think it's not the first time. Shit. I really zoned out there.

"I think we can do it."

"What?"

"I think we can make long-distance work. I mean"—I can see the uncertainty flash across her face—"if you still want to make it work."

"Of course I do, Lila. I'm just worried I'm going to let you down."

"You probably are. And I'm going to let you down too. And we'll both feel shitty about it, but we'll try to do better the next day. That's how relationships work."

I know she's right, but it also feels like she doesn't understand how quickly people's dreams can go to hell when they hitch their wagon to mine. Maybe I should have her talk to my mom. I know Lila's trying really hard to pull me out of this funk, so for her sake, I will try to believe this is something I can do.

Fortunately, the waitress returns to take our order, and I use the time to regain my composure.

Lila smirks at me as the waitress leaves. "It's like you've learned nothing from the romance books I assigned you."

"Wait, are you telling me you've been brainwashing me into becoming a good boyfriend with your romance book recommendations?" I ask. "Damn, that's a long con, Lila. We couldn't even stand to be in the same room when you dared me to read those."

"I'm always two steps ahead of you, JT. Just remember that. And I'm not afraid to make you suffer by any means necessary if you don't meet the book boyfriend requirements. Punishments such as wearing skimpy clothing when we're around my family."

"Like at Thanksgiving?" I ask.

"Well, I think we can both agree you deserved that."

"What do you..." I trail off as a memory of the other night comes back.

"What do you mean?" I ask. "I thought we were on the same page that we were going to go back to not getting along after that night."

"Yeah. You're right. We did agree on that." She starts fiddling with her straw wrapper, curling it around and around her finger.

"Lila?" I ask. "What are you not telling me?"

"It's just—and it's so stupid now, so not even worth talking about—"

I halt her fingers from wrapping the straw wrapper again as I raise my eyebrows. "Tell me," I'm almost begging at this point.

"I'm not sure if you saw it or not—Elise is sure you didn't—but before I went back to my room, I left a note in my spot asking you to get breakfast the next morning."

"I didn't see it, Lila," I say, my heart dropping in my chest, knowing she spent the past year thinking I'd stood her up the morning after we hooked up.

"Right." Her shoulders rise as she takes a deep breath. "It's just that when I asked you about it Sunday morning at breakfast with Jameo and Bryn, you said, 'You've been around long enough to know what happened, Lila. I'm not proud of it, but it is how it is.'"

My mind is frantically trying to catch up. I have absolutely no idea what Lila is talking about. I know for certain that I never saw her note. I'm not saying I would've gone to breakfast, even though I woke up the next morning and was shocked by how sad the cold, empty spot next to me made me feel, but I at least wouldn't have ghosted her.

"I didn't get the note, Lila. I would've at least texted."

"Okay," she says, but I can tell she still doesn't believe me. "But then why would you have said that when I asked you about it?"

"I truly have no idea. I don't remember—" The morning in question comes flashing back into my mind. I was simultaneously excited that my game was going well and worried as hell Lila was going to say something that would clue Jameo into the fact that we'd hooked up Friday night. My game Saturday had been almost perfect, except for my tee shot off of hole one, which I had shanked because I thought I saw Lila in the crowd watching me. It turned out to be another woman with similar hair, but the surprise had been enough to pull me from my game.

"—I thought you were asking me about my shanked drive off of number one tee box."

"What?"

"It was possibly the worst drive of my life. I barely made contact with the ball. My parents both called about it, and I was so embarrassed by it. I definitely didn't want to talk about it with you. I thought you were bringing it up to make fun of me."

"Well"—she thinks about her response—"does it make me a bad person that I feel better about that? Like, I don't love I've been so unkind to you that you assumed I was going to try to make you feel bad about yourself, but I'm also mostly glad you didn't just ghost me after the best night of sex of my life."

"...until tonight." I smirk at her. "And I promise to get you breakfast in the morning too."

She laughs. "I do love breakfast." She takes a drink of her water before turning serious again. "If we're being honest about our past, I feel like we need to talk about that kiss. The one at the pre-Thanksgiving party."

"Lila, I was 23—"

"I know. And I was 18. I get it now, I do. I just...it really hurt my feelings, is all. I thought you liked me. You kissed me. Then as soon as Wes left me alone, you said, 'Fuck, that was a mistake' and left me there by myself. Anyway, I was really embarrassed that you had to save me from a drunk guy at a party and, obviously, that I was a mistake." She holds her hand up to stop me from cutting in. "*I do get I was too young for you at the time.* I just felt like you needed to know why I was such an asshole to you when we were together after that. You embarrassed me, so I wanted to embarrass you. I wanted you to feel as naïve and silly as I did. I'm sorry."

"You have nothing to be sorry for, Lila. I was the one who messed up that night. You were hot and funny, and my best friend's 18-year-old sister. When I saw that jerk hitting on you and not leaving you alone, the only thought that crossed my mind was 'kiss her, you idiot.' So I did. And then I wanted to do it again. And again. But then

I saw you look at that guy you dated your senior year of high school, and I realized how stupid I was. Of course you didn't want me to kiss you. I was an old perv who just kissed you without even asking. I was jealous and ashamed and, honestly, worried about what would happen if Jameo found out. Our fighting was just as much my fault as it was yours."

"You're not perv amounts older than me."

My mom's comment from earlier about Lila being a child crosses my mind, and I realize I still haven't told my parents Lila is here as more than just my date. *Shit.* They are not going to be pleased I'm distracted at a time like this.

"Not now, but at 18 and 23? It's a bigger age gap then."

"Still not. I wasn't looking at some other guy, I was working up the courage to kiss you again."

"Damn, I guess we've got some lost time to make up for, then, don't we?"

CHAPTER THIRTY-FIVE

LILA

"You're not leaning into me enough," JT says later that night, pulling me closer to him as we walk away from the restaurant and straight toward the elevator.

"I'm not sure we have to commit to that level of reenactment."

"Of the best night of our respective lives? I respectfully disagree."

"When have you ever respectfully disagreed with me? And why in the name of all things holy would you start now?"

"I see your point. It would be particularly inaccurate for this portion of the reenactment anyway. We didn't run into that fucktard Alex until we were closer to the elevators."

"Andrew."

"I said what I said."

I laugh at that. Of course JT knew his name was Andrew. JT's the kind of guy who remembers everyone's names and calls them by it just to make them feel good about themselves.

We reach the elevator bank without running into anyone we know, which I'm sure is a real letdown for JT. He's put a lot of thought into making this as close as he can to our first night without making me go hungry. His PA even called the hotel to request he be put in the exact same room as last time. He told me we had to "save ourselves" for tonight. Whatever that means. Whatever it is, it didn't stop us from hooking up in the room a couple of times since arriving yesterday. Sometimes it's hard to remember JT hasn't been in a real relationship in a long time, but then there are times like tonight when it's clear he's outside of his comfort zone: He put in waaay more thought than was necessary for drinks and dinner.

I take in a deep breath as we wait for the elevator to arrive, laughing when I realize that was exactly what I'd done the first time too. Instead of kissing me to piss off Andrew, though, this time JT rests his chin on my head and says, "I'm sorry about dinner."

"Why?" I ask.

"It really got off track. I was hoping for a fun night where we argue a bit before coming back to our room and fucking like there is no tomorrow. I didn't mean to bring up such heavy topics."

"I'm glad you did. You can always talk to me about those things, and you *should* talk to me about it when it involves us. That's what it means to be in a relationship with someone. We help each other carry our baggage."

"You know, Kelsey gave me that same speech to convince me to tell her about my feelings for you, and I'm pretty sure she just made my baggage heavier. Like she added rocks to it or something."

"Really?"

He seems to consider it, and as we reach our floor, I feel him shake his head. "Damn it. No. I feel lighter than I have in a really long time. Shit. Don't tell Kelsey she was right."

"I would *never*," I say as I pull him out of the elevator, stopping just outside the doors.

"You're going to text her the minute you're alone, aren't you?"

"The whole group chat."

"She'll never let me live it down," he says before capturing my lips with his. JT slides his hands down my legs, stopping the movement when he reaches the hem of my dress. He slips his hands back up, under the fabric this time, but seems to stop himself, moving them slightly lower before picking me up. I wrap my legs around his waist, conscious of the fact that my dress is not covering everything that should be covered.

"Fuck," he says, pretending to be upset. "No one else gets to see that. Come on. You and your sexy little dress need to be in our room now before we give the whole floor a show."

I laugh as he drops me to my feet before grabbing my hand and yanking me down the hallway, his long strides eating up the space between us and our hotel room. He slides the key card out of his back pocket and slows down just enough to scan it before he shoves into the room.

Just like before, he wastes no time in spinning around and trapping me against the door. Except this time, instead of promising to forever be annoyed by me, he says, "I think I'm falling for you, Lila. I don't know what next week will bring, but I want to be with you."

If I wasn't sure before that I was falling in love with JT Johnson, that right there would have done it. I know I can't rush him, and I need to give him time to deal with all these new feelings and experiences, but he has burrowed his way into my heart, and I never want to let him go. Based on the way my body reacts to his statement, I'm not sure I could let him go even if I wanted to.

"Me too, JT. I'm falling for you too," I say before standing on my tiptoes so I can press my mouth to his. His lips meet mine in a fiery collision, stoking the warmth in my heart into a blazing inferno that burns through me, body and soul. He moves his hands down my waist, coming to rest on my butt, gently stroking and squeezing before slowly moving his attention between my parted legs. He strokes the wet spot on my black lace underwear with two fingers, and it rackets up my heart rate, making it pound so loudly in my ears, I can barely hear.

He pushes the fabric to the side, pinching slightly before rubbing his fingers back and forth through my slick. As I start to move my hips, seeking the friction I'm desperate for, I cup his erection, making him release a little hiss. With his free hand, JT pushes a strand of hair out of my eyes and whispers, "You are so beautiful, Lila. You make me want to give you the entire world. I cannot believe how lucky I am." He shoves two fingers inside me, the rough thrust in direct contrast to the sweet words, and I almost lose myself to this man. I'm gasping for air and trembling. I've completely abandoned his erection in its time of need, forced to hold on to his shoulders with both hands or risk losing the ability to stand. I feel like I'm going insane. He adds a third finger, curling them all at the same time, and I moan loudly.

"Talk to me," he commands. "Tell me what you need."

I can barely form coherent thoughts, so I let out whatever wants to tumble from my mouth. "You. Counter. It's all I can think about. All I've thought about since it happened."

"Fuck," he says, adding his thumb to run circles around my clit. "You are so goddamn perfect." His voice is reverent, his fingers magical. "But no. I've also been thinking about that counter since October, and there is no way I'm going to be quick about it, which means you need to come before we move there."

He sucks the skin along my collarbone as he presses down on my clit, and my world goes dark before exploding into a wild mass of fireworks. As if there is a sound barrier between us, I hear JT let out a muted "fuuuck."

"That was the sexiest fucking thing I've ever experienced," he says to me, his warm breath caressing the outside of my ear. We're both breathing hard, and, as he leans over me, his arms bracing against the door, I can see the visual evidence of just how much JT wants what is coming next. I slide my hands down my dress, pulling it off and throwing it on the floor before doing the same with my now soaking underwear. JT watches me with hooded eyes, his arms never breaking the cage they have me in.

"Your turn," I say as I drop to my knees and unbuckle his pants. He's still fully dressed, including a long-sleeved button-down shirt that hugs his chest and brings out the blue in his eyes. How he brought me that much pleasure without even removing an article of clothing is beyond me. As I work on his pants, JT peels his shirt off before stepping out of his shoes, slacks, and briefs all in one smooth motion.

I offer him a sweet smile before cupping his balls and licking up the underside of his cock. His thigh clenches beneath my fingers, and I keep my pace slow, loving on the tip of his dick with my tongue while massaging his balls with my hand. His patience doesn't last long, and soon his hands are tangled in the hair on the crown of my head, his hips pistoning himself into my mouth. I add my hand to his shaft, increasing the friction, since I can't take him all the way to the back of my throat each time. He shoves past my lips, and I gag around him. A feral groan escapes him, his hips moving at a brutal pace.

As he continues to pound into my mouth, I look up at him, taking in the view from down here. The ridges of his abs flex and bend as he moves his hips, his shoulders bunching tighter and tighter as he reaches ever closer to his orgasm. His breathing is ragged, and I'm having a hard time keeping up with his brutal pace. My perusal of his body reaches his face, and I realize his eyes are locked on mine, the usual blue of his irises fully taken over by the midnight black of his blown pupils. He closes his eyes before opening them again, his gaze taking too long to focus as if he's drunk.

"I need...more," he says, and in response, I suck in my cheeks, pulling slightly on his balls as I increase the pressure on his cock.

JT explodes into my mouth, and I swallow, doing my best to keep up with his release. He lets go of my hair and uses his thumb to wipe the overflow running from the corners of my mouth, and I slowly pull off him, trailing a line of kisses down his dick as I go.

"Shit, that was good."

"Get it together, old man," I say. "You promised me counter sex."

"I'm not that old," JT says as he helps me off the floor, lifting me up so I can wrap my legs around his waist.

"Prove it," I taunt as my ass hits the cold marble countertop next to the sink. The main lights in the bathroom are off, with the two little ones along the floor keeping us from being in a pitch-black room. There's a huge mirror behind me, but a small makeup one is behind JT, so I can see every inch of him while he can see each side of me. The countertop is just the right height for him to be inside me while I sit on it. The angle it causes is—fuck—if it's anything like last time, it's going to be perfect.

JT keeps my legs locked around his middle and, after a few quick pumps with his hand, he notches his head at my entrance. "Oh, shit," he says. "I forgot to tell you. I got tested last week while I was gone like you asked. Totally clean."

"Some people just have all the luck," I joke.

"I wrapped that shit up, Lila. One hundred percent of the time."

"Well, don't let me get in the way of your perfect record. I'm more than happy to use a condom if that's what you'd prefer. I just figured, since I am on the pill, that if you were clean—"

JT cuts me off by shoving inside of me and bottoming out. I scream, the pain of his unexpected thrust quickly morphing into pure pleasure. "Fuck," I pant as JT puts his physical stamina to good use. I take in his face, his five o'clock shadow, the curl behind his right ear that never seems to want to go the same direction as the rest of them, and my heart starts beating to a fully different rhythm. It's not just the joining of our bodies, but the joining of us at a molecular level.

I moan as JT continues to rock in and out of me, his hips pistoning with the movements. I wish there was a mirror on the other wall, because the small makeup mirror view of JT's ass as it flexes sure isn't big enough to fully appreciate just how strong it is. I'm unraveling quickly, my second orgasm building at a faster rate than the first. The dazed look is back in JT's eyes, and as I'm barely aware of what's going on around me, I'm sure mine are equally as glassy.

"Yes. Right there," I moan out as he slides me forward slightly, changing the angle just enough to hit that spot on my inner wall that makes me want to shatter into a million pieces. His pace increases and I claw at his back, trying anything to keep from breaking before him. "That's it. Don't stop," I say as he groans.

"I'm gunna...I'm..." His eyes lock on mine, his thumb finding my clit with just the right pressure to send me over the edge. He follows me into oblivion, his body shaking around me from the power of it.

One round later, I fall asleep with my head on his chest, happier than I've ever been.

Chapter Thirty-Six

JT

"Damn, you clean up nice," Lila says as she steps out of the bathroom in our room Saturday night. I'm standing in front of the full-length mirror, trying to get my bow tie to straighten out. I look in the mirror to find her reflection over my shoulder, her body wrapped in a bright red dress, somehow looking both classic and sinful at the same time.

Jameson and Bryn are already at the large event space in the Everlight—the hotel the Ferguson brothers just purchased and renovated on the Strip. They coupled the tournament and event with the grand opening. As sci-fi as the name sounds, it's supposed to be incredibly classic in its designs, like you're in an old library or smoking room. All the tournament players were offered the chance to be the first to stay there, but I wasn't willing to pass up the opportunity to relive my and Lila's first time together. Damn did it pay off.

Though, after our amazing night, Lila fell asleep and my mind continued to spin, haunted by the fact that I went the entire night without thinking about my game once. My parents have been relentless, calling and texting reminders about how important it is for me to win this tournament with its large purse. Despite playing well enough to be in the hunt, I'm terrified I'm going to fail them again. I also never seemed to find the right moment to tell them about Lila.

Lila and I walk into the event space thirty minutes later, and I'm overwhelmed by the size and grandeur of the event. There are people in black ties and formal dresses carrying flutes of champagne and tumblers of hard alcohol. There is not one shiny beer can in sight, and if that doesn't scream fancy, I don't know what does. It's clear the invite list has expanded to include a wealthier group, even though, as I start to look closer, I can spot the program directors and parents of the junior players or the recreational golfers who participate in the youth programs. I'm glad the Fergusons made it black-tie optional, though I know I would've felt out of place at an event like this when I was first playing. Hopefully it didn't scare any players or their families off.

As we make our way further into the grand ballroom, I hear Lila's name being called. Bryn is headed our way, her hair pulled into a sleek ponytail. She looks great in a long-sleeved black dress. It's nothing compared to how delectable Lila looks, but that's probably for the best, since she's dating my best friend.

"Hey, Bryn," I say, giving her a one-armed hug while keeping hold of Lila's hand.

Bryn points me in the direction of the bar, where Jameson is already holed up, looking like an advertisement for an expensive cologne. I tell him as much when I join him there moments later, and he falls into a formal commercial pose. Sometimes I forget the man actually does rep a whiskey brand—though surprisingly not Jameson.

"Are your parents here yet?" he asks me.

I take in the space around me. The low lighting and the dark wood finishes make everything seem prestigious. The bar has an old speakeasy feel to it with what I can only assume are hand-carved accents along the sides. Rather than high-top tables around the room to mingle at, there are little alcoves set up complete with deep leather chairs and couches. I don't see my parents, but they could be anywhere, blending in with the other black-clad people.

"Not yet, I don't think. Though I'm sure they'll be glued to my side as soon as they arrive. Probably will send me to bed at eight thirty with a glass of warm milk, so I get a good night's sleep before the final round tomorrow."

"Yeah, Lila told me your parents were really pushing this one."

"I don't love that you guys talk about me."

"I don't love that you guys are doing it in my guest room, but such is life."

When the girls' drinks are placed in front of us, we make our way to where the women have staked a claim to one of the couches. Just as I hand Lila her drink, I spot my parents walking in. "Oh, there are my parents," I say. "I'm going to go say hello."

"I'll come too," Lila says.

"I've got it. No worries. You can stay here and keep chatting with Bryn," I say, not wanting to break the news to my parents that we are dating with Lila standing right there. I know I should've told them one of the one hundred times I've talked to them, but it never seemed to be the right time. I want them to be happy I found someone as amazing as Lila, but I doubt that will be the case. They're going to see her as a distraction I can't afford.

"Oh. Sure," she says with a forced smile, and I feel guilty for putting this off. Now it seems like I'm ashamed of her, which is as far from the truth as possible. I just don't want to have to deal with my parents' reactions to the fact I'm dating.

Knowing I can't put it off any longer without risking Lila finding out, I make my way to the bar in the far corner of the room where my parents are ordering drinks.

"Hi, Mom. Dad," I say, giving my mother a quick peck on her cheek before shaking my father's hand.

"JT. How are you?" my mother asks.

"Your hips are moving through your swing slightly too early," my dad says in greeting.

"Okay," I say in answer to both the question and the critique. "Though, before we start making the rounds, I was hoping to tell you both something." I look around, trying to find a private area to have the conversation. "Can we step out into the hall for a minute?"

I don't miss the skeptical look my parents share before nodding in agreement and following me through the heavy doors into the corridor outside the event space.

"What's going on, JT?" my dad asks.

"I need to tell you both something. Something I'm really excited about."

"Oh, honey, did you finally put together enough money to get us the cash we've been asking for?" my mother cuts in.

"No." I shake my head. "It's not about my finances."

My mother's face drops at the news, and for some unknown reason, tears start to form in her eyes.

"I'm dating Lila Walker."

"You're what?" my dad asks.

"Dating Jameo's sister, Lila. We both ended up in Wild Bluffs this summer, and yeah. We're dating now. I'm really happy about it."

"You know this is the worst possible time for you to be distracting yourself, don't you?" my dad asks, just as I expected.

"Dad," I say.

"How can you be so selfish, JT?" my mom asks.

"What do you mean?"

"You know we need you to be focused on your game. We need you to bring in additional money."

"I know you have a great investment set up, but worst-case scenario, if I don't win this tournament, we'll just press pause on it. I'm sure you can find another opportunity later this year that will be just as beneficial. It's not a big deal."

My mom's eyes are wide, the white scar under her eye standing out prominently against the flush of her cheeks. She looks like she just finished a race against an axe murderer.

"Not a big deal?" she asks.

"Yeah, I'll be back to my usual earnings soon."

"Soon won't work," she croaks, a noise that is so unlike her normal elegance, I can't help but stare at her in shock.

"Why?" I ask.

"Why?" Her voice is now an octave above where it falls. "Why?!"

My dad is shaking his head at my mom, trying to tell her something, but she's not listening.

"Because we *need* the money now. Because we must start paying our construction crews, and the bank won't loan us any more money. Because *your father* is terrible at making investments. Because we lost everything on a deal *your father* thought was a sure thing."

What? They're broke? How could they possibly lose all their money? I pay them a healthy management fee, and I fund most of their extravagant lifestyle out of my portfolio. Shit. Am I broke too?

"Don't you blame this all on me," my father cuts in. "I'm not the one who spent millions of dollars we don't have renovating a house we are already underwater on. I'm not the one who invested in her friend's fashion line that folded within two months. I'm not the one who—"

"Enough," I say, loudly enough to cut him off. "How could you possibly be broke?"

"Bad investments," my mom says, glaring at my father.

"Extravagant spending," my dad shoots back.

"Okay." I wish I had my hat on right now. I'm not sure what to do with my hands. How the fuck could they lose all their money? How is it even possible that I'm standing here in a black tie having a conversation about not being able to pay workers who have *already completed the work*? I'm so mad, I can barely think straight, but, as I look into my mom's tear-streaked face, watching the mascara flow over her scar, I know I'm going to help them out of this mess, in whatever way I need to.

"What about my money?" I ask.

"It's there," my dad says.

My mom glares at him. "Tell him the truth."

"It *is* there."

"The real truth."

My dad sighs, looking anywhere but at me. "Well, anything that was tied up in longer-term investments is there. Your pain-in-the-ass PA has called me about seven times this month about the losses in your portfolio. We've had a couple of large business loans come due this year, and I've needed some cash freed up to pay them. I've been borrowing money from your accounts to keep us afloat for a few months now, but it's no longer enough."

"A few months?!" I roar. This isn't some bad luck, poor timing, type of thing. They've known about this. They decided to renovate their house knowing they didn't have the money to do it.

"Shhh," my mother shushes me, and beneath my anger, I feel guilty. How had I become so distracted that I didn't even notice the funds missing from my account or my parents losing all their money?

"We understand this isn't ideal, but we've always been a team. Seven million dollars will cover the repairs as well as the business loans that are due. If you win this tournament, you'll take home close to ten after taxes. We gave up our dreams, ones that would've earned us far more money than where we are now, to help you chase yours," my father says, his voice defiant. "I'm sure you understand how hard it is to maintain our lifestyle on the pennies we make managing your money."

"Live a less extravagant lifestyle," I suggest.

"And have everyone think we're poor wealth managers?" my mom asks.

"You *are* poor wealth managers," I hiss.

My dad holds up his hands in a placating gesture. "We're wealth managers because we had no other options after I gave up my pursuit of professional golfing to give that dream to you. Managing our child's money was the only option we had. Did you want your mom to continue working the night shift, cleaning offices her entire life? Please, JT. The earnings from this tournament will more than cover our debt. One win and we can all forget this ever happened. Let's just focus on your game."

Inside, we hear the sound of people being called to their seats, and before I can respond, the doors open, a waiter stepping out to ask us to find our table.

I'm in a fog as I introduce my parents to Lila and Bryn and as I listen to Conrad Ferguson talk about his firm's work. My mom keeps shooting me concerned glances, all of which I ignore. My father, on the other hand, is using his proximity to Jameson to pitch their wealth-management services. I want to yell, to tell Jameo to run away fast, but instead, I sit there in silence, unable to comprehend how it came to this. As mad as I am, all I can think about is how much I owe my parents and how I'll do whatever it takes to help them out, just like they did when I was trying to become a professional golfer.

As the speaking portion of the event comes to an end, I clap along with the rest of the guests, trying to clear my head. "I should head out," I say, forcing cheer into my voice. I turn to look down at Lila. Her smiling face makes my guts twist uncomfortably, the sight of it reminding me of how selfish I've been, focusing on my enjoyment instead of winning like my parents asked.

"You should stay here and have fun," I tell her. "Don't let me ruin your night."

"Don't be silly," she says. "Of course I'm coming with you."

I nod, offering a quick goodbye to the table before making my way toward the door. Lila trails after me, blessedly silent, before climbing into the car waiting for us at the hotel entrance.

Lila tries to say something to me once we're slowly creeping down the Strip to our hotel, but I'm spiraling, unable to stop the memories of the tears running down my mother's face, the sound of my father's voice telling me their money is gone, following their dreams into a world where they can never return. The guilt of my parents' sacrifice smothers me, overshadowing everything.

I have to win tomorrow.

CHAPTER THIRTY-SEVEN

LILA

"THE WEATHER IS GOING to be great for your round today," I say the next morning, looking at my weather app to see what the weather will be like when he tees off at 1:13 p.m. today.

JT grunts a response yet again, and as sad as his lack of conversation makes me, I'm not surprised. JT was a zombie last night, all one-word answers and head nods. As he turned his back to me, curled up on his side, and went to sleep, I'd wanted to lash out, to demand his attention, but I knew I couldn't. Because I knew his secret, even if he didn't trust me enough to tell me himself.

Annoyed JT hadn't taken me with him to meet his parents when they first arrived last night, I'd huffily headed to the bathroom after he abandoned me with Bryn and Jameo. On my way back, I'd heard JT's voice and had taken a detour, following the sound to a back hallway. I stopped against the wall just before the corner, able to hear everything without them seeing me.

Knowing I should leave but too intrigued by the argument unfolding between the Johnsons, I stayed, listening to JT's parents confess to spending all their money plus the funds they were able to take from JT as well. At least, that's how I heard it. JT seemed more concerned about getting his parents the money they needed than correcting the injustice done to him.

As their conversation wrapped up, I slipped in a different door to the event space, meeting JT at the table. I tried to ignore the burning in my chest when he introduced me to his parents as Jameo's sister Lila, recognizing it wasn't about me. He's been on autopilot since then, a pleasant smile plastered to his face, but no other sign of life behind his eyes.

"How are your eggs?" I try again.

"Fine," he says before shoveling another forkful into his mouth, his eyes focused on his phone. At least when I ask him about his food he takes a bite of it. I'll just have to figure out how to work it into the conversation about twelve more times. Totally doable.

I'm worried about JT, but I know how important his game is for him today, so I'm doing my best to keep everything positive and lighthearted, knowing I will eventually have to confess to knowing about the situation with JT's parents.

I sigh and then quickly cover my mouth with my hand. Now is not the time to be melancholic over the fact that JT doesn't seem to be inclined to tell me about his family's issues.

JT's knee is bouncing again, the fingers of his right hand circling and circling the stem of his water glass.

"Hey," I say, reaching out and squeezing his fingers. "You're going to do great today."

"Yeah."

"These eggs sure are tasty, right?" I ask, letting go of his fingers so he can take another bite.

"Really good." He scoops up another forkful, and I would find my ability to control his actions highly amusing if I weren't so worried about him. He's not okay.

I manipulate him into eating two-thirds of his breakfast before I give up, and we take the elevator back to our room in silence. I stare at JT in the mirror-covered elevator, taking in the dark circles under his eyes and the downward pull to his lips that is so unfamiliar on his normally sunny face.

Don't say anything, Lila. I'd decided last night it wasn't the time to admit to JT that I overheard his conversation yesterday, but as the morning wears on, I'm genuinely starting to be worried about JT. He's not doing okay, and he's never going to be able to perform like he wants to if he's in this headspace.

As we enter the room, JT bangs his shoulder against the door, and instead of reacting in any normal way, he just keeps moving inside. Okay, maybe waiting to say something isn't the right plan. Shit. Why don't I know what to do here? I'm sure Bryn or Kelsey would, but I can't get their advice without having to admit that I spied on my boyfriend last night. Sure, it was initially an accident, but I intention-ally stood there and listened to their whole conversation, something the Harper sisters would likely find morally repugnant.

Uncertain if it's an appropriate time for an intervention, I decide to ease into it.

"Are you okay?" I ask.

"Mmhmm," he replies, his voice monotone as he sits in the brown chair in the corner, endlessly watching videos his dad has sent him about his game.

Okay, then. You tried. Just drop it.

Except I can't drop it. The man I'm falling in love with is struggling, and I feel like I need to do something to try to make it better.

"Do you want to talk about it?" I ask.

"Nothing to talk about."

"Is everything okay with your parents?"

"Yep."

"JT," I say, exasperation lacing my tone. Is he really going to sit there and lie to me? It's one thing not to tell me everything going on in his life—even though it hurts knowing he doesn't want to share with me—but to have him outright lie to my face? My anger is quickly overpowering my sympathy and my reason.

"You're sure you want to stick with that answer?" I ask, dropping down to sit on the end of the bed across from him.

He doesn't respond, the sound of his father's voice critiquing his form filling the space instead.

"JT!" I yell. Great, I'm yelling now.

"What?" he asks, like he just realized someone is in the room with him.

"Look, I didn't want to do this right now, but you're kinda scaring me. Can you please talk to me about what's going on?"

"Nothing," he lies, his blue eyes meeting mine. They look dull, and my heart aches as I mourn the loss of his normal twinkle.

"That's not true!" I shout. "I know you fought with your parents last night. I know they lost all their money. I know."

"You...know?" he asks, his voice barely rising with the question, so it comes out as a statement instead.

"Yes. I accidentally heard you all talking in the hall. And I'm worried about you, JT. You're not handling it well."

"Oh, really? And you get to decide that, huh?"

I hold up my hands in a placating gesture. "I'm just worried about you. You're...despondent."

His eyes flash at that, and I recognize the signs of JT about to enter battle. As worried as it makes me, I'm also glad to see the flicker of life in him.

"I'm *focused*, Lila. If you listened in on my conversation, which is a real dick move by the way, you know how important today is to me and my parents."

"It was an accident," I defend myself before realizing I'm getting off track. "Look, I'm sorry about invading your privacy, but I'm not sorry I found out. This level of focus is not healthy. You barely touched your food this morning. You ran into the goddamn door and didn't even flinch. You're in your head. You're stressed. That's not conducive for anyone doing their best work."

"And what would you know about it, huh? You've had a job for all of six weeks now. I've been golfing at the highest level for almost a decade. Don't try to tell me how to do my job, Lila. I've been successfully navigating it without you for a long time now."

"I'm just trying to help," I say, and I hate how small my voice is. "Jameo always says he plays worse when he tries too hard. I'm just...trying to help. Trying to support you."

"Well, you're doing a poor job of it." He's leaning forward now, his voice an angry rumble. "And I'm not Jameo. I've carried the guilt of my parents' sacrifice my entire life. I've watched my dad's video commentary, day after day, week after week, year after fucking year since I was nine. It reminds me of all he's done for me. All the hours he's poured into my career and my happiness. Don't act like you know what's best for me."

"Okay. Okay. I'm sorry," I say. "I just wanted you to know I'm here to support you. I can help you."

"Oh, really? Do you have a few million dollars in your purse I can borrow?"

A tear runs down my cheek, and I wipe it away quickly, embarrassed how poorly this has gone.

"No," I say, even though it was a hypothetical question, as we both know I have nowhere near the amount of money he needs to help his parents.

"Well, then, I guess the only thing left you can do to help is to let me focus."

The tears are openly falling down my cheeks as JT turns his attention back to his phone, dismissing me and our conversation. I wipe them with the hem of my shirt as I stand up from the bed and head toward the door.

"I'm going to go get some coffee," I say, though, as expected, JT doesn't respond.

I slide to the floor as soon as the door to our room closes, pulling my knees to my chest as I cry. Knowing it's my fault for pushing when I shouldn't have, but not knowing what I should've done better.

CHAPTER THIRTY-EIGHT

JT

I LOST. I PLACED so low, I didn't even make enough to cover the cost of being here—it's not cheap flying private, staying in a hotel for five days, or paying my caddie.

I let my parents down because I couldn't hit the damn ball straight to save my life—or my parents' life, I suppose.

I'm back in my hotel room, our flight scheduled for tomorrow in the hope we would be celebrating tonight.

"Do you want me to see if Jameo and Bryn want to change the flight to tonight?" Lila asks. It's the first time we've communicated since I got back to the room after the round. Since our fight this morning, really. We've been sitting in silence since I walked in three minutes ago, and the sight of Lila made my heart race with a joy I knew I couldn't let myself feel.

She *knew* how important it was for me to play well today, and yet she chose this morning to pick a fight with me about my parents. Of course I was off my game after having a major fight with my girlfriend. The more I think about it, the more I realize my parents have been right about dating all along. It is a distraction I can't afford. I know she didn't mean to throw me off my game. I know she likely had the best intentions at heart, but I also know the unfortunate truth of the situation is that I can't let another tournament like today happen. Which might mean I need to let Lila go. She can find a boyfriend who will be around and focused on her, and I can spend my time helping my parents get what they need.

"Doesn't matter" is my only contribution to the conversation. Realizing I can't be with Lila feels like someone is slowly constricting my airways.

"Hey, are you okay?" she asks.

"What? Yeah. Sure." I stand up, staring blankly at my closet.

She stands up too, wrapping her arms around me from behind. "I'm proud of you. I know today didn't go the way you wanted, but it will all be okay. No one can win every tournament."

Of course she would say that. She's sweet and caring and—distracting me from what I need to do again. "Yeah. Sure," I say, my posture rigid, trying not to let myself fall into her warm embrace. I know I need to use this motivation to end this now, before we get in too deep. Before I hurt her more than I'm going to.

"Look, Lila," I say, turning around and stepping out of her arms. "I don't think this is a good idea."

Confusion flicks across her features. "What do you mean?"

"I clearly hadn't thought through what it meant for us to be together for longer than the time we had agreed upon, and now that I have, I don't think it's a good idea."

Her facial expression flashes between hurt and anger, and she takes a step back, crossing her arms in a way that is half defiance, half defeat.

"You're breaking up with me? Why?" she asks, her voice barely above a whisper.

I can see how much this is hurting her, and it takes all of my self-control not to go over to her and hug her.

"This just isn't a good idea."

"But…"—her lower lip quivers, and I can feel my heart collapsing in on itself as tears pool in her eyes—"but I think I love you."

"I…I can't be in a relationship right now, Lila. You saw what happened this morning. We fought, and my game completely fell apart."

"Wait, you're blaming me?" She wipes at her eyes, smearing her makeup as she does.

"No. But at the same time, I can't deny the facts sitting in front of me. I have to focus on my game, and you demand my attention. As you *should* with someone you're in a relationship with. It just can't be me."

"You played well in the rest of the tournaments this summer. I was around then."

"Yeah." I sigh. "I thought you might be my good-luck charm there for a minute, but this morning…I can't have that kind of distraction. You should've known I can't have that kind of distraction."

Her face crumples. "That's not fair, JT. You were suffering. I just wanted to talk to you. To be there for you. To *help* you."

"I can't do it, Lila." I throw my clothes into my bag, Lila standing there, silently crying as she watches me pack.

"You can!" she all but yells, the fire in her calling to me. "You just don't want to. At least have the courage to tell me the truth. You just don't want to put in the effort to make us work."

"Sure," I say, because it's what she needs to hear. It's the guy I need to be to make her see that I can't be her HEA.

I grab my toothbrush and bathroom bag and put it in my bag before zipping the whole thing up.

"At least now you can go back to hating me. It'll make everything far less complicated for everyone."

"I don't want to hate you! Don't you understand? I loved you when I was 14 and you were the only one of Jameo's friends who would spend time with me. I loved you at 18 when you kissed me for the first time. I loved you at 21 when I realized you would never feel the same way about me, and I love you now, even as you're ripping my heart out."

A montage of our time together plays before my eyes, every scene changing as I'm given a new perspective of our history together. One that, if I were someone else, might actually turn into a happily ever after. But unfortunately, I can't turn back from my path. My parents need me, and I can't let their comfortable lives be another thing they end up sacrificing because they decided to help me chase my dream.

I can't look at Lila as I prepare to leave. Her fire is slowly draining away from her, and I know it's all my fault. But hopefully, with time, she'll get it back. She'll find it again with someone else.

"I can't be the guy you need, Lila, but I hope you find him."

"JT, don't. Please." The final word comes out as a whisper, the plea of someone about to have everything taken from them, and it guts me. "Please don't leave."

"I'll get Sam to coordinate shipping my stuff in Wild Bluffs back to me," I say, bags in hand as I force myself to walk out the door. "Bye, Lila."

I hear the door swing closed, and I pause, realizing I can hear Lila's sobs out in the hall. I force my legs to move me away from our room and the temptation I have to run back to her and beg her for forgiveness. I promise myself that this is the last time that I will hurt her.

I need another room for tonight, and fast, so even though it's late in New York, I call Sam.

"What's up, boss?"

"I need a new room for tonight."

"Okaaay. What happened to your old one?"

"Lila's staying there tonight. I need somewhere else to go. Preferably in a different hotel and under one of my aliases that Jameson doesn't know I use." I know Jameson is going to have some thoughts about what went down with his sister tonight, but I need to get my head on straight before I'm ready to deal with that. This is exactly why I should've never allowed myself to acknowledge the feelings I had for Lila. I knew I would end up losing my best friend as well as the only thing close to a loving family that I ever had.

"Do you want to talk about it?" Sam asks.

"No," I snap, and thankfully he leaves it at that.

"Okay, I've got you a room at the hotel across the street. I'll text you the booking information."

"Thanks. Can you do one last thing for me?"

"Of course."

"Can you put Jameo and Bryn's names on my current room with Lila? She shouldn't be alone tonight."

"Are you sure they're the ones who should be with her?"

"Unfortunately, yes."

There is a long pause, and I'm not sure if Sam is going to call me out on my bullshit or not. He must sense the defeat in my tone, though, because he simply says, "Okay, consider it done."

With that, I hang up and quickly send Jameson what will likely be the last ever civil message between us.

Me

I ended things with Lila tonight. I'm really sorry. Don't worry, I know this means we can't be friends anymore. I won't make it awkward. She's in room 65890. I had Sam add you and Bryn to the room so you can get a keycard to go up. I think she could probably use a friend.

Jameson

Are you fucking kidding me? How about you go be that friend? And fuck you. We're still friends.

Jameson

Really? You're not even going to text me back?

Jameson

Answer your phone, JT.

Jameson

Don't run away from this thing. You're going to regret it.

Jameson

We are with her now. What the fuck, man? Come back and make this right.

Jameson

You made the wrong call. This isn't how you make her happy. Fight for her.

The next day...

Lila

It really sucks what you said to me last night. It was a total dick move, but it also wasn't you. Can you please answer my calls? I want to talk to you.

Three days later...

Jameson

What the fuck is wrong with you?

Four days later...

Jameson

Really? You're going to fucking avoid me at tournaments now too?

Jameson

You're a dick.

Jameson

If you'd stop running the other direction when I am around, I would tell you that I'm pissed at you, but it doesn't mean we're not friends.

Five days later...

Jameson

Are you okay? Please call me. Or talk to me at the tournament this weekend.

Three weeks later...

Unknown Number

What is wrong with you? You need to pull your head out and come back to Wild Bluffs. Fight for the girl who makes you happy. This is me firmly putting the weight of your problems back on you. Don't be the guy who runs away when things get hard. It's cliche, it's stupid, and it's beneath you. Deal with your goddamn problems and then come back for her. And just to be clear, I'm saying this because you were supposed to be my friend, not because I'm getting involved in the life of my employee.

CHAPTER THIRTY-NINE

LILA

"So what's it like to have a professional golfer for a brother?" my date asks, leaning back in his chair and picking at his teeth with the toothpick he pulled out of his wallet. We just finished our pizza, and this is the first question he's asked me about myself since we got here. Though, to be fair, I was happy to zone out while he went on and on about his new pickup truck, including but not limited to how much it cost, what upgrades he bought it with versus what he installed himself, and how often he cleans it. I tried to steer the conversation away a couple of times, but he was not having it. Apparently, it's the world's cleanest vehicle, and I *need* to know all about it.

I'm not sure why I said yes when Caleb asked me out last week. I was out at Wild Brews with the Harper sisters and Becca, and he'd come over out of the blue and asked me out. I noticed the subtle headshakes from Izzy and Bryn, but I couldn't think of a good reason to say no. JT has made it really clear last month he doesn't want anything to do with me, so what am I to do? Sit around and wait for someone who bailed? I think not. Though, to be fair, it was a huge mistake on my part to bring up his family issues. If I had just handled that conversation better—or not at all—maybe I'd be sitting with JT on our couch right now, cuddled up and reading spicy lines from a book.

"It's a lot like having a brother who isn't a professional golfer, I guess." I shrug. "I watch him golf a lot more than most sisters probably watch their adult brothers play sports, but other than that, we have a fairly typical sibling relationship."

"So you don't think he'll be stopping by here anytime soon?" Caleb asks, sending what has to be his seventy-fifth text of the night.

"On our date?"

"Yeah."

"No, I don't think my brother will be stopping by my date to casually say hello."

"That's too bad." Clearly, Caleb isn't a sarcastic person, because he is most certainly not picking up mine.

I fake a yawn, and the waitress brings the bill by, a pitying smile on her face as she looks between me and my date. "Ready to go already?" she asks.

"Yeah. Tonight's kinda a bit of a bust anyway," Caleb says. And while I wasn't planning on ever going out with him again, it hurts to hear him put it like that. Though I suppose he's just upset that my famous brother didn't come by to say hi.

Caleb looks at the total and throws a twenty and some odd cash on the table before casually sliding the bill toward me. "You don't mind splitting, do you? Your brother is a professional golfer, after all. I've seen how much money he makes."

"Right," I say, pulling my credit card out of the wallet that is magnetized to the back of my phone.

Caleb must realize I'm going to have to wait to pay by card, and with another look at his phone, he stands up. "Well, I'm going to take off. See ya around, Lila."

I manage to offer him a small two-fingered wave, even though everything inside of me wants to drop my index finger and just leave the middle one. Unfortunately, I've felt every pair of eyes on us since we got here—small-town dating at its finest. I highly doubt anyone would blame me for the reaction, but that doesn't mean I should be flipping my date the bird in the middle of the restaurant. For all I know, his grandma is at the table behind us.

As I walk out, I see a couple of people I know at the tables. Janice, the queen of gossip, is at a table in the back, and I know word will be out about this disaster of a date before I even get home. But honestly? I'm not even mad. I'm just relieved it's over.

***

"How was the date?" Jameson asks from Bryn's phone where it's propped on my new coffee table in the house I'm renting. Bryn just arrived, bringing phone-screen Jameo with her. The gossip mill hit must have let her know I was done with my date—if we can even call that snoozefest of a dinner a date.

"Horrible," I sigh, burying my face in my hands. "He thought you were going to stop by and was disappointed when you didn't."

"I'd be disappointed too if I thought I was going to see my pretty face and then I got stuck looking at you all night."

"Blech. Caleb is all yours. The two of you can compete to see who is more obsessed with themselves."

"So the dating isn't going well?" Jameo asks.

"Well, I've been on exactly one date and it was horrible, so no. I would say it's not going well."

"Do you still love JT?"

"Jameo!" Bryn yells, turning the phone so he can see her disappointment.

"What?" he asks.

"We aren't talking about you-know-who," she chides.

I roll my eyes. "It's fine. You can talk about JT. I stopped crying whenever someone mentioned his name like three whole days ago." I'm joking—mostly.

"He was in the group before mine today, and while he still wouldn't even look me in the fucking eyes, I could still tell he looks like shit. I'm worried about him."

"Jameo!" Bryn says again. "How is that helping?"

He sighs. "I'm not really trying to help. I'm worried about my friend, and I wanted to see if Lila is okay with me spending time with him again."

"Of course," I say automatically, wanting to beg him to bring me with him when he does, but knowing it's a lost cause. "I thought he was going out of his way to avoid you, though?"

"Yeah. He is. Unfortunately for him, I'm done playing that game. I'm really fucking pissed at the way he treated you, but I do believe *he thinks* he's doing it for the right reason. He's just a fucking idiot."

"Most men are," Bryn says. A snort of laughter breaks through my lips, and it feels so good to finally feel an emotion that isn't sad or angry. Or annoyed, I suppose. I definitely felt annoyed during my date tonight.

"I saw he's going into tomorrow tied for fifth. He's clearly been playing just as well as before." There is a part of me that's sad his game hasn't suffered from our breakup. Not because I want him to do poorly, but because I want him to be as torn up by our breakup as I am. Though, maybe those weeks we spent together were just that—a few weeks. He always meant for it to end; I guess I shouldn't be surprised he's not suffering because our fling followed his anticipated trajectory.

"Have you watched him play?" Bryn asks.

I shake my head. "No. I've just been watching Jameo's highlights at night. I haven't turned on live coverage of an event since Vegas."

"He doesn't look—" Bryn starts, but Jameo cuts her off.

"He looks like he hasn't eaten or slept since Vegas." It's like he knows he's dropping a bomb on me. Because as frustrated as I am with the man, I do still love JT, and hearing that he's suffering is hard, especially when I know I can't fix it. Look at what happened the one time I tried to help him—I failed epically.

I look between the concerned faces of Bryn and my brother and am not sure how to respond. I know Bryn has been sticking around Wild Bluffs at my brother's insistence. They're worried about how I'm handling everything, and Jameo feels bad he can't stay with me. My parents have both called me so much that I'm worried they're going to show up on my doorstep any day now, a Midwestern care package in hand. Kelsey has brought me in on every meeting she's had in the past three weeks, and I know it's her way of helping me keep my mind off things. To be fair, she's not wrong. We are in the final stage of landing this huge client, and I have been staying at the office until ten or eleven most nights, working on figuring out all the proposal schematics I don't understand.

I'm definitely not staying late because I can't sleep without JT next to me, so I have to be dead on my feet to have any chance of dozing off.

"I don't know what to say."

"Have you reached out to him?"

"I let him down, Jameo. JT doesn't want to talk to me. He could barely get out of our room fast enough."

"God, you're both such idiots," Jameo says.

"What do you mean?"

"He cares about you. You know he did. His parents dropped this huge bomb on him and he played poorly—"

"He blamed that on me."

"Like I said, he's an idiot. An idiot who made an irrational decision because he's got the world's largest guilt complex when it comes to his parents...and a blind spot about them equally as large. But then you don't even reach out? Not even one single text to see how things turned out with his parents, or to make sure he got his stuff, or to confirm he's not wasting away into nothing?"

"He ended things with me!" I'm all but yelling now. It's not fair for Jameson to say I'm not handling this the right way. JT did this. "He was the one who wasn't even willing to try. I made a mistake, I wasn't perfect, and he walked out the door. Plus, I don't even really think it was my fault. I mean, come on, his parents dropped a huge bomb on him the night before and yet my tiny little bottle rocket is somehow blamed for the massive explosion?"

Bryn comes over and hugs me, wrapping her arms around my shoulders as I realize I'm crying. Again. Damn it.

I lean into Bryn, accepting her comfort even as I hate myself for how weak I am. I never wanted to be the type of girl who cried over a dumb boy. One of my friends in high school had a pair of socks that said, "Boys are stupid, throw rocks at them" and *that* is the energy I should be bringing to this breakup. Instead, I'm bringing real supporting-character vibes. If I were in a historical romance, they would've had to revive me with smelling salts at least three times by now, and the main character *never* faints.

"I'm sorry, Lila," Jameo says.

I shrug out of Bryn's hug, claiming her phone so I can talk directly to my brother.

"There's nothing for you to be sorry about. I got myself into this mess."

"Yeah, after I tricked you into living with the guy."

I tap my cheek as if I'm considering it. "Hmm, you know? Now that you mention it, this does seem like it's entirely your fault. Heaven knows I would've fallen in love with any guy I ended up sharing a house with for a couple of weeks."

"You're hilarious."

"I'm just saying you shouldn't feel bad about it. Even though it sucks so much right now, I wouldn't change a thing about us getting together. I would change us breaking up, but that's beside the point."

"So, you do still love him?" Jameo asks, coming back to his original question. Bryn rolls her eyes as if to say "How dumb can this man possibly be?" but chooses not to say anything.

"Yeah. Of course I do. You don't fall out of love with someone in three weeks. I'm not sure I'll ever stop loving him. JT is...well, he's JT. But hopefully I can move on from him."

"So when I force him to talk to me, should I try to get him to talk to you?"

"No."

"No?"

"I don't want him to talk to me because my brother forced him to. I want him to talk to me because his heart is telling him he can't go another day without me. Because he realizes losing me is the worst possible outcome—worse than losing one golf tournament. I want him to realize our relationship doesn't make him lose focus—it brings what's important *into* focus." I take a deep breath, feeling more conviction with every word I say. "If he doesn't feel that way, then...I don't want him at all."

Jameo looks at me for a long moment, his brows furrowing. "And what if he's just...scared of letting down his parents? You know how JT is. He feels like he has to pay them back, even to the detriment of his happiness."

I shrug, trying to be nonchalant. "If his guilt about the decisions his *adult* parents made when he was a kid is stronger than what he feels for me, then maybe it was never enough to begin with."

The pain at the thought burrows deep inside my chest, threatening to pull another round of tears from me. "And I'll just have to find some way to move on."

Chapter Forty

Lila

"Where is the final proposal for—" Kelsey stops herself before saying the name of our client in front of Izzy and Becca.

"I'm almost done with it," I say, though I still haven't figured out what I'm supposed to include in two of the images for the client.

"What do you mean? You were supposed to give me the final version yesterday. You've been here late working on it for weeks. It should have taken you two weeks tops. How are you not done?"

"Well, we're just going to go get some coffee," Izzy says as she and Becca both hastily grab their cell phones and head toward the door.

I feel my face turn red, unsure if I'm more mortified by my inability to do my job or my friends seeing me chastised by my boss.

"I'm sorry," I say as the door swings shut behind Izzy.

"I don't need you to be sorry, I need you to explain how it's taking you this long," Kelsey says as she crosses her arms.

"I..." I feel the tears start to build in my eyes, a curse I have any time I feel like I'm getting in trouble. "I don't know how to do most of the things in it." *Shit.* I can't believe I just admitted that to my boss. Now I'm going to be heartbroken and unemployed.

"Why didn't you ask?"

"You hired me to do this job. I wanted to prove to you I could do it."

Kelsey sighs, her arms still crossed, but there's something softer in her expression now. "Look, I get that you want to prove yourself, but struggling alone doesn't help anyone—not you, not me, and certainly not the client. Everyone needs support at some point. I understand wanting to do things right. I'm a bit of a perfectionist myself," she admits, her voice losing its edge.

I look down, unable to meet her eyes. "I didn't want you to think I couldn't handle it. You hired me to do this job, and I wanted to prove I could do it perfectly, without needing anyone else."

"Perfectly?" Kelsey echoes, one eyebrow raised. "If I expected perfection from everyone, nothing would ever get done. Besides, no one does this work alone. I have mentors, I ask for input. We all need help to grow."

Her words sink in, settling in a way that feels almost painful. The need to be perfect, to prove I don't need anyone else—it's more than just this job. It's why I didn't call him after he left. Why I pretend I'm fine, that I can handle the breakup on my own, even though it feels like I'm barely holding myself together. I've spent my whole life being the smart, strong overachiever. It's how I managed to have my own identity when competing against a sports phenom for a brother.

And now, as an adult, I don't want people to see me when I'm not put together and strong. I don't want people to see my weakness.

I look up at her, suddenly seeing Kelsey as more than just my demanding boss. She's someone who has had to ask for help too, who's needed support at times. "So...you don't think less of me for not knowing everything?"

She chuckles, her tone lighter. "Of course not. If anything, I'd think less of you for pretending you didn't need help. You're still learning, and that's okay. Don't be afraid to reach out when you need someone."

I nod slowly, feeling a weight shift inside me. Her words are like a soft nudge, something that hits deeper than the immediate problem at hand. Maybe it's time to let go of my need to appear flawless, to prove I don't need anyone—even if that someone is the person who left.

Kelsey gestures toward my laptop. "Show me what you're stuck on. Let's work through it together and maybe we can get it done in time."

As we go over the project, she's patient and encouraging, helping me realize that my mistakes aren't the end of the world. Izzy and Becca return later, both of them jumping in to help proofread and review the proposal. Bryn stops by a couple of hours later with pizza, and it turns into an all-hands-on-deck situation.

Strangely, when Kelsey finally hits submit on our proposal, I feel more at ease than I have in weeks. I realize that if it's okay to admit I need help here, maybe it's also okay to reach out in other parts of my life, too.

After everyone heads home for the night, I sit quietly, staring at the blank message screen on my phone. I've been holding on to my pride, my need to show him that I'm perfectly fine on my own. But maybe—just maybe—I don't have to do everything alone. And maybe reaching out to him doesn't mean I'm any less strong.

I take a deep breath and start typing. *Hey, I know it's been a while, but...do you want to talk?*

Kelsey's words echo in my mind, reminding me that sometimes, strength comes from knowing when you don't have to be perfect—or alone.

I delete my message, knowing JT wouldn't read it anyway. Plus, I have a much better plan for how to get through *his* defenses.

CHAPTER FORTY-ONE

JT

THERE IS A PHONE vibrating somewhere near my head, but I can't be bothered to answer it. Jameo stopped calling a week ago, so I'm not even tempted to communicate with the outside world at this point. I bury my head under my pillow, simultaneously blocking out both the noise and the overly bright sunshine. I need gloom. I feel like I'm hungover, but I'm not. I haven't allowed myself to drink even one sip of alcohol since I ended things with Lila. Alcohol would numb this pain, and I deserve to feel every memory like the hits to the heart they are.

My phone stops buzzing, and I consider pulling myself out of bed and getting dressed, but I just can't be fucked. As if the person on the other end of the line can sense my decision to stay in bed all day, the phone starts vibrating again. I'm almost certain I'm not supposed to be playing anywhere today, though, upon further reflection, I don't know what day it is, so it's hard to say if I have somewhere to be.

Snaking my hand out from under the sheets of my bed, I blindly reach around until I find my phone and, with a flick of my hand, send it crashing to the ground. I grab the pillow that's next to me—the one that has been filling in for Lila as I attempt to fall asleep each night—and drop it on top of the phone. I can still hear a faint buzzing sound, but it's not loud enough to bother me anymore. I've been getting really good at shutting things out these past few weeks.

Sometime later, I can't really say how long it has been since the phone forced me to recognize the existence of a world outside of my memories, I hear "JT Johnson!" bellowed from somewhere in the house. Huh. That's unexpected.

Unfortunately, that small spark that I felt at the sound of the unknown voice is now gone, and I can feel myself sinking back down into the thick fog that has clouded my mind and my senses since I left Lila in Vegas. I sat through meeting after meeting with my parents, my body on autopilot, Sam on the phone, providing the collateral and signatory power they needed to extend or pay their loans. Sam hates that everything is mortgaged through the roof to get them the cash they need, but oh well. What do I need equity or cash for? I spend every drop of my willpower making sure I'm focused when I'm at the tournaments—making sure I win enough money to continue to pay the people who rely on me. I can't be expected to interact with the world when I'm at home.

"Um, no," I hear from somewhere much closer to me. "This is completely unacceptable. What is that smell?" The man must be in my room with me, but I cannot summon the energy to lift my head. It sounds like Sam, but he lives across the country. Unless, I'm at home, right? I blink open my left eye, but—

Holy fucking shit. Why is the sun trying to scorch my retinas? What did I ever do to that flaming ball of gas anyway? Ugh, where did my pillow go? I turn my head the other direction, trying, though not particularly hard, to escape the light and the voice that is now saying things to me. Things I'm likely supposed to be listening to.

"JT! Wake up. Listen to me!" I close my eyes, hoping the ghost of Sam will go away if I just ignore him. It's colder now, so I guess he must've pulled the blanket off me. "JT! I'm going to dump water on you if you don't sit up right now." Facing my life right now seems worse than getting water dumped on me—plus it was likely a bluff—so I opt to do nothing.

"Ahh!" I scream minutes later, sitting up and blinking the water out of my eyes. "What the fuck...Sam? What are you doing here?" I focus on my assistant, my eyes slowly tracking from his bright white tennis shoes past his gray joggers and light pink tank top to his clean-shaven face and perfectly styled hair. He's pacing back and forth in front of me.

"Are you fucking kidding me right now? What am I doing here? What am *I* doing here?!" He stops, fully turning to look at me for the first time, and his jaw drops. "Oh, for the love...what happened to your hair?"

I run my hand over my chia pet hair, remembering a few days ago when I saw the curl Lila liked to wrap her finger around peeking out above my collar, and I realized it had to go. I drove to the nearest drugstore, bought some clippers, and gave myself a buzz cut.

"I cut it."

"You...you cut your own hair?"

I nod, considering if it's appropriate for me to lie back down at this point or not.

"Why in the name of Chad Michael Murray would you cut your hair? It's literally the first rule of breakups. Do. Not. Cut. Your. Own. Hair." He pulls out his phone and starts typing something, so I assume it means I'm okay to go back to sleep.

"Do not put your feet back on the bed, JT Johnson. I will take drastic measures."

I drop my legs back down, the cold of the hardwood bringing some awareness back to me. Sam taps a few more buttons before he turns his attention back to me.

"I scheduled you a hair appointment this afternoon. It wasn't how I thought we would be spending the afternoon, but priorities have changed based on that hack job. Thank God you at least had the sense to keep some length to it. If you'd gone for a full shave, there's nothing I or anyone else could've done."

"There *is* nothing that can be done. It's too late," I say, meaning so much more than just my hair.

"There is always *something* that can be done, JT."

I run my hand down my face, silently urging myself to move. To do something other than just sit here. I know I can do it. I've done it every Thursday through Sunday since I shut the door behind me in Vegas. The face the world wants to see is here somewhere. I just have to find it.

Sam gives me another minute before striding into the bathroom and turning on the shower.

"Okay, this is so much worse than I was anticipating, but I'm not going to let that slow me down. First things first, you need a shower. You are seriously malodorous." He wrinkles up his nose in disgust, and after realizing I don't know the last time I showered—likely Sunday morning, if only I knew when that was—I do as he directs, shedding my clothes without a thought on my way into the door.

Sam is clearly unfazed by my nudity, because he follows me into the bathroom, leaning his ass against the counter as I climb into the shower.

"Excellent. We can check step one off the list."

I let the hot water pour down my body, not even trying to listen to what Sam's saying. I'm sure he'll just make me do it anyway.

"Oh, for fuck's sake!" Sam steps into my walk-in shower fully clothed and flips the water handle, causing freezing cold water to spray down on me.

"You are not okay. I do not give one flying fuck if you fire me for this, but I *will not* let you go on like this, do you understand me? We are going to feed you. We are going to get your hair fixed, and then you are going to see a therapist."

"I'm not going to—"

"It's non-fucking-negotiable, JT. I've been researching who in the area would be a good fit for years now, and I've got an appointment with the one who came with the best recommendations for people dealing with emotional trauma caused by their parents."

"What? My parents haven't caused me emotional trauma."

"Really? Is that so?" Sam is standing in my shower, fully clothed, the freezing water hitting him just as much as me, and it's a terrifying sight to see. He's pissed, but I can't figure out what I've done.

"I'm sorry, Sam. I...I know I've let you and the rest of the team down lately, but I'll get it together. I am sorry. I'll get it together." I turn the water back to warm and squeeze some soap onto my palm as if in proof of my togetherness. "You don't need to stay in here with me. Go change into a pair of my clothes, and then we can talk about what my afternoon looks like without the therapy visit."

"No." It's all he says. Just no. And the straight line of his mouth is doing nothing to help me understand any better.

"What do you mean, 'no'?"

"I'm not getting out, and you're not getting out of going to therapy. I can assure you, based on the many years I've spent with my therapist, it's going to suck, but then you're going to get better. You're going to feel better. You're going to get stronger. And then you're going to realize just how strong the version of you that took the terrifying first step into your therapist's office really was. You can do this, but you cannot do it alone."

"I'm fine, Sam."

"Then why did you break up with Lila? Did you know she calls me on a regular basis now? We're friends, but that's beside the point. She calls me to check in on you. She's worried about you after you left her alone in a hotel room after she told you she loves you."

"I didn't leave her alone. I told Jameson and Bryn to go over and be with her."

"Semantics, JT. You love that woman, and you walked away from her. Telling yourself you have to throw your life away to pay your parents back for their sacrifices—the ones they made when you were a child and they were adults, for the record—that is the thought process of a man who is not okay."

"Lila's better off without me."

"She's devastated without you."

"She'll move on."

"Yeah, I'm sure she will if you refuse to pull your head out. She's in love with you, but she also knows her worth. If you don't get your shit together, she won't wait around forever. Is that what you want? For Lila to be happy with someone else? And do you really think some other guy will make her happy like you did? Do you want to curse her to a life of what-ifs and half-loves?"

"I...I don't know." My head is spinning. Was this a mistake? Am I so broken that I pushed Lila away to focus on something that, at the end of the day, is just a job rather than fighting for her—for us? Did I push away the one person who saw me and never asked me to be anyone but who I am?

"Do you love her, JT?" Sam asks, his tone finally softening.

"Of course I do." I don't even need to think about it. If anything, her absence over the last few weeks has made me realize just how much I love her.

"Then turn yourself into the man she needs you to be. And that's not the one who feels so guilty about his parents' decisions that he is willing to sacrifice anything to make them happy. It's the one who puts in the work, every day, to be the guy she deserves. Loving someone doesn't mean you have to be perfect, you just need to be willing to try, even when it's hard—especially when it's hard. You're going to mess up. A lot. Therapy is going to help you figure out how you can still love yourself when you do so you can keep loving her."

He turns and walks out of my shower, stopping on the bath rug to peel off his drenched clothes. "Oh, and I'm moving into your guest room and will be traveling with you until you prove to me that you remember your body needs food and water on a regular basis."

"Thanks, Sam. I don't deserve you."

"You do, JT. And you have a lot of other people in your life you deserve as well. I just happened to be the one who was elected to stage the intervention. Kelsey had *thoughts* on the best way to get you to pull your head out of your ass. And can I just say that I am in love with that woman? She is terrifying and smart, and...I really hope we can get a brunch group or a book club or some kind of travel friendship lined out...I need more Kelsey Harper in my life."

And with that, he walks his naked ass out of my bathroom.

CHAPTER FORTY-TWO

LILA

"Okay, here are the final copies of the presentations. Yours is the one with the forest green cover, so make sure you don't hand it out to Jaxon Steele," I say as I release a small squeal and hand off the spiral-bound presentations I've been spending way too much time on lately. We were selected as finalists despite submitting our proposal at the last hour.

"I cannot believe you get to meet Jaxon Steele! I've always wanted his song 'Forever Starts Here' to be the song I walk down the aisle to." I let out a small sigh, realizing that day may never actually come for me, but that's okay.

I'm learning to let go of the unhealthy expectations I set for myself, including the ones regarding finding and falling in love. If I learned anything from my time with JT, it's that love sneaks up on you sometimes. Lightning strikes just the right spot and the flames spring to life as if from nowhere. Looking for the fire before the lightning is a fool's errand.

Kelsey gives me a sympathetic look but then raises her eyebrow as she asks, "You do know I already know Jaxon, right?"

"WHAT? How am I just finding out about this now? We've been working on this for months."

"He grew up in Wild Bluffs."

"What?!" I ask it again because it feels like this is information that should be blasted across the internet, and it is not. I would know, too. I did a lot of research and deep dives on Jaxon Steele throughout this process.

Kelsey just shrugs. "He's very security conscious." She taps our ninety-eight-page security proposal as if proving her point. "And he didn't graduate from here, so it's a lot easier to scrub from his history."

"Wait, why does he want to scrub—"

"Oh, there's my dad. Wish me luck!" Kelsey says before climbing in the passenger side of her dad's pickup. Ken, like the saint he is, is giving Kelsey a ride to the airport at six thirty in the morning. There's a chance there will be hail in Denver this weekend, and she didn't want to risk her car getting damaged in the airport parking lot. I think they just like spending time together, and the thought makes my heart ache a little, wishing my parents lived closer.

I sit down at my desk, staring at the task list on my screen, wondering what I should dive into first. As excited as I am that the final presentations for Jaxon Steele are here, I'm dreading how much my workload is going to be lightened. I shoot a quick message to Brian, the head of Information Security, asking him for an update on a recent breach we detected in one of our clients' systems. I'm coordinating our rapid response team with our team who will do a deep dive into the system, and I need to make sure our final penetration testers have what they need to both replicate the attack and try to anticipate the next iterations of the attack. I'm not an expert in any of these things, but I know enough to get by. Plus, my project-management skills are top-notch, so Kelsey has been shifting my job more and more toward that side of the work.

I sit at my desk, fingers hovering over the keyboard as I wait for Brian's response. My mind keeps drifting back to the conversation with Kelsey. *Jaxon Steele. In Wild Bluffs.* It's wild to think someone so famous, whose music has touched so many, grew up in this small town.

My desktop pings, pulling me from my thoughts. It's a message coming through from Brian.

Brian: *Got your message. We've isolated the breach but we're still working on patching the vulnerabilities. Pen testers will get the results soon. We're on track, but it's delicate. I'll keep you posted.*

Good. At least that's one thing I don't have to stress about right now.

My mind wanders back to the shocking information that Kelsey knows Jaxon Steele. How have I lived here this long without someone in town mentioning they knew him way back when? That feels like information that would just be part of the standard Wild Bluffs rotation. On the plus side, while I'm not sure who our competition is, it feels like Kelsey growing up with Jaxon will be a positive, right? Unless she was secretly the mean girl growing up. Then maybe it will take more than our kickass proposal. After everything I've gone through with this proposal, I'm far more invested than I should be, and it makes me anxious that it's all coming down to a handful of final decisions. A part of me should feel relieved the finish line is near, but instead, I feel a familiar sense of dread creeping in.

What will I do with my time if we don't get the contract, and I don't have enough work to keep me busy until nine or ten every night?

My work has been the perfect distraction. Distraction from the ache in my chest, the endless loop of thoughts about JT, and the constant questioning of where I went wrong or what I could've done differently. Whenever the feelings get too loud, I lose myself in work. But now, with things winding down, I can feel the emptiness gnawing at me again, threatening to bubble to the surface.

I shake my head, willing myself to focus. One task at a time.

Before I know it, an hour has passed, and Becca and Izzy are both arriving, settling in to start their workdays. I absently reach into my bag for my notebook, and as I pull it out, a paperback tumbles out with it, landing on the floor with a soft thud. *Fighting for Forever*, by Mia Ford. The cover, featuring an illustrated couple locked in an almost-kiss, seems to mock me, but I don't let it. Instead, I see it as a source of inspiration. It's about a brooding hero who pushes the heroine away because he doesn't think he deserves her, only to have a grand epiphany about how much he loves her. I may have reached an unhealthy level of projecting, but until I convince both myself and JT that this isn't just a storyline for novels, I'm going to keep reading.

I deserve a happy ending, and so does JT. Love is worth fighting for, and there is no doubt in my mind what we had was real, even if it was messy and imperfect—hell, I know it's real *because* it's messy and imperfect.

Shoving the book back into my bag, I look over at my officemates. Becca's long blonde hair is the only part of her I can see around her computer monitor. She's explaining something about lowering overhead to increase profit margins to Izzy, who is silently sipping her coffee as she stares intently at Becca's screen. They look busy, but I also need to know more about the Jaxon Steele drama that was casually dropped in my lap this morning.

"Umm, you guys, did you know Jaxon Steele grew up here?" I ask, immediately feeling stupid. Of course they knew that. They also grew up here. You don't miss a kid when your entire grade has less than fifty students in it.

"Yep," Becca says, showing no interest whatsoever in this.

"And?" I ask.

"And what?" Becca replies.

"You guys told me the entire family history of the girl who delivered my coffee last week. You knew her great-grandfather's name."

"Well, his name was Elmer Fud. That's not something you forget easily."

"Okay...but one of the top country artists in the world grew up with you and you didn't even mention it. He would've been like, right around your age, right? Did you know him? Is he awful?" I can feel myself getting carried away here. He was likely just a nobody little kid who moved away when he was like six or something.

"He's roughly the same age as us, yep," Becca replies, shooting a glance at her friend as she says it. Izzy is surprisingly quiet about the whole thing, but who am I to talk? I haven't been the best company of late.

"Did you guys know him? Were you friends with him?" I gush.

"I'm going to go grab some more coffee," Izzy says, standing up and heading toward the door, a coffee cup still in her hand. I watch her go before turning back to Becca. She still has her eyes trained on her friend as she makes her way across the street, headed back to get a coffee that she doesn't need.

"Look, I get that Jaxon *Steele*"—she laughs at the last part, making it clear Steele wasn't always his last name—"is like a superstar, but there is a complicated history between him and a lot of people in this town, including Izzy, so I would be careful who you bring him up to."

"Really?" I ask.

"Yep. Now, if you're finally ready to talk again, why don't you tell me what's going on with you and the guy you most likely love but definitely are also super pissed at."

CHAPTER FORTY-THREE

JT

SAM PULLS MY CAR into the garage at my house, insisting on chauffeuring me everywhere since he rolled into town three days ago.

"Well, another day down," Sam says with a smile. "And all those smoothies I've been feeding you have really helped counterbalance that gray pallor your skin had taken on."

We are just getting back from my third appointment with Dr. Burbanks, the psychiatrist Sam pulled a lot of strings with to get me in same day. I was so uncomfortable as I sat in the leather chair in his office, picking at the seam on the armrest while I tried to figure out how much eye contact I should be making. Based on my answers to a variety of questions and Sam's input, Dr. Burbanks decided I was experiencing situational depression and prescribed me a low-dose antidepressant as a temporary treatment to accompany my daily therapy sessions. If all goes well, the sessions will move to weekly or virtual here in a week or two, and I'll stop taking the medication after a few more weeks of progress.

The sessions are starting to feel less foreign, but every time I leave, there is a heaviness in my chest, like all these tangled emotions have been ripped open, and now I have to figure out what to do with them. I hadn't realized how much I'd buried until I started talking, and now everything feels raw. Still, I know I need to keep going, even if it feels like I'm unraveling a bit more each day.

Today, when he asked me what was on my mind, I willingly shared my anxiety about not having a golf tournament this weekend. I have five whole days staring me in the face and no idea what to do with them. The distraction of golf, and my relative success at it, has always been my way of avoiding what's underneath. We talked for a while about my relationship with my parents. I told him about my dad giving up his chance at becoming a professional golfer to coach me and about my mom working multiple jobs to allow us to afford such an expensive dream. I told him golf is the only thing that has truly made me feel like I'm worth something. Well, golf and Lila, but I don't know what to do with that realization yet.

Sam and I walk into the house, planning what we are going to order for dinner, since he only knows how to make smoothies and takeout is how I cook. Since I started the medicine, or maybe it's the therapy, I haven't felt quite so apathetic, so Sam and I have spent a lot of time hanging out, swimming in my pool, and playing golf on the three-hole course I have in my backyard.

"Knock, knock," I hear my mother call from the front of the house, and my spine straightens. I'm not ready to deal with my mom. Dr.

Burbanks and I have barely scratched the surface of everything—how am I supposed to know what to do with this woman who elicits such a tangled web of emotions within me?

"It's unbecoming to have so many packages on your front porch, JT. Have you considered what your neighbors will think?"

Sam's leaning against the white marble island in the kitchen, his hands casually tucked into the pockets of his joggers, but I can see the annoyance on his face already. "You want me to get rid of her?" he asks.

Yes.

"No. I'll go talk to her. You can stay here if you don't want to come say hello."

"I'm not leaving you alone with her."

"She's my mom."

"She's a bitch."

"Oh, hello, JT." Patricia Johnson walks into the room, her heels clicking as she moves off the runner in the hallway and onto the hardwood floor in the kitchen. "Sam."

"PJ," Sam says with the fakest smile you've ever seen, not bothering to stand up straight to say hello.

My mother's eyes turn into slits at the nickname, one she never has—and never will—go by. "I thought you were the virtual kind of assistant."

"And I thought you were a marginal parent. Turns out, you're a shitty one, so I guess we were both wrong."

Mom stares at Sam as if she's trying to piece together what he just said, or maybe how he had the balls to say it to her, but in true Patricia

Johnson form, she chooses to simply ignore him. Instead, she turns her anger in my direction. "I'll tell Jon to start searching for a new assistant for you."

"No. You won't."

My mom's eyes widen in shock, and if we're being honest, I feel similar. I think this might be the first time I've ever openly disagreed with my mother. Adrenaline starts working its way through my system from either the freedom of speaking my mind or the fear of what it means that I did, and it compels me to keep going. "While I appreciate everything you and Dad have done to get me to this point, things need to change. My team is mine. You will not try to fire my employees or even contact them in any way. My plane is mine. You are not allowed to use it for your personal travel. The airport and pilots will all be made aware of the change." I'm on a roll now, my confidence increasing with each boundary I set for myself. Doctor Burbanks is going to be so proud of me.

"My house is mine. You are not welcome here unless I invite you over. I'm getting the locks changed, and I won't be giving you a key. You will also be taken off my list of guests at the front gate. You can have them call me should you ever be invited back."

My mother's posture is rigid, her arms crossed, hip jutted to one side. "Is this how you are going to treat me? Do you realize the things I gave up for you?"

"I do." I hear Sam's snort of derision, but I know my mom truly does feel like she gave up the best years of her life—her dreams of fame and stardom—for me. Just because she was the one who ultimately made the decision doesn't change that. "But I also realize you are currently a negative influence in my life, and I need to enforce boundaries with you to stay healthy."

"Enforce boundaries? You're...you're seeing a therapist now?" Her tone is dripping with disgust as if she just found out I was spending my afternoons rolling around in piles of dog shit and then licking myself clean.

Sam practically snarls at the condescension in her voice, moving toward her. "All right, Mommy Dearest, time for you to fuck right off."

She doesn't acknowledge Sam, her eyes traveling from my toes to the tips of my short hair, her eyes narrowing even further as she realizes for the first time that my hair is buzzed.

"You don't mean that, JT. Do you?" Her eyes water, and one tear falls. "After everything I've given up, everything I've sacrificed for you?"

My willpower starts to fade, my mom knowing just the right words to say to make me question everything I'm doing. I can't kick her out of my home or my life. I know Doctor Burbanks suggested holding strong boundaries, but I can't do it.

"You wouldn't cut me off," she continues. "Especially if you pull your funds from our firm, how will we get by?"

I clench my fists, keeping my face neutral, but her words hit somewhere deep, somewhere familiar. That old place of feeling guilty, feeling wrong, like I've somehow failed just by playing the sport my dad wanted me to dedicate my life to. But today...today, something feels different. Her words don't cut as deeply as they once did. I don't feel the urge to shrink under her gaze or justify myself.

Instead, I feel a strange, quiet anger—a boundary forming, maybe for the first time.

"I'm scheduled to be in New York next week for my friend's fashion show, and your secretary over here suggested I fly *commercial*." My mom waves her manicured fingers at Sam.

"That will be terrible, I'm sure. Unfortunately, I am currently tight on cash, as I just had to bail my parents out of years upon years of debt and extravagant spending habits."

She pauses, her mouth opening slightly as if to argue, but she's thrown off balance by my response. It's clear she expected the usual apologies, the scrambling to meet her expectations. But I'm tired. Tired of bending myself over backward trying to make up for something I never asked them to give me.

She turns and makes her way toward the entrance, her steps the only noise as she leaves. As she reaches to open the door, it opens wide, revealing a surprising face on the other side.

"Jameson Walker," my mother hisses. "Of course you're part of this too. You've always been a terrible influence on JT."

His eyes dance with amusement despite her ire. "Patricia. It's always such a pleasure to see you." My friend steps to the side, holding the door open for my mom to exit. "Let's do it again sometime," he says as she walks by.

The three of us stand there watching my mom climb into the fancy black sports car I got her last year for Christmas, one with every top-of-the-line safety feature I could find. We wait for her to leave in silence as if there is an unspoken agreement we need to ensure she's gone before we can move on. My mom drives away, and even though I know I shouldn't, I feel a pang of guilt slide through me.

"Hey, Sam," I say, not taking my eyes off the spot where my mother's car just was. "Can you please see if Doctor Burbanks can fit me in for a call this afternoon?"

"Yep," he says, pulling out his phone and moving back toward the kitchen. "I'm on it."

Jameo is still standing by the door, holding it open like he's not sure if he should come in or walk right back out.

"Who's Doctor Burbanks?" he asks.

"The therapist I've been seeing," I say, pulling my eyes away from the street when— "Holy cow," I say, taking in the pile of white mailing envelopes sitting on my front doorstep. "My mom wasn't joking about there being a bunch of packages out there. It looks like I'm obsessed with late-night infomercials."

"You didn't know they were there?" Jameo asks.

"No. I never use that door, and I haven't been in a shopping mood lately."

"You should open them."

There's something about his tone that makes me realize he's not just interested in what scrub brush I ordered off QVC.

"Why? What's in them?"

Jameo sighs before bending down and gently throwing the packages through the door. "Just open them, JT."

I lean over and pick one up, my gaze immediately going to the Wild Bluffs address in the return spot. Suddenly, it feels like my heart is trying to escape my chest, and I'm not sure I can do it.

"You'll regret it if you don't," Jameo offers as he shuts the door, moving into the house with me.

I squeeze my eyes shut, trying to will courage into my veins. With a deep breath, I pull the perforated section off the bag and reach my hand inside. It's...a book. I pull out the paperback novel, the cover giving it away as some variety of contemporary romance.

"It's a book," I say, staring down at the illustration of the woman on the front. "Why did she send me this?"

"Well, I don't know much about books, but they do say you're not supposed to judge them by the cover. Maybe try opening it up to see if you get any more meaning from the inside?"

Slightly terrified of what I'll find, I open the book to a random page in the middle, and realize Lila's annotated it in the same way we did the pirate book. I flip through the pages and find her thoughts, her questions, and her comments meant just for me.

"This at least explains why you haven't reached out to her," Jameo says.

"What...what do you mean?" I ask.

"She's been doing this for weeks now, sending you books about guys who made mistakes but then came back stronger. Well, she's been reading them since Vegas, she only decided to send them to you like a week ago."

"But why?"

"I have a couple of guesses, but I think it would likely mean more coming from her. Maybe you should call her?"

"I'm not sure I'm ready for that," I admit.

"Maybe you should work on getting ready, then."

"I am," I promise. "I swear I am putting in the work to become the man she deserves."

Chapter Forty-Four

Lila

I'M JUST FINISHING UP a chapter in my book when I hear a couple of soft knocks on my door. Assuming it's one of the guys from across the street stopping by to see if I want to come over for their weekly friend dinner, I put a bookmark in and race barefoot across the floor. I throw the door open, ready to beg for five minutes to change. Instead, my heart stops when I see JT standing in the doorway.

My breath catches in my throat as our eyes lock. He looks different—his curly hair is gone, and he looks tired, maybe even a little lost—but still JT. The same JT I've known for years. The same JT I fell in love with.

"Hey," he says, his voice soft, almost hesitant. "Can we talk?"

I blink, not sure if I'm imagining this. I wasn't prepared for him to show up, and certainly not here. He hasn't responded to a single one of the ten books I've sent him in the last six weeks, and yet he flies across the country to show up unannounced at my house. I open my mouth but nothing comes out. Finally, I manage, "What are you doing here?"

He steps into the room, closing the door behind him. "I've been... I've been doing a lot of thinking. About us. About everything."

I don't know what to say, so I just watch him, waiting for him to continue. My heart is pounding in my chest, the old, familiar pain resurfacing.

"I know I hurt you," he says, his voice low. "I told myself leaving was the right thing to do, that it was the only way I could focus on my game and earn the money my parents so desperately needed. But...the truth is, I was scared. I have so much guilt because of the sacrifices my parents made, and I just couldn't have one other person give up their dreams for me."

There it is. The same narrative I've been reading in every romance novel. The hero, broken and convinced he's not enough for the heroine.

But this isn't fiction. This is real life.

"You're right," I say, my voice trembling. "You did hurt me. And you didn't even give us a chance to figure it out. You just...left."

"I know," he says, his eyes filled with regret. "I thought I was protecting you. But really, I was causing the exact pain I was trying to shield you from. I was too caught up in my own insecurities to see that pushing you away was the exact opposite of what I should have been doing."

"It really sucked. I've felt like I wasn't enough—like maybe your leaving meant I didn't deserve the love I thought we had. I kept replaying every moment, wondering if there was something I could've done differently. If I hadn't said anything about your parents...or said 'I love you' too soon." My voice cracks, and I hate how defeated I sound, because I've put a lot of work in the last few weeks combating those lies as soon as they enter my headspace. "You decided for both of us that we weren't worth fighting for."

"I know. And that's what haunts me. I took the easy way out because I was scared and hurt, and I convinced myself it was for your sake when it was my insecurities. You deserved so much more than that, and I failed you. But I'm here now because I don't want to fail you anymore. I want to face whatever comes, even if it's hard, because we are worth it—you're worth it. And, honestly, I've put a shit ton of money and time with my therapist for me to be able to believe that I'm worth it. I'm worth the sacrifices people *choose* to make for me."

He looks at me with a vulnerability I've never seen before. "I'm willing to put in the work, every day, to be the man you deserve. I can't promise I'll be perfect, but I can promise I'll try."

I take a deep breath, my mind racing. This is what I've always wanted, right? For him to fight for us. But now that it's happening, I'm scared. Scared of getting hurt again. Scared of letting myself hope.

I asked him to come back with every book I sent him, every note I wrote him in the margins, every heart I drew around the quotes when the man would find his courage and come back to the woman he loves. I want to take the risk because if there's even a chance we can make this work, it's worth it. He's worth it. We're worth it.

"Good," I say, the spark only JT can ignite in me flaring to life again in my soul. "Because perfect sounds boring, and let's be real—we've never been boring a day in our lives."

"I love you, Lila," he says, his voice uncertain, not at the words themselves but at how I'm going to respond to them. Like maybe I've changed my mind since he's been gone.

"I love you too," I manage, my voice barely a whisper. Tears well up in the corner of my eyes as I take a step toward him. He reaches out and cups my face in his hands, his thumbs brushing away the tears that spill over. He moves closer, pressing his lips to mine. The kiss is gentle at first, but as I respond, it quickly becomes something more. His hands roam down my waist, and I wrap my arms around his neck. Our tongues dance together, exploring each other again for the first time in far too long. The taste of him sends shivers down my spine. It's like I'm coming home while also experiencing the greatest adventure at the same time.

When we finally pull apart for air, he holds my face between his hands and looks deep into my eyes. "I've missed you so goddamn much, Lila." His voice is raw with emotion. "I needed some time to figure myself out, but I promise I am all in." He wipes away the tears still sliding down my face and tucks a loose strand of hair behind my ear. I lean forward and kiss him again, this time more confidently, our tongues tangling in a more desperate embrace.

I can smell the faint scent of his cologne mixed with something else—something that makes me want to sink into his arms and never leave. He tastes like home and coffee and something vaguely sweet that must be from his travels. His stubble scratches against my skin as he kisses down my jawline toward my neck, causing shivers to run through me even as he trails tiny kisses across every inch of exposed skin available to him. His hands explore every curve of my body they can reach, tingles exploding through every nerve ending his skin touches.

As I return the favor, he lifts his head, searching for something. "Where's your room?" he asks, and I realize he's never been to my house before. I push away the pang of sadness I feel at knowing he shouldn't need a tour but quickly drag him through the living room, pointing out the attached kitchen, the bathroom, and the towel closet on the way to my room.

I stop at my doorway, the scent of cinnamon from the candle I was burning earlier filling the air. My bed is made but clothes cover the floor, and I have a few open books lying around. I notice JT glancing at them curiously. "I wasn't sure how many books it was going to take to convince you to come back to me." I shrug. "At least Jameson gave me a heads-up that you're terrible at checking for packages."

He laughs softly and kisses me again before pulling away. "I read every word you wrote," he whispers against my lips, his voice rough with emotion. "You gave me the strength to see myself as someone who could make you happy—as someone who deserved your love. It just took a bit. And I didn't want to come back to you before I was ready to be the man you need me to be." His statement sends shivers down my spine, making me feel alive in ways I didn't know were possible. He trails kisses along my jawline as his hands explore my body once more. I want to talk to him, to hear about how he's doing, about what happened with his parents, but my body has different ideas. His fingers intertwine with mine as he sits down on the side of the bed, pulling me between his jeans-clad thighs.

As he leans in for another kiss, I feel his stubble scratch against my chin, reminding me of our shared past—of memories that make my heart race and stomach flutter all over again. Our lips meet in a bruising kiss as JT pulls on the back of my legs, encouraging me to sit on him. I straddle his waist, aligning the heat of my core with the hard ridge under his zipper. I can't concentrate on anything other than the feel of him under me as I rock slowly in time to our kisses.

"Do you want me to show you just how much I love you, Pipsqueak?"

"Yes." I sure do.

He rolls his hips, and I let out a soft moan. I haven't felt anything close to lust since Vegas, and now that JT is here, my body is ready to go. I'm soaking wet and desperately seeking the friction I've been deprived of in his absence.

JT snags the bottom of my T-shirt, pulling it up and over my head, letting out a breathy "goddamn" when he realizes I'm not wearing a bra. I laugh as his head dips, his tongue finding my right nipple. He traces the puckered tip slowly before pulling the entire thing in his mouth and biting gently.

"Oh my *God,*" I moan into his mouth.

"I've missed you so fucking much."

"Prove it," I taunt, pulling away to stare him in the eye as I issue my challenge.

He stands, and I keep my legs locked around his waist until he unceremoniously throws me down on the bed.

"Your wish is my command."

His hand moves to his zipper, and I gulp as he drops his jeans and underwear. He grins at me, that pretty-boy smile of his taking up his entire face. I lift my hips and pull off my shorts and underwear as well, unwilling to wait any longer for the reunion my body is demanding. JT looks his fill, and it takes every ounce of my self-control not to pull him down to me.

Finally, he stalks forward, his hands hitting the bed by my hips before he crawls forward to meet my mouth with his. I lift my head, bringing my lips to meet his, pressing into his mouth with my tongue. JT reaches between us, bringing the head of his cock to my entrance. Taking a deep breath as if to steady himself, he pushes forward, and I swear my eyes roll to the back of my head.

"Mmm, you feel so good," he moans into my mouth.

I respond by hooking my legs around his waist, my ankles crossing at the bottom of his back to keep him there deep inside me.

"Fuck, you're such a good girl."

His words stoke the fire in me, and I pull him to me, begging him to increase his pace.

We fall into a world of moans and pants, our bodies rediscovering the connection between us. It's almost as if we're making up for lost time with this physical reunion alone, every touch seemingly more intimate than before because we both know how much it means that we found our way back to each other. It's a promise, a prayer, and a whisper of forever.

JT presses his lips to my collarbone, up my neck, and down again. One hand tugs my hair, and I am close. I'm writhing beneath him, my breath hitching as his cock brushes against my G-spot. My body is on fire, my entire being screaming for release. JT removes the hand tangled in my hair and slips it between us, his thumb rubbing against the swollen bundle of nerves in just the rhythm I need.

"Come on, love. Break for me."

My body tightens, and I cry out, pulsing around him. He collapses into my chest, his hips jerking as he follows me into oblivion.

"You're incredible," he says as I continue to rock back and forth, making sure to ride his full orgasm out with him.

I look at JT, the straight lines of his jaw covered in a light scruff, the round globes of his shoulders, the tanned strength of his back, and I can't help the smile that spreads across my face. He's back, and I'm the luckiest girl in the whole world.

Epilogue

JT

I KNOCK ON LILA's door before pushing it open, biting back the urge to remind her to lock it when she's home alone again. She simply refuses to believe anything bad can happen in Wild Bluffs—she may be right, but it's not a risk I'm willing to take. Jameo and I golfed eighteen holes today out at WBCC before showering quickly at the house I'm currently sharing with him and Bryn before heading into town. It's Halloween, and apparently, Kelsey Harper throws a party that's not to be missed. I'm not going to lie; I'm somewhat terrified that Kelsey's favorite holiday is Halloween. I truly don't know if I should expect pumpkin carving or literal axe murderers trying to hunt me down. And I say that as someone who has spent a lot of time with Kelsey over the last few months—I'd go as far as to call us good friends, in fact. The real kicker is that she might even agree.

"Lila!" I call out, wondering how much longer it will be until it makes sense for me to move in. When I decided to move out to Wild Bluffs, I truly considered just moving in with Lila, but Doctor Burbanks suggested I consider a different location—one that would give me the space to work through my issues without relying on her as a crutch. I quickly realized how right he was. It would've been so easy to go from feeling guilty about my parents' sacrifices to feeling guilty about how I left Lila. I still occasionally find myself apologizing to Jameson and Lila, but Dr. Burbanks assures me it's normal to feel guilt when you make mistakes—what matters is being able to distinguish between what you should and should not feel guilty for. It's a slow process, but I'm starting to see the difference between feeling empathy that something doesn't work out the way someone wants it to, and feeling guilty about it turning out that way.

"In here!" Lila calls from her bathroom. I stride down the hall to find her at her vanity, putting on the final touches of her makeup. I take in her sin-red dress paired with the damn knee-high black boots that almost killed me last Thanksgiving. It's hard to believe how much has happened in one year.

I slide into the room behind her, wrapping my arms around her waist and planting a kiss on the side of her neck. "I didn't realize Lucifer gives his demons the day off for Halloween parties."

A wicked grin spreads across her lips as she unashamedly checks me out in the mirror. "Only the ones he's sleeping with," she teases, her eyes catching on the horns I have on top of my head. In an expensive, all-black suit, I'm channeling some *Lucifer* vibes. Maybe if the night goes well, I'll consider opening up a nightclub and lending a hand to the Wild Bluffs PD.

While a devil and an angel are the more common couples costume, it didn't feel quite right. Lila Walker has always been the woman who didn't try to light up the darkest parts of me. Instead, she happily snuggled into them, curled up in a blanket, and stared directly into the dark parts of my life, stargazing. Because sometimes the darkest skies aren't the ones we should fear—they're the ones where profound beauty lies.

Her eyes sparkle mischievously. "You clean up nicely, Lucifer," she says, turning in my arms to face me. "Let's just hope we don't run into any demon hunters tonight." She reaches up to adjust the devil horns on my head before leaning in for a quick kiss. I can't help but smile at her, grateful I was able to make it to the party tonight with her.

Five minutes later, Lila links her arm with mine as we step into the cool night air. The streets are filled with parents out trick-or-treating with their children, though they mostly just stand in the middle of the block as the kids scurry from house to house. Kelsey doesn't live too far away, so we're going to walk rather than figure out who will drive us home. The lack of rideshare in Wild Bluffs is a definite downside to small-town living, though I have to admit the town of Wild Bluffs has grown on me.

The party is in full swing when we arrive, with eerie decorations and costumed guests filling the spacious living room. We don't bother to knock, used to welcoming ourselves into the Harpers' homes un-invited at this point. With Bryn and Jameson getting more serious, the Harper family has essentially embraced Lila as their own and, by extension, me too. I'm not surprised Lila has enjoyed having the women in her life as pseudo-sisters, and I'd never admit it to them, but I've enjoyed having them meddle in my life too.

I spot Ken and Jen Harper in the kitchen, dressed as Bonnie and Clyde, looking every bit the part of the infamous duo. Ken, with his suspenders and fedora, leans casually against the counter, embodying that old-time-gangster charm, while Jen, in a sleek, fitted dress and beret, clutches a bank bag with a mischievous glint in her eye. They share a conspiratorial smile, and it's hard not to laugh seeing this sweet, long-married couple transform into notorious outlaws. Kelsey maneuvers around the large island, two drinks in her hands for her parents.

"Oh my gosh. Kelsey came as Wednesday Addams. I love that," Lila says, following my eyes. "It's the perfect costume for her. Do you think she knows the dance from the new show?"

We both burst out laughing, the image of Kelsey performing the creepy dance painting a hilarious picture.

"Kels! We need more dry ice for one of the cauldrons in the living room!" Izzy says, rolling into the kitchen on a pair of lime green rollerblades. Her pink spandex workout outfit and lime green knee pads complete the *Barbie* outfit. She gracefully turns the corner but runs directly into Wilma Flintstone as she exits the bathroom. "Oh, hey, Janice! Didn't see ya there."

"Tennis shoes. Now," Kelsey demands from the kitchen. Izzy rolls her eyes but lowers herself into a dining chair to take off her skates.

Lila hands me a drink from one of the many black cauldrons positioned around the house, and I give her a quick kiss on the cheek in thanks. Matthew and his friends are the next to arrive, and even though I still feel a slight pang of jealousy when I think about Lila considering dating these men, I have to admit it's been fun having a group of guy friends to watch football games with when I'm in town. As I chat amicably with Matt and the guys, the party seems to be getting livelier by the minute.

The music reverberates through the house, mingling with the sound of laughter and conversation. The atmosphere is festive, with orange and purple lights casting an eerie glow over the room, the dry ice creating shadows that dance along the walls. Lila and I find ourselves caught up in conversations with various people from Wild Bluffs, many of whom I know from my frequent trips to the coffee shop. Kelsey, in her Wednesday Addams costume, maneuvers around the party with effortless grace, ensuring everyone is having a good time and keeping the drinks flowing.

As the night wears on, I find myself with Lila sitting on my lap, sharing a chair as we sit around the firepit with Bryn, Jameson, Izzy, Becca, and Kelsey. Bryn and Jameson showed up a while ago dressed as Ross and Rachel from *Friends*. Jameson has cat whiskers drawn on his face, and Lila has said, "Hello, Mr. Rachel" to him about twelve times tonight. While I know it's annoying the shit out of Jameo, Lila thinks it's so funny, I can't help but smile each time she does it. Lila tried to explain to me why it's funny, and I followed her explanation long enough to understand it has something to do with the episode where they get married in Vegas, but as I've never really been a big TV watcher, it was all kind of lost on me. I love that she loves it, though.

"So, JT, are you coming to Thanksgiving at our parents' this year?" Kelsey asks.

"I am," I say.

With Jameson and Lila both in Colorado, their parents are planning to come this way rather than Lila and Jameo flying to see them. The Harpers were kind enough to invite us all to Thanksgiving at their house, making it so Bryn and Jameo didn't have to decide which family to spend the holiday with. When Bryn texted out the invite, she included me in the group, informing me Ken would be particularly insulted if I didn't come. I've mostly remained out of contact with my parents now that their financial situation is sorted, but Ken has low-key stepped into a father-figure role in my life. When I'm in town and Lila is working, I often go to his men's coffee group with him—it's how I stay on top of the local gossip.

"I'm excited to meet Lori and Steve," Izzy says. "How do they feel about you dating their daughter?" she asks me.

Lila's parents have been great about me dating their daughter, with Lori going as far as to suggest it was "about damn time." Steve just joked it would be nice to finally have some peace during dinner.

"They're just proud both of their kids are dating up," I tease.

"Damn straight," Bryn agrees, offering me a fist bump that Lila bats away.

The group laughs, and as the night goes on and the party winds down, I can't help but realize just how lucky I am to be in this amazing town with a group of good friends. As the night gets late, I feel Lila start to shiver from her place on my lap. I nudge her, silently asking if she's ready to go, and she responds with a dip of her chin.

"Well, all,"—I lift Lila off my lap and stand up—"we're going to call it a night. Jameo, I'll see you in the morning for eighteen?"

Jameo sends me a nod while the rest of the circle waves and says their goodbyes. I grab Lila's hand and walk with her toward the door, looking forward to our night together. Unable to wait, I lean over, pressing my lips to her warm mouth, and when her lips open for me, I deepen the kiss.

"Ugh! You guys!" I hear Jameson yell. "That's wildly inappropriate!"

***

Bonus: Want a sneak peek into JT and Lila's HEA? Use the QR code below to download their bonus scene!

Ready to return to Wild Bluffs?
Don't miss the next Harper sister's story coming Spring of 2025!
And keep reading for an excerpt from Bryn and Jameson's story,
Forever Wild!

Follow me on Instagram @authoremmakate or join my newsletter at www.authoremmakate.com to stay up to date on all the latest Wild Bluffs news!

Thank you for reading *Wildly Inappropriate*. JT and Lila's story means the world to me, and I hope it gave you a few laughs, some swoony moments, and maybe even a craving to hit the back nine. ;)

Now for an awkward author ask: If you enjoyed their journey, it would mean SO MUCH if you left a review. Reviews are like gold in the book world—they help readers find my books, and they honestly make my day (okay, week). Whether it's a couple of lines or a heartfelt essay, your thoughts matter.

Hit up Amazon or Goodreads (or whatever platforms the cool kids are leaving reviews on these days) and let the world know what you thought!

Thank you for being here.

Happy Reading, EK

Acknowledgments

Writing a book is never a solo journey, and *Wildly Inappropriate* is no exception. There are so many people who deserve a heartfelt THANK YOU for helping bring this story to life.

To my husband, the man all my heroes aspire to be, thank you for always supporting my dreams. You're my rock.

To my kids, thank you for making me laugh on tough days and for loving me without fail, even when my head is full of tales that aren't appropriate for bedtime stories.

To my sisters, the Harper sisters wouldn't be near as witty, fun, or smart without you. You're pretty okay, I guess.

To my whole family, your unwavering love and support mean everything. Thank you for cheering me on, talking me up to your friends and book clubs, and giving me the time to write by entertaining the kids.

To Grammee, who we lost this year, thank you for sharing your love of all things creative with your family and for having a bookshelf full of bodice-ripper romances. It makes me infinitely happy you were able to start reading *Forever Wild* and infinitely sad you never had the chance to finish it. I hope Heaven has a robust library system that supports indie authors.

To my friends, thank you for always being my hype squad, for reading my romance books even when it's not your genre, and for giving me such great banter examples to play with.

To my editing team, the biggest thank you. Kelly, you are magic. You took my messy draft and helped me find the heart of the story. Your insights and encouragement made this book what it is. Claudia, thank you for polishing my words until they sparkle. Your keen eye and attention to detail (like how I spelled a nickname in book one!) amaze me every time. And to Amanda, the unsung hero who catches all the little things at the very end—you are a lifesaver. I'm grateful for your meticulous care.

To C, A, and M, thank you for beta reading for me. Diving into an unedited book is a messy undertaking, but you do it with grace. You give me the confidence to keep pushing forward when I'm sure I lost the plot at 70%.

Finally, to *you*, the reader. Thank you for picking up this book and taking a chance on the good folks of Wild Bluffs. Whether you're reading in a quiet corner, on a chaotic car trip with kids, or sneaking in a few pages before bed, I see you. I am you. I love you. Thank you for spending time with these characters and this story. It means the world to me.

Here's to wildly inappropriate adventures and the people who make them unforgettable.

Happy reading,

EK

Also by Emma

Wild Bluffs

(Small Town Romance)

Forever Wild

Wildly Inappropriate

Preview: Forever Wild

Keep reading for a sneak peek of Emma Kate's backlist title *Forever Wild*, available now!

Bryn

"Take any longer and our balls are going to turn blue," my sister Kelsey yells from the next tee box, where she and her friends are waiting for me. I heft the golf bag onto my shoulders, and the straps immediately dig into my skin. Relishing the warm sun on my face, I make my way over to the group. The course looks exactly the same as when I used to caddie here as a teen. Luckily, today I'm carrying my own bag rather than schlepping around someone else's.

Developed in an old cow pasture, Wild Bluffs Country Club was built on the sand dunes that surround Wild Bluffs, Colorado. With its golf holes enveloped by a natural grass rough, you have a hard time finding golf balls if your shot isn't straight down the fairway.

I spent many an hour searching for members' lost balls, working to get a better tip as a teen. Even at that age, I knew college wasn't going to pay for itself.

Today is different, though. We're here for the 32nd birthday party of my oldest sister, Kelsey. The music is blaring—spurred by our mutual friend Becca's recent breakup—and our group is the only one still out on the course. The rest of Kelsey's friends, along with a couple of groups of golfers who flew in for a weekend of fun, gave up after nine holes and headed to the bar for food and drinks.

"When you see my face, hope it gives you hell," I sing along under my breath, loving that Becca is fueling her angst with 2000s pop.

I adjust my stance and take a few practice swings before putting down my Titleist 4 golf ball on the tee. Closing my eyes, I inhale deeply and then launch the ball through the air. It soars but slices right into the rough between our hole and the one next to it.

I swear under my breath. The sun is too bright to follow the ball. It's definitely somewhere between the second or third yucca clump, right?

Why did I let Kels talk me into a bottle of wine each last night? It wasn't even her birthday yet.

Making my way through the sandhills, I search for my ball with my 7-iron, hoping to get out of the weeds before finding any rattlesnakes. Spotting a Titleist approximately where mine landed, I quickly hit it back into the fairway where the other girls had all managed to find their tee-shots.

As I follow its trajectory, I suddenly hear the thud of a bag being set down and somehow know it wasn't my ball that just flew off.

Oops.

Turning around, I see a dark-haired man standing there, looking in disbelief at the ground. I slowly approach him and see my Titleist 4 golf ball lying next to his feet, complete with the small penis Izzy drew on it this morning.

"So you know how to mark a ball, you just don't know how to *use* the mark to identify your ball?"

Looking into his face, I can't help but cringe a bit at the bitterness in his voice, despite being pleasantly surprised by the fact that I am actually looking up at a man for a change, a rarity at five feet, ten inches.

"Oh. Shoot. I'm playing a Titleist 4 too, and I wasn't paying enough attention, I guess. Yours was right over there." Recognizing how ridiculous I look pointing at the spot he had clearly just seen me hitting from, I quickly lower my arm and glance at his face again.

In addition to being tall, this man is all kinds of eye candy. He clearly hits the gym on a regular basis, if how tight his white, collared shirt is pulling across his chest is any indication. His dark brown hair matches a thick beard.

Don't I know him from somewhere? I'm usually pretty good at matching faces with names, and there is something about his dark green eyes that seems familiar. Maybe the facial hair is throwing me off.

Would it be inappropriate to ask if he has a beard all the time?

He crosses his arms, the movement drawing my attention to his defined biceps. "Sure, well, a lot of good that does me. It's still a stroke. Maybe pay more attention next time you and your sorority sisters decide to use Daddy's golf membership, okay?"

Definitely an inappropriate time to ask about the beard, then.

"Excuse me?" I feel my eyebrows shoot up under my baseball cap. "First, you've got to be joking about it being a stroke. You are out here"—I look around—"alone? You get to decide what number you write on your scorecard. Second, fuck you. This is my sister's membership, you arrogant prick."

I turn to point at Izzy, an almost six-foot-tall brunette decked out in Wild Bluffs Country Club attire, nicely proving my point.

The fact that she decided to curtsy with her hot-pink golf skort after her shot does not help my case, but, in her defense, it was a pretty damn good shot.

He pulls his baseball cap off and runs his hand through his hair, a gesture I find irritatingly handsome. "Ahh, yes. A real credit to the sport of golf, that one."

"Again, fuck you. Just play my ball. It will be easy for everyone to identify as yours."

Arms crossed warily across his chest, he shoots me a confused look. "...because you're such a dick?"

Continuing to search his face to figure out who this man is, I'm surprised when I see an almost smile pulling at the corner of his mouth.

"Original. I've never been called a dick before."

Despite his gruff attitude, I feel a pull to keep talking to this man. Okay, yes. By *pull*, I mean a purely physical attraction that is entirely due to his large frame and handsome smile now on display.

"Well, welcome to Wild Bluffs. Home of the honest."

"Wow. What a tagline. I'm surprised they've managed to keep its existence a secret from the world for as long as they have."

I laugh, my annoyance morphing into something else. He's got a sense of humor and can at least keep up with me in a verbal sparring session.

"Oh, the town hired the same PR team that helps keep Atlantis's location a mystery. It's a bit pricey but clearly worth every penny."

He chuckles, leaning casually on his golf club while we banter back and forth.

"Do you think they'd let me in on the secret?"

"Not a chance. It's not for the likes of you."

"Oh really? And just how is that decided?" he asks.

"Multiple rounds of interviews, an IQ test, and an intense psychological evaluation. Unfortunately, I don't think you're going to make the cut," I tease.

"How will I ever recover?"

"I'd suggest therapy, which you can clearly pay for if you're a member here, but I'm not sure it will help. If you can't pass the test, you can't pass the test."

"Of course you'd go there. Whatever." His face changes abruptly, his eyebrows pulling together into a deep crease. He swings his bag onto his shoulders, making me realize again how tall he is. I watch him stomp away, leaving me and my penis ball behind to recover from that emotional roller coaster of a conversation.

***

The back nine flies by in a flurry of stories and laughter. By the time we reach the eighteenth hole, the sun is starting to set, staining the sky with its own watercolor painting of pink and purple.

Becca leads us back toward the clubhouse, talking excitedly about her new plan to stay single for a while.

"Taking a couple months off from the dating scene will allow me to find my sshpecial sshomeone," she slurs slightly at the end, clearly in need of some hydration and likely some food to soak up the booze from today. "You agree, don't you, Bryn? It's working for you, right?"

Before I can answer, Kelsey grins over at us, clearly ready for some mind ninjaing, a side effect of her days with the Marines and now at her cybersecurity firm.

"I don't know if three years can actually be considered 'a couple months,' Becca."

Becca looks at me, her warm green eyes widening at the revelation.

"You haven't had sex in YEARS?" she practically yells.

I grab her elbow as she loses her footing and her bag starts to tip her backward.

"Jesus, Becca, could you say it a little louder? I don't think all the old men in the locker room heard you," I angrily whisper back.

"One"—Becca holds up her finger—"you know most of those men are not that old and would totally be doable at this point. You're twenty-eight. Also, three years is a long, long time to go without...ya know...*companionship*."

I sigh deeply, hoping she'll get distracted if I just stay silent.

"Bryn." She grabs my face so I have to look at her.

I spot Izzy and Kelsey over her right shoulder, waving to the rest of the birthday party already encircling the firepit but clearly planning to stay and enjoy the show.

Just great. The last thing I want is for my sisters to start thinking they need to meddle in my love life. Like I don't get enough of that from my mom, and apparently now Becca.

"Peter was a dick," she continues at a more reasonable volume. "It wasn't fair that he put all the blame on you when you guys broke it off. Relationships are two-sided. He expected a lot from you he wasn't willing to give in return."

Goodness, I'm tearing up a little bit, which I most definitely do not want to do.

Unluckily for me, Becca isn't done. "It's not a good enough reason to go without S. E. X. for"—she drops her voice to a whisper—"three whole years."

"I promise it has nothing to do with asshole Peter. Have you met the men who are on dating apps these days? None of them have been worth a second date, let alone actually sleeping with. Plus, there is no need to worry, Beccs. I can take care of myself, if you know what I mean?" I say with a wink, hoping I can get out of sharing that it has been a hell of a lot longer than three years—twenty-eight, to be exact.

True to Becca form, she turns bright red and starts giggling. She's been this way forever. She so badly does not want to be a prude, but she most definitely is, at least at heart.

Not that I have a leg to stand on, of course.

Becca turns and starts toward the fire, muttering something about needing some damn s'mores in her life if she isn't going to be getting any action, and I can't help but roll my eyes.

My sister Izzy hangs back, the only one who knows about my un-popped cherry. "You could tell them, you know. I don't think they'd make you being a twenty-eight-year-old virgin into as big of a deal as you seem to think they would."

"But they would make it into *a* deal. Which is the exact opposite of what I want. You know I don't care about being a virgin. If I did, I wouldn't be one. It just hasn't happened. And it's not like I'm lying to them."

Izzy gives my shoulder a squeeze, prompting me to continue before she offers me sympathy I most certainly do not want. "They've literally never asked me if I've had sex with someone. Plus, all the men I've gone out with in the last three years have been complete skeazeballs. I wouldn't have slept with them even if it weren't my first time."

"While it was pretty obvious from the fact that you were best friends with all the guys in high school that you were a virgin then, we all assumed you and Peter had sex. You dated for *three years* and never once complained that *he* was the one holding out."

"Meh. The effort of fighting him on a decree from his mother did not seem to be worth the reward."

She grimaces. "It's like he gets worse every time I hear about him."

"You know, he wasn't a bad guy. He was actually a good boyfriend the majority of the time. He just had mommy issues."

"And, apparently, performance issues."

"I want to deny it, but in hindsight, it does feel like there could've been a bit more spark."

"A lot more spark, Sis. A lot more spark," Izzy says as we make our way after our friends.

***

Jameson

After I finish the back nine, I head to the weight room for my second workout of the day.

Yes, I may have gained a few too many pounds in the last year. Yes, it may have been equally due to stress eating chocolate chip cookies and sad beer drinking.

After a month of two-a-days in the gym and walking at least thir-ty-six holes a day, I'm finally back in shape. Okay, fine, it probably doesn't hurt that I've also cut back to a few beers a week rather than the few beers an hour I was consuming before.

But it's mostly the extra workouts.

I finish the final set of my core round, wishing I were back home in my gym with extra fans and air-conditioning rather than sweating my ass off in this little one the course keeps open for nonlocals like me who stay the night in their guesthouses and hotel rooms.

As I start the short trip back to my hotel room in the building just next to the putting green, I notice a group of women sitting around the fire. They're cute, but as one catches my eye, I quickly turn my face away, hoping she doesn't recognize me.

The girl from this afternoon wasn't with them. Maybe she went home? Why do I feel a little sad about that? I mentally shake my head. I've learned my lesson about getting involved with women like her.

After closing the door to my room behind me, I lie down on my bed, letting the air-conditioning cool my sweat. The extra endorphins from my workout didn't even last all two minutes of my walk back, and the scorecard sitting on my desk sapped what little joy remained in me as I walked in.

I bury my face in my pillow and let out a deep sigh.

Ugh. I suck at golf.

My phone rings, and I barely register it's Erica, the head of the public relations team handling my downhill spiral, before I answer it.

"Hi, Erica."

"Just calling to check in on my favorite golfer."

"I can't possibly be your favorite golfer, Erica. Tell me what's really up."

"I just wanted to let you know that my team has been in contact with all your current sponsors, and things are starting to settle down now that you're out of the spotlight. I think we're going to be able to keep them all."

Thank God. While I wouldn't be hard up for cash or anything like that if I lost those deals, I'm not sure my ego can handle any more losses this year. I've always been the go-to golfer for sponsorship deals and ad campaigns, and the fact that I've lost that status hurts far more than I ever expected it to.

"Thanks, Erica. That's great news. Any news of the couple of new ones you were chasing?"

"Nothing yet, Jameo," she says, underemphasizing the "O" in my nickname so it comes out as "Jame-ah" instead of "Jame-oh," like it does for everyone else. "Just focus on your game. Don't get drunk. Don't hit on random women. You know what? Let's just say no women whatsoever."

"Of course. I haven't done anything but golf and exercise since I got here."

"That's what I like to hear."

We make small talk for another minute before Erica has to go. As I hang up my phone, I think about how stupid I've been the last year. Sure, I was hurting, but I made some bad decisions that almost cost me the profession I love and a lot of money in winnings and sponsorships.

But I'm totally focused now. I've barely looked at a woman since arriving at Wild Bluffs until today, and she only serves to remind me what terrible taste I have in women.

With that thought, I roll off the side of the bed and make my way slowly toward the shower, legs burning from the extra eighteen I got in today after the first two rounds ended poorly.

The water pounds down on me like a hundred tiny punches but doesn't put a dent in the feeling of defeat that has settled into my bones. I stand in the shower, my six-foot-four frame slumped as I let the hot water run over me, trying to wash away the disappointment of failing to score more than five under par yet again during my third round.

The round started out fine. And then it had been rough—the trudging through cacti and yuccas to find my balls in the, well, *rough*. That is the essence of golf: the more time you spend in the rough, the rougher the round becomes.

And the hot-as-hell girl who stole my ball and called me a dick before casually mentioning I'm rich? Why is it that women can't help but focus on my money?

Been there, done that. It is the one mistake I'm not interested in making again.

As soon as a woman mentions me being rich, I'm out.

Not that my dick seems to remember the last part.

"Damn it, Jameo," I mutter to myself as I lean against the tiled wall. "Get your head in the game." But the image of her smirking at me from under the brim of her cap refuses to leave. If it weren't for my self-imposed celibacy and her clear interest in me being "rich," she'd be my usual kryptonite, all tanned legs and a fiery mouth.

Just what I need to screw up my already precarious career.

Unfortunately, my brain and my anatomy down south don't seem to agree on what our focus is in Wild Bluffs.

Knowing my head is unlikely to win this battle, I let my mind wander back to the girl from this afternoon. Down her long legs and back up to her adorable smirk, my hand and thoughts wandering into carnal territory. I'm just about to give in to the urge—it's been a hot second since that specific club of mine has gotten any play—when the sound of an incoming text pierces the steamy air.

That, of course, will be Lila, my younger sister and—jeez, I'm lame—my best friend. Unfortunately, and unbeknown to her, she has always had a disturbing habit of interrupting my most private moments. And getting a text while thinking about getting myself off in the shower is actually very low on the list of embarrassing moments she's intruded on.

In high school, as I was losing my virginity, I heard my sister's pipsqueak friends *giggling* about Lila playing seven minutes in Heaven...as I was about to come inside a girl for the first time.

Needless to say, it was not my best showing, and no one had a happy ending, least of all Bryan Godsey, the sixteen-year-old I found behind a tree with my thirteen-year-old sister. He was so scared, he may have left with a bit of pee running down his leg. He should feel lucky it was me rather than my dad who heard her friends.

It wasn't until college that I met Sarah, who fortunately hadn't heard the story of me leaving my date unsatisfied in a field. Unfortunately, Lila called halfway through, and my phone played the "Cheetah Girls, Cheetah Sisters" song she had picked out as her ringtone until I finally found the Decline button through my horny haze. Luckily, Sarah was willing to try again after I figured out how to silence my phone.

I have, thankfully, gotten better since then, although my sister's bad timing remains the same.

Knowing the moment is gone—shit, how pathetic am I that I can't even romance myself these days?—I sigh and turn off the water.

I grab one of the white, fluffy towels from the rack, sling it around my waist, and sit on the edge of my room's extra bed.

Lila

> Hey, Jameo, how's the golf thing going?

I can't help but smile at her nonchalant way of referring to my career.

Me

> Could be better.

> How's grad school treating you? Need more cash for textbooks or late-night pizza?

Lila

> Haha. I asked for pizza ONE TIME. And I was drunk and very hungry, in my defense.

> Plus, you've paid for enough. I told you my internship should be enough to cover tuition this semester.

My heart tightens at the memory of the first time she had to ask me for help with her tuition and how embarrassed she had been. If I hadn't been such a self-centered ass, I would've known the small college fund our parents had saved wouldn't be enough to cover all four years of an engineering degree plus a master's degree. Especially with no sports scholarship like I had.

Me

I'm happy to help you. You get paid shit at your internship, and you should be having fun.

Lila

Like you're having fun right now? When was the last time you saw any of your friends?

Me

You know being seen with me right now is a black mark on someone's image, right?

Lila

That's what private clubs are for. I thought that's why you were out in the middle of nowhere at the only fancy golf course on the planet where you might accidentally step in cow shit.

Plus, JT reached out to me. You've ignored all his texts and calls. FOR A MONTH.

Me

> How did he get your number? I swear to God, if he was hitting on you, I'll shove my driver so far up his ass, it tees up his eyes.

I'm actually very certain Lila and JT haven't been talking about anything other than how pathetic I am. They actively hate each other with a passion so strong, I can rarely be in the same area as both my favorite people at once. My parents set up two tables at Thanksgiving, supposedly because there are so many of us, but really so JT can come without having to fight with Lila the entire time. Still, it's nice to remind her every once in a while that she's too good for every man ever.

Lila

> Super gross, oddly specific visual, bud. Plus, who I text is not your concern.

> You avoiding the world for the last month, on the other hand, is my concern. I know you haven't seen your BEST friend. Have you talked to anyone?

Me

> I would gladly endure the required brain bleach to even know you'd had a one-night stand at this point.

I sigh, running a hand through my wet hair.

Me

> I talked to a hot girl just this afternoon, in fact.

Not *not* true.

Lila

> Ooh. Tell me everything.

> Actually, on second thought, don't. Go find her. Kiss her. Hold her hand. TALK TO HER. And then never tell me what happens.

Me

Lila

> UGH. You are so infuriating. You need a rebound. It has been a year since you broke up with she-who-will-not-be-named. YOU NEED TO GET LAID. I have it on good authority it has been A YEAR. That's too long for anyone, including yours truly.

Me

Lila may be twenty-four and completing her master's in engineering next spring, but I do not need to think about her getting laid. And as much as I want to deny it, I also know she's right. It has been a long time since I've felt any interest in anyone—until that infuriating girl today.

Fuck. No, not the girl today. That zing I felt in my chest was pure anger at her comment, nothing else. No sparks.

Me

And just who is this "good authority"?? Stop talking to JT!

Lila

Gotta run to class. Love you!

"All right, Sis," I say out loud, grabbing my keys and wallet. "You win. I'll go to the bar tonight and see what happens."

Let's just hope the woman from today isn't there. I'm not sure how long my body will let me stay away from her, even knowing she is just after my money.

***

Keep reading *Forever Wild* to find out what happens next!

About the Author

Emma Kate is an author of rom-coms and contemporary romances. She lives in a small Colorado town with her rancher husband, three kids, a dog, and a whole lot of cows. When she's not writing or reading, she can be found chasing after her kids, eating ice cream and cookies, or binge-watching sitcoms.